EVERY OTHER
WEEKEND

**Books by Abigail Johnson
available from Inkyard Press**

If I Fix You
The First to Know
Even If I Fall
Every Other Weekend

Recycling programs
for this product may
not exist in your area.

ISBN-13: 978-1-335-40186-1

Every Other Weekend

First published in 2020. This edition published in 2021.

Copyright © 2020 by Abigail Johnson

This edition published by arrangement with Harlequin Books S.A.

For questions and comments about the quality of this book, please contact us at
CustomerService@Harlequin.com.

Inkyard Press
22 Adelaide St. West, 40th Floor
Toronto, Ontario M5H 4E3, Canada
www.InkyardPress.com

Printed in U.S.A.

EVERY OTHER WEEKEND

ABIGAIL JOHNSON

inkyard
PRESS

For Grady

August 1 used to mark the day I broke my neck.

Years later, August 1 became your birthday.

Because of you, it's the anniversary of
the best thing that ever happened to me.

FIRST WEEKEND

September 25–27

ADAM

*T*he pigeons blanketing the parking lot took flight into the setting sun when we pulled up to Dad's apartment building. I kind of envied the little flying disease bags for escaping until Jeremy killed the engine and they settled back down behind us. As though in sync, my brother and I leaned forward to peer out the windshield and get our first look at Oak Village Apartments, aka Dad's new home and the place we'd be forced to stay every other weekend until we turned eighteen.

Forced wasn't the word Jeremy would use, but it was exactly how I saw the situation.

"Huh," Jeremy said, his blondish brows smoothing out as my reddish-brown ones drew closer together. "I thought it'd be worse." Mom's piano teacher salary and Dad's handyman business might have been a great combination for summers spent slowly restoring our old farmhouse, but it didn't leave much for Dad to live on after he decided to move out last month.

Built just over a century ago, the six-story apartment building looked as if it was one bad day away from being condemned. Water stains from window AC units ran down the walls, and several windows were covered with warped and weather-beaten boards. Describing the green paint on the doorframe as peeling was like saying a tornado was a windstorm.

I could only imagine that the inside was equally inviting. No wonder the owner, an out-of-state friend of Dad's, had been eager to trade a rent-free apartment in exchange for Dad fixing the place up.

I turned slowly to face my brother. "I think it's perfect for him."

Jeremy jerked the key from the ignition and pushed his door open. "We're staying with Dad for two nights, Adam. Cut the crap."

Normally, I couldn't let things go with my brother, even little things, but after the thirty-minute drive from the rural Pennsylvania I'd called home my entire life to the crowded, somewhat congested outskirts of Philadelphia, I was feeling too dejected to bother. As it was, I barely had time to grab my backpack from the trunk before Jeremy slammed it shut. His massive duffel was easily five times the size of my backpack. That about summed up our respective opinions on our parents' separation.

The full impact of our new residence—however temporary—hit me as we drew closer to the glass front doors. There was a tiny spiderweb-like crack decorating one corner, and the maroon carpet inside was worn so thin by foot-traffic paths that it looked striped. Small metal mailboxes were built into the wall on the right, and unpainted plaster covered the left. Mom wouldn't have lasted five minutes in here before peeling back the carpet to check for hardwood. Another ten and she'd have been chipping away at the plaster, hoping to expose brick under-neath. Dad would have been right there next to her, grinning.

He should have been, only not here, there—home. With Mom.

Two and a half years. Jeremy didn't seem to grasp the se-verity of the situation. Then again, at seventeen, maybe he was realizing that he'd have to hold out for only another year. Not that he viewed the inauguration of these weekends as something to endure. He was looking forward to seeing Dad, whereas I would have sooner slept in the alley outside.

I moved past Jeremy toward the elevator, but after pushing the button for a full minute, I started up the stairs. "You're right, Jeremy. This place is way better than our dry, clean, not-broken-down house, where Mom is alone right now."

My backpack wasn't nearly as heavy as Jeremy's duffel—unlike my brother, I was carrying only what I needed for the next forty-eight mandatory hours—so it was only reluctance that weighed my steps up five flights of stairs. We stopped at the sixth floor and peered down a surprisingly wide hall-way with three doors on each side. One of the light bulbs was flickering in a seizure-inducing pattern that increased my nausea at having to be there.

"Which one is it?" Jeremy asked.

"Does it matter?"

Jeremy checked his phone, then pointed to the middle door on the right, 6-3. He was already knocking by the time I stepped up next to him. Each rap of his knuckles made me wince. I hadn't seen Dad in three weeks, and that was only when he'd been packing up the rest of his stuff. He'd tried to hug me before leaving, but I'd backed away. It was his choice to leave and mine not to help him feel okay about it.

"He's not here." Jeremy frowned at the door.

"Great. Let's go."

More door frowning from Jeremy.

"I'm not staying if he's not here. I'll call Mom to come get me if I have to."

Jeremy's head snapped to mine and he glared. "I'm so sick—"

The door to 6-5 opened, and a pretty Korean woman wearing sky blue yoga pants and a matching sports bra stepped out. "Oh, hi! You must be Jerry and Adam!"

The expanse of midriff on display rendered my brother mute. I was too pissed off by the whole situation to care much. "Yeah, but we were just leaving." I grabbed Jeremy's arm.

"Paul asked me to keep an eye out for you. He needed to pick up a few things, but he thought he'd be back by now." She peered down the obviously deserted hallway. "Anyhoo, come on in." She turned and called to someone in her apartment. "Jo, come meet the new neighbors."

Neither Jeremy nor I moved.

"Whoops. Probably should introduce myself. I'm Shelly, I live here with my boyfriend, Robert. It'll be so nice to have some new faces on the floor." She laughed and popped her hip against the doorframe in a way that drew my eye despite my mood. "Those are vacant." She pointed at the two apartments directly across from ours. "And then the Spiegels and their new baby live on the other side of you in 6-1, but don't worry, the baby doesn't cry a lot. There's a guy who lives in 6-2, but he's not around much, and honestly, he gives me a creepy vibe. That's mean, isn't it? It's just that this generally isn't the kind of place that attracts non-creepy people." She made a face. "I know your dad is going to fix it up, but it's kind of a dump right now."

She lifted a hand as if to shield her eyes from the flickering bulb. "We wouldn't be here if Robert's queen bitch of an ex hadn't taken everything in the divorce, and I mean *everything*. The house, the cars, his sports memorabilia." She started ticking things off on her fingers. "You wouldn't believe what he went through just to get Jo every other weekend." Shelly shook her head. "So this is it for now. It's better inside though. We might still have some pizza left over, I think."

She leaned back into her apartment, and I thought Jeremy was going to pass out at the rear view she presented. "Jo, did you eat all the pizza? Jolene?" Back in the hallway, she half rolled her eyes, then smiled. "She's kind of a nightmare, and I'm not exactly her favorite person."

I blinked at the sheer amount of information this complete stranger had just vomited at us. "Maybe you shouldn't call her mother 'queen bitch.'"

"I know, but…" Shelly shrugged. "It *really* suits her." She stressed the word and laughed again. "Do you know she had their dog put down while Robert was out of town? I mean, who does that?" She leaned forward. "Just between us, she's a drunk, too."

I wasn't sure that Jeremy was listening as much as he was watching the way Shelly's chest rose and fell when she took a deep breath—which she did constantly.

I leaned into Jeremy while Shelly continued to grossly overshare. "You realize she's probably wondering what size diapers you wear."

Predictably, Jeremy reacted by slamming me into the opposite wall. His nostrils flared. "I'm so sick of your crap."

"Yeah?" I straightened up from the wall with a smile. "I'm not exactly—"

Shelly had fallen quiet as soon as Jeremy pushed me, but she started up again as Dad crested the stairs behind us. "And here he is." Her voice held a note of relief, like she expected my brother and me to fall in line at the sight of our father. Once, that would have been true.

Dad's arms were filled with bags. Jeremy went to help him; I did not.

"Thanks, Jer." Then he stared at me. Dad looked about ten years older than the last time I'd seen him, with a scruffy half beard and more salt than pepper in his light brown hair. His normally suntanned complexion looked paler, too. But he was smiling, and that made me want to knock his teeth out. "Hi, buddy."

"Don't worry," Shelly called out, drawing all eyes once again. "They only just got here. We've been getting to know each other. Paul, you didn't tell me how cute your sons are. Jeremy looks just like you, and I bet Adam has the sweetest smile." She flashed an inviting grin at me, and I continued not smiling as Dad thanked her and led us inside his apartment.

That was when I discovered Shelly's first lie: it was *not* nicer inside. There were two tiny bedrooms, a small eat-in kitchen, and a slightly-larger-than-the-hallway living room that barely fit a couch and TV.

"So—" Dad clapped his hands "—who wants a tour?" Jeremy and I kept silent. "Guess I should save the jokes for after dinner, huh? I've got a lot of plans and I'm hoping you guys can help me with some of them. This building has good bones, you'll see."

"Yeah," Jeremy said. "We'll help." He tried to catch my eye but I ignored him.

Dad pointed at the closed doors on the right. "I'm giving you guys the bedrooms. One has access to the balcony and the other has slightly more space."

"Adam's the youngest, so he can take the couch."

"And you're practically a hobbit," I said. "I wouldn't even fit." Jeremy had nearly two years on me, but it'd been clear for a while that I'd gotten the height in the family. I'd grown two inches in the past year. Jeremy was five-nine with his shoes on and I was six-two barefoot. I enjoyed Jeremy's reddened face before heading into the bedroom with the balcony.

"Okay then. Adam, I got a pillow for the lounge chair out there, but the balcony is probably held together by rust more than anything right now, so be careful." He moved back to dig in one of his bags. "The lady at the store said it was fine to leave outside even in the snow—which it feels like we're going to get early this year."

I shut the door behind me and heard Dad's voice trail off. The walls were paper-thin, so Dad and Jeremy's somewhat stilted conversation chased me onto the balcony. It shook but felt sturdy enough. The view was… Well, it was the side of another building.

There was an apple orchard outside my window at home.

I pulled my phone out and hit Redial. Mom answered on the first ring. "Adam, sweetie?"

"Hi, Mom."

"Oh, is it that bad?" She could tell from my two-word greeting that it was.

"No, it's swell as long as I breathe through my mouth."

"Two days and you'll be home. You can do anything for two days. And Jeremy's there." My mother lived in denial about the state of my relationship with my brother. In her mind we were still the same little boys who'd built forts together. "Your dad misses you."

I ground my teeth together to hold in my response to that oft-repeated comment. It wouldn't do any good to remind her that if Dad missed us, he had no one to blame but himself.

She asked me a few more carefully worded questions about Dad's apartment. For once I was less careful with my answers.

"It's foul, like rats-wouldn't-live-here foul."

Mom laughed, which was what I wanted. "So I shouldn't tell you I just saw a deer in the backyard?"

"Can you repeat that? I couldn't hear you over the drug bust going on below me." I heard a snicker—not from Mom—and moved forward, following the sound to the edge of the balcony.

"I miss you so much," Mom said, then in a softer voice, "The house is so quiet."

"Yeah, me, too." Distraction leaked into my voice as I leaned around the dividing wall to look into the neighbor's balcony.

There sat a petite girl about my age with olive-toned skin and a waist-length brown braid hanging over one shoulder. She was slowly panning a bulky camera past two pigeons that were perched on the railing in front of her.

"Mom, I gotta call you back." I hung up. "Hey," I said, waiting until the girl turned her camera toward me and then waiting longer until she lowered it. "You could have said something or, I don't know, gone inside."

"Sorry," she said, giving no indication that she meant it beyond the word itself.

She was lounging in a foldout chair with her legs thrown over one side and the bright red glow of a cigarette illuminating her free hand. I was cold in my hoodie, so she had to be freezing in her jeans and black T-shirt that read SAVE FERRIS, but she didn't show it.

"You must be Jolene." Either that, or she was squatting on Shelly's balcony.

She smiled. "I prefer Spawn of the Queen Bitch."

Jolene

It was kinda pretty, the way his face turned red when he realized that I'd overheard Shelly trashing my mom. One of the many perks of Oak Village Apartments was the utter lack of privacy. "Which one are you?" I asked.

"What?"

"Are you Jerry or Adam?"

"Adam."

"In that case, thanks, Adam." When his reddish-brown eyebrows drew together, I elaborated, "You told Shelly not to call my mom 'queen bitch.' That was nice of you."

His eyebrows smoothed out. "Figured she might not be impartial."

I laughed. Then I did it again. It took a lot of effort not to go for a third. "That would be a no. I mean, my mom is awful, but so's my dad and his teenage girlfriend."

"Wait, she's not—"

"She was close to it when I first met her." I mentally and physically shook myself away from that chain of thought.

Adam made a face that echoed my sentiments.

"Yeah," I said.

"Is she for real?"

"Everything but her boobs. I'm pretty sure my dad bought those two—or was it three?—Christmases ago. I can't remember. Wait, it was three. We couldn't afford braces for me that year, but obviously my dad enjoys those more, so it was the right call." I smiled, revealing the slight gap between my front teeth. In hindsight, I liked my gap, but my dad was still a tool. "Hey, do you smoke?" I held up my cigarette.

Adam shook his head.

"That's too bad." I lowered it without taking a drag.

He flushed a little more. "Maybe you shouldn't either."

He was cute. "I don't." I flicked off the ash. "Shelly says the smell makes her sick and forbade me to smoke, so." I shrugged.

"But you *don't* smoke?"

I wrinkled my nose. "I tried, but I felt like throwing up afterward, and the smoke messed with my shots." She nodded at her camera. "Now I just let them burn and enjoy the results. Still, it'd be a lot easier if you smoked. All the stink in half the time, you know? It's not exactly warm out here." He surprised me then by swinging his leg over and jumping into my balcony, sending the two pigeons flying off. Very cute, I decided. He lifted the cigarette from my hand and took several long drags without hacking and coughing like I had. "Thought you didn't smoke."

It was his turn to shrug. "My mom used to. She caught me one time sneaking a cigarette from her purse, so I promised to quit if she did."

My fingers itched to pick up my camera, but that might make him stop. When he hit the filter, he presented it to me like the diamond it was.

"And did she?"

"Yeah."

Such a simple answer, yet the concept completely eluded

me. "I'm guessing that means you won't be my smoking buddy from now on?"

"Sorry," he said, like he really meant it. "Onetime thing."

The problem with cute boys who valiantly smoke cigarettes for you is that they tend to be distracting. In my head I was shooting the scene of him leaping to my balcony with the fading glow of daylight outlining him. I would focus on his hands clutching the railing and zoom in to show how the rust would still be stuck in patches to his fingers when he picked up my cigarette. I was leaning forward to check the angles and was therefore completely oblivious to the fact that we were about to be invaded until the balcony door slid open.

"Jolene, I—" Shelley's nose wrinkled and her gaze dropped to the cigarette butt in my hand. "Seriously? It's like you deliberately do the things I tell you not to."

Scene forgotten, I refrained from tapping my nose and making a bell noise, but only just. "When the sweet, seductive lure of nicotine calls, you have to answer."

Shelly snatched up my pack and plucked the butt from my unprotesting fingers. "It makes it a lot easier not to sugarcoat things for you when you pull this shi—" She broke off when she noticed Adam. "Where did you come from?" Her eyes went wide and her gaze shot to the balcony next door. "Are you out of your mind? You could have died!"

A thoroughly frigid breeze raked over us, and Shelly shivered. I looked at Adam to see if he was noticing what the cold air was doing to my dad's not-so-little gifts. He glanced but didn't linger. Cuter by the minute.

"Are you okay?" Shelly moved forward as if to hug him, but Adam stepped back.

"Yeah, I'd really rather you didn't touch me."

I grinned at him. "I'm going to like you, aren't I?"

Shelly made a distressed noise.

"Calm down, Shelly. He's fine. We're fine. Feel free to go

back inside where it's warm before you put someone's eye out with one of those things."

Shelly did a decent Adam impersonation by going red and wrapping her arms across her chest. She took a step back. "I need you both inside right now." I didn't move and, much to my pleasure, Adam didn't either.

"That's gonna be a pass, Shel, but thanks."

Shelly sucked her upper lip into her mouth and glanced upward. "Jolene, I thought we had an agreement."

"And what agreement was that? The one where you break into my room whenever you want?"

"I knocked. You didn't answer. And our agreement was that you were not going to smoke here." She made an exasperated noise. "And to think I was going to talk to your dad about that summer film school—"

All my muscles tightened. "What are you talking about?" But I knew. I just didn't know how *Shelly* knew. I didn't go around sharing huge personal dreams with anyone, let alone my dad's prepubescent girlfriend.

"The film program in California. They sent this huge info packet. Honestly, I almost threw it away because you never mentioned that you were expecting anything, but then I saw your name when I opened it and…"

Shelly kept going but most of me shut down so that I could silently scream in my head without externally moving a single muscle. From the corner of my eye, I noticed Adam sucking in a breath. It helped, however slightly, to have someone else register the line Shelly had crossed without even thinking about it.

"…I thought you just liked watching old movies. Is that what you're filming all the time?" She reached for my camera, and I snatched it away with a barely repressed snarl.

I guessed, to Shelly, movies from the '80s were old. I preferred them, because they showed me a time before my parents met and lost their minds long enough to get married and have me. You know, the good old days. But I didn't watch only "old" movies.

"Maybe if you didn't hide every single aspect of your life from me, I wouldn't have to go through your mail or barge onto your balcony to know anything. I'm just—" She gritted her teeth. "I'm sick of it. I can't control what you do at your mother's, but over here you need to follow your dad's rules."

I was almost done screaming in my head. Not quite, but almost. If she'd let me finish, I'd have been able to stay silent until she left, but then she had to go and bring up my dad. "He never gave me any rules. See, he'd have to actually show up once in a while to do that."

One of Shelly's eye muscles twitched and her voice softened. "He's in the middle of a really big work—"

"So, Adam, seen any good movies lately?" I don't know if Shelly stopped talking when I interrupted her, or if I just drowned her out. I'd heard that line from her before, and I wasn't going to listen to it again.

"We agreed that I'm in charge when you're here."

Angry me rarely accomplished anything except to invite crying me to make a long, insufferable appearance. So, ignoring all instincts, I forced amusement into my voice. "I never agreed to that. What were the terms?"

Shelly's arms snapped to her sides and her nostrils flared. "You don't get terms when you're fifteen, but fine, do whatever you want. You always do." She tossed the pack of cigarettes at me and flung an arm toward Adam's balcony. "Please do not climb over that when you leave." Then to me she said, "I left the film program packet on your bed. Oh, and I came out here to tell you that your dad's not coming home tonight. I can't *imagine* why he wouldn't want to."

My eyes stung and the air in my lungs swelled painfully, but outwardly I didn't react at all. Shelly closed the sliding door behind her without looking back. It took me two tries, but I managed to light another cigarette. I focused on the thin line of smoke that trailed up in front of me. Adam was staring after Shelly with a slightly agape mouth and wide eyes. "Just wait until you get yours," I told him.

He blinked, then snapped out of his semi-horrified stupor. "Get my what?"

"Your Shelly. Or does your dad already have a girlfriend?"

"What? No. He doesn't have a girlfriend. My parents are just separated. They aren't even talking about divorce."

"Since when does that matter? Shelly was in the picture long before the paperwork went through." Christmas had been a hoot that year. Everybody knew that everybody knew, but since my mom hadn't officially pulled the trigger yet, the holidays were in full swing at my house. This year, they were in an all-out war over who would get to celebrate the birth of our Savior with me.

"No," Adam was saying. "It's not like that with my parents. There weren't any affairs or anything. I can't imagine my dad having a girlfriend."

"But you haven't seen the way he looks at Shelly. Unlike you, he doesn't back away when she tries to hug him." Based on Adam's expression, I was guessing he'd witnessed such an event earlier in the hall. "Or I could be wrong." I wasn't.

Adam was still frowning, but this time at me and not just the unpleasant idea I'd forced on him. "He's not—you have no idea what's going on with my family. Clearly yours is seriously messed up. Mine is..." he hesitated "...normal messed up. My dad isn't going to start dating, and my mom isn't some—"

"Oh, I hope you finish that sentence. Considering your entire opinion of my mother will have been formed by Shelly's, you must have a ton of insight." I rested my chin on my hands and blinked at him with wide, waiting eyes.

The blush that stained his neck and cheeks wasn't nearly as cute this time. He rotated his jaw like he was physically forcing himself to say something other than what he wanted to. "Our parents aren't the same, okay? That's all I was trying to say."

"Then spill. You say no one strayed, but maybe they were just good at hiding it."

Adam looked at me like I was something he'd stepped in. It wasn't a new experience for me, so I let it go. "What's wrong with you? You're messed up, you know that?"

My cigarette had burned low by then, and I was reaching my suffer-in-order-to-piss-Dad-off-via-Shelly threshold in terms of temperature. My skin was covered in goose bumps, and I was rethinking all kinds of things about Adam. The movie in my head suddenly had an ominous, horror-themed score to it. "Fine, whatever. I'm going to slink into my room, but stay, smoke the rest of my cigarettes if you want." I nodded toward the mostly full pack. "Maybe it'll piss off your dad, too."

"I'll pass. I don't need to resort to anything so petty to punish my dad."

I grinned in all my gap-toothed glory. "Enlighten me, oh mature one—how grown-up do you have to be to call Mommy two seconds after you get here?"

He didn't say anything, just walked to the wall and started to scale back over to his balcony.

"Oh no. Leaving so soon? I have all these other petty things we could do together."

Adam's head popped back over as soon as he was in his own balcony. "Look, are you going to be around a lot?"

"Every other weekend."

He hung his head. "Me, too."

I didn't bother with the fake smile. "Yippee."

ADAM

What. The. Holy. Hell.

I glanced down at my calloused palms, scraped raw on one side from my hasty and nearly fatal climb back to my own balcony. The railing was rough from rust along the bottom and slick from a recent rainfall on the top. Nausea, cold and stinging, had flooded me during that split second that my foot slipped and I nearly plummeted six stories to my death.

I was chilled and sweaty and my heart was more than a little jumpy, which I wanted to blame on almost falling or maybe the cigarette but couldn't. It was all her. Jolene. The things she'd said. Back in my room—the room I was staying in—I dropped onto the foot of my—*the*—bed and let my head fall into my hands. I felt kind of like a jerk, but at the same time I couldn't bring myself to care, not with the sound of Dad and Jeremy laughing in the next room.

Dad hadn't left Mom because he wanted someone else. His reasons made him a coward, not a cheat.

I grabbed my earbuds and phone, and turned up the volume to just shy of painful so that I couldn't hear them or myself.

I don't know how long I lay on the bed before Jeremy came in and yanked out my earbuds. "Dad wants to know if you're going to eat."

I started to close my eyes again, but Jeremy dead-legged me. I launched myself at him, tackling him into the dresser. We hit the ground, and the next instant I was bodily lifted and flung onto the lumpy mattress.

"Enough!" Dad was between us, hands outstretched toward each son. "Since when do you guys fight like animals?"

I looked at Jeremy and saw a tiny trickle of blood on his mouth. I must have elbowed him when we went down. We were both breathing hard, and he wouldn't meet my eye. When I refused to answer, Dad turned to Jeremy.

"Somebody start talking."

"It was nothing. We were messing around." Jeremy shrugged.

I couldn't see Dad's face, but I doubted he bought that story. I wouldn't have. So I was surprised when he dropped his arms and the line of questioning.

"This isn't a great situation, for any of us. I know you guys are caught in the middle, but if you can just hang in there, we will get through it."

"Get through it?" I asked, slowly shaking my head. "You *left* Mom. How exactly do you want us to get through that?"

Dad lowered his gaze, and my brother, still dabbing the bloody lip I'd given him, spoke to me in a tone that was the complete opposite of the hostile one he'd used with me earlier. "C'mon, Adam. We just got here. Can't we just..." He trailed off, realizing, I hoped, that we couldn't *just* anything. At least, I couldn't.

"I don't have a plan here. This isn't what I wanted— it's not what your mom wanted either," Dad added when I started to rise from the bed. "It's just the way it is for now. I'm... I'm working on it, okay?" He made a point of meeting and holding both Jeremy's and my gazes, and I wanted to pretend that I didn't notice the moisture in his eyes. "In the meantime, can we agree not to go no-holds-barred in the apartment anymore?"

"Sure, Dad. Sorry." Jeremy clapped a hand on Dad's arm in a gesture I was sure he thought made him seem grown-up.

"Adam?"

I was too busy staring at my sellout of a brother to answer. Before—before *everything*, Jeremy had been the one who clashed with Dad. He'd never rolled over, not even when it would have been the smart thing to do. It was like he'd enjoyed the tension, the way Dad would get riled up. But then everything went wrong. Dad eventually moved out, Mom broke almost worse than before, and Jeremy decided to stand with the wrong parent. He sided with the coward. Unlike my brother, I wasn't going to smile and nod at Dad like I was fine with him abandoning Mom. She'd cried all morning, even as she was telling us how glad she was that we were going to see Dad. She was probably still crying, and my brother was apologizing to Dad. I felt the urge to bloody Jeremy's mouth again.

"I'm going to take that as a yes." Dad clapped both of us on the shoulder, then headed out of the room. "Dinner's getting cold."

Jeremy and I made the briefest eye contact before he followed Dad, and when I was alone, I let my stomach make the call and I joined them.

Dinner turned out to be takeout, some local place I'd never heard of, but it was hard to wreck a cheesesteak in Philly. I think between the three of us, we ate about eight of them. Even better, talking wasn't an option until all that was left on the breakfast bar that we were crowded around was crumpled foil and empty bags.

Jeremy was the first to talk, complimenting Dad on finding a good take-out place already. I clenched my fist so I wouldn't deck him.

Dad launched into a story about how he'd found the place and thought they were even better than our old place in Redding. Some good-natured arguing commenced, and every word caused the food in my stomach to turn into stone.

"We'll let Adam be the tie vote," Dad said. "Who makes the better cheesesteak? Mike's, or are you with me and Sonny's?"

I looked at Dad with his overly eager expression. He was desperate for this "normal" moment with his sons. A sign, I guessed, that the three of us could get through this. It didn't even matter which place I picked. He just wanted us to be talking again. He wasn't delusional enough to think that everything would be perfect from then on, or that his run-down apartment was where any of us would choose to be, but it was like our future hinged on this moment.

While Mom was more alone than she should ever have to be.

"I think they both taste like crap." Then I jumped off my stool and disappeared into the room I'd be sleeping in every other weekend for the foreseeable future. After a minute, I pulled out my phone and listened to the two-year-old voice mail I'd saved, the last one my oldest brother, Greg, ever sent me.

"Adam, Adam, Adam." His half-teasing voice filled my ear and made me smile, even as my chest tightened. "Why do you even have a phone? So, listen, I'm bringing another dog home and I haven't found a home for Baloo, so obviously Mom and Dad can't know. I need you to move Baloo to the other cage in the barn, the one with the blue dog bed. But watch his leg, because he'll bite you if you pull his stitches. Maybe get Jeremy to help—" His voice grew quieter like he'd moved his mouth away from the phone. "You can? Thanks, man." The volume returned to normal. "Never mind. Daniel's gonna swing by and take care of Baloo. Tell Mom, okay? About Daniel, not the dog. Maybe if she's fussing over him she won't notice the chunk this new guy took out of my leg." He laughed at something Daniel said. "Are you telling me you wouldn't bite if a couple guys were trying to remove some barbwire that was embedded in your neck?" A low growl sounded, and Greg's laugher faded. "All right, I gotta go, but I owe you, little bro."

I had it memorized, but I replayed it two more times until my vision grew too blurry to read my phone.

The last thing I did was send a text to Mom: **Heading to bed. Will call tomorrow. Love you.**

Jolene

Shelly made a show of covering her mouth and nose when I reemerged from my bedroom. I didn't bother pointing out that I'd showered. I thought my wet hair was enough of an indicator, but then again, this was the woman who, the day she'd moved in with my dad, had told me—with a straight face—that she wanted me to think of her like a sister. I'm sure I peed a little laughing, which hadn't gone over well with my wannabe sis.

I decided not to bring up the fact that she'd opened my mail. I figured that one was on me for having something important sent here in the first place. But if I'd had the film program info sent to Mom's house and she'd found it, she'd have assumed Dad and I were conspiring to lower her alimony by sending me away for the summer. I'd have suffered a lot more from that than I had on the balcony with Shelly. Mom would have cared too much, and I figured Dad wouldn't care at all. That was my life in a nutshell.

Anyway, I had the info now, and there was at least a semi-decent chance that Shelly wouldn't bring it up again. Besides, if I exhausted all my other options—and I would—and still had to go to Dad for the tuition, I'd be the one to do it, not Shelly. I'd sooner sleep with a rat in my bed.

Vermin aside, I'd intended to grab something from the kitchen and spend the rest of the evening in my room going through the film program application, but seeing Shelly's scrunched-up face in response to my nonexistent cigarette smell made me shift directions. I settled on the sofa and stretched out my legs.

This was a game we played, Shelly and me. There was only one unspoken rule: when I entered a room, she left; when she entered a room, I left. We'd been playing for a while now and I saw no reason to change things, but every so often, Shelly would try. I could tell just by the way she was breathing—deep and through her nose—that this was one of those times.

"I'm sorry I had to do that in front of your friend."

"Hmm?" It was harder to tune her out when she moved to perch on the opposite arm of the couch.

"I figure if we both start treating each other with more respect, things will go a lot easier."

Hearing Shelly talk about respect was like hearing an atheist talk about God. "You mean the respect that you didn't show me just now on the balcony? Or when you went through my mail? Or earlier in the hall, when you trashed my mom to complete strangers? That kind of respect?"

"I'm trying to apologize here."

I let my silence speak for itself.

It had taken me a while to figure out Shelly once she'd grafted herself onto our lives. She wasn't a gold-digging home wrecker siphoning life and money out of my dad; she was worse. She thought she loved him, and the cherry on the deluded sundae? She thought he loved her. I don't know, maybe he had at first. But that was the thing with my dad: he could be so charming. I guess that was what made him such a good salesman. He'd sell something so hard that I think he sort of had to believe it himself. When they'd first gotten together, Shelly must have seemed like a ray of sunshine in his otherwise gloomy life. Always smiling and praising him, never complaining about the hours he worked or the way his hair was thinning. I'm sure she made him feel like a man when, for his whole life, he'd felt like anything but. And in return, he'd lavished her with gifts and trips until her head spun so much that she didn't have to think about the wife and daughter he already had.

Now Shelly was stuck in the lackluster apartment where he'd stashed her—and me—enduring his eighty-hour workweeks and two-plus years of broken promises, including the as-yet-to-appear—and realistically never would—engagement ring.

I guess you could say that Shelly's happily-ever-after hadn't turned out as she'd hoped, and the fallout had been extreme. Every weekend that she got saddled with me was a fresh reminder of the lives she'd helped destroy. If I was being charitable, maybe I could chalk up her not leaving my dad to guilt in addition to reckless stupidity, but regardless, Shelly brought out the worst in me.

Her shoulders slumped. "Fine. I don't even know why I try with you."

"Yeah, your life is super hard."

"But that's just it. It doesn't have to be." Shelly moved to the coffee table in front of me. "Aren't you tired of playing the bratty teenager? 'Cause I gotta tell you, I'm tired of being on the receiving end."

"What can I say? You inspire me."

Shelly made a half-aborted gesture to touch my hair. "I still remember what you were like before." A ghost of a smile.

"You used to let me braid your hair and ask me to teach you new yoga poses. We were friends. I know you remember."

I couldn't forget. When she'd started working for my parents as their personal at-home trainer, Shelly had been like a granted wish I didn't know I'd made. She was energetic and friendly and so pretty. Unlike my parents, who always seemed to be embroiled in some pressing task that required Shelly to hang around waiting for them, Shelly would ignore her phone and focus entirely on me. She'd do my hair and tell me about college and how the guys she went out with were so immature. More than that, she'd ask about my day and my life, and listen like it mattered.

The shift had been so subtle that my thirteen-year-old brain hadn't caught it. She'd gone from asking about soccer practice to coaxing details from me about the caustic relationship between my parents and commiserating with me once I spilled. By the time I'd realized what was going on, it was too late. Dad started meeting Shelly at his office, and Mom, not to be outdone, upgraded to a full-time fitness coach named Hugh who worked her out in ways it was illegal to pay for outside Las Vegas. Three months later, papers were filed, lawyers went to war, and Mom began a passionate affair with Jack Daniels.

And Shelly couldn't understand why I wouldn't let her braid my hair?

It took everything I had to not flinch from her. I wasn't thirteen anymore. I viewed her past friendship with me like the stain it was, and I wasn't about to alleviate her occasional pangs of conscience by pretending otherwise.

I locked eyes with her. "I remember *everything*."

Shelly nodded at me, once, twice, and dropped her hand to her thigh. "Okay. I get it. You hate me. I might hate me, too, except I think I might be smarter about it."

I raised an eyebrow at that.

"I put up with a lot, and not just from you and your mom."

I propped up my head on my arm and raised an eyebrow. "Oh no. Don't tell me there's trouble in paradise?"

"You're trying to get slapped, aren't you?"

My other eyebrow rose. For all her talk—and with Shelly there was always a lot of talk—she'd never once threatened me. I hadn't thought she had it in her. I once saw my mom throw her out of the house by her hair, and all Shelly had done was cry. Was there an actual spine hiding behind the Barbie-doll facade?

I suppose the proper reaction to an adult threatening to hit you would be fear, but Shelly wasn't the kind to inspire anything. She had maybe ten pounds on me—not counting her boobs—and not even as many years. I had friends with siblings older than she was.

I think Shelly realized that her scare tactic had been a bust. She sighed. "Things are going to change around here. I promise you that."

"Sure they are." I successfully fished the remote out from under the cushion and gestured for her to stop blocking my view. She didn't move.

"I know you think I'm temporary, but one of us is sorely mistaken."

I turned on the TV and leaned so that I could focus on the screen. "You don't really think he's going to marry you, do you?"

Shelly shot to her feet and held up a not-quite-steady hand. "Why does he want you here? Did you ever think about that?" Her eyebrows shot up. "Unlike your new friend next door, your dad wasn't here for you, was he? It's the weekend, and he's choosing to be at work. Again."

I gripped the remote tight enough to turn my knuckles

white, but I kept my voice flat. "That's one of the many fundamental differences between us. I know I'm here because my dad enjoys taking things from my mom, even things he doesn't want." I felt my own eye muscle twitch at that admission, convinced of it as I was. I couldn't fully embrace the indifference I tried to show Shelly. I gave her the kind of smile usually reserved for videos of cats failing to jump over things. "You're here because my dad thinks paying for sex is gauche."

I think Shelly would have slapped me if she'd been within striking distance. Instead, she looked at me with tear-filled eyes, then strode purposefully into the room she shared with my dad. She slammed the door so hard that one of the pictures on the wall crashed to the floor.

I left it there.

Grabbing the nearest pillow, I found a *Full House* marathon and spent the rest of the evening in magical TV land. Or I tried. I maybe should have picked a show where the family more closely resembled my own. Something on Animal Planet, where the father left and the mother ate her young.

I clutched that pillow tight enough to burst it.

ADAM

Iknew something was wrong the minute I woke up. It was
a cacophony of little things that combined into that overwhelming roar of wrongness, like when you rent shoes at
a bowling alley. Even before I opened my eyes, I felt the
scratchy stiffness of my sheets when I shifted. The sound was
wrong, too. No birds. Instead there was a muffled rush of
traffic spilling past and the occasional blare of a horn. Then
there was a clicking noise, followed by a deep, groaning
wheeze as warm air gushed into the room. The wrongness
didn't dissipate when I opened my eyes, but comprehension
sharpened its edges.

Thin drapes the color of rust hung over the sliding balcony
doors and let the gloomy September light show me much
more of the room than I cared to see. Last night I hadn't
turned on the lamp, preferring instead to let the shadows
conceal details I detested on principle.

Dad had only just moved in himself and had the entire
building to fix up, so it wasn't like I'd expected him to have
decorated the place, but the spartan, thrift-store furniture

wasn't helping my unease. The showstopper was the print that hung over the bed. It was an apple orchard. I wondered if Dad had hung it on purpose, or if it came with the apartment. Either way, the mockery of it drove me from my bed as though I'd been doused with water.

At home, I could have looked out the window and seen real apple trees and breathed in crisp, slightly sweet air. There wouldn't have been the sound of one car assaulting my ears, let alone hundreds. We didn't live on a working farm or anything, just a house nestled back from the main road surrounded by trees and quiet and, as Mom had reminded me yesterday, the occasional deer.

Had it been only yesterday? Last night, really? I sat on the bed with my back to the orchard print and fished my phone out of my jeans from the floor. It rang twice before she answered.

"Hello?"

"Mom, your phone shows my face and name when I call."

She laughed, but it sounded relieved more than anything. "I know, but what if someone else had your phone?"

"Like if someone stole it? Why would they call my mom?"

"Not a thief then, but a Good Samaritan. Or maybe Jeremy."

"Jeremy has his own phone, and I doubt there's a good anything within twenty square blocks of this apartment." I thought of Jolene and Shelly. There was a pause while Mom tried to figure out how to respond to my antipathy. I yawned audibly. "I'm just tired. The mattresses over here are sacks filled with old laundry."

Another pause.

"That's a joke, Mom."

More shaky laughter. She must have had a worse night than I had. "I can't always tell when you're teasing me."

"All right." I stood up and stretched my back. "No more jokes. You okay? Did you sleep a little?"

"Oh, sure." She forced an overly bright note into her voice. "Just whipping up breakfast for one."

I imagined her standing in the kitchen with one hand clenching the counter in a death grip. She'd probably been up for hours. I wouldn't have been surprised if she'd repainted half the house or something.

"What about you? You have an okay time with your dad last night?"

I thought about how to answer a question I knew it had practically killed her to ask. Anything I said would hurt her. She'd feel more alone if I told her it was good, and she'd blame herself if I told her the truth. So, in a flash of brilliance or insanity, I told her the only other thing I could think of. "I met a girl."

"You what?" Finally an unguarded response.

"She lives in the building, the apartment next door actually."

"Wait, wait, wait." I heard something clinking. "Let me get my coffee, and then I want to hear everything. What's her name?"

I smiled in relief. Mom sounded like Mom for the first time in longer than I liked to think about. "Jolene."

"Like the Dolly Parton song? I wonder if they named her—oh no. Probably not. She's kind of a home wrecker in the song. It's really pretty though."

"She's a really pretty girl," I said, realizing for the first time that it was true, objectively if nothing else. "She has a great smile with this little gap between her front teeth and a twisted sense of humor, but I kind of like that." I found myself telling Mom about Jolene—what I knew at any rate— and carefully omitting details that would not have added to the picture I was painting. When I was done, even I could see how I would have been crushing on this girl if things had gone a little differently.

"What did I tell you?" Mom said. "I knew you'd find something to like. When will you see her again?"

"Um. I don't know. We only just met."

"Oh, of course, but it's nice, you know? Jeremy won't talk to me about girls and—well, it's just nice."

Greg used to talk to her about stuff like that. I felt that old-but-never-gone sadness flare up at the way her voice had thickened. I tried not to let mine do the same. "I promise to keep talking to you about her. I'll try to see her again today."

"Maybe you can get a picture of her," Mom said, and then added, "She doesn't even have to know you're taking it."

"Mom, that's called stalking, and most girls don't like it."

"You're teasing me again, aren't you?"

"Yes, but I'm still not taking pictures of unassuming girls for you."

"My funny boy. You're just making me miss you more."

"More than Jeremy. Not much of a compliment."

"I miss you both the same."

I rolled my eyes, but the effect was lost on the phone. "Right. Did he even call you yet?"

"He will. He's probably still asleep."

"I can fix that." I lowered the phone and distantly heard Mom telling me not to wake my brother as I headed to the other room to do exactly that.

The blanketed lump on the couch showed me Dad was still asleep. Once in the other still-darkened room, I not so gently shoved my lousy brother over. "Get up and talk to Mom." I left off the word I wanted to call him, since Mom would have heard.

"Adam, what the—" not-Jeremy said. Dad was blinking up at me. "What's wrong with your mom?" He moved quicker than I did, seizing my phone before I thought to correct him. "Sarah? Are you all right?"

And then I had to listen to Mom's muffled explanation that I was supposed to be giving the phone to Jeremy. It got more awkward when Dad explained that, after I'd gone to bed, he and Jeremy decided to change the sleeping arrangements. The conversation itself wasn't the problem; it was listening to my parents talk as though they were strangers that hurt. Dad, with his husky sleep voice that he kept trying to mask, and Mom with her painful over-politeness. These were not people who'd been married for twenty years. Who had kids together. The strained *how are you*s that they exchanged before hanging up made it worse.

"Sorry," I said when Dad handed my phone back.

"Might want to rethink your wake-up call."

"I thought you were Jeremy."

"He offered to take the couch."

"Yeah. I got that," I said, ending the longest conversation Dad and I had had in weeks. I left him to get up or go back to sleep or whatever. Jeremy was sitting up on the couch and scratching himself when I walked through the living room/hall.

"What was that about?"

"It's about you being an ass," I said. "Call Mom."

Jolene

The doorbell rang as I was looking over the footage I'd shot on the balcony yesterday and trying to decide if the poor lighting was a cool stylistic feature or if I'd ruined the shot. I was about to hit Pause on my laptop when those last few seconds, the ones of Adam peering at me from his balcony, began playing. The fading sunlight lit only half his face, revealing a slight pinch between his brows that said he was curious despite his annoyance.

The lighting, I decided, had been perfect.

With a sigh, I went to answer the door. It was way too soon for the Chinese food I'd ordered, unless they had a time machine. I didn't really expect it to be my lunch when I opened my door, but nearly as surprising as time-traveling delivery guys was the person actually standing there.

"Come to bum a smoke?" I asked.

Adam started to blush, and unlike the night before, I didn't find the muddled red color marching up his neck to be that appealing. "I have a favor to ask."

I leaned my shoulder into the doorframe. "Yeah, no. You

were a punk yesterday, so I'm not inclined to do much of anything for you."

"You owe me," he said, his blush continuing to spread until his ears glowed pink. "For the cigarette."

"Wrong. Try again. No one forced you to jump onto my balcony and take that cigarette from my hand. I certainly didn't make you smoke it."

"Seriously?"

"Yes, seriously. What do you even want anyway?" I asked, curiosity winning out over the smug superiority I was feigning. Adam's lips thinned, and my interest rose. He was not at all excited about what he was going to ask me.

"I need to take a picture of you."

My eyebrows shot up. "Excuse me?"

Adam was looking everywhere but at me.

"What kind of picture?"

"A normal picture."

"Why?"

I hadn't thought he could get any redder, but he did. "It's for my mom."

"I don't even know what that means, but forget it." I started to close my door, but Adam caught it.

"Look, I'm not trying to be creepy—"

"Well, you totally are, so let go of my door."

"I'll do something for you in exchange. I'll smoke as many cigarettes as you want, whatever."

Our tug-of-war with my door halted. He was serious. His hazel eyes were focused on mine, and even though he wasn't really preventing me from jerking my door free if I wanted, he *was* desperate. For a picture of me. My skin prickled. "Fine, I'm listening."

"Yeah?"

When I nodded, he let go of the door. So trusting. I was

tempted to slam it in his face as a learning experience. I didn't though. My cigarettes weren't going to smoke themselves.

"I told you last night that my parents were separated—"

"You told me many things last night."

"And I'm going to apologize about most of those things, just let me get this out."

I could have told him that leading with an apology when you wanted something was always a better idea but I waved him on.

"My mom likes to pretend that she's fine—both my parents do—but it kills her that we're here. She's not great with being alone." He swallowed, and I wondered for a minute if he was going to tear up. The prospect made me step back. I couldn't imagine feeling my mother's pain so keenly that it became my pain, too. "I think she's worried that Jeremy and I are going to pull away from her, too, and decide we like it better over here with our dad." He shook his head like the idea was ludicrous.

I crossed my arms. "Sounds like you need to send her a picture of your apartment." No one would willingly spend time at Oak Village unless they were legally forced to, like for a court-mandated custody agreement in my case, or if you were trying to convince a judge that you were too broke to pay more alimony like in my dad's case.

"It's more than convincing her I want to stay with her," Adam said. "She can't think I'm miserable over here either, or she'll feel worse and blame herself for putting me through it. I don't want to her upset if I can help it."

Now I was getting pissed. My skin was still prickling but it was growing hot. This was heading into "Gift of the Magi" territory, and I could already feel something rising in my throat. "Get to the point of the picture, Adam."

"I told her I met a girl. You."

"You did meet a girl. Me." I was being deliberately obtuse, but it seemed only fair to make him suffer a little while his parents both fought over him because they actually wanted to see him. The rising bile lodged itself in my throat and burned before I could push it—and the thought that caused it—down again.

"I led her to believe that things went a little better between us than they actually did."

"You mean you didn't tell her about calling my family messed up and denouncing my pettiness?" I wagged my finger at him. "You shouldn't lie to your mother, Adam."

"Thank you for the morality lesson. The point is I told her about the girl in the apartment next door, and it made her happy. I like making her happy, and it will make her *really* happy if I show her a picture of you."

"Why me? Why not find a picture of a girl online and tell her it's me?" Then I rolled my eyes at his nonverbal reaction. "Do you have a condition? You blush a lot." Of course my comment only made him redder.

"You're...unique-looking."

Ah, so he had tried to find a random girl online. I swished my waist-length braid over one shoulder in a dramatic flourish. "Beauty is its own punishment sometimes. I'm constantly told I could be a model if I were taller and had a different face and body." When he didn't so much as crack a smile, I dropped my arms with a sigh. "I believe I was offered an apology."

That same uncomfortable look thinned his mouth again. Apparently, apologizing ranked up there with asking for favors. "I don't know anything about your family, so I was wrong to make assumptions about them."

We both stared at each other for several seconds.

"That's it?" I asked. "Do you ever get in trouble?"

"What?"

"Forget it. You obviously don't, because you suck at apologizing. You should have just told me you were sorry that I was offended. That way you take no responsibility."

He waited for me to say something else and when I didn't, his nostrils flared and he turned to walk away, obviously deciding that putting up with me wasn't worth his mother's happiness.

I tried to remember how I'd felt when my family first imploded. A volatile mix between fragility and... Nope, it was all fragility back then. The thick skin I'd had to develop over long months volleying between lawyers, bitter accusations, and even uglier admissions until I found that indifference served me much better than the hot and cold emotions ever had.

Adam was clearly in the kill-all-humans stage of the process, so pushing his buttons the night before probably hadn't been the wisest course of action on my part. And to be fair, I didn't know anything about his family either.

If I let him storm off, I'd be stuck alone until Shelly came back, and that was reason enough to call out to him. Or it should have been, except there was an uneasy sloshing in my stomach reminding me that he wasn't the only one who'd overstepped last night. "Look, I'm sorry, too, okay, for the crack about your dad getting a girlfriend." I shifted my jaw to one side and willed my insides to settle. I sucked at apologizing, too. "Just take your picture already."

Adam stopped but didn't come back.

It nagged at me, how quickly he'd managed to reverse our situations. I was the one apologizing to him. "Will it help if I promise to be nicer in the future?" At least I could try. I was always trying.

Adam did come back, if somewhat reluctantly.

"And maybe we should avoid talking about our parents," I said.

"Fine by me."

"So are we gonna do this thing?"

His phone was out in a second, and his thumb hovered over the screen. He didn't take a picture.

"Could we go outside or something?" He looked around, gaze snagging on the flickering light bulb a few yards away. "It's…"

"Super bleak and depressing in this hallway?"

"Yes," he said. "Exactly."

As if I had any more promising offers in my dad's equally bleak and depressing apartment. "Can you drive?"

Adam shook his head. "I turn sixteen in February."

"My birthday's in January," I said. "What about your brother?"

"I'd rather stay in the hallway."

"For real?" Adam didn't even respond. "Okay, then we're on foot. There's a good cheesesteak place a couple blocks—" I started to point, but he cut me off.

"We can just find the nearest tree or something."

I shrugged. "It's your photo. Let me grab a jacket."

I snagged my camera, too, and followed him to the stairwell. We played the quiet game the whole way down; me because all the things that I thought of saying were probably not, strictly speaking, in the *nice* category. I was going to have to watch myself around Adam. He, on the other hand, seemed to have the nice thing on autopilot. He even opened the front door for me.

Weirdo.

ADAM

For a place called Oak Village, there were surprisingly few oak trees on the property. Dad had mentioned something over dinner the night before about landscaping plans but that the building itself had to come first.

We found a tree half a block away, and Jolene kicked it and turned to face me. "What's my motivation?"

"What?" I asked.

"Forget it. Is this fine?" She leaned against the oak tree and dipped her head a little to one side. When she smiled, her gap showed, and I kinda liked that she didn't try to hide it.

I lifted my phone and took the picture.

"Here, let me see." She pressed into my side and I inhaled the soft scent of honeysuckle from her hair as she peered around my shoulder at my phone. "Did you close your eyes while taking this?"

"What?" I felt like I was saying that a lot around her. "No."

"That's like the worst photo anyone has ever taken of me." She took my phone and held it out in front of us. "Smile." I heard a click. "There. Much better. See how it doesn't look like I only have one eye in this one? Wow, we actually look good together. Huh."

She tilted the phone so I could see the picture. Of the two of us. She'd taken it so quickly that I hadn't really had time to feel uncomfortable. When she'd pressed into my side, she'd smelled sort of sweet and sort of like the tree she'd leaned against. So in the picture, she was smiling and I was looking at her with an unguarded expression. "Yeah, I can't send that to my mom."

"Why not?" She pulled the phone back to study the picture.

"Right now, you're just a cute girl I met. If she sees that, you're suddenly this girl I'm taking pictures with and—what are you doing?" She was doing something with my phone.

"Sending the picture to your mom. I'm assuming she's the contact marked 'Mom.' Wow, you call her a lot."

I ripped my phone away from her, but I heard the send *swish* sound. "Why did you do that?"

"You said you wanted to make your mom happy. That's the picture that will make her happy. I mean, look at it. How cute am I, and how cute are you noticing how cute I am?"

"Right. Thanks," I said in a clipped tone. The delivered note displayed by the text mocked me while I started trying to figure out how to explain the picture to Mom and defuse the situation. I shoved my phone back in my pocket. "I'll see you." I started back down the street. I made it like two steps before Jolene pulled me to a stop.

"Pissy much? It's just a photo. It's not like I was licking your face or anything."

"You don't get it." I tried to shake her off, gently at first, but with a little more force when she persistently hung on. "Can I have my arm back?"

"So you can storm back to your apartment? No."

I raised my eyebrows at her as if to say, *Are you serious?* In response she raised her own eyebrows.

"Get over yourself for two seconds and explain why you're all butthurt that I sent that innocent picture of us to your mom."

"Of *us*," I said, relaxing my arm so that she might follow suit. "She'll think you're more than just the girl next door."

"Are you saying I'm not?"

I felt my face heat. "I appreciate the photo, but that picture… It was supposed to be of you, not us. You were just supposed to be a distraction so she wouldn't dwell on the fact that she was alone in our house for the first time since—" I swallowed, feeling needles behind my eyes. I puffed out a breath, focusing on the chilly air when I refilled my lungs until I got myself together. "This is way more than that now, or it's going to look that way to her." I pulled out my phone again and brought up the picture. "You really don't see the problem?"

Her eyebrows drew together and she tugged on her bottom lip, studying me, not even glancing at the phone. "You're saying I should have licked your face?" Then she laughed when my jaw tightened. "Wow, you're uptight. I'm kidding. And yes, I see your probably too-anal point." At last she dropped my arm. "So you're in a pickle, and it's my fault." She eyed me sideways for confirmation. I folded my arms. "Honestly, I think you're taking a much too narrow view of all this. You want to distract your mom. Great. Cute girl next door—" she pointed to herself and gave a little curtsy "—in and of herself is good for, what, two weekends of distraction, maybe three? What happens when the novelty of my mere existence wears off? Granted, I am awesome and very cute, so maybe you eke out four weekends, but even I have my limits. So what's your plan after that?"

She barely paused before continuing. "See, this is why you need me for more than my off-the-charts photogenic properties. Me alone, I have a limited shelf life. Me and you—" she bounced her palm between our chests "—us, why, the sky is the limit." She leaned into my side and waved her hand across the sky as though arcing an invisible banner above us. I was smelling her hair like a complete psycho so I jerked away, feeling my face flush.

When I just stared at her fake sky banner, she dropped the showman facade. "Look, all I'm saying is that maybe I did you a favor. If your mom is really having a rough time, then the idea of a reciprocated crush is going to do a lot more for her than your one-sided one. You wanted to give her a picture. Instead, you gave her a story."

I couldn't help but consider the potential upside when she put it like that. Things were only going to get harder for Mom as Jeremy and I spent more weekends away. Maybe that picture wasn't such a bad thing.

Jolene smiled wide when she knew she had me.

"Yeah, okay. Thanks, I think."

"Oh, but I am not done with my benevolent acts for the day."

I started to object when she pulled out her camera and pointed it at me, but fair was fair, so I let her film me, then her, then us, talking and framing her shots all the while.

"Even though you offered, I decided that giving you lung cancer just so I can piss off my dad and Shelly is perhaps a tad on the petty side."

I laughed. It startled me. A couple minutes ago, I had nearly gotten lost in a memory that would have broken me right in front of her. "I didn't really mean the petty thing. And I get it. Having met Shelly, I get it. But yeah, that's good."

She angled her head to the side of her camera, and I

watched her chew her lip before a sudden grin forced her to stop. "You're actually kinda sweet, Adam." When my face heated, she moved back to my side and held the camera out in front of us. "And look at me being all nice."

My mouth kicked up on one side and I gestured at the camera. "Are you one of those post-every-second-of-my-life-on-social-media types?"

"No, I'm one of those capture-the-moments-so-I-can-tell-the-story-I-want types, aka a filmmaker."

"Right," I said, remembering Shelly mentioning something about a film school program the night before. "So you make movies?"

"I make *great* movies. Just short ones so far, and nothing scripted—more slice-of-life type stuff—but full-length feature films are my future." With a sigh she lowered her camera. "Real but better, because I get to control the outcome, cut out what I don't like and frame the rest the way I want."

"Wow, that's cool." Because it was, but also somehow sad. I gestured with my phone. "And thanks again. For being nice, and not just to me."

"The famous mother. Tell me something, why do you care so much about making her happy?"

"Besides the fact that she's my mom?"

Jolene nodded, scrutinizing me in a way that made my answer more transparent than I intended.

"She thinks all of this—our split-up family—is her fault. It's not. My dad is the one who walked out." I closed my eyes, thinking about that morning he'd left and wishing I'd done more. "She hasn't been happy in a really long time, and more than anything, I want that for her."

Jolene's sigh brought my attention back to her. "I want to preface this by saying I'm still trying to be nice here. Try not to take it personally if you can't make your mom happy."

Jolene

"Oh, Mom! Your dearest daughter is home! Come shower me with kisses and lonely sob stories."

My voice echoing back at me from the vaulted ceiling in the foyer was the only response I expected, and I wasn't surprised. It was Sunday evening, which meant my mom was probably still at the gym. I dragged my bag upstairs to my room and tossed it in the vicinity of my bed before continuing to the kitchen. Like most of the house, it was pristine and blindingly white, from the glazed snowy cabinets to the Carrara marble countertops and glittering crystal chandelier. All that splendor faded into the background the second I smelled the lasagna that Mrs. Cho had left for me in the oven.

Technically, Mrs. Cho was only supposed to clean the house three mornings a week while I was at school—a rule Mom instituted to eliminate my interactions with a person I openly preferred to her—but she'd started cooking for me when Mom decided that the elusive key to her happiness was tied to the number of pounds she could lose and had stopped consuming anything that didn't come in a martini glass.

I peeled back the foil, and the scent of cheesy, garlicky goodness wrapped its arms around me. "I missed you, too," I told my dinner. It was too hot, which meant I burned my mouth and had to endure that tiny flap of skin hanging from the roof, but no sacrifice was too big for Mrs. Cho's lasagna.

A thought propelled me across the kitchen to the fridge, and, opening it, I did a happy dance. There was a cheesecake on the second shelf, with luscious-looking red cherries on top. I checked our hiding spot in the bread box on the counter and found the best present of all: a note written in Mrs. Cho's teeny tiny print.

I watch movie with man who drives car. I think I like dog movie best. I make you cheese dinner and cheese dessert. Be good.

My laughter echoed around the kitchen. I knew she'd like the psychological horror of *Cujo* more than the pulpy crime drama of *Drive*—she did work for my mother, after all. Mrs. Cho and I had recently formed a movie club together. She wanted to improve her English, and I was only too happy to recommend titles for her. Next, I'd have to try her on the less gory but arguably more terrifying *Get Out*.

I kept reading. Her notes were never long, and this one was shorter than most, but it was the last line she always added that filled my heart and flooded my eyes: *I miss my girl*. I could remember a time when I'd come home from school and Mrs. Cho would be waiting to hug me and lift me up on the island so that I could help her with dinner. She always smelled like fresh bread and Windex, and she'd scratch my back while I stirred bowls bigger than I was. She spoke next to no English back then, and I knew only the few Korean words she'd taught me, but we always understood each other.

I flipped the note over and in my bolder, blocky hand-writing, suggested a couple more movies for her to watch, and then profusely thanked her for all the cheese that I was going to consume that night and told her I missed her, too. My hand shook as I tucked the note away for her to find to-morrow.

Our notes were better than nothing, but I had to bite the inside of my cheek until that burst of pain chased the tight-ness from my chest before I could lift the first forkful of fluffy cheesecake to my mouth.

If Mom knew how much I ate on a given day, she would cast me out on the street and stone me. Probably. Maybe. More than likely she'd use it as an excuse to rant about Dad and his cursed slim genes, which I'd inherited. The calorie obsession wouldn't last. She'd find out that she was just as miserable at a size four as she was at an eight, and then she'd be onto something new.

Back in my room, I slipped my phone out of my pocket and looked at the picture I'd sent myself from Adam's phone. I tried to imagine what his mom had thought when she saw it. It was a good picture. I looked happy, and my lips weren't curled back in that way they sometimes did that revealed too much gum. The sun had lit the shot at just the right angle, threading my brown hair with gold and highlighting the yel-lows and reds of the last few oak leaves in the tree behind us.

But I didn't study myself for long, and I didn't imagine Adam's mom would have either. He was the one who drew my eye, with his ruddy hair falling forward and his eyes lighting up not for the camera, but for me. It was because I'd surprised him by leaning in and sneaking a photo, but anyone else would look at that picture and envy me. Not because Adam was an Adonis or anything—though I rather liked his jaw—but because his expression, his eyes, his everything, said he was looking at something beautiful.

With a reproachful sound that was directed solely at myself, I tossed my phone onto my pillow and bent to unpack my camera and laptop, ignoring, for the moment, the other few belongings that I was forced to shuffle back and forth between my parents' residences. I kept basic necessities at both places, but I had only one nearly threadbare T-shirt featuring *The Breakfast Club* that I liked to sleep in.

After opening my laptop and Final Cut Pro, I rewatched the footage of Adam and me that I'd imported the day before. None of my footage had captured the magic moment from the cell phone pic, so I imported that image, too. My projects always started the same way: with random footage dumped together until, slowly, the story I wanted to tell took shape. My idol, Suzanne Silver, described her directorial process in a similar way. The current footage was still a mystery to me, but the story would come.

As I was closing my laptop, my phone buzzed, and I saw a text from Dad on the screen. My stomach twisted into a knot before I even read it.

> Busy weekend. You understand. Shelly said everything went well. We'll have dinner next time. Promise.

I clutched the phone with fingers that had gone icy cold. *Yeah, sure we will.* I could barely remember the last time I'd seen him, let alone had a meal with him. My last birthday, maybe? Just for kicks, I scrolled through his last half-dozen texts. They all said basically the same thing. A couple were identical, as if he'd copied and pasted the same words. I wondered if he thought I was dumb enough not to notice, or if he didn't care either way. The knots in my stomach began twisting.

I didn't respond. I never did.

I could put a stop to his absentee parenting act if I wanted to. A single word to Mom or her lawyer, and Dad's no-show weekends would end...until his lawyer dug up something new on Mom. And on and on it would go.

No, thanks.

Besides, how was that a better story than the one I already had?

Hands shook me awake, interrupting my dream that I was Tarzan. During a brief moment of confusion, my dream and reality converged, and then the vine I was swinging on was torn from my grip.

"Jolene. Jolene! Wake up!"

My vines—or sheets, as I saw them with my awake eyes—were discarded at the foot of my bed and Mom was leaning over me.

"Good. You're awake." She smiled, perfectly white-capped teeth on full display.

Mom's declaration that I was awake wasn't a completely observable fact. My eyes were barely open, and my body remained curved around the vine/sheet that was no longer there. In truth, I'd hardly moved except to dip involuntarily toward her as she sat down on the mattress next to my hip.

"You're not taking drugs, are you?" Her thumb lifted my eyelid, and I hissed and jerked away like a vampire confronted with sunlight.

Her hands settled on me again and more shaking commenced. "I wanted to see you. Would it have killed you to wait up for me?"

One eye opened and I glanced at her. "What time is it?"

"A little after two," she said without a trace of remorse.

"Then, yes."

Mom was sitting all prim and proper on my bed, her brown hair sleek and shiny on her shoulders. The neckline of the tank she wore was a little low, and I could see the outline of her sternum in addition to her muscle-shredded, olive-toned arms. Was it possible that she'd gotten skinnier in the past two days? My eyes said yes.

Her brown eyes gleamed a little too bright, but even without that visual clue, I could smell that she'd been drinking and I clutched at the corner of my pillow. These middle-of-the-night chats tended to happen only after a little help from Captain Morgan, and they never went well.

She always started with the same question. "How's your father?"

"Fine."

"And the home wrecker?"

"Mom."

"What? Am I not allowed to ask about the woman your father chose to co-parent with? Is it not within my rights as your mother to want to know that she's treating you well? Is it not—"

"She's fine. Everything is fine. No one beat me or starved me or forced me to join a cult. No, Dad didn't mention you. No, I didn't get the sense that he and Shelly were splitting up. No, I didn't find a secret bag of money marked Hide from Helen. I don't know anything. I never know anything. Now, can I go back to sleep?"

But I couldn't. Because she started to cry. So I had to hold her. Because she never held me.

"Tom says I should be getting more money."

"Who's Tom?" I asked, several minutes and a completely soaked shoulder later.

"Tom. You know Tom."

I did not know Tom.

"I met him at the gym, and he says there's no way Robert's disclosing all his assets." She lifted her head, and after I stopped focusing on the black smears all over her face, I realized she was looking at me like I was supposed to say something.

I sighed and dropped my arms. Just once, I'd like her to wake me up because she actually missed me instead of for what this was: an attempted guilt-trip debrief. I was pretty sure Dad was putting money away somewhere in Shelly's name. Mom thought so, too, but so far she hadn't been able to prove it. Her attempts to get me to spy for her had failed. What did I care which one of them got to enjoy his money? As long as this charade went on, neither of them did.

It was the little things in life.

"I told you I don't know about any money."

Mom snorted and jerked back. "He's hiding it somewhere. You know I'm right." A finger waved in my face and I brushed it away. "Why else would that tart stay with him?"

I no longer thought that either of my parents was especially lovable, so I didn't comment.

Mom rested her head on my shoulder. "Couldn't you just—"

"No," I said, tightening my grip on my pillow and hunching my shoulder to dislodge her. She was trying to play nice, play sweet, but my heart beat erratically from the falseness of it all. "I'm not going to riffle through his stuff. How many times do I have to say it?"

She abandoned my shoulder. "I guess you want me to be homeless."

"You have a huge house."

"What happens if he claims he needs to pay less? I could lose everything."

"Mom, stop. You're getting worked up over nothing."

"Why, because I'm the only one who'll be homeless?"

She made a scoffing sound in the back of her throat. "You'll go gallivanting off to your father's like you do every other weekend—"

"I am known for my gallivanting." I refrained from commenting on the visitation schedule, because she knew—at least, sober, she knew—that I'd had no say in that arrangement.

"—and I'll be in an alley somewhere selling my body for drugs."

I couldn't help it. I laughed at her. "You turned into a crack whore pretty quickly in that scenario."

When she slapped me, my face flamed hot.

"Oh!" Both hands covered her mouth. "Jolene. Honey, I didn't mean that. My Jolene." Then she was hugging me again, rocking and shushing me as if I was the one crying. I wasn't. I never did. My heart limped in my chest, and my face stung, but my eyes stayed dry. "You are the only good thing in my life, do you know that? I love you so much, so, so much…" Then she made me lie down, and she pulled up my sheet and tucked me in.

The last thing she did before leaving was kiss the cheek she'd slapped.

ADAM

I waited in the car while Jeremy and Dad hugged goodbye, opting out of any farewell beyond a single uttered word: *bye*. As a result, Jeremy and I didn't talk on the way home. It was a thirty-minute drive, so the silence took considerable effort from both of us.

We turned off the main road, and even with my eyes shut, the crunching sound accompanied by the vibration of Jeremy's car let me know I was almost home. The graveled road stretched for a half mile before our house came into view and Mom came dashing down the porch, her jaw-length auburn hair fluffing out around her fair-skinned face.

I let Mom hug me as tightly as she needed. Jeremy was next, obediently hugging her and then kissing her cheek as directed. She clung to both of our hands and drank us in with blue-green eyes that were a little too red-rimmed to completely sell the smile she wore.

"You're taller. I swear both of you are taller."

"Don't go giving Jeremy ideas, Mom. Short people are just as good as the rest of us."

Jeremy swore at me, right in front of Mom, but she didn't reprimand him. That, more than anything, killed the fight always simmering between the two of us.

"Who's hungry? I made fried chicken, and there's apple pie for dessert." We both responded eagerly and let her precede us into the house. We exchanged a glance. No smiles or mouthed words, but I knew that we'd both do everything we could to make her forget that she'd been alone all weekend. Jeremy wasn't inclined to place blame on either of our parents, and right then, being half-right was all I needed from him.

An hour later, Mom pretended to be horrified when Jeremy and I polished off the entire pie.

"Got any more?" I asked. She really did look horrified then, but probably more out of self-recrimination that she should have made a second pie just in case. "Mom, I'm kidding. I'm seriously on the verge of throwing up." No joke. I would have stopped after two pieces, but when Jeremy had gone back for thirds, my little-brother inferiority complex kicked in.

"I can make another one." She started to push back from the table, but I stopped her with a hand on her wrist.

"Mom. Sit. It wasn't even that good."

Mom exhaled but it turned into a laugh. "I know you're teasing me, because you ate the whole thing."

"That last piece was pure pity. Awful pie. I mean, I feel bad for the apples."

More laughter from Mom, and each sound was better than the last.

"I liked it," Jeremy said, and Mom leaned over to pat his hand.

"Thank you, sweetie."

She tried to shoo us to go unpack while she did the dishes, but I lingered until Jeremy left. "Mom?"

She was standing at the sink, rinsing plates and loading the dishwasher. She looked at me over her shoulder. "Change your mind about the pie?"

I took a newly rinsed plate from her and put it in the dishwasher. "I'm glad to be home is all."

She kept running another plate round and round in her hands under the faucet. "Me, too. I—I didn't think it would be this hard. How many mothers would love to have their house to themselves for a few days? I'll be better next time. I'll plan some things, and it'll go by faster." She nodded at me and finally relinquished the plate. "Your dad okay?"

"Fine, I guess." I could have added that I didn't really know, because we'd barely spoken the whole weekend, but she'd find a way to feel guilty about that. Instead, I brought up the subject that had served me so well last time I needed to cheer her up. "Did you get the picture?"

"Is that what that was? My phone made a chirping noise and I couldn't figure out what I was supposed to do." Mom had grown up Mennonite and had been slow to embrace technology even as an adult. She wiped her hands dry on a towel and retrieved her purse from the other room. When she handed over her phone, she was already smiling.

"Before you get any ideas, please remember that I just met this girl."

"Adam, I know." She tried to sound calm, but she was practically bouncing up and down on her toes, which ruined the effect. This was either going to be the smartest or dumbest thing I'd ever done. Thinking about Jolene, I decided it was probably both.

I showed her the picture without looking at it too long myself. Based on Mom's expression, I had woefully underestimated the impact it would have. Her smile, which had been big and bright only a moment before, dimmed before my eyes.

"Mom?" When I tried to pull the phone back, she seized my wrist and made a sound like a wounded animal.

"I'm sorry, I'm sorry." She pulled the phone closer, and I watched her gaze flick from corner to corner over and over again. "She's very pretty, Adam." Then she pressed the phone back into my hands. "Take another one for me next time, okay?" When I nodded, she smiled. "I guess all that cooking exhausted me. I'm going to go to bed early tonight." She brushed a kiss on my cheek. "Glad you're home."

When she left, I looked at the phone in my hand, and it took only a second to see what I had missed before. Her reaction had nothing to do with Jolene or the two of us together. It had everything to do with that fact that, in that hastily taken photo, I looked just like my dead brother.

Greg.

SECOND WEEKEND

October 9–10

Jolene

There's this famous sci-fi movie from the '50s, I think, about aliens who come to Earth, only humans don't realize they're being invaded, because the aliens snatch people and replace them with aliens who look just like them. Also, there's something about pods. I should probably watch the movie at some point, but pre-1970s sci-fi doesn't really do it for me.

Still, it would have been helpful to know how the humans defeated the aliens in the movie—they did, didn't they?—because I was 96 percent sure there was one in my kitchen.

It looked like my mother. Olive skin, sleek, dark bun, "Sarah Conner circa *Terminator 2*" arms. But the alien had made one fatal mistake: the apron.

"Try to tell me you come in peace."

"For heaven's sake, Jolene, you almost gave me a heart attack." My mother, the alien, waved me off and bent back over the giant pot she was stirring on the stove. Keeping to the perimeter of the kitchen, I edged closer until I reached the prep sink in the island. I ran water over my fingers, then flicked the droplets at her.

"Stop it, Jolene. What's wrong with you?"

"Hmm, so you saw *Signs*, too. I always thought that aliens with a water vulnerability coming to a planet that's two-thirds covered with the stuff were too stupid to live anyway."

"Is that what this is? You think I'm E.T.?"

"More like the queen from *Aliens*." I fished the candle lighter from a drawer and flicked the flame to life. "And I'm Ellen Ripley."

"You watch too many movies."

"Someone had to raise me."

My mother, the alien, paused, then turned to me. "It hurts me when you say things like that."

In another life, in another movie, that lilt of pain in her voice would have brought me up short. But this wasn't a charming character piece where the mother and daughter fought before one of them broke the tension with a well-aimed handful of flour that devolved into a laughing food fight and a tender reconciliation by the end of the scene. My mother and I didn't do tender, and if I had any doubt about her motives that day, the tiny brown glass bottle that she tried to surreptitiously tuck back into her apron pocket cleared me of them. The contents of my stomach turned cold and familiar. That bottle didn't belong in a kitchen.

I opened my mouth, then shut it, then opened it again. "Sorry."

"How was school? Soccer practice?"

"Enlightening, as always." My hands went clammy as I stared at the bulge in her apron. "How was… What do you do again?"

My mother, the alien, ignored that question. "Are you hungry?"

My stomach clenched. "Wrong. My mother would never ask that question. And she doesn't own an apron."

"She does, actually. She used to cook before you were born. Some anyway."

"I don't believe you."

She lifted a spoon from the pot and held it out for me to taste.

I eyed the soup. Like my mother, the alien, it looked completely harmless on the outside, but I knew better.

Her hand shook when I didn't respond. "It's minestrone soup. I made it for you."

"You first."

The spoon slammed down on the counter, and boiling orange liquid splattered everywhere. "Dammit," she whispered. There were tears then. "Why can't you be good and easy? Why can't you smile and eat a bowl of soup? *Dammit.*"

My whole body trembled as I watched her. I didn't know for sure what she'd put in the soup, but something between too-sick-to-go-to-Dad's and not-sick-enough-to-warrant-a-hospital-visit was a fair assumption. She'd done it before— not often, but enough that I no longer ate anything she'd had prior access to on these weekends. "You burned your hand."

"I know I burned my hand." Red welts were rising along the backs of her knuckles and down her wrist. "It was just soup, Jolene."

It was never just anything.

"It's ruined now." She lifted the massive pot—which held enough soup to feed a dozen people—and dumped the whole thing down the sink. Tiny vegetables and little half macaronis clogged the drain, preventing the orange liquid from disappearing fast enough. She turned and slid to the floor. "Why wouldn't you eat it?"

Watching her, my stomach was churning like I already had. "You've never made me soup. You've never made me anything."

"I'm not an alien."

But she had to be; a real mother wouldn't do this. "That's what an alien would say."

Still teary, she smiled at me. "Good girl."

Several minutes later, nothing had burst out of my chest. Or hers. The soup was still swimming in the sink. She was still on the floor, or rather, back on the floor, this time accompanied by a glass of amber-colored liquid that she tipped to her lips.

I hugged my arms around my chest. "You're supposed to drop me off at Dad's."

A healthy swallow was her response.

"I won't get into a car with you and I don't have time to walk." Dad's apartment was only a ten-minute drive from here, but considerably longer by foot.

She toasted that comment.

I sank down opposite her and my voice broke when I spoke. "Why are you doing this?"

That open-ended question earned me a blank stare until the glass was emptied and refilled. Halfway through her second drink, she paused to trace the welts on her hand with gentle fingers. "I wonder sometimes... Would I still be married if I never had you?"

If my mother had said that, I might have done more than flinch. I looked at the alien. "Was Dad cheating before you had me?"

The alien stared off at nothing. "He was always cheating." Then her gaze shifted to me and the overnight bag still hanging from my shoulder. "Go put that away."

My eyes shut slowly before opening. "You know I can't."

"Jolene. Don't argue with me today."

"I have to be at Dad's apartment by six."

"It's my weekend."

Even if she'd somehow forgotten, which she never did,

Dad's lawyer had taken to calling and reminding her, which had no doubt prompted the display of horror-tinged domesticity with the soup that I'd walked in on. The welts on her wrist and hand were bright red and painful looking. Even sober, she'd have a hard time driving. I had a suspicion she knew that, maybe had intentionally burned herself for that sole purpose.

I drew my knees up. "It's always worse when you fight it."

My phone rang before she could reply. We both knew it was Dad's lawyer before I saw the screen.

"Hello, Mr. Kantos. Yes, I know it's my father's weekend… She's here…" I glanced at the alien, who stared straight ahead and drained her glass. "Unfortunately, she won't be able to drop me off."

A small smile played at her lips.

"I'll call an Uber but I might be a little late… No, that's not necessary…" Dread raised my voice an octave. "I really don't think… Mr. Kantos—" I turned away and tried to whisper, for all the good it would do to keep the alien from hearing me "—we all know that very bad things happen when they get near each other." I bit the inside of my cheek and concentrated on not saying something that would get me into trouble later. "I'm sure you are." I ended the call and stared straight ahead like my mother, the alien.

Shelly was coming to pick me up.

ADAM

It wasn't possible that Dad's apartment looked worse the second time I saw it. Objectively, I knew he'd been working on it since I'd been there, but I could still feel Mom's fingers tight on my shirt when she hugged me and the tremor that transferred from her body to mine as she forced herself to let go.

So, yeah. It looked worse.

"Come on, man." There wasn't a thread of irritation in Jeremy's voice. Mom had clung to him, too. "We can call her after dinner. Tomorrow and Sunday, too." And then he added my bag to his before shutting the trunk. That was the Everest of goodwill as far as Jeremy was concerned.

Two years ago, I'd have appreciated the gesture.

Two years ago, Greg would have not only smoothed out our rough edges but made us forget they'd been there in the first place.

Two years ago, Dad hadn't moved out and I wasn't standing in a pothole-ridden parking lot while my mom spent yet another weekend bereft of her sons. I was a second away from slamming the car door hard enough to royally piss off Jeremy when another slamming car door beat me to the punch.

"Jolene! I'm not done talking to you!"

I looked and saw Jolene walking away from a red sports car with her bag over one shoulder and her braid dangling over the other. She turned, walking backward so that she could respond to Shelly, who was standing by the open driver's-side door.

"But you really, really should be."

Shelly's door slammed shut just as hard as Jolene's had. "It's not my fault that your mother threw a glass at my head."

I felt my eyes widen and glanced over to see Jeremy's do the same.

"No, but you should have stayed in the car," Jolene said, like it was the most obvious thing in the world. "Doors locked, engine running. That's what you do."

"You were supposed to be outside waiting for me."

Jolene stopped. She even took a few steps toward Shelly, and I noticed how frayed her braid looked. "But you don't want to know why I wasn't, do you? You don't want to know that she got drunk and tackled me to the ground when the doorbell rang, or that, before that, she tried to poison me just enough to keep me in bed for the weekend. You don't want to know any of that, because you can't tell my dad or his lawyer without risking the courts deciding that I'm better off living here full-time."

Jeremy and I both swiveled our heads toward Shelly and watched her face turn several shades of red before she looked away.

"Right," Jolene said, turning back to the apartment. "That's why you need to be done talking to me." She yanked open the door, and that was when she finally caught sight of Jeremy and me. To her credit, her expression didn't change at all. She held my gaze long enough for my face and neck to flame hot, and then she went inside. A moment later, Shelly slunk in after her.

"Still feel like complaining about your life?" Jeremy asked, letting his shoulder bang into mine as he headed for the doors.

Jolene held up a finger to her lips when I opened the door to my room and found her sitting cross-legged in the middle of my bed.

I halted with my hand on the door, staring at her and trying to decide if I was hallucinating. Then the sound of Dad and Jeremy talking spurred me into motion and into the room. I pulled the door shut behind me and locked it. "What are you doing here? How did you even get in?"

She lowered her voice to match mine. "I adopted your technique for scaling balconies. Though let me just say it's much more difficult without your height advantage. Also, wet metal is super slippery. Did you know that?"

I half shook my head. "Wait, start with the why."

"Am I here?" She pointed to the bed she still sat on. "In your room?"

I widened my eyes in confirmation before darting them back to the door I was basically barricading with my body. If Dad or Jeremy heard her… But then, Jeremy had already heard her—we both had—down in the parking lot. When she'd said all that stuff about her mom. My gaze slid more slowly over her. I'd noticed her messy braid before, but up close I could see that strands and tangles stuck out everywhere, and one knee on her jeans was torn—and not in a way that looked deliberate. Plus, there was a scrape on her cheek. "Is that all from your mom?" I asked, unable to keep the concern from my voice.

"What?" Then she looked down at herself and half laughed. "Oh, right. No. My hair is mostly from the wind trying to fling me off the side of the building while I was climbing the railing, the scrape is from getting up close and personal with the apartment wall, and the torn jeans are from when I tumbled onto your balcony. It was all very graceful."

I wasn't sure I completely believed her but before I could ask anything else, a fist pounded on the door.

"Adam. Get out here. We're going to dinner."

I looked at the door, then back at Jolene. More pounding.

"Hey, open up. Let's go."

She raised her eyebrows at me, as if she was merely curious as to how I'd handle the situation of hiding a girl in my room while my dad and brother stood right outside the door. Considering that she'd risked much more than a broken leg climbing onto my balcony, the least I could do was blow off my brother.

"Can't. I feel sick." I stood up, took a few steps toward the door, and half turned my back to her.

"You are such a little—" The doorknob rattled as Jeremy tried to force it open. Dad asked what the problem was and the rattling stopped. "It's fine. Adam's sick though. We had to pull over on the way here so he could puke."

The doorknob was tried again, easier this time. "Adam, you all right? Do you need anything?"

Jeremy answered for me. "He's fine. He's gonna stay here and sleep it off."

There was a conversation that I couldn't quite follow, but it ended with Jeremy convincing Dad that they should go and leave me to rest in quiet.

"We'll bring you something back in case you feel better later," Dad said. "You have my cell." The front door opened and shut a minute later.

"You're not really sick, are you?" she asked, eyeing me.

"No, this is my normal skin tone. I'm pale."

"So can I hang out for a while? Not all night or anything, just until Shelly falls asleep?"

"Yeah," I said, sitting on the foot of the bed and feeling pretty good about the fact that I'd gotten rid of Jeremy and Dad so easily. "Stay as long as you want."

She beamed at me, and when I felt my flush start to creep back again, she took pity on me and glanced around my room. "So this is nice. It's like the cheap motel room from a slasher flick." Her eyebrows flicked up. "You know, cozy."

I looked around. That seemed accurate.

"Don't feel bad. Your apartment could be dripping with blood and I'd still find it infinitely more appealing than mine."

"Shelly?" I asked, my gaze catching on the apple orchard picture above the bed.

"Aren't you the smart one?"

I didn't feel smart. I felt…compelled. My focus had strayed from her for only seconds at a time since I'd walked in. She demanded my complete attention without seeming to try. Plus she talked a lot. Sometimes her voice would get a little strangled as she ran out of air, but she'd force another sentence or two out before drawing in a massive breath and continuing. Shelly had struck me that way, too, but her non-stop talking had felt smothering. With Jolene, I didn't mind.

She wandered around the room, looking in drawers and peeking into the closet. All my stuff was in my bag, so I let her.

"Want me to help you unpack?"

"Why?"

"Aren't you going to unpack?"

"I hadn't planned on it."

Jolene dropped onto the corner of the bed. Her brown hair was so long that she was practically sitting on it. I'd never seen anyone with hair that long in real life. "You want some advice? Divorce kid to divorce kid?" She immediately raised her palms when I started to object. "Sorry, divorce kid to separated kid." It was clear from her tone that she considered that distinction a technicality. I felt that irritation from our first meeting stir to life. "Don't waste your energy on the small stuff."

"Small stuff?"

"Yeah, you know, tiny acts of rebellion like living out of a suitcase and—"

"Smoking?"

Her mouth twitched and she bit back a smile, the slight movement effectively snuffing out my irritation. "Okay, yes, and smoking. Although in my defense, I have to focus on stuff that speaks for me even when I'm not here since I've barely laid eyes on my dad in months. The last time he stood outside my door and begged me to go to dinner with him—" she gestured toward my door "—was, oh, never."

"Seriously?"

"No," she said, plucking at her braid. "I'm making it up so you'll pity me."

Why did she have to say stuff like that? "Sorry."

"Yes, he is, so let's not talk about him. Let's talk about you." She scrambled up on her knees again and took out her braid so she could comb through the snarls with her fingers. "You still haven't told me what your mom thought about our picture. Good, right?"

I blinked at her. In that moment I was sucked back to Mom and me standing in the kitchen and the expression on her face when I showed her the photo. I couldn't think about it without seeing it through her eyes, without seeing Greg.

"Let me guess." Jolene rolled onto her stomach and hung her upper body over the edge to search under the bed, her impossibly long hair pooling on my floor. "She thinks I'm way too pretty for you. Don't feel bad," she added. "When you grow into your ears, you are going to be intolerably cute." That was when she looked up and saw my flushed face that had nothing to do with her teasing and everything to do with the thing about Greg. "Oh, wow, are you sensitive." She twisted and sat up to face me, pushing her hair out of her eyes. "I was messing with you. And even if I wasn't, that would put you at tolerably cute now. Tolerably cute is still cute, Adam. Plus, I like your ears. They're the first part of you to light up like Rudolph when you get embarrassed."

As if on command, I felt blood rush to my ears.

"Honestly, it's more than tolerably cute, but you probably already know that. Hey, is that why you blush so much? Can you control it like a flirting superpower?"

She'd been talking so much that she'd completely pulled me back from the brink without even knowing I'd been there or why. The sadness that lingered in the recesses of my mind when I thought of Greg receded further as Jolene's gap-toothed grin filled my vision and kicked up my own lips. And she thought *I* had superpowers.

"Come on, what did your mom think of the picture?"

After she'd gotten over her initial shock, Mom had stared at it long enough to comment that Jolene was pretty. Which I guess she was. She'd worn her hair braided back both times I'd seen her the other weekend, but this time I could see that it was thick and wavy, almost rippled. It was pretty. And when she was smiling, she was, too. Her upper lip was smaller than her lower and her chin was a little pointy, but smiling made her look like an elf or something. Mischievous edging toward dangerous.

I didn't think Mom had looked at the picture and seen much beyond Greg. But she'd asked for another picture, and

I could give her that. She needed something to hold on to when Jeremy and I weren't with her, even if it was only an idea.

"She liked it," I said. "So yeah, mission accomplished. And she's expecting another picture if you're up for it."

"I don't know. Are you going to freak out on me again?"

"As long as you don't actually lick my face, I think I'm good."

Jolene tapped her chin with her index finger a few times. "Hmm. Normally, I don't like to work with these kinds of creative restrictions, but if you insist." She knee-walked across the bed to me and stuck out her hand. "Adam Whatever-Your-Last-Name-Is, I think this is the beginning of a beautiful friendship."

It was the beginning of something.

Jolene

When I woke up on Saturday, the view outside my window was a glittering white wonderland, incredibly rare for the beginning of October. The street hadn't yet been plowed and the cars below were fluffy white balls. This was the first weekend since I'd started coming to Dad's apartment that I didn't immediately pull the covers back over my head, hoping to shorten the day by sleeping through as much of it as possible. It was a strange sensation to view the prospect of getting up with anything but resignation, let alone tingling anticipation. Ideas danced in my head as I hopped out of bed and to the window. I grabbed my camera and captured the fog of my breath on the glass and then traced a smiling sun high in one corner.

I hesitated at my door and listened. Silence. Still, I turned the knob slowly. Shelly claimed she was an early riser, but she'd been up before me only twice before. Not that I was willing to gamble. I scanned every inch of the living room before fully opening my door.

Staying on the balls of my feet, I padded into the kitchen

and scrounged up breakfast for myself and even raided Shelly's vegetable drawer for the one item I knew I'd need for the day I had planned. When I was outfitted with my full regalia of winter wear, I slipped quiet as a ninja into the hall and entertained myself by imaging I was in a John Woo–style action film, hugging the wall and side-walking the ten feet down to Adam's apartment. I stopped short of attempting an elaborately choreographed parkour number that I was in no way capable of doing but would have looked so cool in a series of tight close-up shots.

I stopped outside Adam's door and listened. He'd said he was typically awake hours before his dad and brother, a claim that I was about to test as I rapped softly on his apartment door.

My first thought, when he opened his door, was that it wasn't fair that his bedhead looked so cute when mine looked like I'd slept in a jet engine. The second was that he smiled when he saw me. It made me feel like my coat was suddenly too warm.

"Hey," he said, his voice husky with sleep. He probably hadn't used it yet that morning.

"Hey." I rocked back and forth on my toes, inexplicably excited. "I have an idea about our next picture for your mom that will double as a scene for a film I'm working on if you're okay with a little quid pro quo."

He took in my clothes, including the scarf, hat, and gloves. "Sure, give me a second to brush my teeth and stuff, then I'll grab my coat."

Boy stuff apparently took a really long time. As the minutes ticked by, I sighed and lowered the bag with my camera in it.

A guy with thinning blond hair who looked to be in his late twenties came out of the apartment across and one down from Adam's and smiled at me. I wasn't sure how, exactly, but it was different than the way Adam had smiled at me.

"Hey there. I don't think we've met before. I just moved in."

I shifted a little, giving him my back, and pulled out my phone. I wasn't up for playing nice with the neighbors. Well, except Adam. "Sorry about that," I mumbled.

He laughed too hard for the joke, and I pretended to take a call so he'd take the hint.

He did eventually. "I'll let you go then. Hopefully we'll run into each other again some morning. We early birds have to stick together, right?"

I sort of nodded and raised a hand distractedly in his direction while pretending to be deep in conversation on my phone until he was gone. After that, I still had to wait another five minutes before Adam reappeared wearing a camel-colored coat with a fleece collar. The bedhead was gone and his hair was damp. He'd had the slightest bit of stubble on his chin earlier, but now his skin looked perfectly smooth. I wondered if he'd shaved for the picture, or me.

I picked up my bag. "I feel like being five today."

"Okay," he said with a hesitant smile. "What does that mean?"

I pulled Shelly's carrot out of my pocket. "When's the last time you built a snowman?"

"Kindergarten, maybe."

"Then we're about to go back in time to glue eating and scheduled nap times." I wrapped my gloved hand around his, an act that made his eyes widen for a second and tugged him to the stairway. "Not that I ever ate glue." I glanced over my shoulder at him. "But you sort of look like the type."

"You're pretty mean for a girl I let hang out in my room all night," he said, but there was a hint of laughter in his voice.

"I don't hear you denying it."

"What did you do in kindergarten then?"

"I was a thief. Used to steal all the good stuff from the other kids' lunches. Then I'd try to play it cool walking around with bags of chips stuffed into my tights. Trust me, I'd much rather have been a glue eater."

"So you were the weird kid?"

"Oh no, I was super popular." I grinned at him and reached out to push open the double glass doors that led outside. "I had all the good food."

I took us to the grassy area at the nearby elementary school, which had an easily hopped fence. Sure, the kids might kill our snowman come Monday, but I felt like I was giving him a chance.

I made sure to get a lot of footage of Adam's hands as we rolled the body segments together and stacked them one by one before stepping back to check our progress.

"Um," I said.

"Yeah, I think we did something wrong."

"Or brilliant. Look, he'll be a middle-aged snowman complete with a beer gut. This is what we call serendipity."

"Or we accidentally switched his lower section with his midsection."

"Either way, I'm digging him." I added the carrot nose and found two rocks for the eyes. He still looked unfinished, but there weren't any nearby trees with branches that we could reach, so I unwound my scarf and added it. "Much better." I surveyed our armless creation and took a slow pan shot with my camera before lowering it. "So this is how Dr. Frankenstein felt. Huh."

"Not everything you hoped he'd be?"

"Not quite. I mean, look at him. He has no mouth. He

doesn't know what to feel." I leaned forward. "Are you happy, Mr. Snowman? Are you going to blame us later for your lousy childhood?" I gestured at our snowman and turned to Adam. "Well I can't do anything when he's like this. Maybe you can talk to him."

Adam stepped forward and placed a hand on Mr. Snowman's shoulder, doing something with the other that I couldn't see. "There," he said, stepping aside. "He's forgiven us, and he's ready to raise his own dysfunctional snow kids."

Mr. Snowman had a semicircle carved under his nose. He was smiling. I was, too.

We positioned ourselves a few feet in front of Mr. Snowman, making sure he was clearly visible in the background, and snapped the pic. Adam didn't let me get my hands anywhere near his phone and scrutinized the photo for a solid minute before deciding it was okay.

"Vain much?" I asked as we set out in search of some playground equipment that wasn't iced over.

He shrugged in answer. *Okay then.*

The swings turned out to be our only option. "Do your parents get along?" I asked, filming my knees as I pumped my legs while Adam only swayed slightly.

"Define *get along.*"

"Can they talk to each other without lawyers present? Can they be in the same room without screaming obscenities? Are they constantly after you to spy on each other?"

"My mom baked my dad his favorite pie last week and had my brother drop it off. Just because."

"Wow," I said. "That's… I don't know what that is."

Adam twisted toward me, pulling his arm inside the chain of his swing. I couldn't help lifting my camera for a few seconds to capture him under the guise of putting it away for good. "It's messed up. People split up when they don't like each other anymore. When my dad moved out, my mom helped him pack. Like, they literally did it together."

"You have to have some idea why they split."

Adam looked down at his hands. Clearly I'd asked the wrong question. Maybe it was something horrible, like his parents finding out they were related. I suppressed a shudder and changed the subject before Adam became completely comatose.

We left the swings and our snowman and headed back to the apartment as flurries of snow began falling. Our conversation lagged the closer we got, drying up completely when we reached the parking lot.

"So that was fun," I said.

"Yeah." Adam had his hands in his pocket and was so busy staring at the building it was like I wasn't even there.

Super awesome feeling.

I glanced up at our floor. "And that won't be fun."

His lips barely moved when he answered. "No."

I didn't say that it was already not fun, but I doubted he would have heard that. I suppose it was naive to think he'd keep me from Shelly all day, so instead of showing the disappointment that tugged at me, I adopted a chipper tone and started backing toward to the door. "Well, I guess I'll see you."

"Wait, you're going?" He nearly tripped as he started after me without noticing the pothole in front of him.

I slowed. "You got your photo, I got my footage, and you clearly want to be alone with your brooding, so…" I took another backward step.

He dropped his head and nodded slightly. "Okay, that's fair. I'm sorry, I'm not sure how to do this yet." He flicked his gaze at his dad's apartment before returning it to me.

I lifted and lowered my shoulders, saying softly, "Nobody knows how to do this."

"But we still have to."

I didn't say anything to that.

He strolled toward me, purposefully, and my heart unexpectedly starting beating faster when I had to tilt my head up to meet his gaze.

"It *was* fun today. And honestly, I'm not sure what I would have done if you hadn't come and gotten me. I get it if you have to go, but if you don't..." One of his reddish-brown eyebrows lifted and my pulse rose a touch higher.

My mouth lifted to one side as he flushed. "I mean, I don't *have* to go, not if you can make me a better offer."

"Define *better*."

"Not Shelly."

Adam grinned. "Done."

ADAM

I might be the world's worst poker player.

My dad and Jeremy had gone to dinner, and Jolene and I were sitting on the carpet in my living room with an empty popcorn bowl between us and a growing pile of pretzels, candy, and whatever else we'd had on hand to gamble with. I'd taken her at her word when she said I had only to offer her something better than Shelly, which was how we ended up wandering around the neighborhood before coming back to my dad's apartment as soon as he and Jeremy left.

It had been a surprisingly fun day even though she'd nearly cleaned me out an hour ago and had been eyeing my Philadelphia Flyers T-shirt ever since. When I lost yet another hand, she did her best evil villain laugh and gathered her winnings closer.

"You're cheating."

"Why do losers always say that?" She winked at me and started shuffling the next hand.

"No." I pushed back and leaned my head against the seat of the sofa. "I'm done. I have nothing left to lose."

Jolene sat back as well, spreading her hands on the carpet. "I wouldn't say that." When she eyed my shirt again, I burst out laughing.

"But it will look so much better on me," she said.

"No argument there." She'd looked good in everything I'd seen her wear so far, including the puffy coat she'd had on while we were outside. "I'm still done."

She aimed her camera at me, a sight I was rapidly growing used to, considering it had barely left her hand all day.

"Come on. I really feel like I'm gonna lose this time."

I laughed. "And a liar, too. No way. I'm not going to literally and figuratively lose my shirt playing poker. Leave me with a little dignity, will you?"

"Dignity is overrated. Plus..." She frowned and started pawing through her pile of loot. "I thought I won that in the last hand." I kicked out at her with my sock-covered foot, and she retaliated by ditching her camera so that she could throw an Oreo at my head. I stretched up and caught it in my mouth.

We were both still laughing and throwing things at each other when Dad and Jeremy walked in. My laughter cut off immediately. Jolene, on the other hand, took a full thirty seconds to compose herself. Longer still, to follow my example and stand up. She kept glancing at me as if wondering how to gauge her reaction, like she'd never been caught doing something she wasn't supposed to and gotten yelled at the way I was about to be.

Dad glanced down at our cards and food before turning to the fridge and stowing take-out bags inside. Jeremy strode up to me. "You're worthless, you know that?"

A muscle twitched in my cheek. "I'm not going to go eat with him so that he can feel better about walking out on Mom."

Jeremy took another step toward me, forcing Jolene to back up in order to avoid him bumping into her. Her foot slipped on one of the cards, and she caught my arm to keep from falling. I was about to shove Jeremy back when she regained her balance and smiled.

"I'm good." She eyed my brother. "I'm Jolene, by the way. You must be Jeremy." She introduced herself without a trace of discomfort in her voice, as if my brother hadn't just crowded her into almost falling. He swallowed and for a second looked like he was sorry. Then his expression hardened again.

"I'm just gonna..." Jolene pointed down and dropped cross-legged on the carpet, then gathered the cards and started shuffling them. "What do you say, Jeremy? Want me to deal you in?"

Jeremy and I turned equally incredulous looks at her.

"I'm assuming you're familiar with Texas Hold'em. On a totally unrelated subject, how much would you say your watch is worth?"

Jeremy frowned hard at her, then turned to me. "Get her out of here."

I shoved him back with one hand. "You talk to girls like this, but *I'm* worthless?"

"Yeah, you are," Jeremy said, leaning forward. "You piss and moan about a headache to get out of dinner again and then invite your girlfriend over?"

My face blazed red-hot and I clenched my fists.

"He wishes," Jolene said to Jeremy, turning three cards faceup. "You're not really helping his case."

Jeremy was still trying to stare me down. The effect wasn't as intimidating as he would have wanted, because I was taller.

As if he realized that he needed to get Jolene out of the apartment before his sons snapped, Dad came back into the living room. "Adam," he said. "Are you going to introduce me?"

With great effort, I pulled my gaze from Jeremy to face him. For a moment, my fury for the way my brother had treated Jolene transferred to him. But when he looked at Jolene, Dad's expression was the opposite of Jeremy's. He even smiled at her. I nodded, then extended a hand to urge her to her feet. "This is Jolene. From next door. Jolene, this is my dad."

"Jolene? You're Shelly's—"

"I am Shelly's nothing," she said, cutting him off and for the moment looking as uncomfortable as she should have been in this situation. "Shelly 'dates' my dad." And yes, she added air quotes. Just like that, my anger started to slip away.

"Well, Jolene, it's good to meet you. You're welcome over anytime my son is here as long as I'm home, too, but Adam's not allowed to have girls over alone."

She looked like she wanted to laugh, but she had the good sense to meet my eye first. My mood had lifted, but my mouth didn't so much as twitch.

"Oh, you're serious?" Jolene asked.

Jeremy pointed at the door. "Yeah, so take the hint and get out."

Dad didn't hesitate. He grabbed Jeremy by the upper arm and hauled him to the kitchen, where I could hear harsh whispers flying back and forth.

"I was just leaving anyway," Jolene called out, and then tapped her hand against mine. She mouthed *sorry* at me and dragged her lower lip to the side. When she bent down to grab her camera and the shoes she'd kicked off earlier, I came down, too.

"You didn't do anything wrong, and you don't have to go."

"Yeah," she said, eyeing my dad chewing out my brother. "I think I do. Besides, I have a hot date with Ferris Bueller in my room tonight."

I said something about hanging out the next day, and at Dad's obvious insistence, Jeremy came back and offered the barest of apologies.

Jolene backed out the door, opening it just enough that she could squeeze through it sideways. "Don't think twice, Jeremy. It's understanding that makes it possible for people like me to tolerate a person like yourself. Bye, Adam."

I ducked my head to hide a smile, then walked into my room without glancing at Dad or Jeremy.

IN BETWEEN

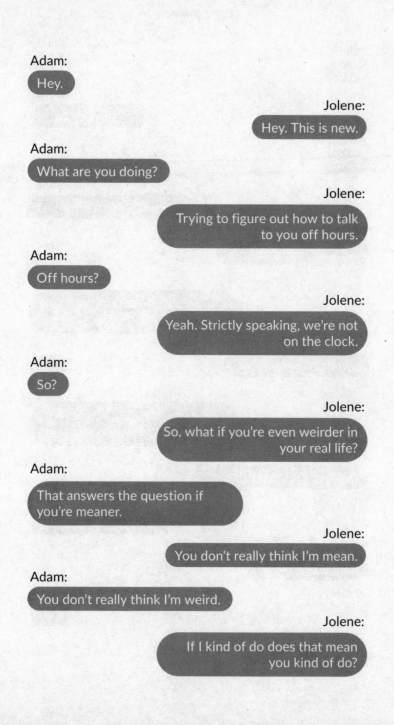

Adam:
Yes.

Jolene:
I'm stymied here.

Adam:
So...

Jolene:
Why are you texting me?

Adam:
Felt like talking to you.

Jolene:
Adam, are you trying to say you miss me?

Adam:
I wouldn't go that far.

Jolene:
I bet you're blushing. Send me a picture.

Adam:
See? It's not that different.

Jolene:
Where's my picture?

Adam:
Camera's busted.

Jolene:
Liar.

Adam:
Are you at home?

Jolene:

Yeah, you?

Adam:

Look out your window.

Jolene:

You don't know where I live.

Adam:

Took you too long to text back.
You totally looked.

Jolene:

Only because you have very
clear stalker tendencies.

Adam:

Says the girl who broke into my
bedroom.

Jolene:

Says the guy who keeps taking
pictures of me for his mom.

Adam:

You caught me.

Jolene:

I bet you have a big heart-shaped
collage of me taped to your ceiling.

Adam:

It's inside the door to my closet.

Jolene:

It'd be cool if you lived nearby.

Adam:

Yeah.

Jolene:

Or you weren't so pathetically still fifteen.

Adam:

Remind me how old you are again?

Jolene:

Fifteen is only pathetic when you're a guy.

Adam:

That's unfair.

Jolene:

But true.

Adam:

It's weird that part of me wishes it was next weekend already.

Jolene:

You miss me being mean to your face?

Adam:

Yeah.

Jolene:

That is weird.

Adam:

Maybe you're not that mean.

Jolene:

Maybe you're not that weird.

Jolene

I ducked to avoid getting hit in the face by a soccer ball as I left my house on the Saturday morning of my second non-Dad weekend of the month. It still clipped me in the shoulder, which was apparently good enough for Cherry and Gabe to high-five each other from where they were standing in front of their minivan. The glint of brilliantly white teeth, the kind that only the kids of two dentists could have, contrasted against the deep brown of their skin as they grinned.

"Awesome," I said without smiling. "That never gets old."

"Then be on time," they said together, then scowled, because they hated when they inadvertently spoke in unison.

Cherry caught the ball, which I'd thrown back at her, and tossed it to her twin before focusing her attention back on me. "Are you ready to fight?" She held a hand to her ear. "Are you ready to win? Are you ready to make those Elkins Park girls wish they'd never been born?"

"Yes!" I jumped off the last step on the porch, and Cherry met me for an impromptu chest bump. We double high-fived before pulling back. She linked her arm around my neck in a half headlock and shoved me toward the front seat.

I was smiling. I was in a half headlock, and I was smiling. It was a side effect of being around Cherry, one I'd taken full advantage of since my parents' divorce. Cherry and I had been friends before then, but we'd been more like the kind of friends who said hey to each other when we bumped into each other outside school. Now we were the kind of friends who asked each other for deodorant checks, which Cherry did then, given my proximity to her armpit.

"You smell like a meadow made sweet love to a bottle of mouthwash," I told her.

"Yeah?" Half of her mouth kicked up as she opened the sliding passenger door. "Awesome."

"Hey, Teen Spirit," Gabe called from the driver's seat. "Let's move."

"Thanks again for the ride," I told him, hopping into the front seat.

Cherry rolled her eyes. "He's such a loser. All I have to do is shake the keys from anywhere in the house and he comes running."

Gabe started the car with a wild grin that reminded me he'd had his license for only a couple weeks. Music was soon blasting, vibrating through the back of my legs and making it impossible to hear what Cherry was saying. She *was* talking, her violet-glossed lips opening and closing like a fish out of water. She leaned forward and clapped Gabe on the shoulder and then pointed to the stereo.

He turned the music up so that the beds of my nails seemed to thrum with the beat. Cherry rolled her eyes at me and doubled her efforts on her brother's shoulders until he lowered the volume.

"We're all deaf now, Gabe." Cherry sat back with a huff. "You probably blew the speakers out, too."

"My car, my rules."

"Mom's minivan, you're pathetic," Cherry said, echoing the rhythm of his words.

I tried to choke back my laughter, but Gabe saw me and barked out his own laugh. "Jealous, baby sister? Uh, yeah," he said, starting to sing. "You are jealous of a minivan, jealous of a minivan."

"You are tragically uncool."

"Says the sixteen-year-old without a license. Burn!" He covered his mouth with one hand and held up the other for me to slap.

I eyed Cherry and tapped Gabe's hand as lightly and quickly as possible. "What? He's voluntarily driving us an hour early to our soccer game. He's getting high-fived."

By way of answering, Cherry narrowed her eyes and showed me the side of her short, bleached afro.

"You need to quit being stupid," Gabe said to his sister. "Get your grades up and Mom and Dad will let you get your license."

That sounded cruel on the surface, except both Cherry and Gabe were super smart. I'd never seen Cherry get less than an A- on any test she'd ever taken. She just didn't like homework. I couldn't believe a driver's license wasn't motivation enough for her, but there we were, nearly a year since her parents had laid down the law where her grades were concerned, and she was still coasting on test scores alone. I, on the other hand, planned to spend my sixteenth birthday at the DMV if I had to walk there myself.

"Hey, hey," Gabe said, lightly smacking my arm a few times. "What did you think of the song before the uncultured among us made you turn it down?" He narrowed his eyes at his sister through the rearview mirror.

"No way!" I turned the sound back up—though not to

the same eardrum-bursting volume as before—and listened to the song.

Now that I was paying attention, I could pick out Dexter's gravelly voice and Gabe's deeper harmony. It was my turn to smack his arm and grin. I normally didn't go much for alternative rock, but Venomous Squid was the exception. I was obviously biased, because I was friends with all of them, but even Cherry admitted they didn't suck. The new song was one I'd heard a stripped-down version of when Grady, the lead guitarist, had been working on the melody while I shot B-roll footage for their first music video (which had turned out way better than I was expecting, as I'd never made a music video before). But that had been without lyrics. As I listened to the song, which was about a guy having to watch the girl he loved choose someone else, I started seeing the couple in my head, the close-up shots I'd start with and then how I'd slowly zoom out from her throughout the song, ending with an extreme long shot showing that distance she'd put between them as I choked tight on him.

"Whoa, are you crying, Jo? Man, I'm good."

I laughed a little and blinked the moisture from my eyes. "Yeah, it's good. I was imagining the video I could make."

Gabe grinned. "Hell yes. We've got over thirty thousand views on the first one. We might even be able to pay you with more than free-hug coupons for this one."

"Send it to me—" I pointed at the speakers "—and I'll start working on it."

"Awesome," Gabe said. "Thanks."

"You know, I could walk to the game faster than this," Cherry said, leaning forward to rest her chin on the back of my seat. "Just saying."

Gabe sped up, then came to an abrupt stop when we reached the school, causing both Cherry and me to jerk forward against our seat belts before slamming back.

Cherry smacked him and he groaned much louder than the hit required. I wasn't the only one who noticed the difference. Cherry and I turned to see what her brother was looking at, and I had to hold back my own groan.

Cherry's on-again, off-again boyfriend, Meneik, was strolling toward us, right arm swinging like he was listening to music only he could hear. Even when she hated him, Cherry always said Meneik had mad swagger. He also had rich dark skin, a lean, muscled physique, and cheekbones so chiseled that they'd landed him a few modeling jobs. Plus, he was a senior and had had his own car long before Gabe got minivan privileges.

I never saw the appeal beyond his pretty exterior—okay, and maybe the fact that he could drive us places—but Meneik didn't look so cute when he was yelling at Cherry for not answering his texts fast enough or laying down the mother of all guilt trips when she wanted to hang out with her friends instead of spending every night with him. He never got violent or cheated or anything, but he manipulated and isolated and tried to control every aspect of her life. She had no choices, no freedom, no support. He made sure the only thing she had was him, and he somehow managed to convince my funny and fearless friend that she didn't want anything else. At least, not when he was around.

Their latest breakup had been the longest one yet, after Meneik lost it when Cherry had visited her grandmother in the hospital instead of going to his basketball game. He flat out told her that her grandmother's hip would still have been broken after his game. No amount of backpedaling and telling her that he needed his lucky charm had worked, which had given me one blissful, Meneik-free month with her that I'd thought would last. One glance at the smile spreading across Cherry's face was all it took to show me they were back on again.

She burst out of the van and ran to him, jumping onto him and sealing her mouth to his and I *accidentally* slammed my elbow into the van's horn while twisting around to grab Cherry's and my soccer bags from the back. If I were Meneik, I'd be able to sell that story. Since I was not, I was treated to a disbelieving glare and one artfully arched eyebrow.

"Cherish," Meneik said, tugging her back to him for one last kiss. "It's all good." He told "Baby" he'd call her later before striding back to his car as I joined Cherry. I guess she was expected to be at all his games, but the same rule didn't apply to him.

"What happened to 'I don't want to waste another second of my life on that jerk?'" I asked in a tone that sounded more weary than angry.

Cherry took her bag and turned toward the field without meeting my gaze. "Don't give me a hard time, okay?"

"Hey," I said, matching her stride. "I'm only quoting what you said to me. But come on, he's not worth it. You agreed, and—"

Her eyes flashed as they finally met mine. "You need to stop." Then she sighed and shook her head at me. "See, this is why I didn't tell you. You don't get it. You've never been in love."

My cheeks flushed hot. No, I hadn't, but I was a walking, talking casualty of it, and that was reason enough not to want any part of it. Love—the romantic kind—existed only in Nora Ephron movies, and we didn't get to live in those.

"Meneik and me? We're always going to get back to each other. You either get that—" she lifted her bag over her shoulder "—or you don't." Then she sidestepped me and jogged across the parking lot to where the rest of the team was waiting.

Cherry and I both moved through the game without our usual trash talk and laughter. Our teammates noticed and started asking what was up, but neither of us answered.

Without discussing it, after the game, we put on a show of normalcy for her parents, but on the drive home Cherry turned the music all the way up the second Gabe started the engine.

ADAM

"Hey, Adam. Got a minute?" On Monday afternoon, Erica Porter waved me over to her table in the cafeteria, eliciting a few grumbled comments from my friends Gideon and Rory. As I headed toward her, Rory muttered, "Lucky bastard," and I couldn't help but smile. Apart from being valedictorian, being noticed by Erica Porter was the epitome of my high school aspirations.

My heart started pounding as I drew closer to her table, so much so that I was sure she'd see it through my shirt. Erica wasn't just beautiful, with her honey-blond hair, hazel eyes, and flawless tan skin, she was the kind of gorgeous that made it hurt to look at her for very long. Seeing her was like staring at the sun. Sure, there was a chance that you'd go blind, but she was so brilliant, you risked it anyway.

"You guys all know Adam, right?" Erica looked around the long rectangular table as heads nodded. I did know most everyone. A few other cheerleaders; their boyfriends; Erica's younger brother, Peter; and her two best friends.

"Hey," I said.

"So," Erica said the second I slid onto the bench seat next to her, "you probably know why I called you over."

I had a split-second thought that she found my uncontrollable blushing as "adorable" as Jolene did, because I could feel myself turning red as a tomato. "You're after my pudding cup?"

Erica laughed and the sound, so close to my ear, sent tingling goose bumps all over my skin. "I was thinking more of a preemptive partnering up for the *Beowulf* project in British literature."

I thought I could maybe die happy, knowing she had looked at me like that once in my life, as if I, and I alone, had the power to do something for her. "Oh yeah, sure."

And then she hugged me. "Adam, you're the best." She released me before I worried she'd feel the copious amount of sweat my body decided to start producing. "I hate these group projects. I always end up doing all the work, and people who do nothing get the same grade." She stabbed a strawberry with her fork. "I refuse to do it again, you know?"

While I hated that, too, my mouth was going to agree with anything she said. "Yeah."

"Anyway, we have the two highest grades in the class, so I figured if we partner up, I won't end up doing the report and the presentation by myself again. Oh, and I promise I'll pull my weight."

I'd gone to school with Erica since the fifth grade, and she'd always been one of the smartest people in the class. I wasn't worried about her being a slacker, I was worried my brain would cease functioning if I sat close to her for too long. "I'd love to work with you, but Mr. Conyer always assigns partners. I don't think we'll get to pick."

Erica chewed on her strawberry and held up a finger. "I've got that covered. He always pairs us based on who's sharing

a desk, so as long as you don't mind sitting next to me..."
She smiled, because even she knew that wasn't a possibility.

"For a good grade, I think I can suffer through it."

Erica grinned at me. "Great."

I had to wait for Jeremy in the parking lot after school. I
didn't have a key to unlock the car, so I stood shivering outside for a good ten minutes before he strolled up. As soon as
he started the car, I turned the heater on high.

"You get cold like a little girl," Jeremy said. "It's 'cause
you're so skinny."

"Not everyone comes equipped with the natural insula-
tion that you have."

"Someone's feeling cocky." Jeremy's smile was tight, but
I'd been expecting a quick slam of the brakes or a sharp turn
as he backed out of the parking lot. Something to bang me
around or smack my head against the window in response to
my insult. A smile of any kind was unnerving. "That have
anything to do with your lunch date?"

Of *course* Jeremy would have heard about that. Even the
seniors paid attention to Erica Porter.

Every guy I knew was half in love with her, and in my
case, I'd been full gone on her ever since she'd beaten me in
our fifth-grade spelling bee. Not that Jeremy was ribbing me
because she was smart—I was betting it had more to do with
how she looked in her cheerleader uniform, a sight that had
rendered me speechless on more than one occasion.

I tried to shut any conversation down as quickly as possible. "I ate with her because we're working on an assignment together." I left out the part where she'd called me to
her table in front of the entire cafeteria and then launched
herself into my arms when I agreed to be her partner.

"Not what I heard."

I knew better than to ask, but I couldn't help myself. "What did you hear?"

Jeremy played coy for exactly one mile. "You know she's single now."

I'd heard that enticing rumor only that morning.

"And she apparently broke up with her boyfriend because she's interested in someone else." Jeremy shook his head. "My baby brother and Erica Porter. And I thought she had taste."

I didn't respond. Talking with Jeremy was challenging under any circumstances. Talking with him about girls was not a thrilling prospect. My relationship with Erica was purely academic at the moment, but as strongly as I tried to point out that fact to my burning-hot face, it kept flushing as red as ever.

Was it possible that she was into me? We'd always been friendly, but today was the first time she'd hugged me, and the hug had been long enough for word to spread back to Jeremy.

"So what does Erica think about your weekend girlfriend?"

That snapped me out of my reverie real quick. Mom had been asking me about Jolene more and more lately, and since I'd made sure that I looked like myself in the subsequent photos Jolene and I had taken, she'd warmed up to seeing them and commenting on every detail quite freely, even when Jeremy was around.

"Erica doesn't know about Jolene, who is just a friend. Both of them are friends."

"Oh yeah? So you wouldn't mind if I showed Erica that last picture of you with your 'friend'?"

He was talking about the one Jolene and I had taken right before Jeremy and I left for home last weekend. We'd been walking around the front of the building while Jeremy said goodbye to Dad upstairs, and we'd stopped under one of the boarded windows when Jolene had noticed a bird's nest peeking out from one broken top corner.

When she'd complained about not being able to see if there were any eggs, I'd bent down and offered to lift her up on my shoulders. It had felt like a harmless gesture until I stood and her chilled fingers wrapped under my chin. I don't think she had any idea how close I came to dropping her when she made that little contented noise and pressed more of her hands against my warmth.

There hadn't been any eggs, but Jolene's ever-present camera had been around her neck and she'd agreed to let a passing stranger hold it long enough to snap a pic of us, which she'd then sent to me. In the photo, Jolene was grinning and pointing at the empty bird's nest and I was grinning and looking up at her.

It was my favorite photo yet.

And it definitely wasn't something I should show another girl I liked.

Jeremy kept trying to rile me up and get me to spill about Erica, but I kept my responses to a bare minimum until he finally gave up. It was strange how easy it was to shift my thoughts from Erica to Jolene with only a twinge of regret.

Erica was the girl I'd dreamed about for years who had invited me over to her house next week to get an early start on our project.

Jolene was the girl who teased and unsettled me more often than not but had willingly become my accomplice in my scheme to keep my mom happy. I'd been a sweaty, nervous mess with Erica that afternoon at lunch, but with Jolene, the more time we spent together, the easier it became.

Even in Jeremy's still-freezing car, I was looking forward to hanging out with Jolene on Dad's next weekend almost more than the promise of one-on-one time with Erica. That was the strange part.

THIRD WEEKEND

October 23–25

ADAM

"Don't move!" Jolene's hand wrapped about my chin and turned it forward again. "You're going to end up looking like Lloyd Christmas, and it's not going to be my fault." She moved in front of me and ran a comb through my hair several more times before snipping the ends with scissors.

"I have no idea who that is."

"Duh. Jim Carrey in *Dumb and Dumber*, the first movie written and directed by the Farrelly brothers. Your life is frighteningly sheltered." She lowered the scissors and frowned. "Actually, I think that's their only film that Peter directed by himself."

I pulled back when she leaned in with the scissors again. "Wait, that was a possibility? I thought you were just going to trim it. That's what you said when you got back from your soccer game."

She stepped on top of both of my feet then, pinning me to my chair when I would have jumped up to check the mirror. She also rested her palms on my knees, which probably had more to do with keeping me sitting than her full body weight on my feet.

"You're so jumpy. I'm very good at this. You're going to look great as long as you stop moving every two seconds. Now, stay still."

I did. She moved to my side and kept cutting. I did wince a couple times, but she hissed at me through teeth that held a fine-tooth comb. "I have seen *Dumb and Dumber*, by the way. I just didn't memorize the characters' names."

"Why not? It's good stuff—the first one, not the sequel."

The cold metal of the scissors brushed my ear and I froze, expecting my flesh to be cut. Instead of pain, the next sensation I felt caused me to place a death grip on the underside of my chair.

Jolene blew on my neck.

Then she did it again.

"Voilà!" She removed the towel from around me and twisted it in a flourish like a matador. "You, my friend, are finished."

I kind of felt like I was as I lifted my hand to trail over my neck and the skin that was still tingling from her breath.

She pressed a mirror into my hands. "What do you think?"

"It looks good," I said, glancing in the mirror and trying to steady my breathing.

"You barely looked. Here." She moved behind me and extended the mirror in front of us. She was pressed into my back this time, but it felt like that day when she'd held my phone and taken our first picture. Only not quite. Her hands were running through my hair, pulling it this way and that, trying to get my cowlick in the back to lie flat. She was asking me questions, commenting on how I no longer looked like a Wookiee in training. Our eyes met in the mirror, hers glinting with laughter, mine trying to drink in every inch of her face. Every inch of her.

The first time I'd felt the impulse to kiss her, it had been little more than a reaction to being close to a pretty girl. This time, proximity played a role, but the reason was that the pretty girl was Jolene. I'd let her shave my head bald if she wanted to, as long as she stayed this close to me. Closer.

But she didn't. We snapped a pic for my mom, then she moved away and flopped onto her couch, her hair twisted and coiled around her head.

"Why don't you ever wear your hair loose?" What would she do if I kissed her? Would she laugh it off? Could I let her if she tried?

"Says the boy with two inches of hair. How long does it take you to do your hair? Like a minute when you're feeling fancy?"

"Fancy?" I couldn't help but smile at her word choice.

"It takes an hour, minimum, to dry my hair. And it's this whole ordeal with hairdryers and frizz serums and brushes and—" she made a sound of disgust "—my arms are exhausted just thinking about it."

"Why don't you cut it?" The only time I'd seen her hair down was that night I'd found her sitting on my bed, and she'd looked so beautiful that I felt a little dizzy from the memory.

"Because I'm vain and I can't."

I laughed at her, because she said it like she was admitting to a crime.

"It's true." She lifted her head from the couch to look at me. "You didn't know that about me, but I'm unconscionably vain. Ever since I was little, people told me I had pretty hair, so I figured the more hair I had, the prettier I'd be. It's ridiculous now. I mean, when I put on my jeans, I have to untuck my hair from the waistband. I know I should cut it, but it's like a sickness. Every time someone compliments me on it, I let it grow another inch. I'll be stepping on it before long." Her head fell back.

"It's beautiful, your hair."

She groaned. "Not you, too. I'm going to end up with a cape. I really should cut it."

"But you're not going to."

"Nope."

"Will you wear it down for me sometime?"

She sat up and folded her legs. "You're not blushing at all. How are you doing that?"

She was just noticing? When we'd first started hanging out, I would constantly turn red around her. She had only to look at me, and I'd feel my face flush. But recently, I'd stopped. At first I'd thought it was because of all the time I was spending with Erica, as if the double exposure to two beautiful girls was burning me out or something, but Erica had never once affected me the way Jolene had even that first night. Jolene still said the same stuff she always had, but I'd stopped feeling embarrassed. I felt something else lately. And it didn't make me turn red.

I felt guilty for how close Erica and I were getting.

"Maybe you've lost your touch." I joined her on the couch.

"Well, that sucks."

"For you maybe. I wasn't a big fan."

"But you won't be as cute if you're just plain all the time."

I glanced at her. "You still think I'm cute."

A sigh from her. "Yeah, I guess I do. But you'll still blush sometimes, won't you? For me? If I'm going to go through the laborious process of doing my hair, you have to turn a little red. Just the ears, hmm?"

Her eyes were wide and her eyebrows rose. Her lips were ever so slightly parted and bright red from the Atomic Fireball she'd been sucking while she cut my hair. I could lean forward right then and kiss her. I could do it. She'd taste like cinnamon.

I didn't need to hear her squeal of delight to know I'd turned bright red.

I didn't kiss her.

We watched *Dumb and Dumber* in her room, sitting against the foot of her bed, and she fell asleep with her head on my shoulder.

Jolene

When Shelly dropped me back at Mom's on Sunday evening, I was surprised to see two cars in the driveway. Mrs. Cho didn't drive, and Mom let her come only while I was at school and Mom was out, so I knew one of them wasn't hers.

Mom pulled open the door the second I reached for the handle. She looked…good. I wished I could say normal, but normal for my mom is a far cry from good. She was barefoot and wearing jeans with a cozy-looking white sweater that had slipped slightly off one shoulder. Best of all, her eyes were clear and bright. Sober bright.

Her gaze hardened as she watched Shelly back down the driveway, but she soon turned her attention to me and smiled. Not a manic, brittle smile, and not a calculating one either. She gave me the kind of smile that meant happiness, pure and simple.

My blood cooled and I felt an instinct to turn and run after Shelly's car.

Before that instinct reached my feet, Mom ushered me

inside with a soft hand on my back. She asked me how my weekend had been, if I'd done anything fun or watched any good movies. She didn't mention Shelly or ask about my dad.

Knots started to tie and cinch in my gut.

She was acting like…before. When things weren't great but were so far from awful that comparison made them seem that way.

And then we rounded the corner into the formal living room I was rarely allowed in, and I understood why.

Mom gestured to the man standing by the white grand piano that had never been played. "Jo, this is my friend Tom." She set her hands on my shoulders and gave them a little squeeze. "Tom, this is my daughter, Jolene."

Tom wasn't a bad-looking guy; he was older than the gym rat I'd been expecting, probably late forties. He didn't have a paunch and still had all his hair, but his teeth were too white and I could see his fake tan on the palms of his hands. His polo shirt revealed short, veiny T. rex arms that looked wildly out of proportion for the rest of his body, which clearly meant he skipped too many leg days.

"The famous Jolene." He strode toward me with his hand extended, and I just looked at him until Mom dug her thumbs into my shoulders. I shook Tom's hand and he grinned, first at me, then Mom. "I know you said she was sixteen, but in my head I was expecting a little girl." His gaze returned to mine. "Sorry, fifteen. Your birthday is on January 26, right?" He winked at me and added in a faux whisper, "I'm an Aquarius, too."

His attempt to establish an instant bond was so aggressive that I wanted to back away. Everything about this guy felt like an assault, from his overpowering musky cologne to his too-loud voice that was still echoing off the vaulted ceilings.

Mom released me and went to stand by Tom. "I've been

so excited for you two to meet. Tom and I have been spending a lot of time together."

Tom slung an arm around her and pulled her into his side. "I've been keeping your mom company while you're at your dad's, trying to distract her from how much she misses you. Though to be honest, I never completely succeed on that front. You've left big shoes to fill, Jolene Timber."

Mom and Tom turned equally expectant expressions toward me, and the knots in my stomach, though they'd stopped clenching, roiled restlessly.

It all felt so…fake. Rehearsed even. I looked at my mom and the easy, carefree costume she wore, and my gut cinched tight once more before I forced it to loosen.

"Yeah," I mumbled. "I need to go unpack." I lifted my tiny weekend bag and then headed up the stairs.

My mother must have been going for an Oscar that night, because she leaned away from Tom's side and said, "Oh, do you want any help, sweetie?"

As far as movies go, it wasn't bad, much better than the alien invasion we'd recently acted out. But I wasn't stupid. It was scripted, a scene that was written to lead to the next, and the next, crafted to manipulate the audience into feeling a specific way. For example, I knew I was supposed to be charmed by the obvious affection on display between my poor, lonely mother and the affable, if slightly corny, Tom. I was supposed to be disarmed and maybe even feel a little wistful.

My eyes weren't supposed to sting, and my stomach wasn't supposed to be churning. I blinked my eyes dry before turning fully to face her—them. "Thanks, Mom, but I've got it. I'm going to head to bed early. It was a long weekend, and my game yesterday wiped me out."

Predictably, they both stiffened. I'd gone off script.

Mom took another step away from Tom. "But you just got home, and I haven't seen you in days."

She could have come to my soccer game yesterday. She liked to claim that she couldn't bear to watch me get hurt, because, as the goalie, I often had to throw myself in front of other players. I got kicked a lot, had had a concussion once, and I did get banged up on a regular basis, but that was not why she stayed away.

She stayed away because there was nothing in it for her.

Unlike the farce playing out before me.

Tom rested a restraining hand on Mom's shoulder and gave her a look before returning his attention to me.

"Of course. These weekends must be a lot for you. I want you to know that I understand, maybe better than your mom, what it's like. My parents divorced when I was about your age, and well, it's the kids who suffer the most. For what it's worth, based on everything your mom has told me and now getting to meet you myself, I think you're doing really well."

I tried to keep the disdain from my face, and I must have done at least a passing job, because he smiled.

"I'm hoping we can spend some time together soon. I think your mom is really special, and I have a feeling that the three of us are going to become great friends."

Another wave of his cologne assaulted my senses, and it was all I could do not to wrinkle my nose. I spared a thought to wonder how my mom was breathing standing that close to him. *Great friends.* Really. I couldn't tell if he was that stupid or was hoping that I was, so I decided to test him.

"Wow, Tom. That's...that's quite a statement."

His chest swelled as if I'd complimented him. "Well, we get what we give, and I'm a giver. How about you?"

"Oh yeah," I said dryly. "Giving is the best." And just

when I was ready to write him off as an idiot, he met my gaze head-on and his voice lost its chummy tone.

"I'm glad to hear you say that, Jolene, I really am, because, well, I think you could be giving a bit more." He made a show of drawing Mom back to his side. "You're tired, so we won't go into it tonight, but I think with that attitude and a little know-how from me —" he tapped his temple "—we're going to be very happy."

Mom's adoring gaze, pointed at Tom, was the last thing I saw before I disappeared into my room.

Sitting on my bed later that night after my stomach finally settled, I stared at the application for the film program. I basically had the whole thing memorized: the film program was in LA and ran the entire summer. If I got accepted, I'd be on the opposite side of the country from my parents for three months, not to mention getting to spend time on major studio lots not just watching films get made but being a part of making them.

I wanted it so badly that every inch of my skin tingled in anticipation.

Unfortunately, there was plenty of info that chased that tingle away. I had to write an essay about why I wanted to be a filmmaker and the kinds of stories I wanted to tell, solicit a letter of recommendation from someone who could "discuss my creative strengths in relation to film and filmmaking," and submit three short films. Between the first music video I'd made for Venomous Squid, the second one I'd already started storyboarding, and the undefined project that I was shooting with Adam, submitting the films wouldn't be a problem, but my school didn't have a film program so there weren't any teachers I could ask to write me a letter, and the essay was weighing heavily on me. I knew how to tell a story visually—I could see it in my mind before I ever picked up a camera—but communicating through images was very different from communicating through words.

The letter and essay weren't even the worst obstacles though.

Asking to go away for three months was going to be an issue with my parents, a hair-pulling, screaming, and possibly homicidal issue. What would they maliciously fight over if I wasn't around?

Then there was the cost. Dad had the money. Mom probably did, too, but getting either of them to part with it seemed utterly beyond me as I stared down at the figure.

My fingers curled around the edges of the pages. I felt the paper cuts I was giving myself, but I didn't care. I had to find a way to glimpse a future where I could tell the story I wanted, instead of starring in the never-ending nightmare my parents had cast me in.

I rose up on my knees on my bed and, feeling very Vivien Leigh from *Gone With the Wind*, made my vow. "As God is my witness…"

For some reason I thought of Adam as I struck my pose. If he'd been there, I'd have tried to get him to deliver a slightly modified Clark Gable line and say, "Frankly, my dear, it's time to give a damn."

I think he'd have done it, too.

He might have even let me draw a mustache on him.

And I know he'd have offered to help me with my essay.

He was still such a new part of my life, but he trespassed into my thoughts all the time. In that moment I imagined him sitting at my desk triple-checking whatever homework he'd brought with him and occasionally glancing over his shoulder to gauge my progress. My mouth curved up a little at the way his eyebrows would pinch together when he saw that I hadn't even opened my laptop.

"I've finished six months of extra credit for all my AP classes and you haven't even started yet?" imaginary Adam would ask.

"My muse will come to me when she's ready," I'd say.

"See, I don't think it works that way," imaginary Adam would say. "I think you put words on a page, and then you put more words, and then after that, you put even more words. Good words, awful words, wrong words."

"That sounds wildly inefficient."

"As opposed to not writing any? Get enough of the wrong words down and see what you have left."

"Hmm," I'd say. "Maybe you're more than just a pretty face."

Imaginary Adam would wink at me. Okay, not even imaginary Adam would do that, but he'd smile at me and he'd make me pull my laptop onto my lap.

And even though he wasn't there, I filled my lungs with air and held it in until it started to hurt, then I let it out in a loud whoosh, opened a new document, and started typing.

I want to become a filmmaker to escape my parents.

I wrote another sentence, and another after that. I filled an entire page with awful, wrong words, and maybe, just maybe, a few that were okay.

IN BETWEEN

Jolene:

You never told me what you're dressing up as for Halloween.

Adam:

I don't know your costume either?

Jolene:

I kind of don't think I should tell you.

Adam:

Why not? Unless it's, like, a sexy lawn gnome or something.

Jolene:

I guess it would be embarrassing if we dressed up in the same costume.

Adam:

Ha ha.

Jolene:

Okay, but prepare to feel bad about whatever your costume is.

Adam:

Okay.

Jolene:

I'm Chewbacca!

Adam:

That's cool.

Jolene:

No, I mean I rented a legit Chewbacca costume. It even has mini stilts in the legs to make me Wookiee height. Like I could walk on the set of a Star Wars movie and everybody would be like, "Hey, Chewy."

Adam:

Awesome! You have to send me a picture.

Jolene:

Totally. My friends Cherry and Gabe have this party every year and I never win the costume contest, but nobody's beating Chewy. Okay, now you.

Adam:

I'm just helping out with the Halloween carnival at my church, so I didn't go all out.

Jolene:

But you're doing something, right?

Adam:

I found a purple suit at Goodwill, bought some spray-in green hair color, and face paint.

Jolene:

Okayyyyy?

Adam:

I'm the Joker.

Jolene:

Heath Ledger or Jared Leto version?

Adam:

Classic Joker.

Jolene:

Ah, Jack Nicholson. Very cool! Send me a pic, too.

Adam:

I will.

Jolene:

What are you doing later? And don't say starting next week's homework or your nerd status will transcend time and space.

Adam:

That's not a thing.

Jolene:

Noooooooooo. I'm right?

Adam:

I have to go to someone's house to work on a group project for school.

Jolene:

That's still technically future homework, nerd boy. What's the project?

Adam:

It's an English thing.

Jolene:

An English thing? Do I detect a note of frustration? Let me guess, the other guy plays video games and ignores you while you write the whole thing?

Adam:

It's a girl, and no, she does her share.

Jolene:

A girl? What's her name?

Adam:

Why does that matter?

Jolene:

I'm just curious.

Adam:

Erica.

Jolene:

Do you always go to her house?

Adam:

So far. Why?

Jolene:

No reason. Are you almost done?

Adam:

Close. You haven't told me what you're doing tonight?

Jolene:

I guess I'm doing my own group project. I started filming a music video for my friend's band.

Adam:

Cool.

Jolene:

It's just footage of them playing the song for now, but I have ideas for the story element that I'll shoot later on. G2G get my stuff together.

Adam:

I gotta go, too. TTYL.

Jolene:

I'd say have fun, but it's you and school stuff, how could you not have fun?

Jolene:

What, no response?

Jolene:

Adam?

Jolene:

I guess I'll catch you later.

ADAM

It wasn't the first time she'd done it, but having Erica Porter wrap her arms around me wasn't a sensation I'd ever get over.

"Adam, hi!" She squeezed me for a few seconds longer than she had the last time I'd come to her house, leaning into me in a way that forced all rational thought from my mind, like the fact that her dad was a few feet behind her and we were on her front porch. "Come in." She pulled back, and I had to remind myself to let her go. "Dad, you remember Adam."

I stepped inside and shook his hand. "Mr. Porter."

He wasn't a big man, but he had a presence, and he kept the pressure of his handshake strong and steady as he held my gaze, communicating very clearly that he was capable of protecting his daughter if need be and that there'd better not be a need.

"How are you, Adam? Ready to get to work?" Even though I'd been to Erica's house half a dozen times since we'd become partners, I'd only met her dad last week, because he'd been away on a military assignment.

"Yes, sir."

"You two have been working hard. Must be almost done."

In truth, we didn't need to meet as often as we were. Our PowerPoint presentation was close to finished, and our report was half-written already.

"It's worth a quarter of our grade. We need it to be perfect." Erica smiled at her dad, and after telling us to call out if we needed anything, he headed upstairs.

"Sorry about my dad," she tossed over her shoulder as she led the way to her kitchen and the rustic oak table we usually worked on. "He thinks every guy I bring over is waiting to maul me the second he turns his back. He'll lighten up once he gets to know you."

I was betting he wouldn't, but I kept that thought to myself as Erica grabbed us a couple Cherry Cokes from the fridge while I set my bag on the table. Wanting to agree with everything she said, I'd made the mistake of claiming it was my favorite flavor, too, when she'd offered me one the first time I came over, and now I had to choke down a can each time. I smiled when she handed it to me.

"What about your dad?"

I coughed, and the carbonation burned in my nose. "Uh, no. He's not much of a tough guy."

"Hmm," she said. "But you don't have any sisters, just brothers?"

"Brother," I corrected, the burn spreading to my eyes.

Her can halted at her mouth. Slowly she lowered it to the table. "Right. It's been a little while and I forgot for a second. I'm sorry."

I shook my head. "It's fine. Like you said, it was a while ago."

"I didn't *know him* know him, but I do have this one memory of Greg helping my friend Missy when her cat fell through the ice in the middle of the pond by the elementary school a few winters ago. He jumped right in, didn't even take his shoes off or anything. She still has the cat." She let her gaze go unfocused from the memory before blinking and taking another drink, oblivious to the fact that my own can was denting in my hand. "He was really brave."

"Yeah," I said, my voice low and gruff. She kept talking about how amazing Greg had been that day but I didn't even hear the words. I knew the cat story. Actually, there was probably more than one. Greg had done stuff like that all the time without ever thinking about his own safety. He could have died saving Missy's cat, found himself trapped under the ice, too, or had the edges break under his fingertips when he tried to climb back out, one-handed because the other was wrapped around a panicked cat. He could have frozen solid while Erica and her friend watched from the bank.

"Oh," Erica said, sliding closer to me and brushing her fingers over my face. I tried to shrug her off, but she only moved closer. "It's okay," she said. "I'm here."

She *was* there and she smelled like cherries, and the skin of her fingers was so soft as she brushed my cheek. The kitchen was empty, and the most beautiful girl I'd ever seen in real life was touching me. I couldn't think clearly. My chest hurt like I was somehow trapped underneath thick layers of ice, feeling my thrashing limbs grow sluggish and heavy as I fought to free myself from a memory that wasn't even mine.

Greg hadn't died in a pond or trapped beneath ice. He'd come home that day half-frozen but exhilarated, laughing as he told Mom about his latest rescue over a steaming cup of hot cocoa.

"Weren't you scared?" I'd asked him.

"Sure," he'd said, sucking a marshmallow into his mouth. "But I was more scared of watching a little girl witness her cat drown and seeing the panic in that animal's eyes and knowing I could have helped but didn't." He'd grinned at me. "Plus, I've got thick skin. A little ice wouldn't have hurt me." But his teeth were still chattering, and there'd been a blue tinge lingering on his lips despite the hot cocoa.

Later that night I'd heard Dad tell him he had to be more careful. Dad said he knew better than to tell Greg to let the next animal go, but to think of all of us, his mom, his little brothers, and how we would feel if he didn't come home. Greg had given Dad his promise.

But we'd still buried him a year later.

And there I was in Erica Porter's kitchen, surrounded by the cookie jars that her mom collected, trying not to let tears track down my face. Instead I tried to focus on her, on Erica and the way her gaze kept lowering to my mouth.

Part of me knew what might happen, in that moment when it was just Erica and me and she was much too close and moving closer. The surprising thing was that, even though I'd thought about it for years, once it was happening, something felt off. It was more than the raw memory of my brother still wrapped around me, messing with my head. I'd expected to be more excited. Well, I was, but mostly I couldn't help thinking that Erica's hair wasn't long enough, and that I wished her teeth weren't so perfectly spaced. But it was one of those foggy thoughts that pass through the mind without any substance or lasting power. It had no sooner formed than it dissipated, and the girl of my dreams was an inch away from me. Only an idiot would have let that moment pass by.

I wasn't an idiot.

FOURTH WEEKEND

November 6-8

Jolene

Adam had become a parasite in my life, except not the gross tapeworm kind that coils in your intestines and steals all the nutrients from your body. He was like the benevolent kind that massaged your muscles and brain cells simultaneously, making you smarter and stronger at the same time. I didn't think that kind of parasite existed, but, how awesome would it be if they did? I would call them Adamites.

Adam took exception to my parasitic metaphor.

"I'm the parasite? Me? You're the one who climbed into my room!"

"After you climbed onto my balcony."

"Still, you are clearly the parasite in this relationship. Also, I'm pretty sure the Adamites were an early cult of some kind."

"Why do you have to be such a know-it-all all the time? Fine, we'll change the name. How about something with *worm*? A lot of parasites have *worm* in the name."

"How about we stop calling me a parasite entirely?"

"Even a muscle-growing, brain-building kind?"

"Yes. And how do you figure anyway?"

"Well. I used to spend my weekends here watching movies in my room. Ever since you moved in, we go places, we talk about stuff. I'm moving and thinking. Those are the exact parasitic perks I attributed to you."

"Huh."

"What does *huh* mean in this context?"

"I'm mildly less insulted."

"Oh, good. I did mildly mean to insult you as well as compliment you, so…where are we going anyway?"

"What do you mean where are we going? I was following you."

It was Saturday afternoon and Adam and I were apparently wandering aimlessly around the neighborhood. It was one of those perfect snowy days. Everything was blanketed in white, and the snow had that iced edge to it that made it glitter in the bright sunlight and crunch underfoot. There was no wind, no clouds. It was the kind of cold that made everything, including the air, feel clean.

Adam hadn't bothered with a hat or anything beyond his coat with the fleece collar. I was already regretting my scarf. It was almost too warm.

"We could walk around," I said. "Shoot the breeze, chew the fat, bandy words."

"That's all we do anyway. Not all we do, but whatever we're doing, we always talk."

"I know, but you realize there is still a ton we don't know about each other. We sort of skipped the usual Q&A that most people go through."

Adam laughed. "'Cause we knew we were going to be stuck with each other regardless."

"Exactly."

"It worked out though."

"As far as you know. What if you find out I'm a closeted Trekkie or I discover you're a Bronie?"

"What's a Bronie?"

"A guy who likes *My Little Pony*."

Adam's voice boomed, "WHO TOLD YOU?" When I stopped laughing, he said, "See? It's too late. We're already friends."

"I still have questions."

"I guess I do, too. You never told me much about that film program."

I hunched my shoulders a little. "It's not a big deal," I said, fiddling with the zipper on my jacket. "There's a thing in LA for high school students. If I get accepted, I'll get to learn all about moviemaking and, in my case, directing."

Adam's eyebrows rose and I couldn't tell if he was impressed or thought it was stupid.

I hunched my shoulders more. "Like I said, it's not a big deal."

"You'll get accepted. You're super bossy, and that music video you showed me was incredible."

I bit back a smile and scrunched up my face. "Am I really that bossy?"

"Oh yeah, but isn't that like a prerequisite for a director?"

Deadly serious, I said, "I really hope so."

Adam laughed. "I think it's cool."

"Yeah?"

He nodded. "So what's the application process?"

"I have to write an essay, send in a few short films, and get a letter of recommendation from someone who can—" here I added air quotes "—discuss my creative strengths in relation to film and filmmaking."

"Who are you going to ask for the recommendation?"

"I have no idea. I'll find someone though." I was glad he wasn't asking about the short films, especially the one he was in, because I wasn't ready to show it to him yet.

"I think my dad said there's a new guy in the building who's some kind of movie critic."

I grabbed one of Adam's arms with both of mine. "Are you serious?"

"I think so. I'll try to find out."

"I will seriously love you forever if you find him for me."

"And just yesterday you made me watch a movie about how I can't buy me love." He shook his head, and I threw mine back with a laugh.

"Okay, my turn for questions."

"Ask away."

"Where do you live?"

"Little town called Telford," he said. "It's a thirty-minute drive north from here without traffic. What about you?"

"My mom's house is in the city. We could go later if we want to forge a suicide pact."

Adam stopped walking. "Are you saying that because of the house or the occupant?"

"Both lately."

Adam got that uncomfortable look on his face that meant I'd made him feel sad *and* guilty.

"Not because of my mom, at least not completely. I told you about the guy from her gym that she's seeing. He claims to be a financial expert—maybe he is, I don't know. He's got her all worked up about the money my dad is hiding from her."

"Is he? Your dad, I mean?"

"Totally. Before the divorce, my dad could buy and sell the entire Oak Village apartment building ten times over, and now he's living here and claiming that he can't afford anything nicer—no offense to your dad, the place is better since he started working on it." I stopped walking. "I'm starting to sound like Tom. He's trying to get my mom to hire a forensic accountant to look through my dad's finances and get more alimony out of him. My dad isn't an idiot though, so I doubt they'll find anything, which means that if she wants more money, then she'll have to get a job and do something besides work out and drink. Maybe she'll grow up and care about someone besides herself. Maybe they both will." I was breathing like a bull, steam billowing in and out. Adam hadn't known half the stuff I'd just unloaded on him. No one did.

I needed to get back to safer, less–uncomfortable-for-both-of-us ground. "Just forget I said all that. My point is that until we can drive, we won't be hanging out anywhere except here." We'd come full circle and were approaching our building again. We passed the sign, and neither of us looked at it.

Adam's response was to nod his head and shove his hands into his pockets.

"Let's just do more questions," I said. "Favorite color?"

"Red. You?"

"Purple. Candy?"

"Jelly beans. You?"

"Fireballs. Holiday?"

"Halloween. You?"

"Same. Candy and costumes for the win." We went back and forth until we both shook off the unwelcome heaviness of my earlier confession. A pair of squirrels with fluffy gray tails darted right in front of us, chasing each other up a spindly birch tree. We laughed, and it was okay again.

"More serious questions. What's your favorite song?"

"Of all time? 'Classical Gas.'"

I smacked him in the chest. "That's mine, too!"

He grinned. "Really?"

"No. Who puts the word *gas* in a song title?"

"Mason Williams. And seriously, don't knock the song."

I held my hands up in surrender. "It's pretty, okay. But the title…" I shook my head.

"What's your favorite song?"

"'Jolene' by Dolly Parton." I lifted a shoulder when he side-eyed me. "What can I say? I'm a narcissist." Plus nobody puts pain to lyrics like Dolly Parton. "Book?"

"*Lord of the Rings.*"

I made a face.

"What?"

"It's just so long. And all the songs?" I made a gagging sound in my throat. "I gave up."

Adam came to an abrupt halt. "Wait, you haven't read *Lord of the Rings*?"

"I *started* to read *Lord of the Rings* and decided I would rather do literally anything else. Okay, you look like I just kicked you in the nuts." He was pale, even for him. "Oh, come on. I saw the movies, okay? Apart from Peter Jackson's penchant for endless close-ups, I liked them."

"The movies are great, but they're nothing compared to the books."

"Well, I didn't like them."

"You said you started and gave up. When did you stop? Was it before *Return of the King*?"

I gave him a blank expression, in response to which he growled a little.

"The third book."

I would have laughed if he wasn't being so serious. "More like the third chapter of the first book."

That kicked-in-the-nuts expression was back on his face. To his credit, he recovered quickly and started walking again. "I'm bringing you my copy of *The Fellowship of the Ring* next weekend. We'll find somewhere quiet and I will *read* more than the opening chapters to you."

There was so much determination in his voice that I didn't argue with him. I liked the idea of listening to his voice for a few hours. Even if he was going to be talking about elves and wizards. "You know, I'm afraid to ask you what your favorite movie is. We almost just killed our friendship over a book about trolls."

"I know you know they're called hobbits. But yeah, I'm never telling you my favorite movie."

I bit back a smile.

We walked for a little while after that, frowning at passing cars that weren't ours. "Oh, I got one. Do you have a girlfriend?" As I predicted, the question made Adam blush. But his answer shocked me.

"Yeah."

My entire body flash froze in place, even my heart stopped beating. "You do?"

He stopped, too, and his Adam's apple bobbed when he swallowed. "Yeah. Is that weird for you?"

"No." It totally was. My heart started up again, but it was beating too fast, too hard. "You never acted like you had a girlfriend."

Adam swallowed again but he was clearly trying to act like our relationship hadn't just undergone a huge, monumental shift, which my hammering heart insisted it had. "How does someone with a girlfriend act?"

"I don't know." We were walking again, my limbs moving jerkily as I tried to hide how unsteady the ground suddenly felt to me. I trailed behind him and stepped into the footprints he left behind, aware of how much bigger his feet were. "Does she know about me? That we hang out for seventy-two straight hours twice a month?"

"We only just got together. She knows I visit my dad, but

I haven't specifically mentioned you. It's, um, Erica, the girl I've been working on that school project with."

I remembered our odd text conversation when he told me about her. He'd been weird, and then he'd left me hanging. I thought he'd been excited about doing homework, but it had been about seeing her. I shivered, and my lungs hurt when I breathed deep. "It's going to be weird now."

"Only if you make it weird, weirdo." He tried to bump my elbow with his but I surged ahead, letting my feet break the snow first.

I *was* being weird, but I couldn't help it. My insides didn't know what to do with this decidedly unwelcome information. "No, it's going to happen. You'll tell her about this amazing girl you spend your weekends with, and she'll get jealous, and you'll end up having to choose between us and of course you'll choose the girl who kisses you over the one who stuffs snow down the back of your jeans." Adam had no clue that I was spiraling and not just playing up the drama for effect. I mean, I was a little, but my heart still felt inexplicably wounded.

"That is her best and your worst selling point."

My stomach sank at the thought of him kissing her. "What was her name again?"

"Erica."

"Erica. When you tell her about me, tell her I hate her." I turned, walking backward in front of him. "Not her specifically, just what she represents."

Adam laughed. "I'm sure she won't care."

"And I'm now sure you've never had a girlfriend before." She was absolutely going to care. Adam wasn't even my boyfriend, and I felt a choking jealousy for this girl who got to claim the parts of him I'd never really thought about. And now, suddenly, it was all I could think about. "Hey, what about our pictures? Does your mom know about Erica?" I stopped walking again, this new thought stampeding over the rest. "Now you've got me thinking not-nice things about your mom. We sent her a picture of us yesterday!"

It was really cute, too. We'd set the timer, then hung upside down off my couch so that our heads were inches from the floor and our legs were bent over the backrest. And he was ruining it. I couldn't get my eyelids to close, and my pulse had to be scarily high based on how twitchy I felt.

Adam was in chest-poking range, so I poked him. "Is your mom fine with you having girlfriends at every port?"

"Hey, ow. You have a really bony finger."

I kept poking him. "Answer the question."

"No, she doesn't know about Erica. Now quit it." He stepped away; otherwise, I'd have kept on poking him. It was either that or hit him. And I couldn't do that, because he hadn't done anything wrong. Not technically. I hated technically.

"So you lie to all the women in your life?" I was sort of playing with him, but sort of not. He usually enjoyed my dramatics, and I was feeling particularly inspired. What choice did I have?

"No, but I'm going to now. Hey, did I tell you about the girlfriend I don't have?"

I let out a breath that sounded wounded when I meant it to sound insulted.

"Look who's the sensitive one now. Why are you making a big deal out of this?"

"I'm not." I was. How could he not see that it was a big deal? Wasn't it big to him, too?

"For all I know, you have a boyfriend." His voice sounded ever so slightly off when he said that, and his gaze shot to my face as though he was searching for a reaction before I answered. That made my stomach twist tighter.

"*I* would have told you. I would have said something like 'Hey, Adam, I know we don't kiss or anything, but I have a guy that I kiss now.'"

His face flamed red. "Are you saying you want me to kiss you?"

"No! I'm just saying…" Heat crept into my own face, and I turned away. I had no idea what I was saying, and for once I didn't know if he was blushing because I'd embarrassed him or because he was embarrassed for me. "I would have given you a heads-up."

"In case I wanted to kiss you?"

I threw my arms up. "For one, yes. But mostly, no."

The color began receding from Adam's face but lingered on his ears. Another burst of jealousy shot through me as I thought about how much Erica probably loved that, too.

"I don't know what to do with that."

"Well, it doesn't matter now. She's already here."

"This is the strangest conversation we've ever had."

"I blame Erica."

ADAM

I ran into Dad in the hall leaving Jo's apartment on Saturday night. He was working on one of the normally flickering sconces that he'd turned off. I raised an eyebrow at the couple of lanterns evenly spaced on the floor behind him.

"Trying not to kill myself with a live wire," he explained, climbing down from the small stepladder. "It'll be a late night, but I want these all rewired and replaced by morning." He pulled his cell phone out and tapped the screen. A second later I heard Jeremy's voice on the speaker.

"Ready?"

"Yeah," Dad said. "Go ahead and hit the breaker for the sixth floor."

A series of steady, bright lights flicked on down both sides of the hall. Dad grinned.

"Did it work?" Jeremy asked.

"One floor down, five more to go." Dad surveyed the perfectly working new sconces, then addressed me as he bent to fold the ladder with one hand and pick up his toolbox with the other. "We could use your help." He was careful not to look at me when he asked. I don't know if he didn't want to see my face when I refused, or if he thought that, if he avoided eye contact, I might say yes.

"Okay," he said when I didn't answer. "I gave you a chance to answer like a man, but if you're going to be silent like a boy, then I'll decide for you." He walked by me like we were strangers passing on the street. "Grab the lanterns and meet me on the fifth floor."

We worked in silence for the whole right side of the floor—four lights—and, despite myself, I was impressed with my dad. I knew he and Mom had practically taken our house down to the studs and built it back up again, but the bulk of that had been done when I was too little to understand all the hats he had to wear. Electrician, plumber, architect, carpenter. And he wore them well. Mom handled the design side, though she did a lot more than pick out paint colors. She refinished floors and restored fireplaces; she made furniture and laid tile. Looking around this hallway, I couldn't help thinking how much she would have loved to be here, working with us.

My expression must have revealed something about my thoughts, because Dad halted in the middle of capping the wires of the next light. "What's that look?"

I handed him another cap, and it was either too late or I was too tired, but I decided to answer him honestly. "Mom would have loved this."

I saw a smile play at his lips as he resumed working. "I ever tell you what we did on our honeymoon?"

"Dad," I said, making sure he heard the warning in my voice.

"No, no." He waved me off before relaying the story. "We'd just bought the house, so we had no money to go anywhere. We decided to drive to the Poconos and get a little cabin by the mountains—this was in the summer, so it wouldn't have been crowded with skiers. We took our time on the drive, taking back roads and stopping whenever we wanted. So we're an hour into the drive when your mom suddenly grabs my arm and yells for me to stop. I slam on the brakes so hard that we both get seat belt bruises across our chests."

"Did she see a deer dart into the road or something?" I asked, curious despite my desire to remain indifferent to him.

"Somebody had the doors open to a big old barn, and somehow she happened to be looking over at the exact right second to see what she swore was a nineteenth-century quartersawn oak dining table set."

I laughed, because that was exactly the kind of thing I could imagine Mom doing. "Our dining table?" I asked, already knowing the answer.

"It took her less than twenty minutes to convince the owner to sell it to us for the money we were going to rent our cabin with, and we spent that night back at the house eating pizza and drinking cheap wine while I stripped the table and she tore the ripped caning out of the seats." He smiled again. "We didn't have any other furniture yet, and the upstairs was missing a good chunk of its roof, so we slept on blankets in front of the fireplace. One of the best nights of my life." Then his voice cracked. "And nine months later we had Greg."

And just like that my chest felt too tight, like there wasn't enough room inside me. I didn't like seeing my dad get choked up. It felt like he was betraying something by showing me his weakness, like he was robbing me of the anger I still held so close. All he had to do was tell one story, let me hear the pain that he felt even as he smiled, and the glare I normally graced him with was gone. Instead I rotated my jaw and squeezed the cap in my hand, all my muscles coiled tight so that I didn't crack with him, *for* him, as I watched him grieve his son.

He didn't try to hide it from me the way he had in the past. This time, there was no getting up and going into another room; he stood on the stepladder and clapped a hand on my shoulder, tight, like it was the only thing in the world keeping him upright when my eyes flooded and I'd never felt weaker in my life.

I couldn't cry in front of my dad—that would have felt like an intrusion. More than that, I knew that if I did cry with my dad, I wouldn't be able to hate him again in the morning.

IN BETWEEN

Adam:

You didn't text me with a million exclamation points so I'm guessing the finals didn't go your way.

Jolene:

Is that your diplomatic way of asking if my team lost?

Adam:

Yeah.

Jolene:

We lost.

Adam:

That sucks. Sorry I couldn't be there.

Jolene:

My own parents weren't there. Trust me, you're off the hook.

Adam:

Was it close?

Jolene:

I'd like to be able to say yes, but lies are unbecoming, aren't they?

Adam:

Must have been up against a good team.

Jolene:

Nope. We beat them early in the season and by all accounts we should have won today.

Adam:

What happened?

Jolene:

No one played great, least of all me, which means if you keep texting me I'm gonna slip and say something mean.

Adam:

It's okay. Lay it on me.

Jolene:

No, it's no fun when you're nice about it.

Adam:

I can be mean. I'll just imagine what you'd say.

Jolene:

This ought to be good.

Adam:

I'd get it if you were upset about losing in a cool sport, like basketball, but soccer is the most tedious sport ever. Like, there are entire games where no one scores. I mean I guess it could be worse, like lacrosse or something. So there's that.

Jolene:

That is not bad. I mean, soccer is everything awesome, but I shouldn't expect much from the guy who thought FIFA had something to do with French poodles.

Adam:

You win. At insults at least.

Jolene:

Now that was a solid burn.

Adam:

I feel like a jerk.

Jolene:

And yet somehow you made me smile.

Adam:

Yeah?

Jolene:

Yeah. Want to feel like a bigger jerk?

Adam:

Not really, no.

Jolene:

I play lacrosse in the spring.

FIFTH WEEKEND

November 20–22

ADAM

"You're not doing it right." I stood on the side of the road, shivering as the moon started its slow ascent.

"What do you know?" Jeremy said. "And will you please stop shaking the flashlight all over the place?"

"I know it shouldn't take half an hour to change a flat tire." But I added another hand to steady my grip.

"Adam?"

"What?"

"Could you shut up for a minute so I can finish?"

I clenched my jaw at the gust of wind that cut right through the coat I wore. It was Friday night, and we were heading to Dad's. Even though my teeth were beginning to chatter, signaling my impending hypothermia, I was grateful for the delay in seeing him. Our last weekend had been... I'd acted like things might be okay, or at least like we more moving in that direction. Helping him with the lights, talking a little, letting him choke up in front of me and never once reminding him that his actions meant Mom was grieving all alone at that exact moment.

When the tire on Jeremy's car blew, I'd half convinced myself it was wish fulfillment. Thirty freezing minutes later,

I was rethinking that conclusion. Jeremy clearly had no idea how to change a tire, and I wasn't much help. It was a skill I'd planned on learning, but hadn't gotten around to. Jeremy obviously had a similar plan.

"Dammit, Adam! If you don't stop moving that light around, I swear—"

"You'll what? Move slower?"

Jeremy lunged to his feet. "You want me to knock you out right now?"

"I want you to fix the tire so we can go. Where was I not clear about that?"

The socket wrench—I think it was a socket wrench, it was pathetic that I wasn't sure—clanked against the asphalt as Jeremy threw it down. "Do it yourself then."

However little Jeremy knew about changing a flat tire— and it was a very little—it was still light-years beyond what I knew. I stared at the socket wrench. Then I stared at my brother. I repeated this process several times before he made a sound of disgust and squatted down in front of the tire again.

"You're worthless, you know that?"

I did kind of know that. I didn't bother with a response. Instead I watched my brother struggle to change a tire for probably the first time in his life. There was nothing especially heartwarming about the sight. Squatted down, his jeans dipped low in the back, revealing plenty of butt crack. He was also grunting and swearing under his breath as he wrestled with one of the lug nuts—a term I was mostly confident I had right. But I felt angry heat sear through me.

"Why didn't Dad teach us this? Why didn't he make sure you knew something this basic before you got your license?"

Jeremy shook his head and forced a laugh. "You don't know when to quit, do you?" He looked up at me, and the pissed-off smile left his lips. I wasn't ragging on him that time, and he knew it. "I don't know. Maybe he forgot. Or maybe he didn't have time. It's not like we were having a party when I turned sixteen."

All our holidays and birthdays since Greg died had been somber affairs. Without him, celebrating was the last thing any of us had felt like doing.

"Did you see Mom before we left?" I asked.

Jeremy's hands stilled on the lug nut he'd gone back to loosening. He said nothing.

"Did you?"

"Yeah, I saw her." He made a grunting noise as he continued forcing the bolts free.

"And?"

"And what?" Jeremy got to his feet and kicked the tire. "Damn thing's rusted tight."

I lowered the flashlight to my side. "Did you say anything to her?"

"Of course I did."

"What did you say?"

Jeremy turned, first his head and then the rest of him, to face me. "What was I supposed to say? 'Hey, Mom, please don't spend the weekend wrapping Christmas presents for your dead son like you did last year'?"

I swung the flashlight beam up to his face and then dropped it when he didn't bother to shield his eyes.

Jeremy finished changing the tire. Not once did he have to remind me about the light.

Without asking, Jeremy blasted the heater when we got back in the car. Stopping at the next light, Jeremy flexed his hands on the steering wheel, the red glow of the traffic light illuminating a streak of grease running across his knuckles. When a cursory search for something to wipe them with turned up nothing, he dragged the back of his hand on his jeans.

"We should be with Mom."

"We were," Jeremy said. "And now we'll be with Dad tonight."

I shook my head. "That's wrong and you know it."

"What's wrong is the way you're treating Dad. When are you going to grow up?"

"The way *I'm* treating Dad? Me? What the hell is wrong with you? Mom is in that house all alone right now, and Dad—"

"And Dad is alone *all the time*. Why don't you care about that?"

I forced my head to turn to the window before I did something stupid like punch my brother while we were going fifty miles per hour. Maybe when we slowed down.

"You need to ease up on Dad. He's not doing real well. You'd know that if you spent any time with him."

"Who do you think helped him with the lights, huh?"

"Yeah, and then you didn't say a word to him all Sunday."

"If he hadn't left, we wouldn't even be having this conversation."

Jeremy shook his head. "You keep doing that. Think about what it's like for him. What it's been like since Greg died. She can't let go."

"She's supposed to let go when we keep leaving her alone like this?"

"I don't know. But it wasn't Dad's idea to leave."

"It wasn't Mom's."

"No, it was both of them. They decided together. However mad you are at him for leaving, you better be just as mad at her."

I squeezed my eyes shut. None of it made sense to me, but Dad leaving, even if he was agreeing with Mom, was wrong. It was so obvious after these past few months that she wasn't coping with Dad being gone. She was crumbling before our eyes each time Jeremy and I left. If Dad was any kind of man, he'd have seen that. Jeremy knew it as well as I did.

"Dad's alone because he's a coward. Mom's alone because she married one."

I wanted to feel satisfied when Jeremy didn't have a response, but I wasn't.

Jolene

I couldn't tell you how long I spent waiting for Adam in the lobby, but it was full dark outside—and not from the weather—when I finally saw his brother's car. I was aware of how pathetic I looked, waiting there for him, but I didn't care enough to pretend that I'd been doing anything besides waiting. For him.

I had cause to rethink my so-called indifference when Jeremy entered the lobby first. He took one look at me, scowled while muttering something under his breath, and stormed toward the stairs. The two-second encounter made my skin feel like it didn't fit. But then Adam was there.

He wore a scowl identical to his brother's until he saw me. He stopped halfway inside the building and took a deep breath without taking his eyes from me. Then he dropped his bag to the floor and crossed the lobby in three long strides, sending my heart pounding.

His arms went around me, and my feet were lifted from the ground as his face was buried in my shoulder. If he noticed how I stiffened when he embraced me, he didn't show it. "I really needed you to be here, right here. I wouldn't have made it another step. How'd you know that?"

Adam was still wrapped around me, almost too tightly. He smelled really good, like spicy apples, and my whole body finally sighed into him. "I was actually just down here getting the mail."

He laughed into my shoulder, and his breath stirred the baby hairs at the nape of my neck, making me tingle. With one last squeeze, Adam released me.

"Easy, Adam. You know, I think you cracked my rib just now," I said, lightly running my fingers along my side.

"Nah, you're just not used to it."

Something prickled behind my eyes, but I ignored it and went to retrieve Adam's bag. I felt his gaze on me the entire time.

"Sorry, that was a stupid thing to say."

"Trouble in paradise, I take it?" I nodded in the direction Jeremy had gone. We could still hear him stomping up the stairs. "And call me nutty, but I think your brother is falling in love with me."

"It's not you," Adam said, dodging the lighthearted life preserver I'd thrown him and focusing on the empty staircase. "He thinks I should be spending time with our dad."

"I already knew you were Team Mom in the split."

"There shouldn't have been a split." One of his eyelids started to twitch. "If Dad had stayed instead of leaving when Mom needed him, we wouldn't be here. We'd be home together, missing him together."

Oh.

I mean, not *oh, I totally get what's going on,* but one big piece just got added to the mix. No wonder Adam had gotten so upset when I'd implied one or both of his parents had cheated. They'd lost someone.

"Who?"

"My older brother. Greg."

He did that guy thing where he locked his jaw tight enough to crack and tried to keep his eyes from doing more than looking extra shiny. I should have touched him or said something—that was what people did when someone revealed something like that, right? But patting his back or saying I was sorry felt woefully inadequate.

"Recently?"

Adam hunched, and his hand moved from his jacket pocket toward the phone I could see in his jeans. "Yeah. I mean no." His fingers flexed like he was forcing himself not to touch his phone. He shoved his hand back in his jacket. "It was a couple years ago, but I don't really want to—"

"You don't have to. I'm just—I'm sorry. That sucks."

"Yeah, it does."

His gaze grew distant—more distant—and I could tell he didn't like any of the places his thoughts were taking him, so I changed the subject.

Gazing outside, I said, "Do you ever feel like the earth hates us? I mean, look at that." *That* was the snowstorm currently obliterating the view, such as it was. It was gray and screaming and completely impenetrable. "How do you interpret that as anything other than deeply held hatred?"

"I am feeling strongly disliked at the moment," he told me. "But that might have more to do with the hour I just spent with Jeremy." He looked at me. "Shelly pick you up today?"

I made a face. "Yes. She didn't get out of the car, and I ran out the second she pulled up. It wasn't too bad." Though that was largely due to the fact that I'd hidden Mom's watch and phone and changed all the clocks in the house back an hour before she had gotten up, so she'd been caught unaware when I ran out.

"She try to talk to you the whole drive over?"

"Hmm? Oh no." I grinned at him. "I pretended to be on the phone with you."

He half smiled. "You know, you could have actually been on the phone with me."

I shrugged. It always took me a little while to recover when I left my mom's on these weekends, and I wasn't sure I wanted Adam to see—or hear—me while I was still frayed.

Another howling gust rattled the glass of the doors, and we both eyed the seemingly thin panes.

"That'll hold, right?" Adam asked.

"It held last year."

"Okay, that's good."

"But maybe it was weakened enough that it'll shatter apart any second and impale us with large shards of glass."

Adam looked at me. "Why do you say things like that?"

I shrugged again. "I don't know. I should probably watch fewer movies."

"Yeah, I don't think that's what's wrong with you."

If he only knew. "So where do you want to go?"

"Away from the potentially homicidal glass doors for a start. I'm assuming Shelly is in your apartment?"

"And your dad and brother are in yours?"

"Yep." Adam went quiet for a moment, the kind of quiet that seemed to scrape my skin. "Hey, how come I never see your dad?"

I'd been walking along a lifting seam in the carpet like it was a tightrope. I paused for a beat, then resumed walking. "What do you want to hear?" When he didn't answer, I hopped off the line and spun to face him. "It wasn't a trick question."

"Yeah, I'm not so sure about that."

"Aren't you the clever boy?" My chin lowered slightly

along with my shoulders. "You don't see him because *I* barely see him. I could tell you about his demanding job, the one that helps him afford his ridiculously expensive lawyers who fought my mom with unprecedented savagery in order to get me here two weekends a month, but that's the pile of horse crap that horses crap on. It's not about the money—it's about me. I don't even think he'd keep Shelly around if he wasn't legally required to have someone with me. He couldn't care less about me. I mean, obviously." I kicked at a freshly painted baseboard.

"You said I was petty the first day you met me." I shook my head with a small smile. "I've got nothing on my dad. Somehow my mom managed to convince him that she wants me more than anything else, so of course he's determined to take me away from her. If he thought killing me would make her suffer, I'd have a dozen hit men after me."

"Geez, Jolene."

"Too morbid for you? Sorry and whatever, but you did ask."

"You just talked about your father plotting to murder you out of spite."

"I believe the word I used was *petty*." One foot in front of the other, I walked my makeshift tightrope again until Adam pulled my arm.

"Would you stop for a minute? Don't you see how messed up that is? Tell your mom or her lawyer or someone."

I laughed. "My mom would try to use it as leverage to get more alimony, and my dad would likely retaliate by having me committed—there, is that better than murder?"

"No," he said, his face frozen in an expression that made me scowl.

"Get over yourself."

"I'm trying to get over you." My gaze shot to his, wide

and unblinking, and he reddened, adding, "I didn't mean it like that. I meant—I don't know what I meant."

"Let's forget it, okay? I don't want us to waste our time fighting about something that doesn't matter. I'm here, you're here. You obviously missed me." I rubbed my side again, hoping for a smile or something besides that half grimace he still wore. "And I'm not in a rush to hang out with Shelly, so…" *Come on, Adam. Come on…*

"No," he said after a pause. "No, it does matter."

I groaned. "Fine, it matters, but…" I groaned again. "You're such an idiot, you're gonna make me say it."

"I'm the idiot?"

"You, stupid. It doesn't matter because of *you*. Two weekends a month. It's not a bad trade-off."

My stomach seemed to twist in two different directions as I waited for his response. The days with him were worth enduring the ones with my parents—the presence of one and the absence of the other. He was a jerk for making me spell it out. The prickle was back behind my eyes, and he needed to say something. Fast.

I was still holding Adam's bag, and his fingers glided across mine, warm and smooth, as he transferred the weight to his.

"Me, too."

"What?" My gaze snapped away from our hands to his face.

"It's not a picnic with my family right now either—for different reasons, but still. Two weekends a month. It's not a bad trade-off."

And then he smiled at me like a dope.

And I smiled back.

ADAM

"What made you think of ice-skating?" Jolene asked on Sunday afternoon as I opened the door to the rink for her.

"Winter. Snow. Ice. The thought of potentially watching you fall on your face before we go back to our respective homes tonight." *And*, I mentally reminded myself as my face warmed, *the excuse to hold on to you if you need help balancing.*

She grinned. "What makes you think I'm not an Olympic-level figure skater?"

"Are you?"

"I don't know. I've never tried."

"What, like, never?"

Jolene shook her head at me. "You couldn't be pretty *and* smart, could you? Yes, *never* means never. I take it you were born on the ice?"

"Not born exactly. My dad used to play amateur ice hockey, so he wanted his sons to learn. We used to skate all the time."

"Oh, are we going to sad skate?"

"What?"

"Are we going to be skating and I finish this stunning triple backflip only to look over and find you in full-on *Field of Dreams* mode?"

"Why would I be crying?"

"Because you'll be thinking about your dad, and because my jumps are going to be so awesome."

I didn't answer her. Instead I seized the opportunity to give the girl at the rental counter our skate sizes. Dad started us skating almost before we could walk. We went as a family almost every week; my parents would still hold hands like they were teenagers. And... I started to mentally swear at myself because I *was* about to lose it.

We started walking to a bench, but Jolene scooted in front of me. "Hey, so that was clearly a bad joke." She took both my hands like she was about to bare her soul to me. In a soft, gentle voice, she said, "If you feel like you need to cry, just give me a sign and I'll collide into you, knocking us both to the ground—that way everyone will think you're crying 'cause I kneed your junk."

I laughed, and not for the first time that day. Probably not for the fifth time, and we'd only met up a half hour ago. My heart settled into its Jolene rhythm, the too-fast hammering rate it leaped to when I stared at her too long.

"Seriously though, you good?" she asked. "'Cause we can do something that doesn't involve rented footwear."

"I'm good." And with her, I was. "Besides I want to show you this. It's like flying."

With a comically wrinkled nose, Jolene took her skates and started jamming her feet into them.

"Here, you have to pull the laces tighter than that." Sitting opposite her, I grabbed Jolene's foot and placed it on the bench between my legs.

"I think you're cutting off my circulation."

"That's what you want. Give me the other one." She did, and I laced her up. "Come here." I lowered her foot and pulled on her hands until she stood. I didn't have my skates on yet, so the added inches from her blades put us at almost eye level. "How do they feel? Are your ankles secure?" My voice was unsteady from being that close to her, but I didn't care.

"I feel like I'm embarking on the first stage of Chinese foot binding."

"Good. I like you this height."

"Oh yeah? Why's that?"

I felt my face flush, but ignored it. "I don't know. One of us doesn't have to look up or down. We're eye to eye."

"And mouth to mouth. Smooth."

Now that she mentioned it—actually, long before she'd mentioned it, like the second I'd seen the height of her blades before she even put her skates on—I'd imagined standing with her, mouth to mouth. I hadn't imagined getting called out on it, but it was impossible to predict anything with Jolene. I loved that. I loved that it was equally impossible to think about anything or anyone else when I was with her.

"And don't forget you have a girlfriend."

Her words were a gut punch. Erica. Right. Crap. That was happening more and more often lately, forgetting about Erica when I was with Jolene. And I really didn't want to be that guy.

"Ready to show me all your moves on the ice?"

"Lead on."

An hour later, I was pretty sure that Jolene was a worse figure skater than I was a poker player. And I was a terrible poker player.

"Movies have lied to me. All the ice-skating montages where the novice turns out to be amazing after a single power ballad of practice scenes? No. Nope. Not even a little." Jolene gritted her teeth as I helped her to her feet for the millionth time. "Ow."

I didn't have nearly as much sympathy as I had for her first half a million falls. "Quit trying to do all these spins. Just skate."

"But the spins look amazing."

"Not when *you* do them."

She burst out laughing and took the gloved hand I'd offered. She was wobbly, even with my support, so I took her other hand and skated backward in front of her. "There's this thing called patience."

"There's this other thing called condescension."

My mouth kicked up on one side. "I'm just saying you can't be amazing at every new thing you try. Ice-skating takes practice."

She squeezed my hands, and my heart rate sped up in response. "I just hate this beginning part, where I want to be so much better than I am. I want to be at the fun part, where I can decide I want to do something and my body is like, 'oh yeah, we got this.'"

"What part of life is ever like that?"

"The movies."

I rolled my eyes, but there was a smile on my face that softened the action. "I meant real life."

"Movies can be more real than life. They're life the way the filmmaker wants it to be, or life the way the filmmaker needs to show the world, or life the way the filmmaker is afraid it is. It's *true* life, even if it isn't exactly real."

We glided to a stop, and my smile halted with us. "That's how you should start your essay."

Instead of responding, her gaze followed a little girl who looked barely out of diapers, skating past with a skill and confidence that she was clearly envious of.

"Jolene." We were standing still, so I didn't need to keep holding her hands, but I did. I kept my voice soft until her gaze returned to mine. "What you just said—that's why you want to be a filmmaker. Write it."

"I've tried," she said, gently tugging first one hand free, then the other. "There's a reason I want to be a director and not a screenwriter. Besides, apparently writers are the least important part of the movie. I mean, look at the one we saw last weekend. The script was awful, but it made like a jillion dollars."

I completely ignored her baiting comment. "I'll help you."

Her arms lifted slightly, as though she wanted to wrap them around herself, but then she forced them back down. "I don't want any help."

This time I let my annoyance pinch the skin between my eyes as I glided back a step. Her hands immediately reached for me, and she steadied herself. "Letting other people help you doesn't mean you're weak or helpless. Sometimes it just means you're smart enough to understand that you don't have to do everything on your own."

I offered her my hand again, just one, because the truth was that she didn't need both.

She eyed my hand, then my face, and a second later she lifted her chin and skated past me.

We stayed for another hour and she kept falling, ignoring every attempt I made to help her up.

I should have felt better at home that night in my own room but I didn't, not really. My body might have been lying on my own bed, but my mind was still in the city, with Jolene.

Why was she so stubborn? Was it so bad to let me help her? I'd heard her talk about movies before. We watched a lot of them together, and while we weren't allowed to talk during the movies—Jolene had practically breathed fire at me the first time I'd made that mistake, when she'd showed me *Rabbit Hole*—she'd pore over them afterward with me. She'd point out aspects of the story I hadn't noticed or geek out about how certain scenes were shot to emphasize a specific emotion or mind-set of a character. She noticed all kinds of things I would have never picked up on, and more than noticing them, she had ideas about how she'd have shot different scenes.

I already knew her essay would be as passionate and insightful about films as she was, and if she needed a little help to smooth out a sentence here or there, how would that take anything away from what she'd done all on her own?

I reached for my phone a dozen times to tell her that, but I knew Jolene. If I pushed her, she'd push back no matter what I said.

With a sigh, I flopped back onto my bed and stared up at my moonlit ceiling.

It might have been an hour or three later when my phone buzzed.

Jolene:

Hey.

Adam:

Hey.

Jolene:

My butt hurts.

Adam:

You'll get better.

Jolene:

I can't get worse.

Adam:

That's what I meant.

Jolene:

It hurts more than it had to.

Adam:

Everybody falls. You got back up.

I waited for her to respond, but minutes ticked by and nothing. My thumbs hovered over my screen but I didn't know what else to say.

Jolene:

Check your email.

A smile bloomed on my face when I opened my inbox, and right at the top was an email from Jolene with the subject line **Essay**.

Jolene:

Turns out you have to land on your butt exactly 429 times before you realize that it hurts a lot less if you let someone help you.

Jolene:

Fair warning, my essay is not good. If your eyes start bleeding at any point you can stop reading.

Adam:

They won't.

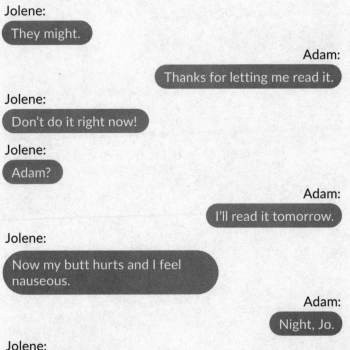

Jolene:
They might.

Adam:
Thanks for letting me read it.

Jolene:
Don't do it right now!

Jolene:
Adam?

Adam:
I'll read it tomorrow.

Jolene:
Now my butt hurts and I feel nauseous.

Adam:
Night, Jo.

Jolene:
Thanks, Adam.

I immediately read Jolene's essay.
My eyes didn't bleed once.

IN BETWEEN

Jolene:

Forget everything you were going to do today. I have a plan.

Adam:

I feel like I need to be alarmed.

Jolene:

The word you were looking for is excited. I would also have accepted super psyched.

Adam:

You do know that we have school today.

Jolene:

And tomorrow's Thanksgiving. You can't tell me you're looking forward to that.

Adam:

My mom's an incredible cook and I make a mean sweet potato pie.

Jolene:

And I like eating my weight in mashed potatoes. Doesn't change the fact that I'd rather stick a fork in my eye than share a meal with my mom and her boyfriend. Also save me a piece of sweet potato pie.

Adam:

That's what you're doing? Nothing with your dad and Shelly?

Jolene:

I'd rather stick two forks in the same eye and do something equally terrible to the other. Thankfully, no. Not this year. Are you seeing your dad?

Adam:

No. We're driving out to my grandparents' and it's a long drive.

Jolene:

Think your mom will cry?

Adam:

Oh yeah. And Jeremy and I will get in a fight, my grandfather will yell at us in Dutch, and my grandmother will forget that Greg is dead and ask about him every few minutes. My mom will excuse herself to cry in the bathroom and then spend the entire two-hour drive home apologizing for ruining the day for us. Or I don't know, maybe it'll be different than last year.

Jolene:

You want one of my eye-stabbing forks?

Adam:

Thanks, but I'm good.

Jolene:

Liar. That is why I have a plan for one awesome day before the suckfest begins. So are you in or out?

Adam:

Tell me exactly what your plan is, oh brilliant one.

Jolene:

First, I totally approve of that nickname. Second, have you seen Ferris Bueller's Day Off? And third, do you know of a parade nearby?

Adam:

Jolene.

Jolene:

This is where you point out that we have no cars and can't drive.

Adam:

Also we have school.

Jolene:

All of those things are true, but you forgot one very important thing.

Adam:

I'm afraid to ask.

Jolene:

My friend has a loser boyfriend that she'd do anything to see, including put a temporary pause on the fight we're having and have him drive to pick you up if I provide an alibi later for her parents. Jazz hands!

Adam:

You're serious.

Jolene:

> We'll pick you up outside your school in 20 minutes. Also, where is your school?

Adam:

> Unless your friend's boyfriend drives a certain DeLorean, it's gonna take you longer than twenty minutes to get here.

Jolene:

> ! You are totally winning for the Back to the Future reference right now. And I stand by my original estimate. Ask me why.

Adam:

> ...

Jolene:

> Because we left fifteen minutes ago.

Adam:

> You're out of your mind. What if I said no?

Jolene:

> LOL

Adam:

> I could have said no.

Jolene:

> You're hilarious. Now give me the address.

ADAM

"What are you wearing?"

Jolene made a face as a girl from inside the car called out, "Told you."

"Yes, I go to a private school. Yes, they make us wear uniforms. No, it's not a Catholic school. The plaid skirt is just something they decided on to torment us."

And me, apparently. It wasn't even short, but I'd almost tripped down the school steps when I pushed out of the double doors and saw her leaning against a car. In tights and that skirt.

It was cold enough outside that I hoped she chalked up my red cheeks to the temperature, but just to be sure, I said something completely at odds with how surreal I found the situation.

"You know that text conversation this morning could have been avoided if you'd just sent me a picture of what you were wearing. I'd have been in."

"Seriously? Boys are so dumb."

Relieved, I shrugged. "So you must be Cherry." I stuck my hand through the car window. "Hey, I'm Adam."

Cherry shook my hand and raised her eyebrows at Jolene. "Polite, too. Are you sure we should be kidnapping him? Someone is going to miss him."

"I have a shared custody agreement with his girlfriend, so we're good."

"You have a what?" My hands grew sweaty at the thought of Erica and the fact that she had no idea I was about to take off with another girl.

Jolene sighed. "I get you two weekends a month. Two. She can give me one measly afternoon, since I'm guessing she won't even know you're gone."

I felt my cheeks heat again, because she wasn't wrong. Erica would be less than thrilled by my friendship with Jolene—and could I even call it a friendship when I thought about her all the time? We texted every day when we were at home, and we barely left each other's sides at the apartment. Jolene was becoming my best friend, except I never got caught checking out my other friends' tights-covered legs or thinking about them while I kissed my girlfriend.

Yeah, I hated myself for that, and I was trying to stop, because that wasn't fair to Erica. Or Jolene, who, despite her initial reaction, seemed fine with me having a girlfriend.

I wanted her to care a little. If it bothered her even a tiny bit...

I had to tell Erica. She didn't always ask me what I did when I was at my dad's, but she had to realize that I did more than sleep and eat. Plus, it was just my luck that Jeremy had spontaneously decided to go out for the school play same as Erica, and I wouldn't be surprised if he let something slip at rehearsal sooner or later. He was constantly telling me what a tool I was being to her—*her* being my girlfriend, not my friend-who-was-a-girl—though I'd have argued I sucked pretty hard to both of them. I knew it was bad when even Jeremy was disgusted with me.

"What's up, man?" the guy in the driver's seat said.

"That's Meneik. He's mine." Cherry snaked an arm around the neck of the lanky guy next to her.

"Hey. Thanks for the ride." I didn't get a response as talking became physically impossible for either of them after that. I turned back to Jolene and found her grinning at me.

"You ditching school for me, Adam Moynihan?"

"I guess I am." I grew sweatier at the prospect. I'd never cut before. None of my friends had cars so it's not like I could have gone anywhere, but the idea had never appealed to me until Jolene. I couldn't think of many things she'd ask that wouldn't appeal to me. Still, I'd have been a lot more nervous if my buddy Os in the front office hadn't agreed to stop the robocall to Mom telling her that I'd missed class.

"It's a cute school," Jolene said, her gaze roaming over the squat, redbrick building. "The white columns are a nice touch. Feels like a president could have gone here or something. Humble but wholesome beginnings and all that."

I didn't bother glancing back. The last thing I needed was for someone to look out one of the many windows and see me leaving with a girl who wasn't my girlfriend. "No presidents yet, but I'll let you know. We should go, right?" I hurried to open the back door for her, and she curtsied before sliding in.

As soon as we were in, Meneik released Cherry and pulled out of my high school's parking lot.

"You do this a lot?" I asked, warily watching the couple in the front seat simultaneously make out and drive.

"Not really," Jolene said, and then she leaned over to whisper in my ear. "I don't think Meneik is qualified to operate a pencil much less a car—an opinion that Cherry takes exception to. We don't hang out a lot anymore."

"I meant ditch," I said, trying to keep my voice steady. She smelled way too good. Honeysuckles were quickly becoming my favorite scent.

Jolene grinned at me. "You are three seconds from breaking out in hives." Then she laughed. "Don't worry. You'll be back in time to hug all your teachers goodbye before school ends."

I side-eyed her. "Part of you thinks I do that."

"All of me knows you do that."

I laughed and tried to force my attention away from Jolene. I was relieved to see that the happy couple were no longer eating each other's faces.

"So what are we doing on this beautiful day?" Jolene asked in an overly bright voice, and I noticed that while she seemed to be addressing the whole car, she was looking at Cherry. I also noticed that she was twisting the hem of her skirt, a gesture at odds with her easy tone.

In a low voice, one so low I almost didn't hear it, Cherry said to Meneik, "We could all hang out for a little bit, couldn't we? Just a little bit?"

From my view in the back seat, I saw Jolene's grip on her skirt twist tighter as she watched Meneik's reaction.

His jaw locked and he flexed his fingers on the steering wheel. He didn't so much as glance at Cherry. "Your mom's been getting to you."

"No," she said, and I picked up a note of panic from her. "That's not—"

"That's what it sounds like." Meneik's voice stayed flat and cold. "She won't let me come around your house, and the one time I get you to myself, you want to go off with your friends. We drop them off somewhere and you get an alibi this weekend. That was the deal. I should have known you'd try to pull something like this on me."

"Meneik..." She reached for his arm but he pulled it away. A heartbeat later, her seat belt was unlocked and she was practically in his lap, telling him that she wanted to be with him, no one else, and she was sorry. She had to repeat her apology so many times that I started to feel ill. When I glanced at Jolene, she had turned to stare resolutely out the window, the hem of her skirt wrinkled but no longer caught in her tortured grip.

A few minutes later, Cherry and Meneik dropped us off outside a strip mall, and I couldn't say I was sorry to see them go. Cherry had made sure every ounce of her attention was focused on Meneik when we got out of the car, even though he remained stiff and indifferent toward her. It was messed up, and Jolene obviously didn't like seeing her friend endlessly apologize for no reason that I could see.

"Hey," I said, drawing Jolene's attention away from Meneik's fading taillights. "I'm sorry about your friend."

Her gaze was weary when it lifted to mine. "Yeah, well, she's the one who wanted a boyfriend."

I started to laugh like she'd made a joke, but Jolene didn't smile. Mine quickly died. "Okayyy, but that doesn't mean she should be treated like that. No girl should."

Jolene shrugged and started to turn away. I caught her arm lightly so that she'd turn back.

"That's not—" I broke off, gesturing in the direction Cherry and Meneik had gone "—the way it should be. Ever." I felt my face heating along with my voice, because the bland expression on Jolene's face told me that she didn't believe me. I started to open my mouth again but snapped it shut, thinking of all the stellar examples of relationships in her life and how they'd probably played a role in the cynical view she held.

"Look, it's just not, okay? I mean, do you honestly think I'd treat a girl that way? Make her—" I was so disgusted by the scene in the car that I couldn't even finish the sentence.

"Erica," Jolene said.

I frowned.

"Her name is Erica. You said 'a girl,' but you have a girlfriend, so the question you should have asked is, do I think you'd ever treat Erica that way."

My face was now blazing for a different reason, because I'd forgotten about Erica. Again. "Fine, okay, Erica then." I half expected her to study me for a moment, as though she had to consider the question, but she answered without even blinking.

"No, you never would, but you're strange and special and there are more guys like Meneik than there are guys like you, so." She shrugged again.

"Strange and special?" I said, thinking that if there was supposed to be a compliment there I couldn't find it.

"You know what I mean."

I wasn't sure I did, but I also wasn't going to stand there and force her to say things about me that she didn't want to on her own.

She spared one last glance after her friend and sighed. "I just hate that he's like that to her."

"Yeah, I get that."

Then she visibly shook herself. "Okay, I really don't want to think about them all day. This was supposed to be fun. Ferris Bueller fun. So what are *we* going to do on this beautiful day?"

I just wanted to go somewhere that wasn't outside. Jolene wanted ice cream. We both won.

She slipped her chilled hand into mine to tug me down

the street, and even though she let go the second I started moving, the heat that somehow suffused my entire body stayed with me.

The ice-cream parlor was empty when we entered. It smelled like vanilla and waffle cones, and Jolene drew in a breath so deep that she practically levitated.

"How can you want ice cream right now?" Her hand had been so cold that I'd made a crack about checking for frostbite.

She shrugged and ordered from the sleepy-looking guy behind the counter. When he turned his half-lidded eyes to me, I shook my head. After he handed Jolene her cone— and it was covered in so many toppings you couldn't even tell there was ice cream underneath—we found a table and sat down. Me to thaw and Jolene to snake gummy bears off her cone with her tongue.

I thawed out very quickly.

I was worried my staring would become creepy in another second, so I said the first thing that came to my mind. "I read your essay."

Jolene paused in the act of biting the head off a gummy bear but said nothing. Even when she finished decapitating the bear, I could see the tension holding the rest of her stock-still.

"Jo, it's really good."

She didn't relax. If anything, she grew more tense.

I usually felt like I was getting only half the story with Jolene. That she was deflecting with her biting humor and brash demeanor. Sometimes she'd let me see more, but not often. Her essay though… It was Jolene stripped raw.

And it was really good.

If I wasn't half in love with her before I read it, I was after.

Except there was no half anything with Jolene.

I really needed to talk to Erica. Whether or not I ever had more than friendship with Jolene, I had no business having a girlfriend when I felt this way about someone else.

Jolene looked tense enough to snap, so I knew I had to come at things in a different way than straight compliments. They always made her uncomfortable, unless she was paying them to herself.

"I couldn't really tell at home but—" I leaned across the table and brought my face close to hers "—did I get all the blood out of my eyes?"

A relieved smile relaxed her face and body. "I'm always so sweet to you, and yet you say stuff like that to me."

I leaned closer and angled my head. "Right in the left tear duct. That one gushed when I read the last paragraph."

Jolene smushed her ice-cream cone in my nose.

I licked at a gummy bear that started to slide down my cheek. "Yeah, you're a sweetheart."

It was cold, but she was laughing, and I'd been the one to make her laugh.

"Really though," she said a few minutes later, leaning toward me and scrutinizing a place on my jaw that she'd wiped clean with a napkin. "You didn't hate it?"

I stilled her hand with my own. There were a few sentences that could be smoothed out, and her opening paragraph was a little scattered, but the heart of her essay—Jolene's heart—beat beautifully through the whole thing.

"No, I didn't."

She gave me a funny look and sat back. "Will you help me though, just a little? I need the film program people not to hate it either."

We spent the next hour going over it on her phone. I made a few suggestions, but I'd meant what I'd said: it was good already.

★ ★ ★

Somehow, Jolene wasn't frozen after all the ice cream she'd eaten, but that didn't stop her from shivering in her uniform the second we walked outside. Neither of us were dressed for spending extended time in the cold, but I gave her my jacket and stoically tried to keep my teeth from chattering while she filmed the snowflakes that floated down around us as we walked. She filmed me, too, and when I asked her if she was ever going to tell me about the movie I was kind of starring in, she smiled and shook her head.

"I had this idea for...something. I'm not sure yet but, I think..." She lifted her camera back to her eye and backed away from me, stepping off the curb and into the side of a parked car. She gasped and then lifted her foot from the several inches of icy slush it had sunk into and laughed. "And impossibly, I'm colder than I was a second ago."

After that she let me talk her into going back inside a heated building, a diner where we drank hot chocolate while we waited for Cherry and Meneik to pick us up. The afternoon ended up being less Ferris Bueller and more whatever movie has the cast wandering around my small, sleepy town and narrowly avoiding frostbite.

It was one of the best days of my life.

Jolene

*T*om was at the house to pick up Mom when I got home from my ditch day with Adam, and when he greeted me with a "there's my girl," I nearly spun on my heel and headed right back out.

Tom tended to leer in a way he thought was charming to women of all ages. I tended to throw up in my mouth each time. We'd spoken a handful of times, all at different levels of awkward, because he almost always tried to turn the conversation around to money: my mom didn't have enough and my dad had too much. How easy it would be for me to help balance things if I would only poke around. And sure enough, he wasted no time that day.

"I'd wager you're looking forward to spending some time with your dad next weekend."

"Then I hope you're not a betting man, Tom." I walked past him to the kitchen and grabbed an apple from the crisper, lamenting the fact that I'd finished off the fried, syrupy spiral *jalebi* that Mrs. Cho had made me the day before. (I'd suggested *The Best Exotic Marigold Hotel* and *Slumdog Millionaire* for her to watch last week and she'd been trying out Indian desserts on me ever since.)

"You know, we've never really talked."

"Nice, isn't it?"

Tom chuckled. It was hella creepy. "Guess I'm gonna have to stay on my toes around you."

I bit my apple.

"Thanksgiving is tomorrow. Are you white meat or dark meat when it comes to turkey?"

I chewed my apple.

"Hey," Tom said, raising his faux-tan-stained palms. "Look, I get it. I'm your mom's boyfriend. It's awkward. I remember how rough it was splitting holidays between my parents but I want you to know that I will never try to re-place your dad."

"Thank you for saying that, Tom. You can't understand what that means to me."

Tom inclined his head. "Sure thing." Then he started to walk away before snapping his fingers as though some idea had just occurred to him. *Yeah, right.* "Hey, next time you're at your dad's, maybe keep an eye out for—" he gestured vaguely like he was coming up with all this from the top of his head "...I don't know, bank accounts or financial state-ments. Snap a few pics and that's it. It'd really help out." He pulled a business card from his wallet and offered it to me.

I looked at it and took another bite of my apple, chew-ing slowly.

Tom's mouth tightened. "Come on, Jolene. It's time to be a team player. Your mom is getting stretched thin here, and we know your dad is hiding money. If he can afford to pay more to make sure you and your mom are taken care of, don't you think he should?"

"My mom is far from destitute, but if you want I'll see if

I can find any spare change in the couch cushions." When I went to throw my apple in the trash, Tom grabbed my arm—not hard enough to hurt, but hard enough to keep me from leaving.

"This isn't a game. Your mom needs you, and we're both a little tired of your unwillingness to help out. Next weekend, I want you to check his desk, take a few photos, and email them to me." He forced the business card into my hand. "That's not too hard for a smart girl like you, is it?"

I narrowed my eyes at him and let his card flutter to the floor. "Let's talk smart, Tom. You picked the wrong woman if all you want is a payday. The reality is my mom's never going to get a cent more from my dad, because he'd rather see it burn than share it with her. So, if you want his money so bad, get it yourself."

"Whoa, whoa." Tom backed away from me and forced a laugh. "That just got weirdly intense. I think I'm already craving that meal tomorrow and I'll let you in on a little secret." He leaned in and lowered his voice as though divulging a secret. "I can get a little hangry if I'm not careful. Let me guess, you, too?" He laughed again. "I, ah, better go grab something before I really put my foot in my mouth. We'll talk more tomorrow, okay?"

I didn't reply as I went upstairs to my room. I'd told Adam I'd rather stick a fork in my eye than share a meal with my mom and her boyfriend. Clearly, I'd grossly underestimated. Scowling, I shut the door behind me, blocking out Tom, and then scowled harder. My bedroom had been featured in some magazine when I was twelve and was supposed to represent the perfect preteen girl's room with light, airy colors and pale wood tones. Nothing overly feminine or youthful. Clean lines, soft fabrics, zero personality. Or I don't know, someone's personality but not mine. I didn't see the point in hanging movie posters or switching the bedding to any-thing that wasn't a sea-foam-green leaf print. It wasn't my room any more than the place I slept over at my dad's was. One day I'd have my own room, my own space. It'd be tacky and mismatched and I'd let the paint get chipped around the doors instead having the whole house repainted every year in the same colors.

That would have felt nice.

Releasing the doorknob, I moved to sit on the plush mat-tress and forced the earlier memories from the day to blot out the conversation I'd had with Tom. No sooner did Adam's face fill my mind than my heart fluttered. He'd been so cute when he first saw me. And nervous. And then cuter still when he tried to downplay how nervous he was. I laughed in my quiet magazine-spread bedroom. The happy feeling faded before the sound did.

He should have been nervous. He just spent an entire af-ternoon with his not-girfriend. *I'd* had to remind him about her. I had to do that more than I liked when we were together. Not that he forgot she existed but sometimes…it was like he let himself stop thinking about her when he was with me. And did that mean he let himself forget about me when he was with her? My stomach lurched and then lurched again. Was I even allowed to feel jealous? I flopped backward on the bed and one of the little peach throw pillows toppled over to rest against my cheek. The smooth satin felt cool and comfort-ing and did nothing to settle the unease swirling inside me.

It wasn't all because of Adam, or even the distaste Tom left me with.

Shifting off my right hip, I pulled my phone from my pocket and had to scroll way too far back to find the num-ber I wanted. It rang and rang before…

"Hey, you're early. My mom's not home yet and if she doesn't see your name on the phone—" Cherry sighed "—actually she'll probably want me to put you on speakerphone or she'll think I'm lying again. I'll text you when to call, okay?"

"I wasn't—I'm not calling about your alibi."

Cherry's voice went so cold I shivered. "No. No way do you get to back out after we drove all that way to Adam's school."

I rolled my eyes and willed my temper to stay in check. "I'm not reneging. I'll tell your mom whatever you want."

There was a pause. "Okay. Good." Another pause. "Then I'll text you when to call."

It was my turn not to answer right away. I rolled my eyes but this time the gesture was directed at myself. It was like we'd forgotten how to talk to each other. "What did you think of him?"

"Adam?" I could hear the eyebrow raise in her voice. "I don't know. He's cute, I guess. Blushes a lot."

I felt my cheeks heat. "Yeah, but it's cute, right?" I scrunched up my nose waiting for her response. It didn't come right away.

"You want to know if I think the guy with the girlfriend is cute when he blushes?"

It was like my mattress turned into a waterbed sloshing underneath me and a queasy, seasick feeling surged over me again. "At least he doesn't berate me for wanting to hang out with my friends."

"Uh-huh. That's 'cause he can't tell anyone when he's with you. He has to lie to his girlfriend so she won't find out about you. So, yeah, Jo. He's real cute."

I curled up on my side, hugging that satin pillow to my chest as my chin quivered once before I stopped it. "It's not like that. We're friends so there's nothing to tell."

"Then why do you care if he's cute? Why do you care if *I* think he's cute?"

My voice went all raspy. "I just wanted to talk to you. Yeah, I wanted to see Adam, but I wanted to see you, too. We never get to hang out anymore."

"Please. You're at my house all the time."

"Yeah, with Gabe and the band. Not you. We never talk and when we do, it's you asking me to cover for you with Meneik."

"So I'm supposed to apologize for having a boyfriend when you don't?"

I shoved my pillow away and sat up. "Ehhh." I made a game show–buzzer sound. "Try again."

"Well then, what?"

"It's not that you have *a* boyfriend, it's the boyfriend you have."

Cherry let out a short laugh. "Wow. Okay. I seriously don't want to get in a fight with you right now. Can't we just—"

"Pretend he doesn't treat you like crap? How do I do that? How do *you* do that? Seriously, Cherry? Deep down I can't imagine you like the person he forces you to become around him. And what about Gabe? You know he's not a fan, and who loves you more than your twin brother? Maybe your mom? Does it feel awesome that you have to lie to her constantly? Meneik's always pitting you against everyone and I think if you stopped for a second and looked, you might see that Meneik is the only person who thinks he's right for you."

"Are you done?"

She clearly was. "He shouldn't treat you the way he does, okay? You deserve better." She was quiet for a long time after that, so long that I started to hope. "You know I'm only saying this because I care about you."

"Yeah, well, I don't need that from you. I need an alibi. I'll text you when to call for my mom." And she hung up.

ONE DAY LATER

Jolene:
How was Turkey Day?

Adam:
The food was good.

Jolene:
What an evasive answer.

Adam:
It was pretty much like I expected.

Jolene:
You didn't talk to your dad?

Adam:
No, he called and talked to Jeremy, but I was conveniently helping with the dishes.

Jolene:
Did you get yelled at in Dutch?

Adam:
Ja.

Jolene:
?

Adam:
That's Dutch for yes.

Jolene:
Say something else in Dutch.

Adam:

Ja is basically the extent of my Dutch. That's one of the things my grandfather yells about. Presumably.

Jolene:

Fighting with Jeremy? Crying mom?

Adam:

Ja and ja. What about you?

Jolene:

Have you ever had Tofurky?

Adam:

That sounds awful.

Jolene:

Awful is too kind a word. Plus Tom and I had words recently and he's being all distant with my mom. It's a toss-up which turns my stomach more: him or the fake meat.

Adam:

Did you see your dad?

Jolene:

Jo. Is that Dutch for no?

Adam:

It's nee.

Jolene:

Then, nee, I didn't see my dad. He texted though.

Adam:

Yeah?

Jolene:

It said "Happy Thanksgiving." Not "Hey, kid, Happy Turkey Day." Not even my name on the end. He probably has an app on his phone that sends out generic holiday greetings to all his contacts.

Adam:

I thought about skipping school with you. It helped.

Jolene:

Me, too.

Adam:

And I saved you a piece of my sweet potato pie.

Jolene:

Did you really?

Adam:

It's a big piece.

Jolene:

I didn't save you any Tofurky.

Adam:

Thanks for that.

Jolene:

Happy Turkey Day, Adam.

Adam:

Happy Turkey Day, Jolene.

ADAM

I hadn't seen Erica in a week. I'd been relieved that she was already in the auditorium for play rehearsal when I got back from ditching with Jolene (very relieved, since our hug in the parking lot went on for longer than I would have been able to explain to my girlfriend). But then she got sick over Thanksgiving and missed a few days of school, giving me abundant time to hate myself for how I'd been treating her.

That self-loathing was still lingering at home the following Thursday as I was helping Mom with the dishes—I rinsed, she loaded—until she propped a hip on the counter and stilled my hand before I could reach for another glass.

"Adam." She brushed a lock of my hair from my bent face. "You're a million miles away."

I was, and I mentally added Mom's name to the list of people I was being unfair to. Next weekend would be the sixth Jeremy and I would spend away from her, and the signs of our impending departure started earlier and earlier each time we left; the tense way she held her shoulders, the light footsteps walking past our bedrooms all through the night, the way she reached out to touch us more and more, like she was trying to store up the feel of us for those days when she'd have to go without. It was like watching her heart slowly break, and normally I tried to keep her talking and laughing, distracted, as the Friday approached. I wasn't doing any of that as I silently rinsed dishes in the sink.

"I'm sorry, Mom. I was thinking about this thing I need to do and how much I really don't want to do it."

I'd have been able to talk to Greg about Jolene and Erica. He wouldn't have made a lame joke the way I knew Jeremy would. He'd have listened to me, offered advice, then clapped me on the shoulder and told me to be the man I wanted to be.

I didn't want to be the kind of man who cheated on his girlfriend, and every weekend I spent with Jolene made it harder to hold back. I'd already come too close to crossing that line and the next time I might charge right past it. I knew I would. Or rather, I'd try, and she'd probably flay me alive. Jolene would never let me make her play the role Shelly had.

And I'd never put her in that position.

"Is this about a girl?" Mom asked.

"Girl*s*," I told her, emphasizing the plural. She stepped back. "Adam Noah Moynihan."

I smiled at her. "C'mon, Mom, you know I wouldn't do that."

She cocked her head at me, smiling back. "Well then, tell me what you mean by *girls*. I thought you and Jolene…"

Dropping my head even farther, I pulled out my phone and thumbed to the first photo we'd taken, the one by the tree near Dad's apartment, the one where I looked just like my brother. "She's not my girlfriend. She's my neighbor, who I didn't even like initially but got to agree to pose for these photos for you, so that I could distract you."

"You *what*?" Mom's voice shook, and I wasn't sure if that was due to the photo that had rattled her the first time she'd seen it or from the confession I'd made.

"It's more than that now." At least, it was for me, but none of that was the point. "I thought I was helping you," I said, because she looked…hurt.

"By lying to me?"

"I wanted you to think about something besides missing Jeremy and me. And Dad." I didn't add Greg, but I knew she understood I was including him, too.

"Adam, that's not your job."

Isn't it?

She led me to the amber-stained dining table with its bead-carved trim, and I couldn't help thinking of Dad, the story he'd told me about it, and the way he'd broken afterward. For the first time, I let myself think about him alone in that apartment while Mom and Jeremy and I were together.

"Tell me about the girls."

I folded my arms on the table and I did, mostly. I told her about Jolene agreeing to help me take pictures, about how we became friends, and how, before I even realized it, I was having more than friendly feelings for her, which made me a complete jerk because I'd finally gotten together with my dream girl here at home.

Mom covered her mouth at that point, and I was starting to worry that my confession had seriously lowered her opinion of me when a laugh slipped through her fingers, muffled at first and then louder as she gave up trying to hide it.

I leaned back. "I'm glad you find my pain funny."

"No, not funny." She reached for my hand. "Honey, you have to be honest with this other girl."

"Erica. And I know. It's just…she knows that I liked her for a really long time, and breaking up with her this quickly makes it look like I was messing with her. I don't want to do that to her."

"If she knows you at all, she'll never think that."

I wasn't so sure. "Plus, Jolene knows I have a girlfriend, and she doesn't seem to mind the way I would if she had a boyfriend."

To that Mom only smiled. "Let me see your phone." When I handed it to her, she pulled up our texts, and, sliding her chair closer to mine so that we could both see the screen, she scrolled thought the photos of Jolene and me, dozens and dozens of photos of the two of us, way more than I needed for Mom. The latest was one of us outside, lying in the snow with a single red scarf wrapping our necks and most of our heads together. Only our eyes were visible, but it was obvious that we were laughing.

I wanted to object that these were photos that were taken specifically to make her believe something that wasn't real, but the more I looked at them and the more I remembered each moment, the less sure I became.

"Maybe she minds more than she's letting on," Mom said, handing me back my phone. Before she let me take it, she added, "And I don't want you lying to make me feel better anymore, okay?"

"I just want you to be happy again," I told her, and for some reason that admission brought tears to her eyes. "Mom?"

She shook her head, trying to stem them, but they fell.

"Mom," I said again, wrapping my arms around her.

She cried for a very, very long time.

I sighed on Friday morning when I saw Erica standing by her locker. I knew this was the moment; it had to be. And not just telling her about Jolene either.

I'd been avoiding the conversation for way too long. I didn't want to be just Jolene's friend, and the more time I spent with her, the more I wanted.

And that meant ending things with Erica.

I'd texted her while she was sick, but I wasn't about to break up with her over the phone, so I'd taken the reprieve like the coward I was.

I didn't have any more excuses.

"Erica," I said as I closed the last few feet between us. "I guess you're feeling bet—"

She turned around and slapped me across the face.

SIXTH WEEKEND

December 4–6

Jolene

"Hello, Adam."

He rolled his eyes at my formality and joined me on the stairwell. It was snowing hard outside, so hard that I'd wondered if Adam and his brother were going to drive in it.

The apocalypse could have been happening and Dad's lawyer would still have made me come. By foot if necessary. So I'd been there, sitting on the thinly carpeted step for over an hour when Adam finally showed up.

"Oh, you've got—" He reached one arm around my back to support his weight as he leaned in to pluck a piece of lint from my braid. But then he didn't lean back, he stared at me and when his eyes lowered to my mouth, I shot to my feet.

"First of all, no. Second of all, I'm tired of being the one who constantly has to remind you of your own girlfriend. You—" and I spun to stare right at him "—are better than that."

"I haven't forgotten anyone. I—"

I cut him off. "From now on I think it's better if we keep a little more distance between us." To illustrate, I sat back down on the step but I made sure there were two full feet between us.

Adam glanced at the space between us, then raised an

eyebrow at me. "I thought you didn't mind me having a girlfriend."

"Okay, fine." I tossed my hands up. "I don't like that you have a girlfriend. And no, I'm not asking for the job. And no, I'm not saying it would be a job to be your girlfriend. I don't like that I have to weigh everything I do in light of how some girl I don't know is going to feel about it, or literally measure the distance between us." I gestured to the space separating us. "I'm exhausted already, and you've only been here two minutes."

"You don't have to worry about that."

"Ah, but I do." I made my eyes go all wide and buggy. "I have to be obsessive and paranoid like a girlfriend would be, and I don't even get any of the benefits. Trust me, I've thought about this a lot."

"No wonder you're tired."

"Just wait," I told him. "You haven't heard my unhinged and overly complicated solution. You ready?"

Adam leaned his back against his side of the stairwell wall. "Go."

"Okay. First, the facts." I poked him in the chest. "You have a girlfriend. You also have a friend who is a girl." I poked my chest. "These two coexisting relationships are going to destroy you and consume your soul. We want to avoid that, if at all possible."

"I appreciate that."

I inclined my head. "The way I see it, we have three options. One—we quit being friends. I object to this option for several reasons. First…" I held up a finger. "Shelly. If I'm forced to endure her company for extended periods of time, it will result in her death and my incarceration." I held up another finger. "Second, Shelly." Another finger. "Third, I refuse to quit being your friend on the grounds that I find you infinitely more tolerable than anyone else I know. Also, Shelly. Fourth—"

"I'll stipulate that option one is a no go. What's option two?"

"Oh, okay. Option two—I meet Erica. We become best friends and I slowly but surely break you down in her eyes until she can't stand the sight of you and she moves on."

"Interesting, go on."

"Option three is that you break up with her in a completely non-recoverable way, like saying, 'Welcome to Dumpville, baby. Population, you.' Or something along those lines. Here, I made you a list." I handed him the folded sheet of paper from my pocket.

He silently skimmed it.

"I'm especially proud of number five." I leaned over and pointed.

"That's...that's... I would never say that to a girl. Also, I'm judging you a lot for coming up with it."

"It gets the job done."

"Yeah, but I'm not doing it." He gave me the paper back. "Or rather, I don't need to do it. She's not my girlfriend anymore."

I couldn't keep a smile from spreading across my face. After we'd played my little game, I had planned on talking to him realistically about the girlfriend situation. I was going to calmly and rationally persuade him that the single life—with me—was infinitely more fulfilling than the dating life with anyone else.

But I didn't have to.

He'd broken up with her. Already. On his own, without any long-drawn-out discussions with me. I grinned at him. "You broke up with her? When?"

He blushed. "This morning. And I wasn't exactly the one who did the breaking." He rotated his jaw a little. "But I would have," he added. "I mean, I was going to. Before I saw you again."

I swallowed and had a slightly hard time of it. So what if she'd dumped him and not the other way around? Adam no longer had a girlfriend, which was all I'd wanted. I pulled my braid over my shoulder and fiddled with the elastic. "Adam, it's fine. You don't have to—"

"I'm not! That's the truth." He reached to still my hand but stopped just shy of touching me. "She, uh… I guess she saw us in the parking lot after we ditched."

For the first time since I'd met him, my face was the one that went red. All we'd done was hug—maybe for a touch too long, but nothing more. Though if she'd seen the way I bit back a smile when he released me… Yeah, it couldn't have been a good feeling.

And that sucked. She was a girl I didn't know, one I'd resented from the moment I'd learned she existed, but she deserved better than what I'd done to her, what Adam and I had been doing together.

We'd never crossed the big lines, but we hadn't stayed away from them either.

Adam was frowning at his hands.

"Are you upset?"

"No," he said. "I hurt her, and I'll never feel good about that, especially since I should have broken up with her weeks ago. Really, I should never have gotten together with her in the first place."

I had complicated reactions to that statement. He was referring to me when he said he shouldn't have gotten together with her. I couldn't deny that even if I tried. But it was scary to suddenly feel like he might be looking at me without any reason to hold back. It made my hands clammy and my breath feel as if it would soon start coming out in panicky gasps. It wouldn't be good for me to be anything more than his friend, and I would only disappoint him if he tried to make us into something more.

I had to remind him that friends were all we could be.

"I mean, I liked Erica," Adam said, still staring at his hands. "But I realized that you were right. If she had some guy that she spent this much time with, it would be weird."

"Or if I had a boyfriend."

Adam's head snapped up. "Don't tell me you do now? I just broke up with a girl I've wanted since middle school because of you—your friendship."

"No," I said, "I turned all the boys down. They were crushed, of course, but they always are."

Adam let out a sigh. "Okay, good."

"So now we can be friends and it doesn't have to be weird?"

He didn't answer right away, and for a moment it looked like he was about to say one thing but then changed his mind. "Right. It doesn't have to be weird."

"Great."

"Yep."

Then it was my turn to pause. I scrunched up my face. "Except it's weird, right?"

"Oh yeah," he said.

We both sighed, and I leaned back on the steps until my butt fell asleep. It *was* weird, coming to a place in our friendship where we had both objected to the other having a significant other while at the same time not wanting to be that significant other ourselves. "You're still my friend, even it's it weird," I told Adam. As long as he didn't expect more, we'd get past weird.

"You're still mine."

Relieved, I stood up—super weird feeling when you can't feel your butt. "Then let's make it not weird. Let's do something."

He looked up. "Like what?"

"Well, we're broke and there is a blizzard outside, so the

options are endless. I spent all my brainpower solving your problem, so this one's on you."

"*My* problem? I didn't even know it was a problem until you went off about it."

"Oh, please." I grinned. "That whole thing would have blown up in your face the second you accidentally kissed me."

Adam's eyebrows shot up and so did he. "I was going to accidentally kiss you?"

"I don't know. Probably. Then I'd have to slap you, because you'd be making me into the 'other woman' and Erica would show up at my house in the middle of the night and we'd get into a fight—that I would win, by the way—and then we'd realize that you're the one we're mad at, so we'd egg your house, and then your mom would find out and she'd never look at you the same way again, and then..." I made an explosion sound.

Adam started slowly down the stairs, one step at a time like he was in a trance. "I've made a huge mistake. Maybe there's still time if I call Erica right now and—" He grunted, then started laughing when I leaped onto his back. "I'll tell her how you threw yourself at me, and beg for her help." He locked his hands under my knees when I would have let go and hoisted me higher onto his back. "And there is no way you'd win in a fight with Erica. You're like a buck ten soaking wet, and I'm betting most of that is your hair. She'd snap you in half."

We were both grinning now. I almost said *weirdness adverted* but that would have been weird. "This, right here," I said, as he started jumping down the stairs in a way that bounced me up and down with each step and added a staccato to my words. "We couldn't—do this—if you had—a girlfriend."

"A friend can't give another friend a piggyback ride?"

"Not if he has a girlfriend. Not unless he's a scummy boyfriend."

"I don't, and I'm not. So hold on."

ADAM

On Saturday morning, Dad was already up when I wandered into the kitchen.

"Morning. Coffee?"

"Yeah, hey." I grabbed a mug from the cabinet and held it out for him to pour.

"I was thinking we could go to the rink today and play a little ice hockey."

"I'm hanging out with Jolene." I turned to take my coffee back to my room, but Dad stopped me.

"Why don't you come with Jeremy and me? You love playing."

"I don't think so."

"Adam." Just my name. I turned to him. "I thought we were turning a corner after last month. Are you ever gonna let up on me? I mean, ever?"

"What do you want from me, Dad?"

"For starters, I want you to come play hockey with your brother and me." He slammed his own mug down on the counter, and coffee splashed over the edge. "I never see you.

I get you for a few days a month, and you spend them in your room or with the girl next door."

"And whose fault is that?"

"I'm trying here. I need you to try, too."

"Yeah, you tried real hard." I held my arms out and gestured around the room. "Look how hard you're trying."

"I'm doing the best I can."

"No, you're not. Your best is all of us home together. Mom not alone. Jeremy and me not living out of suitcases. This is pathetic. You're not trying, so why should I?"

"Adam." He let his head drop forward. "You don't—"

"No, forget it. It doesn't matter. Nothing you say is going to matter."

"And that's you trying?"

"No. That's me not giving a—"

Dad's head snapped up when I started that particular phrase, and the way his eyes widened and then narrowed took some of my bluster.

I finished with "Crap."

But he knew what I'd been going to say, what one look from him had quelled. I wasn't nearly as indifferent to him as I claimed.

He took his victory—and his half-spilled mug of coffee—and went into his room. I had no time to reflect on any of that before I saw Jeremy sit up on the couch.

"What are you going to do when he really stops trying?"

I sipped my coffee.

"Yeah, you're so cool. I keep forgetting." He threw off his blanket, and his back cracked when he stood up from the couch.

"Sleep well?" It was a rhetorical question. The couch was more of a love seat.

Jeremy lumbered past me to the bathroom. He never both-

ered to shut the door even at home, but this bathroom's proximity to the kitchen made it especially grating. I kicked the
door shut when he started to piss.

"So are you really not coming today?" Jeremy asked when
he came out.

"I have plans."

"I heard. That girl again. Jolene. She's cute," he went
on. "I'll give you that, but Erica Porter." Jeremy shook his
head. "You're either the biggest moron on the planet or...
No, you're pretty much the biggest moron on the planet."

I almost told him it wasn't like that with Jolene and me,
but that smacked too much of having an actual conversation
and we weren't having a ton of those lately.

"Oh, so you're not talking to me either now?"

"I'm talking. I asked how you slept."

Jeremy muttered something and poured himself a bowl
of Apple Jacks. "Tell me about your girl," he said between
bites. "I already know you ditched Erica for her." He shook
his head at that one.

"I didn't ditch anybody for anybody. We broke up, that's
all. Besides, I was barely with Erica."

"Half the school saw her slap you."

I said nothing.

"Oh, come on." Jeremy lowered his spoon. "You've
wanted to be with her since forever. You get her, and then
you screw it up in less than two months?" He took another
bite. "That's a waste."

"Not to me." And it wasn't. I worried that I might feel a
little regret the next time I thought about Erica, but the only
thing I regretted was how we broke up, not why. Even if
Jolene had seemed nervous instead of happy when I told her
I wasn't with Erica anymore. I wasn't expecting her to leap
on me and start kissing me—well, she had leaped on me, but

the kissing part hadn't happened yet. I was really hoping it would though. I just needed to show Jolene that being more than friends was a good idea, and I couldn't do that if I kept wasting what little time we had every other weekend talking with my brother.

"You hear Mark Phillips asked her to the winter formal yesterday? She said no. Like, wait two seconds, you psycho."

"She can go out with whoever. Ask her yourself if you want." The idea bothered me a little, but much less than I would have thought possible a few months ago.

Jeremy snorted, then paused like he was considering how serious I was. "You really like this girl." He sounded impressed. I guess he would be. Jeremy had had a couple girlfriends, but he would have pushed either of them from a moving car for the chance I'd had. I knew this, because he'd told me in those exact words when I'd first started hanging out with Erica.

"Your biggest mistake—well, your second-biggest mistake— was telling Mom. She's going to be all over you. She's already been pumping me for info. Like I don't have better things to do than watch you over here."

"You don't."

"Yeah, but she doesn't know that. I keep telling her about all this stuff we're doing with Dad and—"

"Wait, you're what?"

"Telling her about all this stuff we're doing, which, you know, we're not, but she doesn't need to know that."

I dropped both hands on the counter and leaned toward my brother, who was still shoveling cereal into his mouth like someone might take the bowl from him at any second. "Yes, she does."

Jeremy paused between bites.

"She's...she's..." It took me a minute to find the words.

"She's so afraid that she's losing us. That we're not going to come home one day. She lost Greg, then Dad. She panics every second we're away. How do you not know that?"

When Jeremy just stared at his bowl, I knocked it away into the sink. "You'd know that if you talked to her, if you called her or sent or a text or something while we're over here. And you've been rubbing it in her face that it's awesome over here with Dad?" I pushed away from the counter in disgust. "Have fun playing hockey."

I grabbed my coat and let the door slam when I left.

Jolene

"Curse this winter." I shook my fist at the flurry-filled sky. At least three inches of snow crunched under my boots.

"You could walk on the sidewalk," Adam said. He was wearing sneakers, and they looked mostly dry because he'd taken his own advice while I preferred to trudge alongside him in the snow-covered grass, or what would be grass when spring came. If spring ever came.

"Not because of the snow. Who doesn't like snow?"

"The entire driving population."

"So not you then?" I grinned, and Adam kicked a spray of snow at me. "Oh, come on." I stretched up to sling my arm over his shoulder, loving the fact that I could touch him without feeling guilty about it. "I promise to drive you anywhere you want when I get my license. You won't have to worry your pretty little head about anything."

Adam was a whole two weeks younger than me. In less than a month, I'd be sixteen and free, relatively. Those weeks ate at him incessantly.

"So why are you cursing the winter again?" he asked.

I knew he was trying to pull the conversation away from his driver's license-challenged state, and since I didn't want him to get all moody, I let him. "Duh, because of your hat."

Adam had this expression where he would curl one side of his mouth up and frown whenever something made no sense to him, as if he were questioning the intelligence of whoever had said it. He could be arrogant like that sometimes. I knew he was still chafing over the driving thing, so for once, I didn't call him on it. I did, however, explain myself to him in a super patronizing way.

"When it's cold out, your nose and cheeks turn red." I tapped his nose. "But your ears are hidden under your knit cap." I lifted it and lightly pinched his ear. "See? Nice and toasty."

Adam leaned away and pulled his hat back down over his ear. "Right. 'Cause it's cold."

"But I can't see your ears. How am I supposed to know when you're embarrassed? The rest of your exposed skin is all rosy and—don't scowl, Adam, it's very fetching—but I feel like I can't read you. It's frustrating, hence the winter cursing."

Adam's scowl lingered for a second longer as he looked down at me, but it smoothed out. "You're such a strange girl."

"You're still thinking about the fact that I said you were fetching, aren't you?" Then, before he could stop me, I yanked off his cap and was rewarded with the sight of ears flushing bright red. "Ha! I knew it!" When Adam tried to reach for his cap, I held it above my head, which made him laugh.

"You know you're only making it easier for me."

I looked up. With my arm stretched up, the hat was well within his freakishly long grasp. I dropped my hand as he lunged. When I tried to step back, I sank into a drift that sent me sprawling, or would have if Adam hadn't looped his arm around my waist and pulled me up.

"Gotcha." Red ears and cheeks filled my vision. And his smile, too, 100 percent scowl-free. My heart whooped inside me and started pounding at the feel of being in his arms.

I thought about kissing him then. I hadn't had a ton of kisses to compare it to, but apart from the cold, my wildly beating heart was betting that kissing Adam Moynihan would be rather nice. He smelled nice. Crisp, with that super clean, fresh-snow smell, but also a bit like the cologne he'd let me spray on him at the mall earlier. It had some fancy name, but it basically smelled like a Christmas tree.

I pulled away before I did something I'd regret, and then I was the one frowning. Not in his you-must-be-stupid way, but in a truly puzzled way.

"What just happened?" he asked out loud, just as I was posing the same question silently to myself.

"Nothing. I had a random thought." I shook my head, trying to clear it from wondering how soft his lips would be.

We started walking again, him on the sidewalk, me in the snow. I kept glancing at him and not covertly either.

"What?"

"I don't know," I said. "You look different to me."

"You're kind of making me uncomfortable."

"Sorry." I was, but I didn't look away from him. When he stopped suddenly and sighed, I turned my head straight ahead. "Okay, okay. Eyes to the front."

We walked another half a block. We were supposed to be heading to Wa-Wa for hot chocolate, but I would have walked right past the store if Adam hadn't caught my sleeve.

"Don't you want hot chocolate?"

"Yeah. Lead on."

Adam was the one who liked hot chocolate. It was too

sweet for me, but I enjoyed holding the cup to my nose and letting the steam and scent wrap around me. Back outside, I was doing just that when it finally hit me. "It's because of Erica," I said, relieved to realize where the impulse to kiss him had come from. "Well, and the fact that I watched *Eternal Sunshine of the Spotless Mind* last night."

Adam stopped walking. "Um, what's because of Erica?"

"I had this impulse to kiss you a minute ago and I couldn't figure out where—"

"Wait. You wanted to kiss me? Just now?"

I started walking again, and Adam hesitated before joining me. Visible ears or not, I could tell he was embarrassed based on the way he'd hunched his shoulders against a nonexistent breeze. "No, it's fine. I mean, I obviously didn't. And then I realized it's probably because you broke up with your girlfriend yesterday, and then last night I was watching Jim Carrey and Kate Winslet in this bizarrely surreal romance in the snow." I gestured around us with my cocoa. "I can't believe I told you that I thought about kissing you."

When Adam didn't respond, I was the one who sighed. "Okay, you have to tell me what you're thinking, because I can't see your ears and it's like I've only got four senses."

"It's fine, Jo. I mean it's not like I haven't thought about kissing you."

That time when he kept walking, I was the one who fell behind. I felt my face shift like someone had asked me explain the plot of a Darren Aronofsky movie. "When?"

"I don't know. A few times, I guess."

"Cryptic much? When?" When he didn't answer, I relented. "Just the first time then."

"When we took that first picture for my mom," he said at last.

"That was like the first time we met." I laughed, covering

for the tingling heat blazing through me. "You didn't even like me then and you wanted to kiss me?" I almost said, *I don't even want to know what you want to do with me now*, but even I had enough self-control to hold that back.

"I thought you were pretty," he said. "You *are* pretty."

My glance was covert that time. He hadn't put his cap back on, and I could see his ears—not even the slightest bit pink. Mine flushed hot.

Then his mouth lifted up on one side. "And there was a moment when you stopped talking—I mean, it was a tiny moment." He held his thumb and index finger close together. "And I wondered what it'd be like to kiss you." He dropped his hand. "But then you were talking about licking my face and…" He shrugged and made a face.

I pushed him, and he laughed. "At least my impulse came after I actually liked you as a person. I mean, talk about shallow."

He chucked his empty cup into a nearby trash can and held his hand out for my full-but-no-longer-hot cocoa. "You know, it's stupid to keep buying this if you aren't going to drink it."

"Like $0.65 is really going to kill me. Besides, it warms my hands."

"So do gloves. Okay, your turn. Why'd you want to kiss me?" he asked.

I let my boots kick up clumps of snow as we walked. "It was just this idea. One second I was about to eat a face full of snow, and the next, you were catching me. And then you were right there, like inches from me with your arm still holding me. If we were in a movie, that would have been the perfect moment for a kiss."

Next to me, Adam nodded, but he was fighting another frown.

"No, come on. Nobody kissed anybody. We're just talking, sharing the random stuff that sometimes flies through our minds. That's what friends do."

Adam's frown smoothed. "Well, what if I wan—" But his words kind strangled off as his gaze drifted past me and locked. I saw the blood drain from his face, and I turned to see a pale, black-haired guy with strikingly dark eyes walking toward a navy Jeep with a coffee in one hand and keys in the other. He looked to be a few years older than us, and he went still when he saw us.

"Adam?" I asked.

He didn't respond, just started moving toward the guy, who had changed course and was heading directly toward Adam, too. I started to worry that they were going to charge each other, because neither appeared to be slowing down, but instead of colliding, they embraced, hands clapping on each other's backs like brothers.

ADAM

It should have bothered me that I was about to cry in front of the girl who had my heart, but it didn't. That had as much to do with Daniel as it did Jolene. He clapped me once more on the shoulder and then pulled back. And just as quickly as I'd been about to cry, I was laughing. It was so good to see him. It felt like going back in time, and I half expected to see Greg walk up behind him.

Daniel didn't join in my laughter, but he did smile.

"What are you doing here?" I hadn't seen my brother's best friend since Greg's funeral two years ago. My laughter faded with that realization.

"I've been gone some." Daniel had tossed his coffee into a trash can before reaching me, and he shoved both hands into his pockets, but not before I noticed that the knuckles on his right hand were split.

He and Greg had been friends for as long as I could remember, and we all knew how messed up his home life had been. He was old enough now that he must have moved out, but things were apparently still bad. Growing up, my parents had called the police more than once when Daniel had shown up hurt on our doorstep. It had never gone anywhere, because Daniel's mom refused to press charges even when it was clear that her husband was beating her, too, and Daniel cared too much about her to contradict whatever stories she invented to explain their injuries.

As he'd gotten older and bigger, Daniel's injuries had become less frequent, but I doubted his mom had fared as well. I knew that, for Daniel, his mom getting hurt was worse than getting hit himself. But she wouldn't let him help her, would even blame him for making her husband angry in the first place.

I think that was why he'd helped Greg rescue injured animals. He couldn't help his mom, but he could help them.

"How's everyone?" he asked, drawing my attention away from his hand. "Your mom?"

I'd never been jealous over the close relationship Daniel had developed with our mom. She'd taken him under her wing as much as he'd allowed and had been the only one he'd take any comfort from when things went more wrong than usual at his home. When Greg was alive, Daniel had spent more nights at our house than he had his own. Mom had been talking about turning the attic into a bedroom for him until Daniel made it clear that he couldn't leave his mom. Still, I remembered plenty of nights when I'd woken up to find the two of them talking over tea in the kitchen, and once, when he'd been much younger, he'd even let her hug him while he cried. Greg had been like a brother to him, but I almost think he loved Mom more.

"She's, um... Yeah, she's okay. We're okay."

Daniel didn't nod. He knew me well enough to know I was lying.

"How's your mom?" I didn't ask about his dad, because while I hoped he was dead, there was a new scar splitting Daniel's left eyebrow that told me all I needed to know. Daniel's hands tried to push deeper into his pockets. His silence was answer enough.

Jolene joined us then, glancing between us with a cautious smile on her face. "I'm going to go out on a limb here and guess you guys know each other?"

I had to stop myself from reaching for her hand. I felt so overwhelmed by seeing Daniel again that I needed something to ground me, and I suddenly felt nervous and proud all at once that she'd get to meet Greg's best friend. She'd never know my brother—and one of these days, I was going to tell her everything about him—but having her meet Daniel, who'd been like a brother to me, too, somehow made it feel like I was getting to share a part of Greg with her.

"Yeah, this is Daniel. He was Greg's best friend." Daniel flicked a glance at me when I said Greg's name without having to include the fact that he was my brother, and I saw him turn back to Jolene with more interest than before. "And this is my—this is Jolene."

"Hi," she said, and Daniel returned the greeting.

"I haven't seen Daniel in a while," I explained.

"I guessed that, too," Jolene said.

Right. I didn't exactly go around launching myself at strangers.

"So, are you going to college somewhere or...?"

Daniel ran a hand—not the one with the busted knuckles—through his hair. "No, I'm actually getting ready to move. My mom... She's in the hospital and, um, when she gets better I'm taking her... We're leaving. She always wanted to go somewhere warm, so we're gonna try Arizona."

I swallowed. I was more sorry than I could say that his mom was hurt. I glanced toward the hand still concealed in his pocket, and I prayed that he'd busted each one of the knuckles on his bastard of a father. Greg would have been happy, too.

"Arizona sounds good," I told him. I would have said something more if Jolene hadn't been there, but he met my gaze and nodded, understanding.

Jolene glanced between us, then made a show of shivering. "Wow, I am cold. I think I'm gonna head back to my apartment."

"I guess we have been walking for a while. We can go."

Jolene put her hand on my arm. "Stay," she said in a soft voice. "It's not like I don't know the way by myself."

Daniel ducked his head. "Actually, I have to get going. But I can give you guys a ride."

I was glad for the excuse Jolene's presence gave me not to explain about the apartment I had Daniel drive us to. He'd assume Jolene lived there and I was hanging out with her.

We climbed into Daniel's Jeep, me in the back, Jolene in the passenger seat, and I felt such an overwhelming sense of déjà vu that I couldn't breathe. How many times had I sat back here with Daniel and Greg in the front? Greg had never minded when I wanted to tag along with them. Or, I don't know, maybe sometimes he had and I couldn't remember. A lot of the time, Jeremy had been there, too, and the two of us would push at each other, fighting to lean forward between the front seats.

Jolene and Daniel were talking while I drifted back to the past, and I liked the sounds of their voices mixing together.

Greg would have liked Jolene. I knew it with such a strong bolt of conviction that my heart skipped a beat. And then it skipped another as I realized that moment was the closest they'd ever come to meeting each other.

Jolene glanced back at me, took in the moisture I could feel in my eyes, and went back to talking to Daniel. Without being obvious about it, she extended a hand between the seats and found mine.

The whole drive back to the apartment she held my hand, releasing it only when Daniel parked.

"I'll meet you inside," she told me before saying thanks and bye to Daniel.

We watched her go. Well, I watched her go. Daniel watched me.

"So that's your girl?"

"Yeah." I nodded, still staring after her. "I don't know if I'm hers, but she's definitely mine."

"I like her," he said. And I knew he was telling me Greg would have, too.

"I'm sorry about your mom." And because I couldn't help asking, I said, "He won't be able to hurt her anymore?"

Daniel's jaw locked and his injured hand tightened on the steering wheel. "No, he won't ever hurt her again."

I nodded, not caring how or why Daniel knew that. His mom would be safe, and though I'd never met her, I was glad for his sake almost more than hers. "When do you leave?"

"It depends." He swallowed. "On when she gets released and how soon she can handle the move. Few months."

"But she will—heal, I mean?"

"Yeah."

Daniel pushed the passenger seat forward for me to climb out. When my feet hit the asphalt of the parking lot, I turned back to him. "I know my mom would like to see you. I think… I think it would help her to see you."

The way Daniel lowered his gaze told me he didn't agree.

"Daniel," I said. "She knows it wasn't your fault. We all know that." When he didn't respond, I said, "I'm glad I got to see you. I've missed you."

"Yeah, me, too," Daniel said, meeting my gaze again. "It's good to see you finally growing into those ears."

I laughed, and it hurt only a little knowing that I was probably laughing with him for the last time.

"Be good to Arizona," I told him.

"Be good to your girl," he said. "And tell your mom—" He pressed his lips tight together. "Tell your mom that I'm sorry, okay? Tell her it should have been me."

Then he was gone, and I waited a long, long time before going inside.

SEVENTH WEEKEND

December 18–20

Jolene

For the first time in months I felt nervous about seeing Adam. He hadn't said much after Daniel left on our last Saturday, and on Sunday all we'd done was watch movies. I'd had to bite my tongue, literally, to make myself stay silent.

We'd texted a little over the past two weeks, but he was busy finishing a project for school that he'd been working on with Erica, but…yeah. I guessed they'd decided to finish individually.

My weeks hadn't been any more fun. Between dodging my mom and her edginess over Tom's increasingly less frequent appearances at the house, I'd been staying up late to work on the idea I'd finally gotten for the footage I'd captured of Adam and me, one that I wanted to finish while it still seemed good. I'd also been at Cherry and Gabe's filming the music video.

I'd been hoping to see Cherry and that her latest reunion with Meneik would have run its course, but no such luck. We'd said hi and everything, but otherwise she'd been out with Meneik as much as her parents allowed and on the phone with him every second they didn't.

Those whole two weeks between seeing Adam had sucked,

and because we'd talked so little, I had no idea what kind of headspace he was in. It wasn't like I could be mad at him for not opening up about his brother. I couldn't imagine what losing Greg had been like, what it still was like, but I wanted to. I wanted to know about the person he loved so much that, even years later, mentioning Greg's name or running into one of his friends physically affected Adam.

He and his brother weren't talking when they entered the empty lobby, and Jeremy's shoulders slumped as he saw me sitting on the second-floor landing.

"Give him a break, would you? He'll come find you when he wants you."

"Now," Adam said, shoving his bag at Jeremy as he took the steps—two at a time—to reach me. "Now's good."

I tried to disguise how happy that made me by shrugging at Jeremy. "Why don't you go on up? He'll come find you when he wants you." Then I caught Adam's arm and we sped not down the stairs but up. In the past, we'd encountered a few too many neighbors on lower levels, but the last flight didn't see a lot of traffic even when there wasn't a blizzard outside to detract people from the roof.

"I feel like we need to hurry," I told him.

"Hurry with what?"

"Anything. Everything." He was acting like Adam again, there and present with me instead of lost in thoughts he couldn't share. "What is the most awesome thing we could possibly do in this stairwell?"

"You're looking at me like there's an obvious answer to that question." And then he half frowned, half smiled at me. "Are we going to make out?"

It was a teasing, throwaway comment, and it made me grin even as my heart thumped. "Better." I pulled a deck of cards from my jacket pocket and dropped it on the stair between us.

He looked at the cards, then back at me. "So we're not even going to talk about my idea?"

We didn't end up talking about his idea, but we did talk about a lot of other stuff, mostly movies, because with me it's always movies.

I growled when he told me he'd never seen *The Godfather*. "We'll both be dead before I can show you all the awesome movies you haven't seen." Then I leaned against the wall and drew one knee up, my cards forgotten. "Doesn't that depress you? If we watched one movie every night for the rest of our lives, we'd never see them all before we die. And I'm not even talking about all the new movies they make every year. It drives me nuts. I'm doomed to ignorance about so much of something I love."

"Would you really want to do that?"

"Maybe I don't want to see *every* movie ever made, but even half, the good ones, would take more years than I have left."

"You're talking about a medium that's only a century old. Think about all the books you'll never read or the songs you'll never hear."

"You're not helping me," I said.

"You brought up the movie thing. I'm pointing out that there are a lot of other things you won't get to experience. No one will."

"That's my point. Doesn't it bother you?"

He shrugged. "Not really." He leaned toward me. "Look, if you only see the world as a list of things you'll never get to do, then you'll never enjoy any of the things you do get to do. You'll always be thinking of something else, wanting more, when maybe what you have, what you've seen or read or heard or whatever, is pretty great. You'll never appreciate anything." He sat back against the opposite wall. "Now *that's* depressing."

"You sounded really wise just now." I tilted my head at him. "You figure all that out on your own?"

"I had some help."

"Who?"

"My brother… Greg."

I picked up my cards again, casually shifting them in my hands so he wouldn't see how much I wanted him to keep talking.

Sometimes I could tell it surprised him when he brought up his brother. He'd go all tense afterward, like he was bracing for pain that I couldn't see, much less imagine. But it wasn't there that time.

"You could tell me about him if you felt like it. I know you loved him a lot. And don't let it go to your head when I say this, but there's no way he didn't love you."

I lowered my gaze when he stood, both because I didn't want him looking at me while I basically told him that everyone loved him, including me, and because I didn't want him to think I was trying to force him into doing something he might not ever want to do.

With my head bent, all I could see were his feet. They'd been pointing away from me when he stood, but then, then turned back.

He started talking about Greg.

ADAM

*I*hadn't meant to bring up Greg. I'd promised to tell her about him sometime, and it wasn't like he was a secret. Most of my friends had been my friends back before Greg died, so I'd never needed to try to explain how amazing he was to someone who'd never know him. It felt like an impossible task.

But seeing Daniel again had made me realize that, with Jolene, I wanted to try.

"Greg was five years older than me and three years older than Jeremy, but we were close—closer than I'll ever be with Jeremy." That was a sad thing to admit even though it was true. Having the role of oldest thrust upon my remaining brother didn't suit him. Or me. Jeremy never knew the right thing to say or when to say it. He couldn't get away with half the stuff our brother had without even trying. He wasn't Greg, and it was a toss-up on any given day which of us felt his lack more keenly.

"He died a week shy of his eighteenth birthday. My

brother was—" I broke off, because no matter what I said about Greg, it wouldn't be enough.

"What did he like to do?" Jolene asked, giving me a place to start when I couldn't find one on my own.

"Animals," I said. "He rescued animals, ones that were hurt and would have died without help, and not just the cute, cuddly kind either. He'd get Daniel and they would come home bleeding from scratches and bite marks, barely hanging on to some filthy, furry monster that was still trying to claw their faces off...and Greg would laugh." I laughed, too, at the memory, and it felt good to be able to remember something that didn't hurt. "He'd promise the little—and often not-so-little—terror that he was going to take care of them. Daniel wasn't as lighthearted as my brother, but he never complained about the injuries he got rescuing a hurt and scared animal. They were never as bad as the ones he got from his—" I closed my mouth, and Jolene pretended not to notice. She'd met Daniel, but she didn't know him. Plus, I was supposed to be telling her about Greg, not Daniel.

Mimicking Daniel's favorite pose, I shoved my hands into my pockets. "Anyway, Greg always kept his promises. He'd get the animals clean and fed, pay vet bills with money he got from hustling pool with Daniel, and he'd set up places for them in our barn that looked more comfortable than my bed. He even slept out there next to some of the more hurt and skittish ones."

Jolene's face lit up as I talked about my brother. She laughed when I told her how Greg had stolen our dad's truck once when he was fifteen because he wanted to pull a buck out of a sinkhole, only he ended up falling in himself as he tried to get a rope around its antlers.

"He had to call home for Dad to get him out. Our dad

was so mad, and Greg didn't even care how long he was grounded, because they pulled the buck out, too."

"How long *was* he grounded?" she asked.

"It was supposed to be a month, but I think my parents let him off after a week. He was hard to stay mad at." My smile slipped, but I kept talking.

Jolene watched me break apart piece by piece from the inside as I told her about the best person who'd ever lived. I heard the step squeak as she stood and moved toward me. My heart didn't race like it normally would have when she slipped her arms around my waist and rested her head against my chest; it slowed and steadied.

Later, I'd care that she saw me like that.

Later, I'd care that she was pressed that close to me.

Later.

"The last one, a wolf-bear-hybrid-looking dog that Greg dubbed Fozzie, took such a big chunk out of his leg that my parents had to take him to the ER. Nobody but my brother could have convinced them—while he was bleeding and limping across the kitchen—that Fozzie just needed a little TLC instead of a call to animal control. To this day, I don't know how he did it, but when they got home from the hospital, Mom was carrying a chew toy and Dad had a bag of dog food in his arms."

Jolene looked up at me and smiled, but her expression held a twinge of sadness.

"The compromise was that Fozzie had to be tethered to the oak tree in the yard and Greg wasn't allowed to sleep outside with him until his leg healed. Daniel said he'd stay over with the dog, but something happened with his mom and he never showed."

There was a pause before Jolene said, "I'm guessing your brother didn't sleep inside."

I shook my head and felt my chin quiver.

"Adam." Jolene's voice was soft, drawing my gaze back when I tried to look away.

"We don't know exactly what happened. Maybe Greg untied the dog, or he got loose on his own. Greg was blind to anything but the animal in front of him. He'd belly crawled across frozen ponds before, climbed trees so high that I got dizzy watching him to save them—he wouldn't have blinked at following a dog down a dark stretch of road at night."

My chest felt like it was on fire. I'd never done this, never said these words out loud before.

"The driver who hit my brother wasn't drunk. He wasn't speeding or driving recklessly. He said he narrowly missed a dark shape darting in front of his car, and Greg was about half a second behind."

Half a second between not a scratch and killed instantly.

Jolene tightened her arms around me, and I sucked in a breath, holding myself away from the comfort she was trying to give me so that I could get it all out.

"Two years later, and the pallets and empty cages are still in our barn. Everything in Greg's room is the same." My voice broke when I said, "My mom still changes his sheets once a week."

Her arms tightened further, but I kept talking, like I had this compulsion to share everything with her.

My mom wasn't in denial about Greg's death so much as she was engrained in a habit she couldn't bring herself to break. That, and she lived for those moments when she'd see his things exactly as he'd left them and the lie that he was still alive would almost fit, like an old coat. For a second or two.

Sometimes I had those moments, too. When my heart would surface and float along a memory before that suffocating, can't-breathe-can't-move-can't-anything, gaping maw drowned me all over again.

It wasn't a trade-off I sought. Dad and I were alike in that. He'd resorted to using the back stairs so that he wouldn't have to walk by Greg's room. Whenever Mom accidentally—right?—set an extra plate at the table, he'd get up and leave. All night sometimes.

Sometimes even when she set the right number of plates.

Jeremy was the only one who seemed surprised when those all-night absences stretched to two nights, then three, then... Yeah.

"It was better and worse when my dad moved out," I told her. "Better in that there was one less emotional bomb to circumvent. Worse in that, with him gone, Mom started vacuuming Greg's room twice a week."

I felt Jolene flinch.

Greg would have known what to say to Mom, how to find her smile. Jeremy simply took up Dad's practice of leaving the room whenever she did something uncomfortable, like bake Greg a birthday cake.

Or nearly drown herself after passing out in the bathtub with an empty bottle of brandy later that night.

When something wet seeped through the front of my shirt, I realized Jolene was crying silently.

"Jeremy couldn't even nut up enough to help me get her out of the tub. All he kept saying was that maybe we should call Dad. He didn't understand or wouldn't understand that Dad had moved out to get away from exactly that kind of thing. Calling wasn't going to help, but he did it anyway, and my dad moved back home. For a month.

"When he moved out the second time, Jeremy and I got packed up with the rest of his stuff. Here. Every other weekend."

Jolene

On Sunday, I chewed on my lip and watched Adam open my gift. Of course, he would be the kind of person who carefully peeled off the tape and literally unwrapped the gift instead of tearing into it.

We had decided to exchange Christmas gifts early, because we weren't going to see each other on December 25. At this rate the weekend would be over before his was half-opened.

"Adam," I said, trying not to grit my teeth as he unfolded one end of the box and then turned his attention to the other side. "It's gonna die before you get it out of the box."

Adam paused his surgical gift unwrapping and stared at me. "You better be talking about a plant."

I grinned at him, putting the gap between my front teeth on full display. He always seemed to like that. "It's not a plant, but seriously." I nodded at the gift. "Before we're dead."

Eyeing me, Adam carefully slid his thumb under a taped edge.

"Oh my gosh, just give it to me." I lunged for the gift but

all Adam had to do was raise his arms above his head and I couldn't get to it.

"Didn't anyone ever tell you patience is a virtue?" He kept leaning one way or another to avoid my leaping grabs.

"What do you—" I made another attempt and failed "—think?"

Adam took pity on me, and I didn't even mind, because he finally ripped off the rest of the wrapping paper and let it fall to the ground of the top-floor stairway. And then he was holding it. For some reason, I felt like looking away when he lifted the lid.

It wasn't a huge deal. It hadn't even cost me anything, but I was nervous and I desperately wanted him to like it.

The flash drive spilled onto his palm, and I pushed my laptop toward him.

"What is it?" he asked, but with a kind of wonder and anticipation that made me take a step back as soon as he opened the laptop.

"Just..." I nodded at the computer.

He inserted the drive, and then his eyes widened. Tugging at my braid, I watched him smile, softly at first. "Jo, did you—" He pointed at the screen but I shushed him.

"Just watch."

And he did; we both did. He watched the movie I'd made, and I watched him.

His smiles—there were a lot of those, and laughs that seemed to catch him unaware—gave me the courage to draw closer to him instead of backing away. Even the moments when his smile dimmed, his eyes never did.

I was still staring at his face several minutes later when he looked up at me.

"You made that."

"What gave it away, my name or—" I broke off when I felt his hand slide into mine, fingers threading together.

True, I'd held his hand before and leaped on his back a time or two, but those were always moments that I'd initiated and he'd just sort of…gone with.

This time it was all him. His warm skin against mine, the gentle squeeze that I somehow felt in my heart. I could swear I even felt his pulse echoing the rapid beat of my own.

"It's still a rough cut but…you like it?" I asked, in a voice that almost came out timid except I knew my body wasn't capable of being timid.

Adam's hand increased its pressure and sent tingling waves rippling through me. "It's the best thing anyone ever gave me."

I told myself that he was just being nice, kind in the way he always was without even trying, but his hand and his eyes and his voice all said it was more than that.

"This is what you've been filming, but how did you do it? I mean, with the pictures…?"

The film—and I was using the term loosely—had been a compilation of the pictures we'd taken together and all the footage I had shot of us taking the pictures. Plus, some random footage of us. I'd started with the footage and then inserted the still photos at the exact same angle—they'd been a huge pain to match. I'd layered the still images on top of each other, using some of our outtakes to blend the transitions between moving images and the final still photos, letting the background movie continue so that there was always movement.

Like us.

There wasn't a story exactly from just the photos, but I'd created one from the additional pictures and videos I'd taken that he hadn't known about. Thanks to a kindly janitor who happily opened a door for me, I'd even gotten some of the security footage from the recently installed cameras outside so I'd have footage of both of us arriving and leaving the apartment complex over and over again, showing unguarded expressions with each other and the opposite with everyone else.

It was a love story. Not romantic exactly, but the kind of love that maybe lasts beyond passion and heartache. It was a story of friendship, with all its possibilities laid out in front of it.

That was what Adam and I had.

I slid my hand free from his to eject the flash drive and close the laptop, because it felt like too much in the moment, touching him.

"I feel like my gift sucks now."

My head snapped up. "Are you kidding? It's the coolest thing I've ever owned." No joke. I glanced at the gift that had been too big to wrap. Instead, Adam had stuck a giant gold ribbon on it.

It was an old director's chair that he'd found at a yard sale and spent weeks restoring. It looked like it had come off the set of a movie from the '50s. My heart swelled at the sight of it, but looking at Adam wasn't any better.

"You're gonna use this for your film program application, right? You have to."

"I was thinking about it. It still needs work, but...you don't mind?"

"Mind?" Adam glanced at the flash drive as I handed it to him. "You're gonna make me famous."

I laughed. "Merry early Christmas, Adam."

"Merry early Christmas, Jo."

IN BETWEEN

Jolene:

Merry Christmas, ya filthy animal.

Adam:

I know that one. Home Alone, right?

Jolene:

They only run it on TV for the entire month of December. Though technically it's from the sequel.

Adam:

Merry Christmas to you, too.

Jolene:

I just ate a bag of Christmas candy corn. I'm gross.

Adam:

Oh, I finally found out about the movie critic in the building.

Jolene:

Sweet!

Adam:

He does live there but I guess he travels a lot and he's gonna be gone until February.

Jolene:

I don't have to send in the application until the end of April, so that's okay. Thanks for finding out. You asked your dad?

Adam:

I needed something to say to him.

Jolene:

Then I guess you're welcome for the topic...?

Adam:

How did it go at your dad's?

Jolene:

The whole bag of Christmas candy corn, Adam. Between my mom calling me every hour because Tom spent the day with family and my dad texting delay after delay to Shelly, it was my most magical Christmas ever.

Adam:

Jo...

Jolene:

You don't get to do that.

Adam:

Sorry. I wish I'd gotten to see you.

Jolene:

Blame our stupid parents for splitting the day the opposite ways.

Adam:

Yeah.

Jolene:

Tell me your Christmas was better.

Adam:

My mom put presents for Greg under the tree. Each year she adds to the ones that she wrapped the year before, so it's like digging through land mines.

Jolene:

Adam...

Adam:

What happened to not doing that?

Jolene:

Are you at your dad's now?

Adam:

Yeah. It was basically the same only with less crying from my dad and no attempted smile from me.

Jolene:

I'm thinking about eating another bag of Christmas candy corn in your honor.

Adam:

Don't. I hate those things.

Jolene:

Then tell me something good from today.

Adam:

Now. Talking to you.

Jolene:

Something before now.

Adam:

Jeremy sat on a Christmas ornament and broke it. Shocked us all into laughing, even our mom. I didn't think I'd get to hear that from her today. Okay, your turn.

Adam:

Are you still there?

Adam:

Hello?

Jolene:

I was thinking. Mrs. Cho made me a gingerbread house that I probably wasn't supposed to eat but did. And she gave me the Die Hard special edition box set since I told her the first one is my favorite Christmas movie.

Adam:

Die Hard is a Christmas movie?

Jolene:

Die Hard is THE Christmas movie. Why, what's your favorite?

Adam:

I don't know. Elf?

Jolene:

That might be the saddest thing you've said yet.

Adam:

It's funny.

Jolene:

It's... Okay, we're bingeing a bunch of Christmas movies on our next weekend, starting with Die Hard.

Adam:

Yippee ki-yay.

Jolene:

You are so much better than candy corn.

ONE WEEK LATER

Adam:

Jolene:

Adam:

8

Jolene:

We're already behind. 4

Adam:

3

Jolene:

2 & 1! Happy New Year!

Adam:

Happy New Year!

Jolene:

Where are you?

Adam:

At my friend Rory's house with some people.

Jolene:

Ooh, a party.

Adam:

Four guys and an Xbox, so sure. Did you make it to Venomous Squid's show?

Jolene:

Yes, and sketchy doesn't cover this place. I'm trying not to touch anything.

Adam:

Like unsafe sketchy? 'Cause Rory's parents are asleep. We could come get you.

Jolene:

It's cool. I'm right by the stage with Grady's girlfriend, Audra, and Gabe and Dexter are there if anyone bothers us. Which they haven't so far. Our underage wristbands are doing more than keeping us from drinking.

Adam:

Cherry there?

Jolene:

No. Meneik picked her up like five minutes after we got here.

Adam:

How much longer is the set?

Jolene:

An hour, I think. Then we're going to Denny's for pie. Yum.

Adam:

You having fun?

Jolene:

Sure. You?

Adam:

Not bad.

Jolene:

It's too bad you couldn't come.
Are you winning at Xbox?

Adam:

That is the exact right way to
phrase that, BTW. And yeah, still
wish we could have rung in the
New Year together.

Jolene:

And you could have met the guys!

Adam:

I was more thinking about kissing
you at midnight.

Jolene:

That's such a cliché.

Adam:

I'd call it classic.

Jolene:

I don't know. I just saw a guy
belch into his date's mouth. You'd
have had stiff competition.

Adam:

No, I don't think so.

Jolene:

Cocky much?

Adam:

Next year we're spending New
Year's together.

Jolene:

I don't know where I'll be.

Adam:

What does that mean?

Jolene:

It means I go at the behest of my parents' lawyers. I've been to two different schools since the divorce. I could be at another one next week. I could be in another apartment. Or you could.

Adam:

Your birthday is January 26.

Jolene:

So?

Adam:

Mine's February 10.

Jolene:

I know. So?

Adam:

I'm assuming your dad wouldn't be allowed to move you out of state.

Jolene:

I doubt it.

Adam:

Then in just over a month, I'll be able to drive to wherever you are. Or in a few weeks, you can drive to me.

Jolene:

Are you for real right now?

Adam:

Yes.

Jolene:

You'd really drive to me?

Adam:

Wouldn't you drive to me?

Jolene:

This is the first time I thought about it.

Adam:

It's not a trick question. If something happened and we didn't have these weekends, would you still want to see me?

Jolene:

Yes.

Adam:

Good, 'cause I'd want to see you.

Adam:

Still there?

Jolene:

I don't know what to do when you talk like that.

Adam:

Say it back.

Jolene:

I'd want to see you.

Adam:

You're getting better at this nice thing.

Jolene:

You think?

Adam:

Oh yeah.

Jolene:

G2G but have fun Xboxing.

Adam:

I'll see you tomorrow.

Jolene:

Technically you'll see me today.

Adam:

Even better. Night, Jolene.

Jolene:

Night, Adam.

EIGHTH WEEKEND

January 1–3

Jolene

When he knocked, I called for Adam to come in.

"You should check who's at the door before you invite them in. I could have been a serial killer."

"A serial killer who knocks? That's behavior we should encourage, don't you think?"

Adam joined me on my couch, and I made room for him by drawing my knees up. "I'm pretty sure being polite isn't going to offset all the stabbing. Anyway, why aren't you dressed?" He tugged the pant leg of the teal-green pj's I was still wearing.

"Because I feel lousy, and real clothes aren't as depressing as I want to communicate right now."

"Your pj's have little grinning sharks all over them."

I pulled my leg out of reach. "Irrelevant."

"This is the happiest thing you could have worn."

"Well, I don't feel good."

"You look good. What's wrong with you, and can I catch it?"

"Thanks. Cramps. And no."

Adam's gaze swept over me, assessing. "I'm guessing you don't want to go out."

"Do you want a medal for that?"

"No, but maybe don't bite my head off for making an observation. Can I ask another question?"

"Depends on how inane it is."

"I have another favor."

I groaned and flopped back against the cushion. "No pictures right now. I feel like a cat box."

"It does involve pictures, but not for another couple weeks."

"I don't have the brainpower to figure out what you want, so out with it."

Adam frowned. "I might be having second thoughts. How long will you be 'out of commission'?" He added air quotes.

I smiled without meaning to. "I'm not going to be great company today. Maybe you should come back tomorrow."

"Nah. My dad already roped Jeremy into helping him retile all the bathrooms on the first floor. And anyway, I still prefer you in a bad mood to just about anyone else."

All the blood rushed to my head and pounded behind my eyes. He said it so casually, like the nicest thing anyone had ever said to me. How could he throw away compliments like that? He wasn't even throwing it away, he was saying it without having to think about it, like it was a given.

Nobody preferred me. Ever.

I was two seconds away from crying, which was ridiculous.

"Besides, it's your fault that I'm in this position, so it's only fair that you be the one to get me out of it."

"Uh-oh," I said, the cryptic wording distracting me from my impending tears.

"You know Erica and I broke up."

"Who?"

Adam half smiled at my feigned ignorance. "What you don't know is that we broke up right before winter formal."

"Uh-oh." If I wasn't feeling so uncomfortable, I might have had some other feelings at the direction his words were heading.

"Only if you turn me down."

"Are you asking?"

"Yes."

"Ask me for real. Like in a complete sentence."

He didn't hesitate. "Jolene, will you go to winter formal with me?"

For a tiny split second, the cramping knives in my belly turned to feathers tickling up through me. "When is it? The actual date?" If it fell on a Dad weekend, I'd probably need a court order.

"January 22."

Not a Dad weekend.

"Are you going to wear a suit?"

"Yes."

"Will I get to meet your mom?"

"If she drives us."

"She thinks we're a couple though, doesn't she?"

Adam flushed red and cleared his throat. "Um, she sort of knows about the whole fake-picture thing."

"Honestly, I'm surprised you made it this long before telling her. You're kind of a mama's boy, Adam."

"It just came up. She still likes seeing the pictures of us even if we're just...whatever."

"Just whatever?" I batted my eyelashes at him. "This is officially the most romantic way a boy's ever asked me to a dance."

His flush began to recede. "I was trying to say that my mom's not going to expect me to maul you in front of her if that's what you're worried about."

"So we're clear, I'm going to pass on the mauling entirely even when she's not watching."

Adam started to smile. "That sounds like a yes…"

"Because it is."

"Yeah?"

"Yeah, I'll go with you."

Adam grinned full out, sending warmth humming through me.

"You look surprised."

"I figured you'd say no."

"Adam, how many times do I have to tell you, I'm only a *little* embarrassed to be seen in public with you. Plus the dance is going to be at night, so…"

"Be sure to say stuff like that to my mom. She'll think you're more of an angel than she already does."

"That's a new one for me."

"To be clear, *angel* is the word she uses because she hasn't met you."

"And what word would you use?"

"Jolene."

"Hmm." The way he said my name, all slow and confident, made me shiver in such a delicious way.

"So back to the dance. Maybe a little mauling?"

"That's a firm no."

"Wait till you see my suit," he said, stretching and folding his arms behind his head. "We'll see who wants a little mauling then."

"Wait till you see my dress," I said. "They put sharks on anything these days."

ADAM

*T*he suit I owned was too small, like the-pants-were-halfway-up-my-calves too small.

I slid into the hallway to show Mom on Sunday night. "That's not gonna work," she said. "You'll freeze to death."

I extended my arms stiffly at my sides. The fabric was so tight that when I tried to bend my elbow, the seams started to pop. "Yeah, *that's* the problem with this suit. It's not warm enough."

"I didn't think you'd grown this much. Jeremy can still wear his suit from your cousin Becky's wedding."

"Jeremy could still wear his footed pajamas if he didn't care about zipping them up."

Mom looked up at me from where she'd been checking the hem of my pants. "I wish you wouldn't say things like that about your brother. He's sensitive about his height. Please try."

Mom had this way of making me feel like I'd just gotten caught burning our photo albums or something when she used that tone. It was so laden with hurt and disappointment that I probably would have hugged Jeremy in front of her if he'd been around instead of at a last-minute play rehearsal at somebody's house. I was supposed to be making her feel better, not worse. I mumbled an apology and a request to go remove the ridiculously ill-fitting suit.

"Wait. Wait." Mom popped into my room and came back carrying my phone. "Tell me how to take a photo so we can send it to Jolene."

I looked down at myself. I'd somehow gotten the pants up, but the jacket wouldn't close and the overall impression was that of the Hulk mid-transformation. "Ah, no?" I said. "I will not be doing that. That's a horrible idea."

"She'll love it."

She would, just not in the way I wanted. "You only know Jolene from cute pictures. Real-life Jolene would never stop laughing if she saw this."

"Whoops!" Mom said as my phone made the sound that indicated a photo had been taken.

She let me take the phone from her and I quickly deleted the photo, noticing as I did that Mom's smile dimmed.

"If your dad had sent me a picture like this when we were young, I would have thought it was adorable."

I stopped trying to tug the constricting jacket off my shoulders with the limited range of motion it allowed. Every time she brought up Dad like nothing had changed, it was like a mosquito buzzing around my ear. Normally, I mentally swatted it away as an easily ignored annoyance, but I couldn't dismiss the somewhat dreamy look that slipped onto her face at the mention of Dad.

We were standing in the upstairs hallway, the doors to all the bedrooms surrounding us—mine, Jeremy's, hers and Dad's. Greg's. Our family used to sleep on the same floor, in the same house. Now we didn't eat in the same city, much less at the same table. I was the one who didn't get why, and I got it even less when she mentioned Dad with such easy longing. Dad did it sometimes, too—more than someone who had amicably split from his wife should. If they couldn't stand each other or fought or were even indifferent, I'd understand. I wouldn't agree or accept it, but I'd understand why they were living apart.

What they were doing didn't make sense.

"I don't get how you can talk about Dad like that, miss him, but still want him gone." I didn't talk to her the way I would have Dad. I wasn't struggling not to yell or lose my temper. I could never talk to her that way.

"Oh, Adam."

"No. Mom. I'm trying to understand. Jolene… Her parents are going to throw parties when the other dies. She never has to wonder why they aren't still married—she wonders how they ever got together in the first place. I know why you and Dad got married. I've known it every day of my life. What I don't know is how you can want to be apart when you still love him…when he still loves you…?"

"This is hard for me."

I almost asked her if she thought she was the only one it was hard for. "Then why are you doing this?"

She wouldn't look at me. "Because we make each other sad." She swallowed. "After Greg… It nearly destroyed us, I know you know that." She stood and took my hand in both of hers. "We made it day by day, hour by hour. Sometimes minute by minute. It was all we could do."

I did remember. Waking up at night to the sounds of Mom crying and, worse, Dad crying with her. Holidays where one or both of them would leave the room and not come back for hours sometimes. The way she was squeezing my hand as she spoke.

"We decided that maybe we would be less sad apart. I love him too much to make him hurt if he doesn't have to. He loves me the same."

"And is it working? Are you less sad now, or are you just sad and alone?"

Neither of us had expected me to say that. It wasn't cruel and hadn't been spoken harshly, but my own sadness had bled through, and I could tell that she felt it.

"I don't know. Sometimes both."

NINTH WEEKEND

January 15–17

Jolene

"You should have sent the picture! Did you really delete it?"

"Hell yes, I deleted it. I don't need you mocking me until the end of time."

"Adam, that's sweet that you think we'll be friends that long."

"You don't?"

The Saturday matinee crowd at AMC was growing increasingly intolerant of our talking over the previews. A couple a few rows ahead hissed for us to lower our voices. "Well, how do you figure?" I whispered. "Are we both going to go to the same college? Live in the same state? No. You'll go to an Ivy League school, marry Erica 2.0, and live in Virginia, coach your son's hockey team and jog along the Potomac River with your golden retriever on the weekends. Whereas I am going to go to UCLA to pursue film studies, become the next Sofia Coppola, and then die tragically in my apartment alone before the age of fifty." I gathered a fistful of popcorn from the bag Adam held and started munching. "See? Radically different life trajectories." I went for another handful, but Adam pulled the bag away.

"First of all, I'm a cat guy, so no golden retriever for me. And second, if you become a famous director, I'm coming to every one of your premieres. Third, you're not going to die tragically young or alone, even if that means I have to travel the world to find a doctor who'll keep you alive long past what ethical medicine deems morally acceptable."

I threw popcorn at him. "Okay, I changed my mind. Now *you* stay single forever, and I occasionally get you pity casting auditions, which you ruin by showing up drunk and without pants."

Adam's laughter drew more glares from the couple in front of us. "So no middle road? I can't end up divorced with a dead-end job that keeps me in pants if nothing else?"

"No," I said. "You'd never get divorced. And I can't imagine any Erica leaving you." That was a big statement for me to make—big and true. No one would willingly let go of Adam unless they thought he'd already let go of them. It was more than a little scary to realize I was including myself in that category.

The film's opening credits started playing.

"You want to know how I see our future?"

I nodded.

"Okay. Watch the movie and I'll tell you when it's over."

I almost called him on his cop-out. I hadn't gotten two hours to come up with a future, but I let it go because the movie was finally starting. It turned out to be a mediocre sci-fi flick that didn't keep my attention from wandering back to Adam every few minutes, wondering what he was thinking up for us and if it was half as bleak as the scarred landscape on screen.

When the movie ended and we trailed out, Adam requested an Uber for us and then he started telling our story.

"I end up at Brown and you go to UCLA. You cry at the

airport when I drop you off. After you get your hysterics under control, I chuck you under the chin and send you away. We video chat every weekend for the next four years. I fly to you for spring break, and you come to me for Thanksgiving. During the first summer, we backpack across Europe, and we get jobs with a traveling circus the next. Our third summer we spend apart, because you get an internship working with J. J. Abrams."

I couldn't help but interject with a cough and the name "Suzanne Silver," followed by another cough.

Adam smiled. "Fine, you get an internship with Suzanne Silver. Better?"

"No offense to J. J. Abrams, but yes."

Adam shook his head and kept going. "After graduation, I drive across the country for the premiere of your first movie, and I get there in time to catch the leading man kissing you."

"Plot twist!"

"My life feels meaningless for a while, and I bounce between jobs because, as it turns out, majoring in philosophy was as big of a waste as my dad warned. I'm complaining about this to you one night via video chat, because you're on location shooting your first big studio film."

"Okay, can I just say that your future for me rocks?"

"You can. I'm complaining, and you end up telling me that I'm miserable enough to write a book. And the idea sticks. I write it, it connects with the world, and suddenly movie people are knocking at my door, begging and pleading for the film rights. I refuse, because, by then, I'm too pretentious to consider selling my art. We still talk, but we're both busy—you're too busy, in fact, to read my book."

"Future me is starting to suck."

"You eventually read it after the financing on your latest movie falls through. You recognize its unmatched brilliance and want to make the film. I've never been able to say no to you, so I agree. Three years later, we stand onstage together with matching Oscars, you for directing and me for adapted screenplay. It's a great night with many more great nights after it."

"Wow," I said, my voice thick and a tremble starts to work its way up my body Not because of the professional success he saw in our future, but because he saw us together. Not just for a year or throughout college, but always.

Adam shrugs. "I guess both futures are possible, but I like mine better."

"What about Erica 2.0?"

"Who needs an Erica when I've got you?"

The tremble shook my hands until I clasped them tight to hide it. Inside, I couldn't stop the way my heart forgot how to beat or my lungs how to hold air. I forgot everything but the simple, unconscious honesty in Adam's face. My version of the future seemed much more plausible, but I decided to pretend, at least for a little while, that his could be true. That we stayed in each other's lives forever. "You could be a storyteller," I told him softly. "You came up with all that in two hours?"

"Maybe I've been thinking about it—the college stuff anyway."

I didn't respond. Knowing he thought about things like that, that he made plans that included me...that he could pluck people out of their lives and graft them into his and make them better, stronger... Sometimes I couldn't believe people like Adam existed. Other times, I thought it was unfair that he could be like that when I couldn't.

ADAM

Jolene was quiet on the way back to the apartment. Not angry quiet or even sad quiet, just…quiet.

"We've seen worse movies," I told her after a particularly long stretch of silence.

"What?" she said, not glancing up. My fingers itched to reach out to her, glide along her hand. I'd gone too far with our futures, planning out our entire lives. I knew that was a stupid thing to do when we weren't even sixteen, but Jolene made me want to try for stupid, probably impossible things. She made my heart sink just from knowing hers was heavy.

"That thing we just spent two hours watching. Don't you want to pick it apart?"

She shrugged.

I slowed my steps as we reached the entrance to the apartment. "Is this about what I said? Our future? 'Cause I was just talking, you know."

"I know. It was just…" She chewed on the inside of one cheek. "Do you really think we'll have any of that?"

My response was automatic. "I think we can have as much as we want."

Her features went a little slack as she looked at me. I could almost swear she was going to cry, and my heart twisted, but then she looked away and muttered something about needing to go lie down because she had a headache.

"In your apartment?" Incredulity colored my voice. Jolene never voluntarily sought out her apartment. Her head would have to be literally splitting in two before I'd expect her to choose to go there. "We could go sit down somewhere, or—"

"I'll find you later if it goes away, okay?" She didn't look back as she started up the stairs.

I didn't have the same dread for my apartment that Jolene usually had for hers. We'd been doing this every-other-weekend thing for nearly half a year now. Dad didn't hassle me too much about being with Jolene most of the time and behind my closed bedroom door the rest. Having to be here at all was far from ideal, but I'd figured out a way to interact with him as little as possible.

It was working.

And usually Dad was, too.

When I closed the apartment door behind me, Dad and Jeremy looked up from the mountain of old metal light switch covers they were stripping on the coffee table. Frowning more over Jolene's hasty departure than anything else, I gave Dad a one-word greeting and tried to slip off to my room.

"Adam, hold up," Dad said. "Why don't you lend us a hand today?"

Even though the question was rhetorical, I answered like it wasn't. "What, like you want a list?"

Jeremy's eyebrows lifted. The disrespectful tone of my voice coupled with my insult-laden words was asking for trouble.

I got to see Jolene so infrequently as it was. If I got myself grounded, the level of suckage would be unprecedented.

But the volatile, hotheaded part of me had been spoiling for this fight since the conversation with Mom and her faulty explanation for why they lived apart. That and my frustration over Jolene's cryptic behavior told my brain to shove it.

So instead of lowering my head and mumbling an apology, I stared my father down. "We shouldn't be here—*you* shouldn't be here. And if Greg were here, he'd have said it to your face the second you started packing your bags." I heard Jeremy's intake of breath. "I'm just so sick of this." I shook my head, my sudden burst of anger fizzling out as I listened to my own words. "How can you expect me to just sit on the couch and pretend that Mom isn't at home getting ready to go visit Greg?" She went every Saturday at sunset without fail. "And you…" I slid my gaze to Jeremy. "Is this where you want to be right now? Do you even think about what it's like for her at the cemetery without us, huh?"

For once Jeremy lowered his head rather than shout back at me. Mom going to Greg's grave alone was something that even he could agree was wrong. We used to visit Greg together as a family, but it had just been the three of us since Dad moved out. I know Dad went on his own, because we always found the sunflowers he left when Mom and Jeremy and I went, but thinking of her going to his grave by herself the way she'd been for months… I lost the strength to stand and sank into the nearest chair, my gaze unfocused on the floor. I didn't have enough goodwill left with Dad after the way I'd just spoken to him to ask if he'd let me go with Mom for a few hours, but maybe Jeremy did. I'd swallow any amount of pride I had to make that happen. It wouldn't be nearly enough, but it was something. I dragged in a breath.

"Dad, would you—"

"Sarah," Dad said and my gaze shot to him to see the

phone to his ear. "No, we're fine. We just thought—*I* thought we'd visit Greg with you this afternoon. Would that be all right? You're sure? Okay, we'll leave right now. Should take us about forty-five minutes. Thanks, Sarah." He stood up and, without looking at Jeremy or me, said, "Get your coats."

Dad tried to start a few conversations while we drove, but I didn't give him a lot to work with. And for once it wasn't because I was trying to make a point. Jeremy at least recognized that, so after the first time he caught my eye in the rearview mirror, he didn't give me crap about it.

Greg had always been the family mediator. He could still do it without even having to be in the car.

This was the first time that we were going to visit Greg via separate vehicles, as separate families. I wondered if anyone else felt as ashamed by that fact as I did, like we were letting him down. Not that it mattered or that Greg would even know, but I almost suggested we pick up Mom so that we could at least arrive together.

Thoughts of my older brother swirled in my head like the snow parting around the car. I looked at each with the same sense of wonder. I hadn't always been able to do that, think about Greg and not hurt down to the marrow of my bones. Talking about him with Jolene had helped, but I still felt the twinge of pain when a memory caught me unaware, like getting the air knocked out of me. I liked to keep those memories near me now that I'd discovered I could.

On the days that we visited, it was harder to hold on to the happy memories. Not because of Greg himself, but because my family pooled our collective sorrow, and it overwhelmed us as we sank under not just our own sadness but each other's, too.

I noticed Dad's shoulders tense before I saw the sign or felt the car turn into the parking lot. We kept silent as we piled

out and hunkered deeper into our coats. Mom was already
there. She withdrew a gloved hand from her pocket and held
it up in greeting. We were too far away for me to see whose
face she was staring at, but Dad's gaze was locked on her.

She kissed both Jeremy and me on our cheeks with lips
cold enough to make me jump, then she took the hand Dad
offered her, and we walked through the arched wrought iron
gate of Montgomery Cemetery.

Greg's headstone was indistinguishable from those around
it, but all of us picked out the well-worn path to it without
hesitation. Mom was first to approach and bend down to remove twigs and leaves that stabbed through the freshly fallen
snow. The bouquet of flowers resting against the headstone
was barely withered, but Mom knelt and replaced them with
the fresh ones she'd brought. After she removed one glove,
her fingers drifted over the engraved letters.

Dad moved to kneel next to her, and she leaned into him.
As they spoke to Greg, murmurs reached Jeremy and me,
but not the words themselves.

Long minutes passed. Mom cried. At one point Dad took
her hand in his and said something to her. She shook her
head and tried to pull her hand away while Dad spoke again.
I could tell he was asking her something, pleading with her
by the look on his face, but she went still until he released
her hand. When she finally turned back to Dad, she cupped
his face with her hand but said nothing.

Eventually, she looked over her shoulder to beckon Jeremy and me to join them.

Dad and I walked ahead as we left the cemetery, Mom,
with her arm around Jeremy, following several paces behind.
I kept casting looks back at them until Dad stopped me with
a hand on my shoulder.

"She's fine. Jeremy's with her."

I wasn't going to say anything. I'd determined not to for Greg's sake, but the words came out before I could stop them. "What did you say to her?" Somehow I knew he hadn't been asking to come back home.

Dad didn't answer me for several steps. "I love her" was what he finally said. "Despite what you think, I want our family to be together again, but it can't be like it was before. We have to let go, and your mom isn't ready to do that yet."

No, she wasn't. She clung to Greg more tightly every day.

Letting go didn't mean forgetting. Angry as I was at Dad, I couldn't pretend he was saying that. He meant the rest. She had to stop living as though Greg would come home again at any moment. She spoke about him like he was gone, but that wasn't how she lived, and because of that, none of us had been able to fully let go either.

That didn't mean I agreed with Dad moving out. If anything, I thought that had made her cling even tighter than before. It certainly hadn't helped her let go.

We needed to be together to do that.

"We should all be with her tonight," I said. "All of us."

Instead of tightening his jaw or increasing his pace like I expected, he said, "I know."

Those words revealed more about his leaving than anything he'd said since the night Mom had helped him pack.

A biting wind stole the breath I needed to respond, and I'd slowed enough by then that Mom and Jeremy were walking abreast with us. None of it made sense to me. Not the way Mom took Dad's hand again, or the way he tilted his head to rest on hers when more tears spilled onto her cheeks. How could he not see that she needed him so that they could let go together?

When we reached Mom's car, Dad confounded me yet again when he opened the back door and told Jeremy and me to go home with her, even though it was his weekend.

Jolene

Stupid Adam.

He texted last night to explain that he wasn't coming back to the apartment that weekend. He felt bad about ditching me, which was sweet and I got why he did it, but Sunday still sucked for me. Instead of hanging out with him and forgetting that anything else existed, I sat in my room hiding from Shelly and stewed about winter formal.

I'd agreed to go but I couldn't just be excited about seeing Adam in a suit or what it would feel like to have his arms wrapped around me—my toes curled a little as I imagined resting my cheek against his chest and hearing his too-fast heartbeat—no, I had to deal with the problems first.

Of course it wasn't as easy as the dance not falling on a Dad weekend. For one, I needed a dress. I'd never really gone for pretty around Adam, but I could do it in theory. I had all the parts, and my hair would compensate for the less impressive ones. I'd wear it down. He'd like that. *I'd* like that he'd like that.

But I'd need help with the logistics, and that meant a dress.

Cherry was out of the question. I'd kept my word and covered for her with her parents so that she could go out with Meneik, but she'd gotten caught trying to sneak back into her house at 3:00 a.m. Then she got caught the next night trying to sneak Meneik into her bedroom. She was massively grounded. Her parents took her phone and wouldn't even let her hang out in the basement when I was working with Gabe and the band on the music video.

I probably could have asked one of the other girls from the soccer team, but I'd never been awesome at making friends and I wasn't super close with anyone besides Cherry.

So that meant Mom. When Shelly dropped me off that evening after a blissfully silent car ride and I found Mom getting ready to go out with Tom, I knew I wasn't going to get a better chance.

She was dragging a black pencil along the inside of her upper eyelid when I stepped into her bathroom. One finger lifting up her eyelid made her eyeball look like it could pop out of the socket at any moment. She glanced at me in the mirror and kept lining.

"I didn't hear you get home."

"I was quiet." I stared, hypnotized and slightly grossed out by her eyeball.

Mom straightened. "Come here."

I didn't want to, but I pried my hands free from the doorframe and moved to the place she gestured in front of her.

"Tilt your head and don't blink."

"I don't really—" But she was already lifting my eyelid and bringing the pencil to my exposed eyeball. It tickled more than anything when she ran the pencil back and forth. I blinked furiously as she turned me by the shoulders to face the mirror.

"See how much thicker your eyelashes look?"

I looked but I didn't really see a difference and my eye still felt ticklish. "Wow." I tried to move away, but her hands tightened on my shoulders.

"I could teach you. Maybe for special occasions." She brushed the side of one finger down my check. "You wouldn't need much."

My gaze shifted from my reflection to hers. "Like a school dance?"

Still stroking my cheek, she said, "I was thinking dinner tonight. I could do your hair and you could smile and tell Tom that you're going to help me, that you want me to be happy, hmm? Doesn't that sound nice?"

I lifted my hand to move hers slowly away from my face, but she only lowered it to rest on my shoulder along with the other. "Mom. Tom isn't—he's not—" But then I stopped. Because it didn't matter. I'd told Tom that there was no money coming Mom's way, and he'd been pulling away ever since. I saw it; Mom saw it. The truth was, I couldn't help even if I thought more money would make her happy. Dad wasn't stupid enough to leave anything around the apartment that could be used against him. I'd told her that so many times, and she never heard me. She never heard anything. And soon, Tom would be gone for good and all her playacting with me would be over.

So I sucked in a deep breath and took my shot. "I want to go to a dance. With a boy. And I need a dress."

As soon as I'd spoken, the dark side flooded thick into the bathroom. I wouldn't have been the least surprised to hear Darth Vader's voice come out of Mom. Her hands dropped from my shoulders.

Shelly was painting her toenails when the Uber dropped me off at Dad's apartment thirty minutes later. She looked up with surprise when I let myself in. "Jolene. Hi. Did you forget something?"

"Is my dad coming here tonight?"

"Oh, um." Shelly started fiddling with the cap of her nail polish. "He has this—"

"He does it to you, too? Whatever, I don't care." I smoothed my face. "I need to ask him something."

A wrinkle appeared between her perfectly groomed brows. "Okayyy."

I gritted my teeth. She was gonna make me say it. "Can you give him a message? He doesn't take my calls anymore."

I had to think about Adam and his flushing cheeks and the chance to see him in a suit, and not the perfect O Shelly's mouth made when I admitted that my own father wouldn't answer my calls. Not that I called him anymore.

"That can't be right. I'm sure he would if he knew you—"

"Can you not be the complete cliché right now? Come on, Shelly. You went to college. I know you had a job before my dad whisked you away to this paradise. *He knows.* Now, will you give him a message or not?"

Shelly twisted her nail polish bottle shut. The wrinkle didn't disappear from her forehead. "What's the message?"

"There's a school dance that I want to go to. With Adam from next door. It's not one of Dad's weekends—I know how much he treasures those—but I need a dress. My mom—" I tried really hard to block out my memory of the way she'd screamed at me, the accusations she'd made and finally the way she'd shoved me out of the house with hissed orders to ask Dad for the money I wanted. "She made it clear that I need to ask my dad cover it." My face was burning. I would have rather licked the scuzzy carpet in the hallway than ask Shelly for help, but at least it was done. I hadn't looked away the entire time, though she had.

"I'll call him right now." And before I could stop her, she was dialing. Right in front of me.

I backed up a few steps until I couldn't hear the ringback through her phone. Until I was sure I wouldn't be able to hear him either.

"It'll be real quick," she said after he presumably answered. "It's about Jolene."

My mind was an evil thing, and it all too easily invented responses for Dad.

You deal with her. That's why you're there.

"There's no problem. It's good actually."

What is it?

Shelly glanced at me. "She needs a dress for a school dance."

Her mother can take care of that.

"Apparently she can't."

There was a rather extended pause and I imagined several unflattering but not untrue things were said about my mother. Possibly a few that weren't true, too.

"Well, with the dress and shoes and everything…" Shelly rattled off an amount that sounded extreme until she added in a low voice, "That's less than half what we spent on dinner the other night. I know you bought her a laptop for Christmas, but…"

I stopped listening when Shelly started arguing with him, because even my brain decided it wasn't a good thing to imagine Dad's objections. And that was what they were.

I left the apartment without a word. If I'd been smarter, I would have told both my parents that the other wanted to buy me a dress. Then I could have just sat back while one threw money at me to spite the other. But I wasn't smart. I was something else, and I didn't care to spend another second thinking about what that was.

★ ★ ★

I took another Uber to the movie theater and watched something I'd already seen until it was late enough that I thought Mom would be asleep or passed out, assuming her date with Tom had ended as early as all the others lately.

Someone leaped out at me as I walked up my driveway. I realized it was Shelly within half a second, but that was enough time for all my internal organs to try to evacuate my body. "You're just determined to star in all the scariest moments of my life, aren't you?"

"I was five minutes from calling the police, Jolene. Five minutes." Shelly held up her open hand, then crossed her arms. "I didn't know where you went or if something had happened to you. I couldn't call your mom. What was I supposed to do?"

"How about not hide out in the bushes like a complete psycho? Why are you here? I mean, how else will you two lovebirds keep the spark alive if you're not in the apartment during the five minutes a week my dad's there?"

Shelly's face went expressionless. "You really are a self-righteous little bitch, you know that?" She let out an audible exhalation and made like her knees were giving out on her. "You have no idea how good it feels to say that. I don't even feel bad. I used to, but that was before I got to see what a conniving and entitled—" Her lips pursed. "No. Forget it. I'm done trying to cater to your emotions. Did you get a bum deal? Yeah, you did. Are you the only person on the planet whose life didn't turn out the way you wanted? No. So it's time for you to suck it up. This is not the fairy tale I dreamed of either."

I was almost impressed that Shelly was calling me out. Not that she wasn't a total hypocrite, but that was easy enough to point out. "And yet you did all the right things. You found a guy twice your age, had an affair, broke up a marriage. I mean life is *super* unfair sometimes, huh?"

"There." Shelly pointed a shaking finger at me. "This is why I want to slap your smug face every second of every day."

"But then you risk giving up precious moments like this." My voice had risen slightly, but I dropped it back down. However unpleasant this conversation was, adding Mom into the mix meant risking more than just Shelly's life.

Which she knew. Mom had legitimately tried to electrocute her using a stun gun and a well-timed sprinkler once. It made no sense that Shelly was there, ostensibly waiting for me.

"You could have just called me, you know. I'd have told you I was exactly where I wanted to be." Alone in a movie theater.

"Except I can't. Because you blocked my number. So I had to come here and skulk around your house trying to find out if you were inside, and then when you didn't respond to the rocks I threw at your window, I had to wait out here for you while I froze my tits off because I couldn't risk the queen b—your *mom* seeing my car." And then Shelly burst into tears. It was horrifying. I took a step back and watched her convulse and leak all over the place.

I hated crying. I'd have rather she vomited on me than break down like this. With Mom, crying was a regular occurrence, one I knew I could wait out if I stayed completely still and silent. But Shelly didn't look like she was going to stop on her own.

"I just hate you so much sometimes."

"Okay," I said, glad that she was controlling herself enough to speak. "I'm fine with that, just stop crying." I grabbed her a tissue from my bag. "You look gross."

Shelly half laughed, then scowled at me. "You're just awful all the time, aren't you?"

"You've seen my gene pool. What'd you expect?"

That comment sobered her up. "I'm not waiting up for you again. Stay out all night for all I care."

"I don't remember asking you to, and we both know my dad didn't." Heat suffused my face at the mention of my father. Wow, did it gall that she knew exactly how low I ranked in his estimation.

I stared at her.

She stared at me. "Here." She twisted her purse in front of her and dug around inside before pulling out several folded bills and slapping them into my hand. "This is to buy your dress."

IN BETWEEN

Adam:

Bad news.

Jolene:

The other girl you asked to the dance said yes, too, and now you're in a sitcom situation trying to figure out how to juggle two dates?

Adam:

Jeremy is driving us to the dance tonight.

Jolene:

So the other girl said no?

Adam:

Funny. Jeremy got a date to the dance and it didn't make sense to take two cars.

Jolene:

I'm sorry I won't get to meet your mom.

Adam:

Me, too. Her, too.

Jolene:

I'm also morbidly curious about the girl who agreed to go out with Jeremy.

Adam:

I think she's someone he met working on the play. He's got the tiniest part ever but he never misses a rehearsal.

Jolene:

That'd be sweet if I hadn't witnessed his turd act firsthand. Though I'm guessing he's sweeter with her than he is with me.

Adam:

Whoever she is, we're sharing a car with her tonight. You can go, right? We don't have to sneak you out of your bedroom window or anything?

Jolene:

Sneak me out of my third-story window?

Adam:

I'd catch you Princess Bride–style.

Jolene:

!!!!

Adam:

Is that a yes?

Jolene:

That's a yes but I kind of want to do the window thing now anyway.

Adam:

I vote for the front door.

Jolene:

I'd probably ruin my new dress going out the window.

Adam:

You got a new dress for me?

Jolene:
I got a new dress for me.

Adam:
I got a new suit for you.

Jolene:
What time are you picking me up?

Adam:
6

Jolene:
I need to prepare you for my mom.

Adam:
She's letting you go. How bad can it be?

Jolene:
You sweet, naive boy.

Adam:
So prepare me.

Jolene:
She hasn't spoken to me in four days. That's a new record.

Adam:
Why the silent treatment?

Jolene:
Because I called her bluff.

Adam:
?

Jolene:
She told me to ask my dad for money for a dress and I did.

Adam:

You didn't need a new dress.

Jolene:

You sweet, naive boy.

Adam:

I don't care what you wear as long as you come. Return the dress. And stop calling me naive.

Jolene:

I had to take money from Shelly for that dress. I can't go back from that.

Adam:

I'm serious. Return it.

Jolene:

I look really good in the dress.

Adam:

You look good in anything. Think your mom will stay silent through me picking you up?

Jolene:

Here's hoping. So tonight we'll be an awesome teen dance movie, right?

Adam:

Tonight we'll be us, so the awesome is a given.

Jolene:

How do you always say the right thing?

Adam:

I'm learning.

Jolene:

Oh, I'll get to meet the famous Erica!

Adam:

We'll probably want to give her some space, but she'll be there. This guy John pulled off an elaborate ask involving the entire marching band.

Jolene:

Wow, seriously?

Adam:

Yeah. Wait, should I have done something like that?

Jolene:

What could possibly have been better than asking me while I lay on the couch with a heating pad on my stomach so I wouldn't die from cramps?

Adam:

I suck.

Jolene:

I'm messing with you. Besides we don't go to the same school.

Adam:

I could have done something.

Jolene:

The point of the big ask is to get a yes. You got that just from saying the words. No pomp and circumstance needed.

Adam:

And you say I'm the one who always says the right thing.

Jolene:

G2G. It takes a zillion hours to do my hair.

Adam:

Is it weird that I've been dreaming about seeing you with your hair down?

Jolene:

Totally. See you at 6. Don't be late!

Adam:

For you? Never.

Jolene

"**W**ould you believe they were all out of shark dresses?"
Adam acted like he hadn't heard me. The second I'd
opened my front door, his face had gone blank and I couldn't
tell if he was struck dumb by my overwhelming hotness or
didn't recognize me. "Well, *you* look nice." I stepped forward
to straighten his tie, but Adam caught my hands.

"You're so beautiful."

I stilled at the reverence in his voice and it was like the
sun was rising inside me, all bright and warm.

Okay. That felt good. I'd wanted a sort of *La La Land*
thing, specifically the blue cocktail dress Emma Stone wore.
My dress was full-length instead of knee-length, but the royal
color was spot-on. I was going to freeze to death for sure,
but Adam's rather awestruck expression made it worth it.

I twirled, because it is impossible not to when wearing
a flowy skirt. My hair—which had taken two full hours to
dry and curl and make look shiny and soft—swished around
me like a chocolate cape. Adam swallowed.

Worth it.

Just then a prolonged horn blared from the driveway.

Adam's mouth thinned. "I need to talk to you about my brother and his date."

I waved him off. "We need to get a quick pic for your mom." I sized up his jacket and then grinned when I correctly guessed which pocket held his phone. I squeezed against his side and he smiled without any prompting from me as I took the photo. "Tell her we'll keep sending them until we get too drunk to work the phone."

"Jolene says hi," Adam intoned as he typed out a quick message and sent the photo.

I laughed. "Already editing me? Aren't you worried I'll do irrevocable damage to your reputation by the end of the night?"

"You're definitely going to do something to my reputation."

The sun inside me went supernova. I almost glanced down at my skin to make sure it wasn't glowing. I grabbed my coat. "Adam, are you trying to say you like my dress?"

"I'm actually afraid to touch you right now."

"Okay, now I am the one blushing." I could feel my face heating and it was nothing compared to what I felt inside. He was way too smooth with the compliments, and he wasn't even trying to be smooth.

"But seriously, about Jer—"

"Jolene! I found them!" Mom came running down the stairs, breathless but triumphant, with her fist held in the air. She brushed past Adam and, taking me by the shoulders, spun me to face the hall mirror. A second later she draped a delicate string of pearls across my collarbone and fastened the necklace. "There. You're perfect."

My fingers rose to caress the pearls. They were lovely and made me look too sweet, but I said thank you because she was smiling, something she hadn't done since I'd mentioned Adam and the winter formal.

She'd kept up the silent treatment until about an hour earlier when Tom had shown up, and then she'd thrown herself into the role of fretful mother sending her daughter off to her first dance.

I had to keep reminding myself that it wasn't real, because it felt nice to have her fussing over my hair, invisible wrinkles in my dress, and her last-minute quest to find the necklace she'd worn to her prom.

She'd gone into a panic over locating it for me, like it was some symbol of mother-daughter bonding for us both to wear the necklace. Or that was what I'd thought until I realized it was Tom's reaction she was looking for instead of mine. It was the first time that he'd been by in a week, and she wasn't going to waste it.

She'd angled her body as she stood behind me so that he could see her face as she lifted it to catch the light. It was all so *Stepford Wives*, and not the original one either, the crummy remake that Nicole Kidman was wasted in. If I'd had more time, I'd have looked for a control panel to switch her off.

"Lovely," Tom said, joining us in the foyer and sliding an arm around Mom's waist. "I can't decide who's prettier."

"Jolene," Mom-bot said, her computer programing releasing enough fluid to add an alluring shine to her eyes when she looked at me. "She's a vision." She kissed both my cheeks, leaving lipsticks smears that I'd have to rub off, before turning to Adam. "Jolene, aren't you going to introduce us?"

"Mom, this is Adam Moynihan. Adam, this is my mom and her boyfriend, Tom."

I couldn't tell what Adam was making of my mother. She was on her best behavior. It was a show she was putting on for Tom, but I didn't care about her motive so long as she stayed that way until we left.

Adam nodded to Tom before extending his hand to my mom. "It's nice to meet you, Mrs. Timber. Your home is lovely."

"It's wonderful to meet you, as well. Jolene has told me so much about you. Please call me Helen."

I hadn't told her squat about Adam, but I was too grateful for this moment of normalcy, however artificial, to contradict her. And really, what would be the point?

They schmoozed for approximately thirty seconds before Jeremy laid on the horn again, this time without any indication that he planned to stop.

Mom-bot surprised me again by responding with laughter when Adam apologized for his brother. "Must be eager to start dancing with his own date. I won't keep you, but I do want one quick photo." She held up a finger and dashed into the other room for her phone.

Our smiles were strained because Jeremy honked the entire time, but he did give us the excuse to leave the second the photo was taken. Mom-bot's parting words that Adam take care of her baby followed us out.

The horn didn't stop until Adam was opening the back door of the car, by which time he was redder than I'd ever seen him, not from embarrassment either. He didn't say anything as he closed my door, then walked around to the driver's side and opened Jeremy's.

"If her mom wasn't watching us right now, I'd knock your teeth out." Then he slammed the door and slid in next to me. "I'm sorry," he said.

"Got us out of the house quicker."

"You," Jeremy said, turning around to face me, "are welcome."

"And you," I replied, "are a tool." Then I noticed his date in the front seat and apologized.

"It's fine," she said, turning in her seat to look me over. That felt...weird.

I glanced at Adam, and it was possible that his face was ever redder.

"Oh, right," Jeremy said, twisting to grin at his brother. "You two haven't met. Jolene, this is my date, Erica."

ADAM

The second Jeremy started the car and the music started playing, I leaned toward Jolene and whispered, "I swear I didn't know until we picked her up."

"Oh, I believe you," Jolene whispered back, her gaze focused on the back of Erica's head. "You said some guy asked her with a marching band?"

"He asked but she said no. And Erica is the girl from rehearsal..." I figured Erica would be at the dance and that she and Jolene would see each other, but I'd planned to keep them well apart. I'd tasked my friends, Gideon and Rory, with helping me if necessary, but sharing a car had been beyond anything I could have planned for.

Jeremy lowered the music. "What are you guys saying?"

Before Jolene or I could answer, Erica spoke up. "He's probably trying to convince her that deep down I'm a nice person who lashes out in violence only when half the school tells me they saw my boyfriend cheating on me in the parking lot." She turned her head a little, smiling so that we could see both rows of her teeth.

I was so screwed.

"No, he was explaining how his giant jerk of a brother failed to mention you were his date." Jolene leaned forward. "And for the record, I'm fine with you slapping Adam. He never cheated on you, but I get that it looked that way."

Erica turned more fully in her seat. "Just because he didn't kiss you, that doesn't make what you were doing okay."

Jolene didn't respond, and I swore to myself that I was going to make Jeremy hurt so bad when we got home.

The drive took forever and the tension in the car grew worse. I'd tried to talk to Erica at school a few times since we'd broken up, but the second I mentioned anything beyond the *Beowulf* project we'd already committed to doing together, she'd walked away. There had been a ton of rumors going around school—massively exaggerated rumors—but the fact that some of them held a thread of truth were enough to make me feel like I had deserved that slap.

"You know what, no," Jolene said, breaking the silence. "Did it suck that people at school were talking about you? Yeah, but all Adam did was hug me. That's all Adam's ever done. And I don't know if him not telling you about his friendship with me is any worse than you showing up on a date with his brother. And you—" she said, turning her attention to Jeremy "—seriously? Isn't there, like, a code between brothers that you don't go out with each other's exes?"

"I told him he could ask her," I mumbled, and saw Jolene slowly close her eyes and keep them that way. "He was always talking about her, and when we broke up, he wouldn't let up about what an idiot I was." Jolene went stiff. Her stunningly gorgeous hair slid forward over one shoulder, and I swallowed. "I told him he could ask her out if he wanted, just to get him off my back, but I didn't think he'd do *this*."

Everyone in the car stayed silent. I squeezed my eyes shut, realizing I'd just insulted both Jolene and Erica.

"Wow," Erica said from the front seat.

"No," I said, glancing at Jolene as I started to sweat. "I didn't say it because he was right." Then I looked at Erica. "Or that I didn't care about you. I do. I just—"

"Care about her more. Thanks, Adam. It feels great now that you've broken it down for me." She turned to Jeremy. "So you talk about me a lot, huh?"

Jeremy's neck went bright red, and Jolene made a sound beside me. She was covering her mouth with both hands.

"Jo, please don't be mad. I'm seriously messing this up."

She shook her head and when she lowered her hands, I saw that she was smiling. "Look," she whispered. "He likes her." She nodded at Jeremy's flaming-red neck.

I was too relieved that she wasn't pissed at me to care about what was going on with my brother. "You're not mad?"

"Not at you. Should we see how red we can make him?"

Jeremy was doing a bang-up job of that all by himself, and based on Erica's smile, she was loving it.

"Or...does that bother you?" Jolene started braiding her hair as she looked from Jeremy to Erica, then to me.

"No." I stilled her hands, making sure I didn't glance at my brother or my ex-girlfriend, who were having their own whispered conversation in the front seat. "Jo, I can't even see anyone else when I'm with you."

I'd like to say my gym had transformed into something other than my gym for the dance, but apparently the decoration committee had really taxed themselves hanging streamers and a few balloons.

Jolene had barely blinked since walking through the doors. I tried to see what she saw with such bright eyes. Students spit shined to uncomfortable perfection, some swaying under a basketball hoop, others crowded around tables. Squealing over dresses, high-fiving over dates or lack thereof.

My small-town high school had only a few hundred students, and most of us had known each other since kindergarten. We were a pretty incestuous bunch—take my brother showing up with my ex-girlfriend, for instance. I was one of maybe a dozen who'd brought an outside date. And not just *a* date, Jolene Timber.

My gym was a gussied-up gym full of gussied-up kids.

Jolene, on the other hand...

Her hair shone in soft brown waves that fell to her hips, and every time she turned, it flowed around her to dizzying effect. I could feel my pupils dilate, and Jolene took full advantage.

"The hair," I said, lifting a strand and letting it run through my fingers.

She grinned. "You like it." Not a question, but I nodded anyway.

I would say it took two turns, three tops, before every guy I knew was coming up to meet her. After one even asked her to dance, I pulled her away to meet my actual friends.

"Hey, man," Gideon said, trying not to look at Jolene. He was lanky with thick brown hair that he was constantly shaking back from his tanned face. He'd been one of my best friends since we played T-ball together. I'd told him a little about Jolene, but I still felt nervous introducing them for the first time. Jolene couldn't help but be impressive, and she could be nice when she wanted to be—which she apparently wanted that night—but after Erica, I had no idea how my two separate lives would hold up meeting each other.

I introduced everyone, including Gideon's date, a girl named Julie from my chemistry class, and then Rory, the pretty boy of our friends, with his sandy-blond hair, brown eyes, and easy grin. And while he might not have come with a date, several girls were watching him while we all talked, and they encircled him the second I pulled Jolene away. I introduced her to a few more people until I felt like she had enough names to remember and we headed for the dance floor.

I wouldn't call her a great dancer, but the way she moved—and that hair—it was mesmerizing.

"We need to stop," I told her as the fifth fast song ended.

"Don't tell me you're tired already." She twirled around in front of me, heedless of the people gazing at her, or maybe because of the people gazing at her.

"I'm pretty sure even my brother is eyeing you at this point." He wasn't, but that might have been only because Erica was laughing at something he'd said. Or not. I couldn't actually remember seeing him glance at another girl all night.

Jolene made a face and tugged me away from the dancing. "I cannot believe how much fun I'm having. Yet another reason that private schools suck."

"Maybe you just need me." I grinned as she slugged me, ridiculously happy that I was the cause of her happiness. "You're stunning, you know that?"

"It's the hair."

It was so much more than the hair.

Jolene scanned the room. "Are you going to point out your ex-girlfriends to me? I mean, besides Erica."

I played dumb. "Who?"

"How quickly he forgets. The latest of your conquests, she of the shattered heart, the jilted one. You know, the girl currently making out with your brother."

I didn't glance in Jeremy and Erica's direction. Whether it was true or not, Jolene was testing me, and I honestly didn't mind if they were kissing. Instead I said, "Where do I start?" I pretended to wink at a girl over Jolene's shoulder. She laughed and almost choked on her drink.

"Exactly how many of the girls here are in love with you?"

"Including you?"

"You wish."

Was I that obvious?

A slow song came on that I knew she loved, so I got to put my arms around her. With the added height from her shoes, I could lean my head down and reach her ear. She shivered when I spoke. "Would you believe me if I said I didn't care if Erica was kissing my brother?" Which was 100 percent true. From the moment Jolene had opened her front door, it had been impossible to take my eyes off her.

"Either way, you get mad points for saying it." She didn't lift her head when she spoke, so I couldn't see her expression, but I could feel her happiness.

"Yeah? Are these points redeemable?"

"Sure. Earn enough and I'll get you something pretty."

I could joke about winking at girls who weren't actually there, and teasing with Jolene was just the way we were— usually it was the other way around—but ever since that almost kiss in the snow—longer than that, really—I'd been the one trying to ruffle her composure. At first it was just to see if I could, to see if I possessed over her even a fraction of the power she held over me. But it wasn't a game to me. I wanted it not to be a game to her either.

I don't know if it was the lights or the music or the fact that I was getting drunk on her laughter, but I tightened my arms around her without a moment of hesitation. "I can think of something."

Her breath caught, and she pulled back to look at me. All her bravado fell away as I held her. Not in a joking or a teasing embrace. Not catching her when she tripped or while we posed for a photo. We were in a gym that still smelled like sweat under swirling clouds of cologne and perfume, surrounded by hundreds of people and the seizure-inducing flash from the world's fastest photographer in the corner.

All I could think was, how long would she let me hold her?

But then a smile crept onto her face, and I felt the shift even before her words confirmed that the game was back on. And it was over. Whatever *it* was. Whatever it might have been.

"Well, okay. I'm not sure it will fit, but if you like the dress that much, Adam, it's yours." I didn't resist when she stepped out of my arms mid-song. Her eyes were too wide, and her fingers were twisting in her hair like she wanted desperately to braid it. Seeing her unnerved made it easier for me to let go. For now.

"You want to get in line for photos?"

"Yes!" she said.

When it was our turn, we took our place in front of the winter-wonderland backdrop, and the photographer started maneuvering us into one of the standard awkward poses, but Jolene was having none of that. Her eyes sparked back to life as she shrugged off whatever had dimmed them when I'd pulled her close.

"Adam," she said, ignoring the continued orders from the photographer. "We're not posing like mannequins. What would your mom think?"

Probably not much. I looked around at the rustic wood bench, then back at Jolene. "I don't know that we have tons of options."

"Or time," the photographer deadpanned.

"C'mere." I pulled Jolene in front of me and slid my arms around her—that was going to get addicting quick. I felt very smooth...until I tripped over the fake snow blanket on the floor. But that was worth it, because Jolene laughed, I smiled, and the flash from the camera captured it all.

Jolene

I almost had an Audrey Hepburn moment after Adam dropped me off. *I could have danced all night.* Instead, I spun around my room with my arms outstretched, humming under my breath. I wiggled out of my dress and into my oversize *Breakfast Club* T-shirt before indulging in one last spin and falling backward on my bed.

But then the pearls from my mother's necklace rolled against my collarbone, and I heard a door slam downstairs. Mom and Tom were fighting, and that wasn't something I'd heard them do before. Tom always played nice with her, talking her down and cajoling her into doing things his way. Mom was usually too eager for the attention she thought would make her happy to truly let her facade drop when she was with him.

I'd told Tom the truth about never getting my dad's money, and it seemed that Mom's assurances to the contrary were growing thin, based on their raised voices.

My hand reached up to trace the pearls. None of her loving, motherly act was real. I knew that. It was costumes and sets.

I sat up and started braiding my hair. Adam might not have noticed all the eyes on him during the dance—even some of his friends' dates—but I had. I wasn't surprised. Adam was always so easy with everyone. He expected people to like him unless he chose to give them a reason not to. When I wasn't dancing around my room and remembering the way his arms had tightened around me, I resented him for that.

My fingers faltered. He'd liked my hair down. He'd told me in a million silent and not-so-silent ways all night. I hurried to finish the braid, then coiled the whole thing in a knot on my head. From the bed, I could see my reflection in the mirror on my wall. That was how Adam usually saw me.

My phone buzzed. I knew it was him before I looked at the screen.

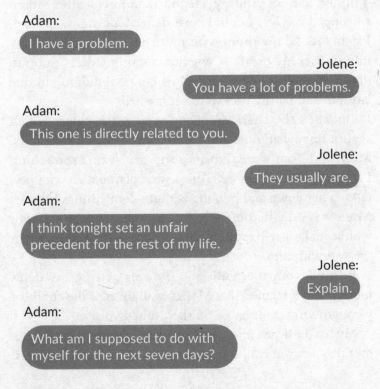

Adam:
I have a problem.

Jolene:
You have a lot of problems.

Adam:
This one is directly related to you.

Jolene:
They usually are.

Adam:
I think tonight set an unfair precedent for the rest of my life.

Jolene:
Explain.

Adam:
What am I supposed to do with myself for the next seven days?

Jolene:

It's after midnight, so technically six days now.

Adam:

That's a long time to wait for something pretty.

I hesitated before texting back. Was that how it was going to be from then on? Was he going to keep digging and digging until he got so far under my skin that the only way to get him out was to rip it off?

Adam:

Jolene?

Jolene:

I'm not used to you like this.

Adam:

You'll get there.

Jolene:

I'm not sure I like it.

I bit my lip waiting for his response. Guys were so sensitive. If I shut down his flirting, I could end up shutting down a lot more than that.

Adam:

Fine. I'll stop, but as long as you keep sending me texts like this, it's game on.

He pasted in a text I'd sent him the previous weekend: I'm here. Why don't you back that thing up and come over?

Jolene:

I was quoting a song.

Adam:

Is that the rule?

Jolene:

I was being funny. It's different.

Adam:

So I'll be funny.

Jolene:

You weren't being funny at the dance.

Adam:

Nothing about holding you felt funny.

Jolene:

That's what I'm talking about.

Adam:

Fine. Next time I have you in my arms, I tickle you instead.

I started to type **Instead?** but that would have invited all sorts of other responses. I deleted it.

Jolene:

Dream on.

Adam:

We'll see. Night, Jolene.

Jolene:

Night.

A door slammed, and a moment later a car peeled out of the driveway.

I unclasped my mother's pearl necklace and set it on my dresser.

ADAM

Jeremy had been smiling all weekend since the dance, and I'd avoided confronting him over springing his date on me, because my night with Jolene had still been amazing. But when he started whistling as we drove to school on Monday, I'd had enough.

My hand lashed out and I turned the radio on. Loud.

Beside me, Jeremy laughed and flicked it off. "All right. Say it."

I kept my mouth shut as I let my gaze travel over the cars we passed.

"I can't believe what a pissy little brat you are sometimes." Jeremy gritted his teeth. "Fine, I should have told you about Erica, okay?"

"Hell yes, you should have told me about Erica."

My brother's jaw relaxed since I'd decided to yell at him instead of stay silent. "Hey, I told you you'd regret letting Erica go. You can't be mad that she's into me now, especially since you told me to ask her out."

"I don't regret breaking up with Erica." I shook my head

at how dense he was. "And I don't care that you're going out with her, if that's what she wants."

"Oh, it's definitely what she wants." Jeremy grinned.

I locked my jaw. "I swear, if you think about whistling again…"

Jeremy started laughing. "Well, then what? You got the girl you want and I got the girl you were too stupid to want." The back of his hand slapped my chest. "Cheer up."

I glanced down at where he'd slapped me before turning to face him. "You're a tool," I told him in a calm voice.

"Whatever, man."

"No, not whatever." I twisted and the seat belt pulled against me. "I don't care that you're with Erica. In fact, great. Good for you." I felt a weird twinge that she could be into him after being into me, but my feelings for Erica had been nothing like my feelings for Jolene, so that was my pride bugging me more than anything else. "I care that you set out to screw me over, and you didn't care that you were hurting Jolene and Erica in the process."

Jeremy pulled his mouth to the side and quickly frowned. "So now you care about hurting Erica? I was the one who was with her every day at rehearsal. You don't even know the number you pulled on her."

My neck heated. "Yeah, I was a jerk, but I didn't *mean* to hurt her. You didn't tell me who your date was, and I'm betting Erica had no idea she was about to be trapped in a car with me and the girl she thought I cheated on her with."

"Oh, she knew." When I stayed silent, Jeremy actually looked offended. "You really thought I'd do that? To a girl I liked?"

Yeah, actually, I had. My brother's emotional range was pretty stunted, in my experience. "Erica knew?"

"Fair's fair. You didn't exactly prepare her before you

let half the school catch you making out with Jolene in the parking lot."

"We weren't—" I ground my teeth. What people thought they'd seen me doing with Jolene wasn't the point anymore. "Erica isn't vindictive. She wouldn't have done that."

"Maybe you don't know her as well as you think."

I frowned at that, and Jeremy shook his head.

"You were at her house all the time. What'd you guys do if you weren't talk—" His jaw twisted and he closed his mouth with an audible click. I watched his fingers clench around the steering wheel, and I let him squirm for a good minute, imagining all the many non-talking things we might have done. When his face started to turn purple, I figured he'd had enough.

"I only kissed her a few times, and never for long because her dad kept coming to check on us." That and my thoughts had kept straying to Jolene, and I hadn't wanted to use Erica like that, but I wasn't about to confess that to Jeremy.

Jeremy shot me a sideways glance as though he was trying to ascertain if I was lying, before his head jerked in a quick nod. He still seemed a little skeptical, and if our situations were reversed and he'd gone out with Jolene before me—the thought alone made me want rip his throat out—I'd have had a hard time believing he'd been able to resist her.

"We worked on our project and we…"

"What? You what?" Jeremy kept veering into the lane next to us as he shot looks at me.

"We talked about Greg," I finally said.

The tension didn't leave Jeremy's body, but it shifted so that I was no longer concerned he'd run us off the road.

I rolled my shoulder to try to alleviate some of the discomfort I suddenly felt weighing on me. "She remembered some things about him from when we were kids, him saving cats and stuff." Shifting again, I remembered that each one of our kisses had been prompted by me talking about Greg, reaching that breaking point of grief where I wanted to feel anything else, even if that meant kissing a girl who wasn't the one I really wanted. More than that, I realized that talking to Erica about Greg had been entirely different than talking to Jolene.

With Erica, I talked about Greg, but not about what it'd been like to lose him, not about what I felt. And whenever I'd reached that point where it hurt too much to go on, I'd stopped. With Jolene, I hadn't wanted to hold back. I'd wanted her to see and feel and know not just who my brother was, but who I'd become since he died. I felt the pain of losing Greg, but with her I hadn't wanted to hide it.

With one, I'd talked; with the other, I'd shared.

The difference felt huge.

"I'm glad she knew him," Jeremy said after a while. "I mean, it's not—" He rolled his eyes. "We're not together yet. We had fun at the dance, and not just because we got to stick it to you. I like her and if something more happens between us... I'm glad I won't have to deal with trying to tell her about him."

"Yeah," I said, my throat squeezing the word so that it barely came out. "It's hard."

"But you did?" he went on. "Tell Jolene?"

I nodded. "Yeah, it was after we...we actually ran into Daniel." I hadn't intentionally withheld that fact from my brother; it was just that we didn't talk, except to fight. I lowered my head though, because, intended or not, I should have said something.

I made sure not to look at Jeremy when he spoke, but I heard the break when he did.

"You did? When? Where? Is he...okay?"

I told him the details, feeling worse with every word. Daniel had been more than Greg's friend, he'd been ours, too—both of ours.

"He's still got the Jeep."

Jeremy's mouth lifted. "Does it still smell like every animal in the state has pissed in it?"

I laughed. "Every animal in the state did piss in it. Do you remember when he and Greg got the badger in the back seat?"

"No, the time they had the two swans..."

And that was how it went for the rest of the drive. My abs hurt from laughing, and for the first time since Greg died, the tears in my eyes weren't from crying.

Jolene

It was late when I heard the front door open, but not as late as I was expecting. I was normally dead asleep by the time Mom got home from a date with Tom, but they'd been gone only a couple hours. I was still finishing the last few bites of the early individual-size birthday cake—pineapple upside-down—that Mrs. Cho had left me along with her thoughts on the most recent films I'd suggested to her—she'd gotten the bittersweet coming-of-age brilliance of *The Way, Way Back* but couldn't get past that scene in *Planes, Trains and Automobiles* where Steve Martin lays into the lady from the car rental place. The cake was supposed to be for tomorrow, but I hadn't been able to wait. And Mom's unexpected appearance meant I didn't have time to wash the caramel off the plate. It didn't matter that I could shove the rest of the cake in my mouth. She'd know. I decided to enjoy my cake, because I was going to pay for it one way or another.

I was lifting a bite to my mouth when Mom entered the kitchen. She froze like she'd walked in on me snorting a line of cocaine off the countertop, which I guess, in her mind, might have been the less grievous action. If I was on drugs, she could send me to rehab. The same couldn't be said about consuming processed sugar.

I took in the mascara streaks under her red eyes and knew that I'd made the wrong decision by not hiding my cake—and myself. This wasn't going to be a film starring movie-studio Mom. This was going to be the underground, black-market edition that only the most twisted people would watch.

I had no choice but to costar.

"Don't," she said, raising a shaking hand in my direction.

I took the bite.

She screamed, smacked the plate away from me, and threw it into the sink so hard that it shattered.

I turned my fork over to lick the other side clean.

She pulled it from my mouth with enough force that one of the prongs sliced the inside of my lip. I tasted blood.

"It's a cake. Why are you acting like this?"

"It is *not* a cake. It is poison that makes you fat."

"Well, it was delicious."

One eye twitched. "You think I didn't look like you when I was your age? That I couldn't eat garbage all the time? Well, I did until one day, bam!" She clapped her hands in front of my face and I flinched back. "I'm a fat middle-aged woman whose husband is screwing his personal trainer!"

"Can you stop telling the same story over and over again? None of that has anything to do with your size, because he would have done it anyway. Plus, he's not your husband anymore, and his personal trainer has a name—Shelly."

It felt as if my eyes opened twice as wide as hers. The pineapple upside-down cake in my stomach tried to turn itself into a right-side-up cake. I didn't care about Shelly. I hated Shelly. She was awful, and she'd used our former friendship to get to my dad. I didn't understand how my brain and my mouth could have become so disconnected, but I didn't have time to think about it, because Mom took a step back from me.

"How could you say her name to me?"

And just like that, I was done. She was supposed to come home from her bad date, see me sneaking my birthday cake, and shake her head as she smiled. She was supposed to slip off her heels, grab a fork, and dig in with me. We could have laughed together, talked together, and when the cake was gone she could have hugged me, and told me she loved me, and that she was sorry for all the times she'd let me think she didn't.

That was what Adam's mom would have done. For his birthday, she'd probably fill their kitchen with cakes and hug him once for every year that he'd been alive. She wouldn't just tell him how much she loved him, she'd show him over and over again, and he'd never spend a single sleepless night counting all the things that were wrong with him.

He'd never feel like he wasn't enough.

Like he was the reason everyone was miserable.

Like his mom was unhappy because of him.

"Because it doesn't matter if I say Shelly's name. And it doesn't matter if I eat a birthday cake for my birthday made by someone who actually cares about me. I don't care what size I am. Why do you care more about what I eat than how I feel? Why can't you care about me, *me*?" I said, pressing my fingers into my sternum. "Not how you can use me to hurt Dad or make you look good in front of Tom or—" I scoffed "—how the two of you can use me to spy on Dad and get you more money. For what? Will money make you happy? You weren't happy when you were married and had Dad's money. You've never been happy with me, and judging from the makeup you've cried off, Tom isn't making you happy either. So, what do you want, Mom, because it looks like the only thing that makes you happy is when other people feel worse!"

And still, after saying all of that, there was a stupid speck of hope beating in my chest that wanted her to shake her head, to gasp and realize with a shock that although she'd been hurting me all these years, she hadn't meant to. That hope imagined a scene in which she'd fall down in front of me, hugging me and begging me to forgive her.

It could have been the ultimate climax, with swelling music and an unsteady, handheld camera capturing it all.

But in the movie of my life, the characters never changed or grew. My life would never be the movie *I* wanted.

She slipped off her right earring, pulled out her phone and dialed, and lifted the cell to her ear.

She never once broke eye contact with me as she spoke. "Yes, I'm sorry for the late hour, Mrs. Cho, but this couldn't wait. I don't need you to come in tomorrow."

"Mom," I said, my voice more breath than sound as I clutched the edge of the island, my heart plummeting.

"My financial situation has become more difficult of late and I won't be able to keep you on any longer."

"I'm sorry. I'll look at Dad's papers, whatever you want. Please. Please don't." For a second I thought she heard me, not just my voice but the plea that came straight from my heart.

"Yes, of course. Thank you for understanding."

She ended the call and replaced her earring. "You think that woman cares about you? Ask me what she said when I fired her. Ask me what her concern was."

I shook my head, feeling like I might throw up the last thing Mrs. Cho would ever make me.

"A reference letter. *Not* you." She strode across the kitchen until she was right in front of me. "She didn't even say your name."

My lungs emptied in a sob and my arms came up to wrap around myself.

"Look at me."

And when I couldn't, she lifted my chin herself.

"One day, you'll thank me for teaching you the most important lesson you'll ever learn—caring about people who can't get you anything in return is a waste."

Then she pressed her lips against my forehead and told me to clean up the kitchen before I went to bed.

ADAM

*T*he second hand of my bedroom wall clock was passing the nine, ten, eleven, and the moment it ticked past the twelve and hit midnight, I pressed Call on my phone. The lateness of the hour made the phone slip in my slightly sweaty hand as I waited for her to pick up.

And waited.

Waited.

I was beginning to wonder if she was asleep when her voice, low but clear, replaced the continuous ringback.

"Adam. It's midnight. Are you dying or super rude?"

"No," I said, and then I laughed. "You can't think of a single reason why I'd be calling you at exactly midnight on this particular day?"

"Let me think for a moment," she said, but I could hear that she was smiling.

"Happy birthday. I wanted to be the first one to say it to you."

"Well, congratulations. That honor belongs to you."

"How do you feel? Older? Mature? Too cool for fifteen-

and-eleven-months-old guys?" I heard Jolene shifting, and for some reason I imagined her flipping around on a bed I'd never seen with her legs propped up on a padded headboard.

"I don't know. I've been sixteen for like a minute, so maybe? Although I've always been too cool for you, so definitely yes to the last question."

"I would take issue with the use of the word *always* in that statement, but come morning, I'm not going to be able to argue with a driver's license when I'm stuck riding a bike. You're still going, right? Gabe is taking you?"

"Yeah, we were going to blow off first and second periods, but there was some damage to the roof from the snowstorm over the weekend so there's no school tomorrow. Want me to call you after?"

"No. I mean, yes, normally I would want that, but my mom decided we should take an impromptu drive up to Lancaster for a couple days to visit my grandparents. We're leaving in the morning and they're conservative Mennonites, which is only a few steps away from being Amish. They don't go for a lot of technology around the farm. My mom wants us to leave everything with a battery at home. I know, I know," I said, forestalling a predictable remark from Jolene. "It's like traveling back in time instead of driving a couple hours away."

"I wasn't going to say that."

"Why not? It's true."

"I think it's nice that your mom is being so thoughtful of your grandparents."

"Okay," I said. "Age is definitely making you more compassionate. I don't know what to do with you if you aren't making fun of me."

"Is that how you see me? As the mean girl who insults you all the time?"

Age was also making her more sensitive, apparently. "No. I wouldn't be calling you on your birthday or wanting to hang out with you all the time if that's what I thought. I'd be hanging out with that other girl, the one I broke up with because I'd rather be friends with you." And then I added, "Is everything okay? I mean, you just turned sixteen. Why aren't you happier right now?"

"Do you remember me telling you about Mrs. Cho, my housekeeper?"

"Sure," I said.

"My mom and I got into a fight tonight, and afterward she called Mrs. Cho and fired her. She told Mrs. Cho it was because we couldn't afford her anymore, but that's not why. It's not even because she caught me eating the birthday cake that Mrs. Cho left me, or that Tom broke up with her because I refused to spy on my dad for them. I was happy for a split second, and she couldn't have that. So she fired the only person who ever cared about me, just because. She even tried to tell me it was for my own good, a way to teach me that caring about people who can't get you anything is stupid."

My hand clenched around the phone and so much blood rushed to my face that it seemed to seep into my vision. It didn't seem possible that Jolene had come from two of the most miserable and worthless people who'd ever lived.

"I've been lying here trying to sleep," Jolene went on. I could hear her too-fast breathing through the phone, and the sound was a fist tightening around my heart. "But all I can think about is that I'll probably never see Mrs. Cho again. And maybe my mom was right. She said Mrs. Cho didn't ask about me on the phone."

"Your mom is a liar," I said, raising my voice. "I don't believe for a second that she didn't ask about you. And neither do you." When Jolene's end of the line stayed silent, I felt a weird wash of anger crash over me—not toward her, but toward the people who were responsible for the way I knew she looked, sitting in her room miles away. Like she wanted the earth itself to swallow her. "You're amazing, you know?" But she didn't, and that was the problem. "Jo, I—" I didn't want to tell her on the phone that I loved her.

"Adam, I'm kidding. Obviously. I mean, it's not even really just my birthday. Every year I'm alive is like a gift to the world."

She was trying to deflect from the rare honest words she'd let slip, and I knew I couldn't let her. "Remember my prediction for our future?"

"The one where I win an Oscar? Um, yeah."

"I started it too late. Before you get into college and you're crying over leaving me at the airport—"

"Uh-huh. Let's see who ends up doing the crying."

"—you submit an incredible application to that film program, and to no one's surprise but your own, you get in. After a single summer, you start realizing that all the crap your parents have made you think about yourself all these years is just that. Even when you come back home, it's not as bad as it's been, because you don't just tell other people what an amazingly talented, beautiful, and funny person you are, you actually believe it. It's not just some joke that only you're in on."

The silence on the phone made me worry that I'd gone too far and she'd hung up. I pressed the phone harder against my ear. "Jo?"

"Yeah?"

My eyes fell shut in relief. "Did you hear what I said?"

"Uh-huh."

"Then tell me you know I'm right."

But she didn't, and I realized that she couldn't, not after

everything that had happened with her mom and Mrs. Cho.
I was going to keep telling her though. And I'd show her,
too. "I *am* right. About all of it. Even you sobbing as I leave
to catch my flight." I told myself that that last part made her
smile. "And I'm sorry about Mrs. Cho."

Jolene let out a sigh that was an acknowledgment of the
sympathy I offered, but not much else. I probably had pushed
her too far and, more than anything, when we hung up, I
wanted her to feel better than when I'd called her. I wasn't
doing a great job of making that happen yet.

"Leaving aside your wretched mom, you know that Mrs.
Cho isn't the only one who cares about you just because,
right? I mean, I'm right here on the phone. At least wait until
we've hung up before you dismiss me out of hand."

Jolene laughed a little. "I forgot about your fragile boy
emotions."

"And we're back to making fun of me." I hoped she could
hear me smiling.

"You want an ego boost?"

I wanted anything she wanted to give me. "Sure."

She laughed again, but when she started talking, she
sounded completely serious. "I like that you're such a huge
nerd that you sat up watching the clock so you could call me
the second it was officially my birthday."

"Anytime you want to start with that ego boost."

"You want me to tell you that I like talking to you better than I like sleeping? You want me to tell you that no one
has ever given me a midnight birthday call and the fact that
you did means I don't think I'll ever be as cool as you are to
me right now?"

"For starters," I said, going for a lame joke because my face
felt so hot that it was borderline uncomfortable, which meant

I was reaching record-breaking blushing territory. Since I knew Jolene would like hearing that, I told her.

"Yes!" was her response, hissing the word so that it tickled my ear through the phone. "You did that just for me, didn't you?"

I did blush for her. I almost always blushed for her.

When she spoke again, her voice started to crack, and she had to swallow and start again. "You're a really good friend, Adam Moynihan. Better than the best."

"You're worth being a really good friend to, Jolene Timber. I hope I get to be there when you realize that." For some reason, that made her cry, though she tried to hide that from me, I could hear it. "You know, if you lived near me, or I had a license, I'd be at your window right now with one of those gross banana cupcakes that you like. Wait, no, I'd be wearing a trench coat, and I'd have found a giant old stereo in a pawnshop or something and I'd be holding it above my head playing...playing..." I smacked my palm against my head trying to remember the song from the John Cusack movie she'd made me watch a few weeks ago.

"It's Peter Gabriel's 'In Your Eyes.'"

"'In Your Eyes.'"

"That's pretty much the biggest romantic moment in movie history," she told me. Her voice was back. So was my blush.

"It's possible I might have fallen asleep during part or all of that movie."

Her laughter was a little shaky, but it told me she wasn't mad about my narcoleptic tendencies. "I'm surprised you remembered even that one scene."

"You rose up on your knees at that point, and you were digging your nails into my arm the second the song started. Not real sleep conducive."

"I love that scene. I love that whole movie, but can I still get the cupcake?"

"The fake cupcake that doesn't exist? Sure, you can have it."

"Did you put a candle in it?"

"I put sixteen candles in it. You can't even tell it's a cupcake anymore. It basically looks like a wrapper full of fire."

"Sounds perfect. And you'd sing to me?"

"Nope, because that sounds as far from perfect as you can imagine. But I would sort of speak the words to you in an almost singing way that you'd really like."

"I think I would like that."

"Next year," I told her, making a promise to myself as much as her. "It'll be just like that—your birthday, midnight, me at your window, a gross banana cupcake, but with seventeen candles in it."

"I actually believe you'll do that."

"If I wasn't chronologically challenged at the moment, I'd do it now."

"Thanks, Adam."

"Happy birthday, Jolene."

Jolene

Shoes in hand, I tiptoed down the stairs and slipped out the front door on Tuesday morning, my first as an official sixteen-year-old, sighing with relief when I made it down the driveway without Mom noticing I'd left. I rounded the corner and sped up with a grin when I saw Gabe's minivan only to slow when I noticed Cherry in the back seat.

I couldn't afford to stand there feeling confused, so I kept walking and let myself into the passenger seat. I said hi to Gabe, then immediately twisted in my seat, and addressed Cherry. "Hey. So no more grounding?"

Gabe smothered a laugh and started the van.

Cherry glared at him before giving me a somewhat less hostile look. "I'm still a prisoner, but since it's your birthday and we made these plans months ago, not to mention the fact that I have a babysitter, they let me out."

"Oh," I said. It wasn't exactly happy-birthday hugs and I'm-so-glad-we're-not-fighting, but it was more than I was expecting given how our last conversation had ended. She clearly wasn't thrilled with the grounding reprieve she was getting, which kept my voice quiet and soft. "Well, free is free, right? Sucks you have to spend part of it at the DMV."

"Yeah." Her face smoothed and she sighed when Gabe made a show of clearing his throat. She rolled her eyes at him. "She barely got in the car. Chill." Then she bit her lip and glanced at me. "I got you a present. I had to order it online since I couldn't go out but…" She handed me a tiny holographic gift bag stuffed with purple tissue paper. "It's fine if you don't want it."

"I do," I said, taking the present. "Um, thanks." A few months ago, I'd have climbed into the back seat to tackle her in a hug before we tore into my gift together. Now I bit my own lip and I wasn't sure which of us looked away first.

"You get that this is my gift, right?" Gabe pointed at the steering wheel and breaking the tension. "Taking you to get your license at 7:00 a.m. when I could be sleeping?"

Cherry flopped back against her seat. "He's lying. He and the guys chipped in to get you a new lens for your camera. Gabe did a ton of research picking it out. They're planning to give it to you at the house later."

"Um, we did not," Gabe said in a bad acting voice while shooting daggers at Cherry in the rearview mirror. "None of us even like you, Jo. It's super embarrassing how you come over all the time and make us free music videos."

Nothing in the world could have stopped me from grinning. A new lens was awesome, but knowing that the whole band had planned a gift for me… My heart felt too big for my chest. I leaned over and brushed a kiss on Gabe's cheek. "Thank you. Also, it's sweet that you think I'm not going to bill you."

"Hey now," he said, side-eyeing me and smiling. "Don't think that gets you out of a thank-you card. And you have to act surprised with Grady and Dexter."

"Deal." Then I looked down at Cherry's gift in my lap. I almost didn't want to open it, as though good or bad, thoughtful or not, it represented the future of our friendship. We hadn't been good for a long time, and I didn't know how we were going to get back there or if we even could at this point. Cherry nodded when I told her I'd open it later.

Gabe tried to ask me a few questions about how my film program application was going after that, but I was too focused on the life-changing test I was about to take, so he gave up and said I could tell them later.

At the DMV, I flew out of the vehicle almost before Gabe stopped. I'd expected getting through the lines to take a disgustingly long time, but I was wrong. It took longer.

I hit neither cone nor small child during my test. I stopped when I was supposed to, and my parallel parking was a thing of beauty. I mentally declared myself an excellent, excellent driver. And my instructor agreed. I rocked a full-on nerd dance, knees bent and arms flailing, when we got back to the DMV. Gabe wasted no time joining me in the parking lot. Cherry was too cool for us, but she did hug me. I was momentarily distracted by that hug, our first since Meneik had come back into the picture, and it was bittersweet since we both pulled away quickly.

I ended up looking somewhat crazed in my photo, lots of teeth and neck tendons on display, but I strutted out of that place like I was John Travolta in *Saturday Night Fever*.

It was sweet.

Having to ride shotgun when the state of Pennsylvania had just declared me fit to drive was less sweet, but at least Gabe played good music.

I half turned in the passenger seat to talk with Cherry and ask the question I both wanted and didn't want to ask. "How's Meneik dealing with the forced separation?"

Her lips pressed together. "Look, maybe we shouldn't talk about him, okay?"

Which meant she was still with him. I could only imagine the guilt trip he was laying on her over being grounded. No doubt he'd found a way to blame her for that, too. I seriously hated that guy.

I felt somewhat stymied by her request though. Without soccer or her sucky boyfriend, what did we used to talk about? I was still trying to come up with something when Cherry's shoulders slumped.

"He's frustrated that we can't see each other right now. And Gabe—" she lowered her voice to a whisper, forcing me to lean farther in to the back seat "—won't pass on any more messages between us."

I made a mental note to hug Gabe more often.

"That's something I was hoping to ask you about."

The hairs on my neck lifted and I *knew* I wasn't going to like what she said next.

"Could you maybe give me your phone, but—" there was so little volume to her voice as she slid her hand around the far side of my seat that I had to read her lips "—don't let Gabe see."

"I can't do that," I whispered back.

"Tell your mom or dad you lost it and ask for a new one."

I half laughed, thinking she was kidding. Cherry knew I'd been psyching myself up for having to ask them to pay for the film program, and after the horrific ordeal I'd gone through getting a dress for the dance with Adam, I was expecting it to nearly kill me.

But Cherry didn't laugh with me, she frowned.

"I need to talk to him," she said.

"Um, no," I said, all the humor fleeing from my face. "You don't."

Her jaw tightened. "Fine. Then call him for me. Tell him—"

"Cherry, no. Let him go. Seriously I—" I almost told her I knew what a good boyfriend should be like and Meneik wasn't it. Except Adam wasn't my boyfriend. As a friend, he was kind and thoughtful, and he went out of his way to make me feel special—he'd almost made me believe him when he said all those things the night before. That was what a boyfriend should be like, not Meneik's controlling, manipulating garbage. Cherry deserved someone who would treat her the way Adam already treated me.

Whether I was worth it or not.

"You can either be my friend and help me or…" She stared me down, the rest of her words unnecessary.

"I'm trying to be your friend," I told her. "I've watched this guy turn you into a meek, paranoid…thing, constantly apologizing for the slightest offense he imagines, forcing you away from your friends and making you feel guilty for every second that you're not thanking him for putting up with you." I'd stopped whispering at some point, and Gabe was obviously listening. "A year ago, you'd have smacked me if I'd wanted a guy like that."

"Except someone would have to want you in the first place, and *no one* ever has."

The air rushed out of me, and my lungs refused to expand. It was like the worst impact I'd ever felt on the field, and she hadn't even touched me. She didn't just mean no guy had ever wanted me; she'd meant no *person*.

It didn't help that her eyes shot wide the second the words left her mouth. She tried to take them back the rest of the way to my house, but between the rushing in my head and Gabe yelling at her, I heard nothing. And besides, how do you apologize after voicing the deepest darkest fears of some-one's soul?

I wanted to get out of the van and I flung my door open as soon as Gabe pulled into the driveway despite the fact that my mother was waiting for us on the porch with a phone to her ear.

"No, wait, she's here. She just pulled up." My mom ended her call as I climbed out of the minivan.

Cherry and Gabe got out, too.

"Jolene, wait, please," Cherry whispered as Gabe's voice rose loud enough to keep my mother from hearing her and asking questions.

"Sorry we kidnapped your daughter on her birthday," Gabe said. "We brought her back in one piece though." Cherry kept shooting desperate glances at me but I wouldn't meet them. I couldn't. It hurt enough to keep breathing.

"Thank you for bringing her home, Gabriel, but it's time for you and Cherish to leave now."

Gabe hugged me tight like I needed. "Don't forget I love you, okay? Promise or I won't let go."

"I promise," I whispered back. "I, um, have a feeling I might not make it over later, so thank Grady and Dexter for my present."

Gabe finally released me. He didn't look at his sister either as he got in the car. Cherry brushed a tear from her cheek as she followed.

As soon as they were gone, every last ounce of civility left my mother.

"Where were you?" Dragons breathing fire scorched less than my mother's voice. If I wasn't so shredded over Cherry's words, I might have felt apprehensive, but she'd already taken Mrs. Cho from me; she could scream all she wanted now.

"The DMV. Look." I pulled my license from my pocket

and held it up. "It wasn't a big deal." I brushed past her to the front door. "And anyway, it's done. I'm starving, so I'm going to go find something to eat."

"No."

"No?" I turned back to her where she was still perched on the bottom step. "No, I can't go in, or no, I can't—what is that?" I pointed past her to a snow-white Lexus parked beside her silver BMW with a giant red bow on top of it.

"You got me a *car*?" Excitement burst inside me like a firework, bright and shocking, only to vanish a second later. "Why?"

"I didn't get you a car."

"Uh, yeah, you did." I was still pointing at it. My arm refused to lower as I walked toward it. I shook my head. It was still there.

"I told you, *I* didn't. And it's going back." Her phone rang and she immediately answered it. "Yes? And? What did he say? No, I absolutely do not agree. Where did he get the money? Tell him that's what I want to know. No, no, that is complete fiction. I can't believe he's doing this to me today." She pinched the bridge of her nose. "He can't let me win this one. Even when he loses, he pulls something like this. Oh, you can bet he's going to regret it. I know, I know, yes. Okay. I will. I won't." She hung up and strode toward where I stood fingering the red ribbon on my car.

"This is from Dad? Did he bring it himself?" I'd coiled the ribbon around one finger and the satin fabric was starting to cut off my circulation.

"I doubt it." She was staring at the car without blinking. "I saw it from the window."

"Was there a card or a note?"

"Yes."

"Can I see it?"

She blinked. "No."

"Why not?"

Another blink. "Because I threw it in the fireplace."

"What did it say?"

"I don't know. I didn't read it."

"Okay then." I wrapped my whole arm in ribbon and yanked. The giant bow snapped and fluttered into a bleeding pile on the ground. I leaned to one side to peer into the cab. I saw what I was looking for: the keys were right there in the ignition.

Mom came to life as I opened the door and slid into the driver's seat. "What are you doing? Jolene, get out of the car *right now*."

I closed the door. I even thought to lock it a second before she thought to try to open it. Her eyes grew wide so that I could see the white rims around her irises.

"Open the door."

I started the engine.

"Open the door."

I shifted into Reverse.

Self-preservation forced her back a step. I adjusted my mirrors and fastened my seat belt before I peeled out, the stink of brand-new tires burning rubber causing my eyes to tear.

"Where are you going? *Where are you going?*" my mother screamed after me. "Baby, come back!"

I curled my fingers around the steering wheel and went to see my father.

ADAM

When I'd told Jolene that all electronics had been banned from our little family road trip, I had assumed the rule was restricted to devices with communication capabilities, like cell phones, tablets, and laptops. I wrongly thought my old MP3 player would be fine, considering we had a two-hour drive in front of us.

Mom's Geo was packed with our bags, Jeremy was driving, and I was more than content to claim the back seat for myself. No sooner had I climbed in and turned on my MP3 player then she yanked the buds from my ears and confiscated it.

"Seriously?" I asked her.

"Grandpa will not be okay with this on the farm." She waved the earbuds back and forth before winding them up and putting the whole thing in her purse. "Besides, I don't want you checking out for the whole drive. When's the last time we went away for a couple days as a family?"

I thought of Dad alone in his apartment. Jeremy was the moron who actually brought that up out loud. "We drove to Niagara Falls last summer, but Dad was with us, so this isn't the whole family."

Mom stilled, then said she needed to take my MP3 player inside, and left us in the car.

I kicked the back of Jeremy's seat. "What the hell?"

"Quit it. What's wrong with you?"

"Me?" I said. "You just had to bring up Dad. Look what you did." I flung a hand toward the house.

Jeremy settled more into his seat. "Maybe she needs the reminder."

That wasn't Mom's problem. It wasn't that she forgot anything that had happened, it was that she *couldn't* forget it. I imagined it as if all the most painful moments of her life were playing on a continuous loop in her head, and when Jeremy went out of his way to bring up something raw, it jolted the volume up louder. She was inside the house agonizing over Dad's absence, the effect that it was having on Jeremy and me, the guilt from all her decisions, and the reasons she'd made them. Greg. Over and over again.

"It's different with her than Dad," I said.

"I know that. You think I don't care? That I like making her hurt or knowing Dad's rotting away in that apartment all the time?"

Sometimes, yeah, I did think that. "You don't act like you care. How is saying stupid stuff to Mom caring?"

"How long has it been?" Jeremy met my gaze in the rear-view mirror and held it.

"Five months." My stomach sank saying those words out loud. It had been five months since Dad moved out and nearly as long since we'd started shuffling back and forth between them. Nothing had changed. Not a damn thing.

"Five months. You've been off with your girlfriend over there, and I'm the one who's been around watching him.

It's not getting better for either of them, and it sure as hell isn't getting better for me. You wander around at Dad's like a zombie, only coming to life to mouth off, and then over here, you're on eggshells trying to make sure Mom doesn't feel anything that might upset her. You're too busy pissing off Dad and protecting Mom to realize you're doing it wrong!" Jeremy slammed his hand against the steering wheel.

My blood rushed and my fist clenched beside my thigh. "And what are you doing that's so brilliant besides making her cry and keeping Dad complacent?"

"Dad's already mad all the time. He doesn't need any help from you to stay that way. And Mom—"

"Is sad all the time," I said. "She doesn't need your help either."

"Yeah, she is, but she's not letting go. Maybe if you let her think about what her sadness is doing, that she isn't the only one who's sad, maybe she'll realize she doesn't have to be sad all the time. That all of us together could help." Jeremy shook his head. "Five months, Adam. *Five months*. I don't want to live like this. I don't want them to live like this." His gaze slipped away when he added, "You either."

There wasn't much I could say after that. It was one thing to know that my brother loved me. Of course he did; he had to, just like I had to love him. I didn't always like him. In fact, I rarely liked him, but I did love him.

Greg had been easy to like, and Jeremy had idolized him. We'd all suffered when Greg died. But it had been easier to focus on Mom's suffering, and my own, than consider that Jeremy was suffering, too. I was beginning to realize that just because he didn't show it the same way didn't mean he didn't feel as deeply. It was totally foreign for me to think of Jeremy that way, to know that he not only had those feelings but that maybe all along, he'd been considering mine, too.

It was a mind trip, and it messed with my brain, making me feel like I needed to apologize and hug him. I couldn't remember the last time Jeremy and I had hugged. I felt like I needed to apologize for that, too. The words formed in my mouth, but I couldn't give them breath. Instead I focused on the problem we shared.

"So what do we do?"

"For starters, we don't take any family trips without the whole family. I don't want her getting used to the idea of us without Dad."

That made sense. We were fragmented, but that didn't mean we needed to form potentially good memories that way. But even though I agreed with Jeremy—a fact that astounded me—I didn't see that we had a lot of options. "We are literally packed and in the car. Little late to get out of this one."

Jeremy was thinking. His face tended to scrunch up when he was concentrating hard on something, like the effort was painful. Brotherly breakthrough notwithstanding, I fell into my old habit and laughed. Jeremy reacted just as predictably by turning around and drilling me in the arm.

It was going to take more than one conversation to turn Jeremy and me into the kind of brothers who liked each other as well as loved each other. I didn't need the throb in my arm to tell me that.

When Mom came back, her makeup was completely redone, which told me she'd cried the first application off. I wondered if Jeremy noticed. Maybe. His face wasn't contorted, so I assumed he'd abandoned any deep thought as to how to get this road trip canceled, but I hadn't. I wasn't going to be able to communicate with him in front of her, but as I rubbed my arm, an idea formed…the barest fragment of one.

"I think that's everything," Mom said. Jeremy only

grunted. "Grandma and Grandpa are really looking forward to seeing you two. You'll be fine for a couple days without your electronics."

I didn't have any more time to think once Jeremy started the car. "Fine," I said, deliberately letting my annoyance seep through.

"Ignore him," Jeremy said. "He's crying because he won't be able to call his girlfriend for two days and the world is going to end as a result."

What a predictable ass. I tried not to smile. "Careful. Forty-eight hours might be long enough for Erica to realize she'd rather not date a guy who has to shop at Baby Gap."

We didn't end up visiting my grandparents. We did, however, back Mom's Geo into a tree, because Jeremy, short though he was, could still twist around and try to beat the crap out of me all without removing his foot from the gas pedal. Not at all like I'd planned.

We also didn't get our phones back, nor were we allowed to go anywhere apart from school. That didn't end up sucking as much as I thought it would, because for the first time in a long time, my brother and I actually talked.

Jolene

barely remembered driving to the apartment, much less climbing the stairs to Dad's floor, but when my toes stopped inches from his door, reality jolted back.

He was there. He had to be. I'd barely seen him in months, and he was going to open the door and see me, talk to me.

And it was my birthday.

He'd gotten me a car.

With a card. Or a note.

Maybe it had said things.

Maybe it had said a lot of things.

Maybe Mom had read it, and that was why she'd burned it.

Maybe it just said "Happy Birthday."

Maybe it was just a card that he'd signed.

Maybe he hadn't even signed it.

Maybe.

Maybe not.

I didn't have my keys. So I knocked.

And he didn't answer.

I knocked again. And I kept knocking. Rap, rap, rap. Boom, boom, boom.

And then I was crying in the hallway.

And it was my birthday.

And he wasn't there.

He was never there. He'd probably never been there. No one ever was. No one wanted to be there.

Mrs. Cho was gone, and Cherry had been gone for longer than I'd realized.

My knuckles hurt, so I switched hands.

And then I stopped knocking on a door that would never open.

I turned until my back was to his apartment, and I slid down to the floor. So what if there had been a card or a note. So what. There'd been nothing—less than nothing—for so long, it wouldn't have mattered. Nothing he scrawled on a card for my birthday would undo the fact that I'd barely seen him since my last one. All of my insides squeezed tight, as memories from all those missed birthdays piled on top me. It was pathetic, and it didn't matter. And I had a car. That was great. Tons of sixteen-year-olds would love to get cars on their birthdays.

A tear splashed onto my cheek.

I could go anywhere, do anything.

Another tear, another splash.

It was my birthday and I was free.

And I cried.

The hallway made my eyeballs crawl. It had to have been designed intentionally ugly. The carpeting on the lower floors had been replaced during the past month, but Adam's dad hadn't gotten to our floor yet. It had the old forest green carpeting with tiny burgundy swirls everywhere. And it looked dirty. The carpet was packed with so many years of accumulated filth that it no longer matched the paint on the walls. And I'd been sitting on it for hours, even knowing that my dad would most likely never show up. Maybe especially knowing that he would never show up. He probably had a different place, a nicer place where he actually lived.

I turned my head with an indifference I didn't have to fake when I heard footsteps dragging up the stairs.

It wasn't Dad or Shelly or anyone I knew. It was a guy in his thirties with thinning blond hair and pale blue eyes. I vaguely remembered him from months ago when I'd been waiting for Adam so that we could build a snowman. He carried a bag of groceries in one arm and a bicycle helmet in the other.

I didn't scramble to my feet and try to rush past him. I didn't move at all.

"Hey," he said with slightly narrowed eyes. He'd stopped with one foot on the top step, the other still down behind him.

I didn't reply.

"Forget your keys?"

"Yeah, that's it." I turned back to the wall in front of me, staring at the ugly paint.

He finally fully ascended the stairs and walked toward a door one down and across from Adam's. He kept glancing at me as he shifted his helmet up under his arm and dug keys from his pocket. "You call somebody?"

"Nobody with keys is coming here."

"Then what are you doing?"

"I'm sitting."

He shook his head before he unlocked his door and let himself in. He was back a second later, sans bag and helmet. This time he walked right up to me. "Hey, so I'm thinking

I need to call somebody to come get you. Whose apartment is this anyway? Ex-boyfriend?"

I closed my eyes and breathed in deeply through my nose. "Sorry, guy, but I don't know you, so I'm not going to talk to you right now." I pulled out my phone and my shiny new car key and held them up for him to see. "I'm not stranded or anything, so feel free to go inside your apartment."

"It sounds like you know me."

"What?"

"My name," he said. "It's Guy. You just called me guy, and we met once before right in this hallway, so…"

I stared at him with my snottiest teenager face, but he didn't back away.

"What about you?"

"What about me?"

"What's your name?"

I didn't answer, but I saw his eyes flick to the number on the door above me and then back with a different question in his eyes. And I knew. "You've met Shelly."

His silence was answer enough.

I let my head tilt backward until it was resting against the door. "Great," I said. "Then you probably know that my mom's a bitch, I'm an ungrateful brat, and my dad is the long-suffering saint who tirelessly puts up with us. Did she read you the full transcripts from the divorce hearing, or is she saving that for when she knows you better, so, like, the second time she sees you?"

"Whoa," he said, holding up a hand. "I haven't been here much since I moved in. I've spoken to… What was her name? Shelly? I've talked to her maybe a couple times passing in the halls, but I don't know anything about anything."

It was impossible to tell if he was lying or not, but it was just another thing that didn't matter. "Whatever. Look, I don't really care what you think of me." He still didn't move. He was just standing there a few feet from me. "Are you going to leave or what?"

"Are you?"

"No. I'm fine. I like being exactly where I am. When I want to leave, I'll get into my car and go."

"And when is that going be?"

I scowled at him. "What, are you planning a party out here? Go back into your apartment and quit hulking over me."

"Sorry," he said. "But you're depressing the hell out of me sitting here. Why don't you come inside with me until you feel like going somewhere that isn't the hallway?"

"Pass," I said. "You're starting to sound super creepy, Guy. In fact, I'm pretty sure Shelly referred to you as the creepy guy from down the hall. And anyway, what are you, thirty-five? Today is my sixteenth birthday. I'm so illegal it's not funny."

He laughed like I hadn't just insinuated that he was a pedo. "For the record, I'm twenty-eight. But good to know I look midthirties."

I didn't apologize.

After a good thirty seconds of silence, he left. He walked into his apartment without closing the door, and a second later he was back, leaning against the frame with a carton of ice cream in one hand and a spoon in the other. I watched him eat several bites, and he watched me watch him.

"Want some?"

I made a face and went back to watching my wall. Though I did want some. I hadn't eaten all day, and the sight of food, even ice cream when I was chilled through from sitting on thin carpet for hours, looked really good. "Are you seriously doing this right now?"

"It's really good ice cream. It's got candy bars chopped up in it."

"Why do you care?"

He didn't answer, just continued eating. And it suddenly seemed like the best offer I'd had all day, so I stood up, leaving the door to Dad's empty apartment behind me, and literally took candy from a stranger.

I came to a dead halt the second I stepped into his apartment. My eyes went so wide that I'd swear my eyelashes passed my eyebrows. Like a magnet, I flew to the nearest shelf in front of me and started dragging my hands down row after row of movies. Every wall in the apartment was lined with them. Thousands.

I let out a laugh.

"Yeah, occupational hazard," Guy said, coming up behind me. "I'm a film critic and—"

I tore my eyes from the shelves and spun to find him right behind me. "*You're* the film critic?"

"I'm *a* film critic. *The* film critic? That's got to be Roger Ebert."

"No, I mean..." My eyes widened impossibly farther. "I've been waiting to meet you. I heard that a film critic moved in and... I love movies."

"Yeah?" Guy said, his lips curving up. "Guess it's a good thing we found each other."

ADAM

My arm went numb all the way down to my fingertips before pain crashed back up, all courtesy of the dead-arm Jeremy just gave me. The worst part was that I couldn't hit him back. It was all part of the moronic agreement we'd reached to help reunite our family.

The first thing I had to do was stop being a jerk to Dad. Anytime I started, or Jeremy perceived that I was starting, he got a free shot.

Jeremy grinned at me and readied his fist for the next hit.

I just stood there. Outside Dad's apartment. When I didn't have to be there. It wasn't a holiday or special occasion. It was a Wednesday. It was nothing. Which was why Jeremy said we should visit him. *We.*

Mom had looked like we'd asked to shove her into a small, dark box filled with spiders suspended from the top of a sky-scraper. There it was, all her fears rolled into one: her sons wanted to leave her. She managed to smile and cry at the same time. She wanted us to go, but clung to our shirts a little too strenuously to really sell it.

But we'd gone. We were there; Jeremy was letting us in with his key, while I tried to force my jaw to unlock. It was harder than I'd thought. All I had to do was speak first, say hi or anything before Dad could. That was what Jeremy and I had agreed on in the car.

But it wouldn't come, that tiniest of almost all words. I wasn't even especially mad that day. Yeah, Mom had started crying when we left, which had made me want to kick Dad in the nuts, but then Jeremy had stopped the car and run back to hug her on the steps. It was nice. It was the kind of thing I would have thought of, if I hadn't been so preoccupied with having to choke out impromptu civility with Dad.

Greg would have done it.

I looked at Jeremy again. The grin was gone. I could see him pleading with his eyes as I stood in front of Dad. *We need this.* They *need this.* One word.

"Hi."

I never knew a word could physically hurt, but that one did. It clawed up my insides so that every breath after felt raw. But I did it. Jeremy's whole body relaxed, and he jumped right in, taking over the burden of the conversation both for me and Dad, who looked as stunned by my greeting as by our unscheduled arrival.

Seeing Dad, I believed what Jeremy had said about him, which made me realize that I hadn't before. Dad wasn't doing well; he just wore a better mask around us than Mom did. But that day, he hadn't had time to disguise his red eyes or hide the photos he'd been looking at.

It was microscopically easier after that.

He hugged Jeremy and looked back and forth between us. "No, of course I'm glad you're here. I just didn't know you were coming."

That was obvious, given the coat he'd been shrugging into when we'd come in and the keys in his hand.

"If you're going to grab food, I could eat." Jeremy looked to me to make a similar statement, and though it hurt as much as my greeting, I nodded.

"Food sounds good."

Dad looked pained. He kept glancing at the door, then back again at us. "Yeah, I was gonna eat...after."

Something vile squirmed in my gut and my entire body clenched. "He has a date." I spit the words at my father and Jeremy looked almost as disgusted as I did before denials started pouring from Dad.

"What? No. *Never.*"

But I didn't believe him, and Jeremy wasn't rushing to his defense either.

"I've been going to a place and—" His face contorted a little. "Look, come with me, all right? I'll show you."

Jeremy and I hesitated, but when Dad moved into the hall, my brother gave me a look, and we followed.

"Church?" Jeremy said, drawing his brows together as we walked up the steps to a large old redbrick Byzantine-inspired building with a sign that read Tenth Presbyterian Church. I shared my brother's frown. Church wasn't a new thing for our family. We—Jeremy and I—went every Sunday we were with Mom to the same church we'd been baptized in as babies. We hadn't gone with Dad during his weekends yet, because he'd said he was still trying to find the right one—not that I'd ever seen him looking. If he'd found one, then why not say so? Why drag us outside in the freezing cold as night fell?

Dad walked forward and opened one of the doors for us to go inside.

There were massive marble columns, floor-to-ceiling stained

glass windows, and rows and rows of carved wooden pews inside, both on the ground floor and in balconies that lined the sides of the sanctuary. The building appeared to be empty.

Dad led us down a narrow, steep staircase and through a hall that branched off in several directions before we stopped in front of the last room on the left. Inside, a group of people had arranged themselves in a circle of chairs in the center of the room.

I knew what this was, though I'd never been to one before. A support group.

Dad greeted a few people and introduced Jeremy and me as his sons before directing us to grab a few more folding chairs. Jeremy moved right away, and the people already sitting began to move back and make room for us, but I stayed in the doorway. I flinched when Dad put a hand on my shoulder.

"Okay." He quickly drew his hand back. "Right. Well, this is where I've been going." Dad lowered his head along with his voice. "These are all people who've lost someone."

My face felt hot, and I couldn't seem to inhale enough air. I closed my eyes, not wanting to see any of their faces. "Since when?" I asked. I didn't know what exactly was bothering me. The fact that he was in a support group, or that he hadn't told us about it.

"A while," he said. "First back home, and then when I moved out, I found this one."

I took a step back into the hall. "Does Mom know?"

Dad's hands were in his coat pockets, and it seemed to take everything he had to hold himself back from me. "I wanted her to come, but she..." He shook his head. "I needed to talk about it, to be able to talk about what happened—about losing my son." His eyes were wet, but he laughed a little. "Sometimes I want to talk about the stupid stuff he did and how—" the laughter turned hoarse as suddenly as it had appeared "—I wish he was still here to do more. I need to talk about being angry at God for taking him from me and being grateful that He gave him to me for all the years that He did. I know your mom needs that, too, and I wish…" His voice caught, and we both knew he couldn't say more.

My chin quivered before I could stop it, but when Dad took a step toward me, I retreated farther into the hall.

At Greg's grave, he'd been asking Mom to come here with him. I knew it without him having to tell me. She'd said no. And he was standing in front of me, silently asking me the same question.

I didn't know what to do, and ultimately Dad didn't make me decide. He went back inside and took one of the two empty seats beside Jeremy, and I stood in the hallway.

I listened to them talk, the tear-filled stories they told and the watery laughter that hit me in the gut.

Jeremy didn't say anything, but Dad told a story about Greg, one that I'd never heard, about him peeing in our cat box once during a thunderstorm because Mom was taking a shower in the only working bathroom. Greg had been so impressed with himself for thinking of that solution that he'd bragged to Dad about it, not realizing that the cats would—and did—pee everywhere but in the cat box after that.

Dad and Jeremy and I laughed, but I knew Mom wouldn't have. She'd have cried, because she still held her grief so tight that none of her memories—or ours—made her happy.

Back at Dad's apartment, Jeremy didn't dead-arm me when I said it was time we headed home. Instead, he gave me a small smile and nod.

I didn't hug Dad, but I said one word. Without any prompting or threat of physical pain from my brother.

"Bye."

Jolene

I texted Adam a picture of my license along with a message for him to suck it, and he texted back a picture of his middle finger. I wonder what he would have sent if I'd taken a picture of my Lexus? Not that I had the option anymore. I got to drive it only that one day. It was gone by the time I woke up Wednesday morning and learned that Mom's lawyers had made Dad take it back.

If Dad wondered why I'd never sent a thank-you note, it never got back to me.

Adam texted back with a picture of a bike and the word Jealous?

A smile I didn't know I had in me crept onto my face. I hadn't heard from Adam in a few days—long, empty days. I'd tried texting him after he was due back from his grandparents, but his mom had responded and explained that Adam was grounded until Thursday. Perfect Adam got in trouble? I was so curious about what he'd done that I almost asked her. But I liked thinking that his mom liked me, or liked a pho-

tographic version of me. I didn't want to wreck that by coming off as nosy and rude, even though I was nosy and rude.

But he was finally texting me back.

Adam:

> I can't believe I had to wait this
> long to see your license.

Jolene:

> And I'm dying to know what you
> did to get grounded for three
> days. Chew with your mouth
> open? Forget to say thank you?
> Get less than 105 percent on an
> extra credit assignment?

Jolene:

> Hey, was it a self-inflicted
> grounding? I'm betting it was.

Adam:

> I got into a fistfight with my
> brother while he was driving to
> my grandparents' house and we
> crashed my mom's car.

Jolene:

> You tore the tag off a mattress, didn't you?

Adam:

> You think I'm kidding?

Jolene:

> I know you're kidding.

Adam sent a picture of a car with the back smashed in.

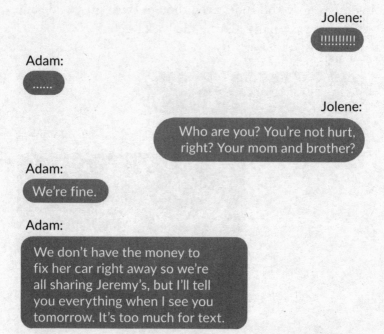

Jolene:

!!!!!!!!!!

Adam:

......

Jolene:

Who are you? You're not hurt, right? Your mom and brother?

Adam:

We're fine.

Adam:

We don't have the money to fix her car right away so we're all sharing Jeremy's, but I'll tell you everything when I see you tomorrow. It's too much for text.

I ran into my bathroom and blasted my hairdryer in my face while letting my jaw go slack. You couldn't see the hairdryer in the picture I snapped with my phone, it looked like I was so stunned my hair was literally blown back. I sent the picture.

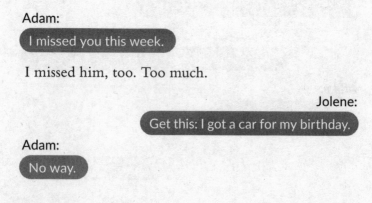

Adam:

I missed you this week.

I missed him, too. Too much.

Jolene:

Get this: I got a car for my birthday.

Adam:

No way.

Jolene:

Yep, and my mom let me keep it for about twelve hours before her lawyers motioned to have a forensic accountant go through my dad's finances to find the money he spent on it.

Adam:

I want you to be kidding.

Jolene:

But you know I'm not.

Adam:

At least tell me you got to drive it first.

My thumbs hovered over my phone. I wanted to break out in hives thinking about the hours I'd wasted sitting outside my dad's apartment. I knew what Adam would say—or text—if I told him the truth. It'd be my name followed by a single period. Pity was the last thing I wanted, especially since the night had turned out okay hanging out with Guy, or more specific, hanging out with Guy's movie collection. But it wasn't like I could tell Adam one thing without the other.

Jolene:

I starred in a shot-for-shot remake of Easy Rider, but in a Lexus instead of on a motorcycle.

Adam:

Is that a road trip movie?

Jolene:

Wow.

Adam:

> So I should probably stop admitting that I haven't heard of half the movies you talk about?

Jolene:

> Probably. Want to hang out?

Adam:

> Don't we always?

Jolene:

> I mean today.

It was already Thursday, so there was only one more day until we'd be at the apartment together, but those stretches between seeing him were feeling longer and longer to me lately.

Adam:

> Did the picture of my bike not come through? I could leave now and still not get there before the weekend.

Jolene:

> I could take my mom's car.

Adam:

> Do you mean take or borrow?

Jolene:

> Well, I plan to hot-wire it, so...

Adam:

> I want to believe you know how to do that so you can teach me.

Jolene:

> Haven't you gotten in enough trouble lately?

Adam:

But now I've developed a taste for it. Seriously, do you know how?

Jolene:

I lived a life of crime before I met you. I'll never fully leave that part of me behind.

Adam:

So your dad's a mob boss?

Jolene:

Yes, and I'm a mob princess. They call me Jolene the spleen remover.

Adam:

That's terrible.

Jolene:

The only other thing I could think of is Mean Jolene.

Adam:

Those are both terrible.

Jolene:

Now you see why I had to leave the life. So, am I hot-wiring my mom's car?

Adam:

I can't tonight. I've got this thing with my mom.

Jolene:

What kind of thing?

Adam:

Just a thing.

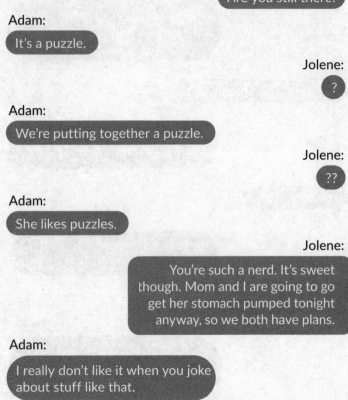

Jolene:

An embarrassing thing?

Jolene:

Are you still there?

Adam:

It's a puzzle.

Jolene:

?

Adam:

We're putting together a puzzle.

Jolene:

??

Adam:

She likes puzzles.

Jolene:

You're such a nerd. It's sweet though. Mom and I are going to go get her stomach pumped tonight anyway, so we both have plans.

Adam:

I really don't like it when you joke about stuff like that.

I typed out **You think I'm kidding?** but I deleted it before sending. Mom and I had done that before, but not in a long time. She'd actually been drinking less since she and Tom broke up. I didn't know if he'd realized that his grand plans to become a kept man were never gonna happen, or if she decided to learn her own lesson and find someone more capable of getting her what she wanted. Whatever that was.

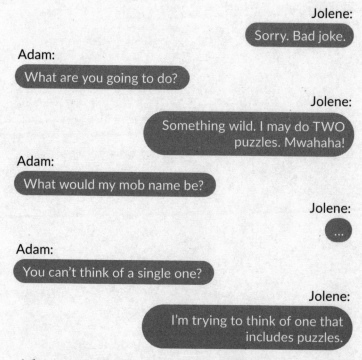

Jolene:

Sorry. Bad joke.

Adam:

What are you going to do?

Jolene:

Something wild. I may do TWO puzzles. Mwahaha!

Adam:

What would my mob name be?

Jolene:

...

Adam:

You can't think of a single one?

Jolene:

I'm trying to think of one that includes puzzles.

Adam resent the picture of his middle finger.

TENTH WEEKEND

January 29–31

Jolene

Adam didn't show up.

I always got to the apartment before him, thanks to the militant insistence of Dad's lawyer, and I'd been there for thirty minutes already. Apart from when he and Jeremy got a flat tire—and he'd texted me to say he was running late that time—he'd never been this late.

I chewed on my nails and peered through the glass door in the lobby. It was new, as was the frame, and it didn't shake like it was going shatter during a snowstorm anymore. Glancing down, I took in the fact that the old, disgusting carpet was gone, too, replaced by long rectangular tiles laid in a herringbone pattern leading directly to the stairs. Adam's dad had been busy. All the baseboards and molding were new, too. Everywhere I looked, things were shiny and fresh. Except for the out-of-order sign on the elevator. It was nice to know Adam's dad couldn't fix everything.

As my gaze traveled around the lobby and I thought about the steadily increasing improvements that were being made throughout the building, a strangling panic began to wrap itself around me.

I pushed open the glass door and, when I was outside, I

turned to look at the building, feeling that panic constrict from my belly to my chest. Stains were gone, broken windows replaced, and the loose stones had been secured with new mortar. The concrete steps leading up to the entrance had even been repoured. It wasn't all perfect—like the broken elevator inside, there were still signs of the decades of neglect the building had endured, but I almost couldn't see them.

Adam's dad had done so much since moving in. I was sure the building owner was thrilled with the progress, but how thrilled would he be to keep letting Adam's dad stay rent-free in a building that no longer needed to be restored? What then? Adam told me his family didn't have a ton of money, not enough to pay for an apartment in the city *and* the mortgage on a house in the country. They wouldn't stay.

Adam would leave.

I spun away from the building, trying to draw air into lungs that had been squeezed shut.

Why couldn't Adam's dad slow down? Take his time? Why couldn't he take up drinking like my mom had following her divorce?

The pressure bore down tight around my head and coiled through my temples. He hadn't done that because Adam's parents weren't mine. There were no Shellys or Toms or teams of frothing lawyers. There were no hastily scrawled notes waiting to greet Adam and Jeremy when they showed up here, and there was an actual person hurrying down porch steps to hug and welcome them back when they came home.

Sorrow separated his family, not loathing, and if Adam's dad ever figured out how to fix the kind of broken that his family was... With a shudder that was more a convulsion, I realized that, for all I knew, he already had.

Adam had texted me about the grief group his dad had taken them to when he and Jeremy visited on Wednesday. Not on a weekend. Not when they had to. They were starting to talk, first Adam and Jeremy, then Adam and their dad… How much longer before his mom was in that picture, too? How much longer before the thing that had divided them brought them back together?

I wanted to be a better person, one who could be happy for Adam as I looked ahead to a time when the broken pieces of his life would mend, but I wasn't a better person. I was me, and I was afraid of losing the one thing I had left.

Already he wasn't here when he was supposed to be, and there wasn't a blizzard raging outside that I could blame.

I checked the time on my phone, hope freeing all my limbs when I saw an unread text from him from nearly an hour before.

Adam:

> My mom dropped us off early since we only have Jeremy's car right now. Come to my apartment when you get here.

Adam's dad opened the door to his apartment when I knocked. He wore the same friendly expression Adam defaulted to. "Jolene, hi."

I hadn't seen his dad since that day he'd found Adam and me playing cards, so I was thrown that he remembered my name.

I shifted my feet and felt the urge to lower my gaze. "Um, yeah, hi." I wanted to make fun of myself for the awkwardness controlling my voice and body. "Is Adam here?"

Behind his dad, Adam peeked his head out from his room and the moment he saw me, he smiled. Butterflies filled my stomach and I took a step back. He was the only person who unsettled me like that. "Hey. I was just coming to get you." Then his face fell and he looked first to his brother, who widened his eyes significantly in return, and then his dad. "I mean, I was going to make sure you got here okay, but

then, I, um… I'm going to grab something to eat with…"
He eyed his brother and dad again.

Oh.

Right.

The butterflies fled, a slick nausea flooded my stomach
in their absence.

It was too fast. Too soon.

I needed to turn around and leave before I did something
that'd be worse than getting sick.

"Oh yeah. Sure. That's fine. I'll catch you later." And
then, somehow, I was turning and stepping into the hall
with no earthly idea where to go. The thought of hiding in
my room all weekend made me feel so alone that my eyes
stung. Where had I gone before Adam?

"Why don't you come with us?"

I froze.

The invitation wasn't shocking in and of itself. It was the
person who'd made it.

Adam's dad.

Somehow that made my eyes sting more. I rapidly blinked
the sensation away before turning to face them.

"What?" Jeremy's reaction was the one I'd been expecting. He stared at his dad looking somewhat put out. I'd also
been prepared for the shocked way Adam's mouth fell open.
But their dad… I knew he'd invited me only to try to get
Adam to thaw toward him, but I couldn't understand why
he was looking at *me*. Worse, the smile on his face, the one
that was nearly identical to Adam's a moment before, was
focused directly on me without so much as a glance at the
audience he had to have been playing for.

"Sure. You gotta eat, right? I know a good cheesesteak
place around the corner. And I like to try to get to know
the people who are important to my sons."

I blinked. "I—"

"See, Dad," Jeremy said. "She's not hungry."

I really didn't like Adam's brother, but I was grateful for his presence and general turdness that day. It was familiar and normal, and I clung to it.

"If you mean Sonny's, I'm in."

Jeremy groaned and his dad laughed. Adam still hadn't closed his mouth.

Jeremy brushed past all of us, checking his brother in the shoulder. They exchanged a look that seemed to communicate volumes. "Whatever. Whoever is going, let's go."

We all went.

"How uncomfortable should I expect this to be?" I asked Adam as we trailed behind in the hallway. "Jeremy's always been *super* subtle, but I have picked up on the fact that he might not love having me around."

Instead of laughing like I'd wanted, Adam locked his jaw. "If he pulls any more of that tonight, I'll shove his cheesesteak down his throat."

I clasped my hands under my chin. "My hero." Then I pulled a face and shoved Adam ahead of me.

Halfway down, we ran into Guy. I smiled, getting ready to introduce him and Adam even if that meant giving Adam a massively abridged version of the events surrounding how I'd met Guy. But then Guy did something weird—or, maybe not weird, just unexpected. He completely ignored me.

My smile slipped, making me feel embarrassed that it had ever been there at all.

"Hey, Paul. How's it going?" Guy said to Adam's dad.

"Good. Just heading out to dinner. You haven't met my sons. This is Jeremy and Adam. And this is Adam's friend Jolene. Everyone, this is Guy from across the hall. Adam, Guy is the film critic I was telling you about."

Adam brightened. "That's so cool. Jolene is really into movies, too." He glanced at me as if expecting me to take over the conversation, but before I could say anything, Guy gave us each a dismissive nod, acted like he'd never met me before, and turned back to Adam's dad. "Hey, did I hear you're getting the elevator fixed this month?"

They went on like that for several minutes, having a totally normal conversation about totally normal things. There wasn't a single thing wrong with what they said, but each word jostled nauseatingly in my stomach.

Seeing Guy talking to Adam's dad like they were friends—peers—was super weird. He shouldn't be friends with my friend's dad, but watching him in that stairwell made it obvious that he was. Which in turn made it very obvious that *we* weren't friends, no matter what I'd thought the other night.

We'd spent my sixteenth birthday together, eaten a carton of ice cream, then shared a Hawaiian pizza, and talked about movies. Guy had written reviews for tons of magazines and websites. I hadn't worked up to mentioning the film program or asking him to write a letter of recommendation for my application, but he'd been cool on the whole and hadn't peppered me with invasive questions about why I'd been crying when he found me. I'd thought we'd had fun, and considering how not fun my birthday had started, that was saying something.

It wasn't like I'd been down in the lobby waiting for a glimpse of him like I did with Adam or anything, but a smile? An acknowledgment of any kind that we weren't perfect strangers? I'd kind of expected that.

His ignoring me just felt off.

Jeremy settled against the wall and crossed his arms, impatience clear on his face.

"One of yours is ready to eat," Guy said, nodding at Jeremy. "Looks like you've got your hands full with all these kids, so I'll leave you to it."

Guy didn't glance at me at all, and when Adam asked me why I hadn't said more to Guy considering he was the film critic I'd been wanting to meet for months, all I did was shrug.

ADAM

The cheesesteak place was small, but fortunately not packed. We ordered, then claimed one of the round tables in the corner. The place smelled enticingly like roasted meat, and my mouth was watering before I could unwrap my cheesesteak.

I watched Dad as he asked Jolene a few polite questions. I knew he wanted to show me that he cared about what I cared about, that he was trying. It was kind of working. Ever since I'd found out that he had in fact been trying with Mom, at least a little, it had become harder to keep my anger focused on him alone.

Plus, I liked seeing him with Jolene. I liked seeing him talk to her, show her that another person was interested in what she had to say even when her answers were…blunt.

"You know, I don't think I've met your dad yet. What does he do?"

"Commercial real estate."

"Oh." Dad let his voice convey that he was impressed. "Guess that's why we don't see much of him."

Jolene opened her mouth, but I pressed my foot down on top of hers to get her attention and subtly shook my head.

Jolene didn't understand that my dad was the kind of dad who wouldn't be able to hear that she hadn't seen her dad in months and not do something about it. He'd get involved, and neither of us would thank him for the outcome.

"And what does your mom do?"

"Alimony," Jolene said, then caught my pained expression and gave me a what-did-I-say look before adding, "I mean, I guess she's a stay-at-home mom?"

"That's kind of like every job at once."

"Ah," Jolene said with a touch more sarcasm than I thought was necessary.

"She must miss you a lot when you're over here."

Jolene choked on her soda. "Yeah. Probably why she spends so much time at the gym. Sometimes I think she'd live there if she could. Her goal this year is to get her body fat down to 21 percent."

Dad frowned but tried to hide it. "Is that for a weight lifting competition or something?"

"Nope, that's for an I'll-show-him-I'm-still-hot kind of thing, since my dad left her for his twenty-six-year-old personal trainer." Jolene gave me a thumbs-up under the table to indicate how well she thought she was handling my dad's questions.

I kind of wanted to kiss her.

Well, I always wanted to kiss her, but I wanted to more than usual in that moment.

When Dad excused himself to go to the bathroom, I seriously thought about it.

"Shelly?" Jeremy finally decided to stop scowling long enough to join the conversation. "She's only twenty-six?"

I threw a curly fry at his head. "Idiot. Don't you have a thing going with Erica?"

Jolene's hand froze with a fry midway to her mouth. "No way, you're dating Erica now? Like for real, not just to mess with Adam?"

My brother's skin did its best impression of ketchup, and
I felt my own face turning red. Was that what I looked like
when I blushed? And Jolene claimed she thought that was *cute*?

Jeremy shot a pleading glance at me, but I grinned and
shook my head. He was overdue for a little squirming.

Watching us, Jolene's laughter bubbled up out of her as
she leaned toward him. "You have to tell me how that happened." She nudged my shoulder with hers. "Tell me you're
not made of questions right now?"

I didn't care nearly as much as she did, but I propped my
forearms on the table. "Yeah, Jer, and I'd make it quick if
you want to finish before Dad gets back."

"There's nothing to tell." Jeremy reached for the basket
of fries, but Jolene hooked a finger around it and slid it out
of reach.

"But I mean, she had to have hated you by association.
And, offense intended, you can be a massive turd, like, *all* of
the time." She popped a few fries into her mouth.

His ears were the only part of him that were still red and
I was guessing that was due to annoyance rather than embarrassment. I figured he was about to mouth off and prove
her point but he surprised me.

"Cut me some slack. He—" Jeremy flicked his gaze at me
"—was supposed to be spending time with our dad, and he
was off with you from the first day. Was I a turd to you?"
He wobbled his head from side to side. "I could have been
nicer, and I was considering it before he got together with
Erica and was still off with you the whole time we were here.
That's how she started talking to me, by the way. We were
both pissed at him—and you by extension."

"For the record, you were the king of turds." Jolene
nudged the fry basket back toward him. "But I get that I
didn't exactly make things easier for you here. And the Erica
thing was not awesome."

Jeremy studied her. She studied him back. He took a fry.

"So you literally sat next to her at play rehearsal and said, what? We both think Adam is a tool?"

"Hey," I said. "I'm right here." Neither of them glanced at me.

Jeremy took another fry. "Basically."

"And whose idea was it to go to the dance together?" she asked.

Jeremy grinned. "Mine. Took a little convincing, but she came around."

"Big-time turd move," Jolene said, but she was smiling, too.

"Worked out though. Turns out we have other stuff in common than wanting to knock him out most of the time."

"Still here," I said, though once again they ignored me.

"Good for you," Jolene said to my brother and I could tell she meant it. "Though I feel sorry for her, since she obviously traded down."

My heart puffed up at that comment while Jeremy threw back his head and laughed. "I tell you what. Give my brother a little breathing room over here, and I'll be moderately less of a turd to you."

Jolene sat back in her chair and one side of her mouth lifted. "Deal."

They were still smiling when Dad came back.

"What'd I miss?"

"Um. These are really good," Jolene said, picking up her cheesesteak. "Thanks for letting me tag along."

I could see the automatic response form on Dad's lips before he squashed it, and I also saw Jolene grow uncomfortable. She set her half-eaten cheesesteak on the table and spent a solid minute wiping her hands clean on a napkin.

He'd been going to say *anytime*, except he didn't mean anytime. If we'd been back home with Mom, he'd have gladly offered Jolene a seat at our dining room table whenever she wanted it. But we weren't sitting around the table he and Mom had restored on their honeymoon. We were in a greasy fast-food place miles away.

That was Dad's version of trying. He'd asked Mom to do something she wasn't ready to do, but instead of staying and helping her get to that place with him, he'd cut and run.

Somewhere between talking to Jeremy and witnessing Dad at that support group, I'd started to forget that fact. Dad had just given me a huge reminder.

As the conversation died around us, my high from the newly minted truce between Jeremy and Jolene went with it. I found myself glaring at him. I felt Jeremy's eyes boring into me, and I could practically hear him saying, *Not the plan, bro.* I turned to Jolene and stood up.

"Let's go."

Jolene looked from me to Dad as he said, "Go where?"

"Out. I don't know."

To Jolene, Dad said, "We'd love to have you join us for dinner again sometime, but I think we need to spend time together as a family tonight."

"What. Family?" I said, biting off each word. "Mom didn't get out of the car when she dropped us off, and I didn't see you waiting on the curb."

Wrong. Wrong thing to say. Jeremy tossed the rest of his sandwich on his plate and rolled his eyes at me.

Dad looked at me. "Sit down. Now." His voice was low so as not to carry to the surrounding tables, but a few people were looking anyway.

Heat rushed to my face. Jeremy was glancing back and forth between Dad and me like he wasn't sure what I was going to do, if I really was going to try to stare down our father. *Try* being the operative word, because we both knew how well that would turn out.

Jolene made things both better and worse. Her presence

gave me the guts to consider holding my ground, but she was also the reason I sat back down. Watching Dad drag me out of a restaurant by the collar was not the cool image I cared to present her with. And Dad's expression said he'd do it. I sat down while it was still my decision to do so. At least Dad gave me that.

We finished our awkward dinner in silence. When we returned to the apartment, we trailed single file back up the stairs. Jolene squeezed my hand briefly as she passed my door.

"I'll call you later," I told her.

"Not this weekend," Dad said. "If he can't talk to me with respect, he's not talking to anyone else," he added to Jolene.

Our standoff in the hall was significantly longer than the one at the restaurant, but the result was the same. I caved, he won, and I left Jolene in the hallway.

"This ends right now." Dad didn't waste any time once he got that door shut. "Do you hear me?"

"Yeah, I hear you." I was standing toe-to-toe with him, saying the words he wanted to hear but not fooling either of us that I was capitulating.

I'd broached new territory by confronting him in public. I'd felt kind of brilliant for standing up to him instead of only shutting him out, but that feeling had withered quickly. He hadn't been impressed or intimidated by my challenge. He'd gotten mad—really mad.

Jeremy, who normally considered me getting chewed out to be the finest spectator sport ever invented, disappeared into Dad's room and shut the door. I was going to have to deal with him, too, and explain why I couldn't make it two hours before relapsing into my old hostility even after we'd agreed it was the wrong move. It had *felt* like the right move, standing up for Jolene when no one else did. But Dad wouldn't know that, and it wasn't an excuse.

"You don't get to call the shots over here. If you try to

pull anything like that again—" He lost his words. "It's not happening. You can hate me, you can think whatever you want, but you are going to quit the isolationist act right now. I'm not putting up with any more of the attitude or the silent treatment. That room—" he pointed to my bedroom "—is for sleeping. You don't hide in there the second you arrive and stay in there the whole weekend. You don't blow off your brother and me to hang out with anyone else either."

His anger abated for a moment. "I get that that girl might not have a lot of people in her life that care about her, and I'm glad you do, but..." His anger built back up. "I'm done letting you dictate how things go. I miss my son." Somehow that last statement was the angriest of all. "I mean, what *is* this? I know you're mad about your mom and me—and you'd better not be pulling any of this with her—"

"I'm not."

"—but you need to get over that and get on board with reality right quick. *This* is your reality. Right here. And it's mine and Jeremy's and your mom's, too. This is what we have. Not forever, I promise you that, but you're making it harder for everyone, yourself included. If you could try—"

"Like you're trying? It's not enough, Dad. Every weekend that she's there and we're here—" and I made sure he knew I was talking about more than Jeremy and me "—it's not enough." I wanted him to listen to what he was saying and realize his words were just as true for him as they were for me. I was tired of it. All of it. That was why I'd agreed to try with Dad. But it was a lot harder than I'd thought. I had months of resentment built up, and I couldn't make it go away in one night. "Try harder."

Of all the stuff I'd said that night, those two words seemed to hurt him the most.

I went to my room without another word.

Jolene

Adam's dad had found his spine at the cheesesteak place, and he wasn't losing it anytime soon. The "family night" he referred to wouldn't be fun for either of them. Either way, we'd said goodbye, and I lingered in the hallway, eyeing the door to Dad's apartment like it was Pandora's box and if I opened it, all the evil in the world would come rushing out.

Or, you know, Shelly.

"What is it with you and hallways?"

I turned my head and there was Guy, casual as could be, leaning against his doorframe. "Me?" I asked. "Are you talking to me? I thought we'd moved on to barely nodding at each other in stairways."

"Come on. Don't be mad about that. You were heading out. I figured you wouldn't want me explaining that you spent your birthday with me after I found you crying alone out here."

The memory of that night stung. "So you ignored me for my benefit? Thank you for that. Let me repay you." I turned and walked down the hall—away from Dad's apartment. I made it only a few steps when I slowed. That direction didn't hold many more options for me than the other one did.

"I wasn't ignoring you. I didn't want to embarrass you in front of your boyfriend."

"Adam's not my boyfriend."

"Whatever you say, Jolene." Then he stepped to the side, leaving the door to his apartment wide-open. "You want to come in or...?" His gaze slid past me to rest on the door to Dad's apartment.

What I wanted was to hang out with Adam, but that door had literally been shut in my face. My other option wasn't an option at all. And Guy knew that.

It would have been awkward to explain how Guy and I had met. Plus, Adam's dad might have gotten the wrong idea, and it wasn't like I needed to give him another reason to dislike me. Adam might have gotten the wrong idea, too, and I definitely didn't need that.

Sometimes, when I thought about it, *I* got the wrong idea. Even though Guy hadn't done anything besides feed me and listen to me. He hadn't tried to touch me or anything. The whole thing was innocent. And I needed his help if I was going to submit my application for the film program. Still, it nagged at me that I had to mentally tell myself that it was okay for us to hang out.

"Yeah, I'm coming."

We ended up watching a movie. It was an old black-and-white film that didn't make a lot of sense to me. Guy loved it. He kept commenting on the brilliance of a camera angle, or a line of dialogue that I had to admit was impressive. He wanted me to watch another movie after that, and when I said sure, he pushed himself off the couch by putting one hand on the armrest and the other on my knee. The touch lasted like two seconds tops. He didn't look at me or let his hand linger or anything. But I still jumped a little. I mentally shook myself, grateful he hadn't noticed my reaction, as Guy busied himself switching the movies.

Remote in hand, Guy joined me back on the couch, where I was still sitting rather stiffly despite telling myself to relax. "Cold?"

I shook my head.

"You look cold." His upper body leaned over mine, against mine, and my breath strangled in my throat. Guy didn't pull back. He turned his head and flicked his eyebrows up at me. "I'm just grabbing you the throw." He drew my gaze to a fuzzy gray blanket that I hadn't noticed. He was already fisting it in his hand when I looked, had been since the second he leaned—not over me, but past me. I tried to shrink back into the cushion, worried that he'd suggest I leave because I kept freaking out over nothing. But he didn't.

He dropped the throw, and his hand sank into the cushion by my thigh. He was still leaning across me, so we were face-to-face when I looked up. "Jolene. You don't have to be scared around me. I have an idea of what your life is like. I get it, okay?" He shifted, and my leg rocked against his wrist. "I know what it's like to feel like no one wants you, like you don't belong anywhere. You don't have to feel like that. I don't care what's going on out there." He jerked his head toward the hall. "It never gets past that door. You can always come here. Do you believe that?"

No. It was stupid. He was trying to force a bonding moment between us. He was being so serious, like I was fragile or something. He barely knew me. I belonged everywhere. Wherever I wanted to be.

He stayed just as close to me, but I stopped worrying about it. He was acting concerned about me, which, maybe he was. Maybe I'd given him reason to be, considering my birthday meltdown. He didn't know that had been a onetime thing. A weird convergence of events that had erupted in a never-to-be-repeated way. But the concerned look on Guy's face, and the way he'd lifted one hand to my shoulder and rubbed tiny circles on it with his thumb, made me realize he wasn't going to take my word for it. He'd been nice, or what passed for nice to me, and even though I was growing uncomfortable, it would make him uncomfortable if I said anything; that was the last thing I wanted.

"You're offering your apartment as a neutral zone. Got it." Then I pointed toward the TV. "We should probably start the movie though, before it gets too late."

"Right," Guy said. "Wouldn't want you to miss bed check." He tried to soften the sting of his words by smiling, but I regretted sharing some details with him the other night when I hadn't had my usual filter on. I'd told him plenty. He knew no one was going to come check on me.

I shrugged his hand off my shoulder.

"Hey, hey." He sighed, and his breath ruffled my hair. "That wasn't directed at you, okay? People should care enough about you to wonder where you are. That's all I meant."

"Sure, fine, but can we please watch the movie now?"

He relented, eventually, after pulling the almost forgotten throw over me, then he left one arm across the back of the couch.

I had the weirdest thought while the opening credits started. There I was with a near stranger, and he was taking better care of me than my parents. My own dad didn't even know where I was. He didn't care, so long as he kept me away from Mom for the exact same window of time every month. And she was no better.

Guy had to wake me up when the movie ended. His arm

had slid around my back, because I'd slumped onto him. He said he didn't mind, and I got the sense that he was telling the truth. Nothing I'd done had bothered him. Maybe he really was a nice guy.

I didn't stiffen when he hugged me at the door. I was starting to get used to the fact that he was a touchy-feely kind of guy.

"So," he said, still in mid-hug. "Next time I run into you with a bunch of people, what do you want me to say?"

"*Hi* usually works."

"Is that it?"

I pulled free from his hug easily. He was talking about more than proper greeting etiquette. It made my skin prickle uncomfortably that this was something we had to have a conversation about. "What do you think?"

Guy looked me straight in the eye before answering. "I think that there are lots of different kinds of people with lots of different kinds of ideas. We don't always consider things from all angles before we make judgments."

"You don't think we should let anyone know we're friends."

"That's not what I said. I don't want to risk a new friendship on what people may or may not decide is okay. Do you?"

What he meant but wasn't saying was that no one was going to understand a thirty-year-old guy hanging out with a sixteen-year-old girl alone in his apartment. It sounded skeevy even to me, but it wasn't like that. People weren't going to reserve judgment while I explained about my broken home and empty room. They weren't going to understand that Guy was offering me a refuge, a place where I didn't have to be alone. And that was what he was doing. He was being a friend when I didn't have anyone else.

"No, I guess not."

"I'm not telling you what to say. You're old enough to make your own decisions."

"No. No, I think you're right. People can be dumb." I couldn't believe I was admitting that to him.

"Right. I'll nod if I see you out there. No one will object to that. But in here," he said, "we can be as close as we want."

It was nice to have somebody who cared enough to think about how things would affect me. I knew Adam cared about me, but he had a whole family that cared about him, and he couldn't always be there for me. Based on how quickly the building was improving, soon he wouldn't be here at all.

I pushed that thought away and smiled at Guy. "I'd like that."

Based on Guy's smile, he did, too.

ADAM

Jeremy's intention was crystal clear when he came into my room later that night. He leaped on me and nailed me rapid-fire in the arm at least half a dozen times before I could get him off. All of this was done with almost no sound, because we were both aware of Dad only a thin wall away.

At last Jeremy stopped trying to find new parts of me to hit, and I released the choke hold I had on him. We sat at opposite ends of my bed, heaving—quietly—and glaring at each other. I was the first to quit scowling, and Jeremy seized the opportunity to get in one last cheap shot.

And I let him.

Because, yeah.

In a low voice, he said, "Two hours. And you couldn't do it."

"I'm trying."

Jeremy reared back to hit me again and I jerked away.

"Okay. Okay." I sighed, because he was right. Saying two words to Dad the last time I saw him wasn't trying. Deliberately picking a fight with him wasn't trying. None of what I was doing was trying.

And I did want to try. I did. I had to, because what Dad was doing wasn't enough.

"I won't run my mouth again. I'll try, okay?"

Jeremy wouldn't look at me. "You better. And it can't just be this weekend. It has to be every time." He didn't mention Jolene specifically, but the point was clear enough. If I was going to do this thing with Dad, really do it, I wouldn't be able to spend every waking moment with her. I'd have to pull back. A lot. Even thinking about that made me clench my jaw and want to yell at Dad again for taking me away from yet another person I loved.

"How do you do it?" I asked, knowing I was going to need help.

Jeremy looked up, a frown on his face.

"How are you not mad at him?"

His frown increased. "You think I'm not?"

"You don't act like it."

"Because it's not just Dad. I'm mad at Mom, too, and I'm mad at you." Jeremy snorted. "I'm even mad at Greg."

That last admission took me aback. "That's messed up."

Jeremy shrugged. "But it's true. And it's not most of the time. Most of the time you're being such a punk that I don't have any mad left for anyone else."

I smiled a little.

"But if I'm mad at everyone, then we're all the same and it doesn't have to matter as much. Is Dad a coward for leaving? Maybe. But so is Mom. And you, you come here and rail at Dad and try to make him jump through all these hoops while coddling Mom constantly. And Greg with his stupid—" Jeremy closed his mouth and blinked a few times. "We all suck, okay? Let's just get us back together and then you can pull all the crap you want."

Jeremy snapped his head to mine when I didn't respond

right away. "Yeah," I said. "Okay. Tomorrow. I'll try, for real this time."

Jeremy shoved me on the way out, but he didn't look half as pissed as he had when he came in. Still, I had to say one last thing even if it didn't make him any happier with me.

"Jer. I'm sorry."

He hesitated at the door. "Yeah, you are. Don't be tomorrow."

IN BETWEEN

Adam:

Hey.

Jolene:

Hey. You got your phone back.

Adam:

I would have texted you as soon as I got home last night and charged it but I didn't want to check out on my mom.

Jolene:

I get it.

Adam:

We were watching a movie and I crashed.

Jolene:

It's okay. Or actually, I'm going to reserve judgment until you tell me what movie you watched.

Adam:

Anne of Green Gables. The first part anyway. It's her favorite.

Jolene:

I've never seen it.

Adam:

Don't tell my mom or she'll tie you to our couch and make you watch all of them with her.

Jolene:

That actually sounds nice.

Adam:

I'm not saying it's a bad movie or miniseries or whatever, but it's long. Like all day long.

Jolene:

And yet you've watched it with her multiple times, haven't you?

Adam:

Well, yeah. It's not her fault she only had sons.

Jolene:

I'm sure she wouldn't trade you.

Adam:

No, she wouldn't. So do I really have to wait two weeks before I get to see you again?

Jolene:

It won't be that bad. I mean, think how many times you can watch Anne in two weeks.

Adam:

One and a half? It's seriously long.

Jolene:

It'll go by fast.

Adam:

It never does.

Jolene:

This time it will. Trust me.

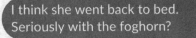

Jolene

"I can't believe I fell asleep. I meant to call you at midnight, and I'm, like, twenty minutes late, but it still counts, right?"

"What counts?" Adam's voice had a slightly gruff quality to it that tickled my senses when he spoke.

"You know. Happy birthday. Are you awake?"

"Yes, I'm awake. Someone programmed my phone to play a foghorn every time I get a call from you." Adam's voice dropped to a whisper. "I think you woke up my mom… Yep. I'llcallyourightback." He hung up before I could say another word.

So far my plans weren't turning out as I'd hoped. If Adam's mom really was awake, she was going to make things a lot harder.

Minutes passed before my phone buzzed with a text.

Adam:

I think she went back to bed.
Seriously with the foghorn?

Jolene:

I think you're exaggerating. It didn't sound that loud.

Adam:

Trust me, it did. If you were within a mile of my house, you'd have heard it.

Jolene:

All I hear is the wind. I can't believe you live out here. There's no traffic at all.

Adam:

Jolene?

Jolene:

Yes?

Adam:

Are you standing in my backyard?

Jolene:

I'm standing in A backyard, but since I haven't heard any foghorns, it's somewhat debatable whether or not I'm in yours.

I looked up at the big white farmhouse and saw the curtains move aside in one of the upstairs windows. I took a gamble that it was Adam's room, and not his mom's, and waved. I couldn't see if he waved back, but the curtain fell closed.

Adam:

Give me a minute. Are you freezing?

Jolene:

Yes.

Freezing had long since come and gone. I was impressed with myself for still being able to text legibly and not go all *The Abyss* on him. It was starting to snow, and the soft white flakes were no longer melting on my skin when they landed on me. The drift I was standing in was over my ankles. But it was worth it. Less than a minute later, the back door opened and Adam came out. He was wearing red-and-black plaid pajamas with his thick, fleece-collared coat hanging open as he jogged toward me. He didn't stop until his warm breath fogged with mine.

"You're nuts."

"What I am is freezing." And happy. I couldn't stop smiling up at him.

Adam turned his head back and forth, looking around. "How did you get here?"

"Remember that whole conversation we had about hot-wiring my mom's car? Turns out it's super hard, so I took her keys instead."

I'd been fully prepared to pay for an Uber or hitchhike if necessary, but ever since my mom had broken up with Tom, she'd been going to bed earlier. Or at least going to her room and shutting the door.

"I can't believe you're here." His gaze roved all over me and the chill fled wherever he looked.

"I am, but you're about to end up with the solid block of ice version of me if you don't get me somewhere warm." I'd already been outside way longer than I'd intended, because I'd had the brilliant idea to park down the block in case Adam's mom heard my car pulling up. Only it turned out Adam didn't live on a block. The road I'd trudged up had turned into rocks, which had turned into dirt long before his house finally came into view. The snow was letting up, but the temperature felt somewhere close to two degrees, and the wind was kicking up. *Too cold.* My teeth were chattering.

Adam took my hand and flinched. He felt like toasty heaven, so I added my other hand and let him lead us to a big red barn a few hundred feet from his house.

"Do you have cows and pigs and stuff?" I asked in a chill-laced voice.

"No, it's empty. Come on."

"You realize that your house looks like a Norman Rockwell painting whereas mine looks like it could be the film set of a *Real Housewives* series."

The barn was moderately warmer than outside. I couldn't see our breath anymore, but I didn't have time to think about that before Adam took off his coat, still heated from his body, and wrapped it around me.

"Better?"

"Mmm," I said, snuggling into the warmth.

There were only a couple windows set high above a loft on one end so I could only make out his outline as he moved away from me and knelt in a corner. A second later strings of crisscrossing lights glowed to life in the rafters above us.

"It's beautiful," I breathed.

"Greg's version of night-lights for the animals," he explained. I heard his teeth chatter and I laughed.

"You're going to freeze in just those pj's, which by the way, you look great in."

There was enough light to make out his blush.

"Be right back." Then he jogged back into the cold and returned a few minutes later wearing another coat. There were a few boxes and a trunk in one corner next to an entire wall of cages in various sizes, and that was where we sat. He shook his head and smiled while he watched me start to thaw. "You're unbelievable, you know that?"

"You did sort of set the bar with your midnight call and promises for my next birthday. The least I could do was wish you a happy birthday in person."

He was looking at me like I was the best thing he'd ever seen, and my heart started racing. It was so intense that it took everything I had not to look away. "So…happy birthday." I didn't think there was anything special about the way that I said that, but Adam swallowed and dropped his gaze to his hands.

"How do you keep doing this to me?"

"Um," I said. "This is the first birthday where I've shown up at your house in the middle of the night, so either you're still half-asleep, or you're confusing me with some other girl. In which case, ow."

Adam didn't even crack a smile. "This wasn't supposed to be a good year for me. My parents split up, and my brother and I can barely have a conversation without one of us hitting the other. Greg's been gone two years, and when I think about him sometimes, I still can't breathe. I've been so mad at…everyone for so long, because if I'm not mad…" His voice went whisper soft. "If I'm not mad all the time, then I have to be something else, something I don't want to be, because if I start, I don't think I'll ever be able to stop."

I should have felt uncomfortable, watching him peel back the innermost layers of his heart, and while I did wish I could help him stop hurting, I didn't want to make him stop talking.

"I'm realizing that I'm even mad at my mom. I tried not to be, because she's so broken that if I let myself be angry at her, I'll end up hating myself more, but I am. I'm angry that she let my dad go. I'm angry that she won't let us all miss Greg together. I'm angry that, because of her, we can't miss all the parts of him. We can't let ourselves remember him without going back to the night he died. I thought if I could just be mad at my dad, then I wouldn't have to be mad at her, but I've been just as stuck as she is and I—"

He finally looked up at me, with that same too-intense expression on his face. "I don't want to do that anymore. I don't want to be stuck. I don't want to be mad, not even at my dad."

I didn't understand everything he was trying to say, but if he was telling me he wanted to let go of all his anger, then I was glad, and I told him so as I reached for his hand.

"Jo." He smiled as he watched our fingers intertwine. "How can you still not know?"

Adam could make someone feel stupid by just raising an eyebrow, but that wasn't what he was doing. He wasn't being condescending; he was being patient with me, carefully trying to show me something that had been hidden for a long time. My heart hammered painfully against my chest as though it was trying to escape.

"That day we took our first picture for my mom, you told me not to take it personally if I couldn't make her happy."

"I don't remember," I said, hating that my voice was shaky.

"But that's what I've been doing. Not just taking it personally, but holding everyone else responsible, too. So I became angrier and angrier, and my family didn't get any better. I'm not saying my anger is the reason my family isn't together, but it's part of why we've stayed that way. If I'd been trying from the start...then maybe... I don't know." He took a huge breath. "I know that it's not my dad's fault. It's not my mom's fault, or Jeremy's. I know it's not my fault. It's all and none, and I know that because of you."

My heart lurched so violently I nearly toppled over. I tried to pull my hand free, but Adam hung on to me. "You made me want to be happy again."

Tears sprang so forcefully to my eyes that I had to squeeze them shut, and still, he kept talking.

"You made me want to try when all I'd been doing was blaming everyone else. You don't do that, and I don't think you ever have. You are so much braver than I am, and I think I—no, I *know* that I lo—"

"Adam!" I didn't think my heart was trying to escape anymore so much as it was trying to smash itself to a pulp. My ribs felt splintered and I didn't trust myself to open my eyes. I could not let him say what I thought he'd been about to say. The terrified, desperate thing in my rib cage was frantic now.

"I will say it to you eventually, but if you're not ready tonight…"

I opened my eyes again, my heart collapsing in relief.

He shrugged. "This—you here with me right now—it's enough."

I felt bruised and battered inside and my heart moved in shaky half beats, weary but ready to start slamming again if given the provocation.

"You here on my birthday?" He smiled. "It's the best gift I've ever gotten."

"Oh, I almost forgot," I said, glad for the reprieve and the reminder that I had something else for him. My fingers still felt stiff from the cold and the adrenaline my heart had been flooding my system with, but they functioned enough to dig into my bag and pull out a small cardboard box. I handed it to Adam. "Open it."

He did, and his smile made me feel warmer than when he'd given me his coat. Seeing his face was worth the cold. Way worth it.

"It's apple cinnamon," I said, nodding at the cupcake. As if he couldn't tell. It smelled amazing, all spicy and buttery vanilla. I hoped it tasted almost as good as his mom's apple pie, which he'd once said was like eating summer. I dug back into my bag and pulled out a candle and a pack of matches. The tiny flame flicked to life and made both our faces glow as I lit the wick. "I'm not going to sing to you, but you do get to make a wish."

He glanced at the cupcake and the flame added liquid gold to his hazel eyes. "That's easy. I already know what I want."

My heart missed a beat, then made up for it with two more right on top of each other, not painful, but fast. Adam said what we had right now was enough, sitting together, talking together, keeping those last few crucial inches between us. My insides warned me that if I let him get any closer I wouldn't survive, but I knew with a burst of heat that chased away every last bit of cold from my body that I'd never truly live if I tried to keep him away. I was ready for my heart to make one last brutal assault trying to protect itself, but it never came.

Because when Adam blew out his candle and his gaze locked with mine, I knew he'd wished for me.

I could feel it in the way his lips fit to mine: warm and so soft, with a trace of the mint toothpaste he must have used that night. I inhaled when his mouth touched mine, and it wasn't just air that filled my lungs, it was Adam. That too-heady feel and scent and taste. My heart was racing again, only this time I wasn't afraid of the way I felt. He overwhelmed me in the most frighteningly perfect way. A camera could never capture it, and for once I didn't get lost trying to imagine the moment as any better that it was. The kiss made me light-headed, and when his still-warm hand rose to lift my chin so he could kiss me deeper, that dizzy, tingling heat consumed me.

It wasn't just the sensation of Adam's mouth against mine; it was what I knew he meant when he said I made him happy.

Me. Comparing every other touch or hug or kiss I'd had before Adam was like comparing salt water to sweet. One took
and the other gave. They'd all carried baggage and motive,
but what Adam gave me was free. He kissed me because I
was exactly what he wanted. He made me feel all the things
he'd said on my birthday—that I was amazing and beautiful and the one thing I'd never let myself hope I'd ever be.

The thing I hadn't let him say.

In his empty red barn that was a million miles away from
anywhere I'd ever imagined, Adam Moynihan made me
feel loved.

ADAM

I woke to the smell of bacon and what I thought were voices downstairs. Jeremy typically woke up just early enough to put on pants and grab a handful of whatever Mom had made for breakfast—he was notorious for eating scrambled eggs out of a paper towel with one hand while driving us to school with the other. But according to the clock, that still left him a good forty-five minutes.

I was groggy from the late night with Jolene, and my senses overflowed with thoughts of her. I smiled, hoping they stayed that way until I could see her again, kiss her again.

She'd tasted better than summer. And she'd let me kiss her, hold her. She hadn't made a single joke about how shaky my hands had been, or the one time I'd accidentally banged our teeth together. It was like she hadn't noticed any of that.

She'd noticed me.

And I hadn't noticed anything beyond how right she felt in my arms and how maybe I'd found my way into the heart she pretended not to have. If she didn't know before last night, she had to know after that she was forever in mine.

I'd had one panicked moment when I'd tasted her tears. I'd thought I'd done something wrong, or she hadn't wanted me to kiss her, but then she'd given me the most achingly beautiful smile I'd ever seen. She hadn't been crying because I'd done something wrong, but because I'd done something right.

I'd kissed Jolene.

My stupid/happy smile lingered as I showered and got dressed, and it was still on my face as I sauntered downstairs, replaying the night in my mind.

When I walked into the kitchen, it felt like I'd traveled back in time. Mom, still in her rose-print bathrobe, flipped a pancake onto an already high stack by the stove while Dad manned the toaster. She had only to glance at him before he silently moved closer to her and reached up to grab the powdered sugar shaker from the top shelf for her.

I couldn't stop my head from snapping to the kitchen table and the spot where Greg always sat. But of course he wasn't there, and the rush of grief that punched me in the gut told me never to make that mistake again.

Everything else was the same though. It was exactly the same.

Only the longer I stood in the doorway, watching my parents watching each other when they thought the other wasn't looking, the differences began slamming into me.

Mom was still in her robe, but Dad was dressed, and there was gravel and mud on his boots from the driveway. Faint tracks on the floor from the back door where he'd come in, too. Not to mention the snow that had melted on his head and shoulders, leaving both wet. Mom's hands didn't reach out to touch Dad whenever she passed behind him, and he wasn't whistling some off-key song that he'd insist was perfectly in tune even when Mom played it back for him on the piano in the next room.

Dad also wasn't yelling to Jeremy to get his butt downstairs, and Greg and I weren't at the table arguing baseball over glasses of orange juice.

We weren't laughing. We weren't happy. We weren't together anymore.

The old floor creaked when I shifted my weight, and my parents both jumped before turning toward me.

"It's the birthday boy." Mom, metal spatula still in hand, hurried over to hug me. "Sixteen. I can't believe it."

My gaze slide past her to Dad. "Me either."

She tugged the sash of her robe tighter. "He called last night," she said, her hands shaking, along with her voice. "He didn't want to miss your birthday. I thought maybe you wouldn't want him to either." Then she returned to the pancakes, probably needing to stay busy before she started feeling more than she wanted. "I'm making you sixteen, so I hope you're hungry."

I told her I was, but I was distracted by the fact that our whole family was apparently about to eat a meal together for the first time in months. He'd called her? Invited himself over? Where the hell was my brother? Not that he'd know any more how to respond to the situation than I did, but he'd talk, say *something*, which was more than I appeared to be capable of.

I moved all the way into the kitchen and pulled out a chair to sit down.

"Juice? Coffee?" Mom was hovering halfway between the fridge and the coffeepot as she waited for my answer.

"I can get my own drink." I started to stand up, but she was at my back in a second, her hands urging me back down.

"It's your birthday and you're going to let your mother make you breakfast."

"You're already making me breakfast." I plucked a piece of crispy, hot bacon from the plate on the table.

"Juice or coffee?" she repeated, not moving from behind my chair.

"Coffee would be great. Thanks."

She smiled and a second later a mug was in front of me. "Give me one second to finish this last batch of pancakes, then I'll grab some syrup and heat it up for you."

Dad set the toast next to the bacon and eggs and joined me at the table with his own mug, taking the chair next to me instead of the one at the head of the table, where he usually sat.

He stirred his coffee with a spoon to busy himself as though he thought I might forget that he always drank his black, but then he sighed and let the pretense go. My shoulders hunched, because I knew he was waiting for Mom to leave before saying anything to me, and as soon as she disappeared downstairs—our house was old, which meant our kitchen didn't have a pantry upstairs—I felt his gaze settle on me.

"I should have told you I was coming."

I didn't take my coffee black, so I had every excuse in the world to stir mine. Bent over my mug, I said, "Yeah."

"I was worried you'd tell me not to come."

My spoon stilled, weighing the statement in my mind. It was sad that I had to consider it, but we'd changed a lot since the last time he'd been in our kitchen.

"No," I said. "I wouldn't have told you not to come."

I felt more than saw him nod. Then he drew his chair closer to mine and rested his arm on the table where I could see it in my peripheral vision. "I wanted to be here for your birthday, but I also want you to know that I heard you, okay? I've been doing what I thought was best, but if you're say-ing it's not—son, look at me." There was no command in his voice. He was asking me to face him, all the while being fully aware that I might not be able to.

I might have surprised us both when I met his gaze.

"If you're saying that it's not enough, then I'm going to do more." He glanced at the open cellar door, the one he'd made with his own two hands before I could walk. "I'm going to try as much as she'll let me."

I dropped my gaze then, not because I couldn't look at my dad anymore but because I didn't want him to look at me. I was blinking too fast, and every muscle in my body was pulling too tight.

My dad put a hand on my shoulder and squeezed. "Happy birthday, Adam."

I nodded and let him add a couple pieces of toast to my plate. "I'm, uh—" I had to push the air from my lungs and suck in a new breath before I could say "—glad you're here, Dad."

ELEVENTH WEEKEND

February 12–14

Jolene

I was waiting for Adam in the hallway outside his dad's apartment when he and Jeremy got there.

"Hi," he said with a smile I knew Jeremy would mock him for later, but when his eyes traveled over my hair, hanging loose and free down my back, his smile grew, and I knew he didn't care. I'd worn it that way for him, and as he closed the distance between us, looking at me like he was remembering exactly what I tasted like, I wondered with a huge leap of my heart if he was going to kiss me in front of his brother.

And I wondered what he'd do if I kissed him first.

ADAM

I wasn't used to Jolene being shy around me, but for once she was the one with too much color in her cheeks (though I liked it), and she was the one chewing on her bottom lip (I probably liked that more). If my brother hadn't been standing right behind me, I would have said something like *how the mighty have fallen* and touched her cheek. But I wanted to make her blush for me, not because I'd embarrassed her. Assuming such a thing was possible. Looking closer, I realized that the redness in her cheeks probably wasn't from blushing but due to being windblown and cold. But the lip bite, I thought, was for me.

The hair, too.

Jeremy said hey to Jolene—a first since we'd started coming here, and it made me happier than it should have to see the truce between them was still holding—then gave me a look as he brushed past us. I knew what he was telling me, what I'd agreed to. "Five minutes, yeah?"

"Yeah," I said to Jeremy before he went inside and left me with a confused-looking Jolene.

Jolene

"You only have five minutes?" I liked to pretend that I was impervious to pain, but either I wasn't trying very hard with Adam, or he knew me well enough to pick up the trace of hurt in my voice.

He drew closer. "I want way more than five minutes." He swallowed and dropped his gaze to his hands. "I didn't want to tell you about it over text, but my dad came over for my birthday. He's going to try harder to get us all back together." He tried to keep elation from his voice, but there was no missing how happy he was.

ADAM

Apart from Jolene coming to dinner with my dad and brother, I hadn't gotten to spend any time with her on our last weekend, and after that night in my barn when she'd finally started looking back at me the way I'd been looking at her for months, all I wanted to do was spend time with her.

Well, that wasn't *all* I wanted to do.

But my family had eaten breakfast together. All four of us. I'd been silently—and not so silently—screaming at my dad for months to make something like that happen, and the fact that he'd done it meant that I had to try more, too. Not the one-word responses that I'd worked up to either.

But it was hard to think of any of that when Jolene looked like I'd just hit her.

Jolene

I stepped back as unobtrusively as possible. I'd known it was coming, that his family wasn't severed the way mine was. I'd known they'd start finding their way back to each other. I just hadn't known it would happen so fast...or that it would hurt so much.

After the night in his barn, when I'd felt our hearts beating together, it was like a cruel joke to feel mine breaking when his was so full.

ADAM

She moved away and nodded too many times. "Oh, wow. That's great. I'm really happy for you," Jolene said, but her tone lacked conviction. Not because she was lying, I knew, but my birthday had gone very differently than hers. I hadn't meant to brag or rub my happiness in her face, but maybe it had come out that way.

"It's not like everything is going to be better overnight," I told her. "My dad—he's not moving back in, and when my mom dropped me and Jeremy off just now, she still wouldn't come up to see him."

And I'd really wanted her to, a fact I hadn't tried to disguise the way I would have in the past.

Which just meant we'd have to try again next time—me, Jeremy, and Dad.

Jolene

How could he not see that he was making it worse? He stood there trying to convince me that nothing had changed, when I could tell that everything inside him was screaming that it had. It didn't matter that his dad had come back to our building, or that Adam and his brother were still spending every other weekend here with him. All of that was technically true, but it wasn't going to last. It was as though someone had put a giant countdown clock above our heads, and the numbers were racing.

My heart was racing, too, pounding so fast and so hard in my chest that I felt sure he could see it.

ADAM

I didn't know who I was trying to convince, me or her, but I could tell that neither of us believed me. The truth was that everything had changed, and not just because Dad had come over on my birthday. *I'd* changed. I could see how much my anger had further driven in the wedge that was keeping my family apart, and I was beginning to understand that no one person had been responsible for putting it there.

I'd already decided to go with my dad to his next support group meeting, and this time I wasn't going to stay in the hall. And when he dropped us off at home on Sunday, Jeremy wouldn't be the only one inviting him inside. It was starting to feel like we might have a chance, and it hadn't felt that way since Greg died. But Jolene…

Jolene

I saw the exact moment he realized what it would mean for us if more days like that one on his birthday followed. If his dad started coming around his house more and his mom saw both of her sons wanting him to be there. If his parents started to realize what he and Jeremy had known from the beginning: that they were better together, as a family.

His words cut off midsentence, and his hands stilled. He went the opposite of red, and if I could have seen into his chest to his heart, I thought I would have seen a crack split right down its center.

My heart had seen the crack coming, and since it had never been whole to begin with, the fissure didn't show as much on the outside. For me, there had never been any hope for a happy ending. I didn't have to lay my anger aside in order to help heal my family, because anger had never been my problem, and my parents were never going to reconcile. My problem was something that made me so much more vulnerable than I'd ever wanted to be.

My problem was that, just when I realized I could be loved, that love was being pulled away.

ADAM

I didn't mean to rush at her, but I didn't have time to check the impulse before I had my arms around her.

"I'm not letting you go," I said, more than a flicker of the anger I'd decided to abandon surging into my voice. "I only just found you, and I won't give you up. I don't care what that means." I didn't let go, not even when it took way too long for her arms to come up and hold me back. I'd been so happy since my birthday, both from that night with Jolene and the morning with my family, that I hadn't for a second considered what that potential happiness would cost me, cost Jolene. If things went the way I wanted them to with my family, these weekends would end, and Jolene and I would… What? Drive out to see each other twice a month in the cars we didn't have?

The thought of not seeing her, touching her… It hurt. Staggeringly so.

"We'll figure it out," I said, drawing back so she'd have to look at me. "You're still gonna cry at the airport when I go to college, and I'm gonna be there when you win your first Oscar, right?"

Jolene

But I couldn't give him the answer he wanted, because how could we? Adam was determined enough that I believed he'd find some way for us to still see each other even if he had to bribe Jeremy to bring him to me. He'd leave his newly mended family to spend time with me...and he'd continue to alienate the only brother he had left in the process. He'd give things up so that we could have a taste of the future he wanted for us.

He'd made me want that future, too—the one where we stayed in each other's lives and that neither of us had voiced; one where there was no Erica 2.0 for him and the only leading man for me was him.

The future where there was only us, together.

The problem was that he'd made me want his happiness more than my own. And his future could be happier without me in it.

ADAM

Everything about her laugh felt wrong. "You're always so dramatic. So you start spending more time with your dad when you're here. Honestly, that's fine with me." She swept the full length of her hair over one shoulder and started to braid it. "I'm way behind on finishing my application for my film program."

I'm pretty sure I flinched. "Yeah, but—"

"Once I get in, I'll be gone in a few months anyway, so you might as well start figuring out some way to survive without me. Hey, cheer up!" She clapped me on the chest, and I felt so shaken that the light pressure forced me back a step. "We both own phones, and I promise to check mine before I go to bed unless I'm super caught up in working on something, okay?"

I didn't respond, because Jeremy swung open the door and leaned against the frame. "Five minutes are up, lovebirds."

As he started tugging me inside, I thought I saw something flicker over Jolene's face, like she wanted to reach out and stop him. But her hands stayed at her sides, and after saying bye, she left, her braid swinging behind her.

I hated myself for not hating the next two days more. Jolene and I texted a little on Saturday, but mostly I spent time with Dad and Jeremy. We ate out, hit up the home improvement store, reframed windows, played video games, hit up the home improvement store again. We also visited Greg, and when Dad once again offered to send Jeremy and me home with Mom, when she said no, we didn't push it. In short, we acclimated to each other again. There were still stretches of silence and moments when I had to grit my teeth in order to keep my temper in check, but I did it.

I did such a good job that Jeremy didn't balk on Saturday evening when I said I needed a couple hours to myself the next day. Once Dad left to fix a drippy bathroom faucet on the second floor, I pulled up the Danish pastry recipe Mom had texted me earlier along with the stuff she'd helped me pack from home. I'd made it with her before, but I was still hoping Jolene would judge me more on the intent rather than the taste.

Jeremy frowned when I told him what I was doing, then frowned further when I told him why.

Tomorrow was Valentine's Day, and fledgling relationship with my dad or not, there was no way I wasn't seeing Jolene.

I hadn't wanted to go the flowers-and-candy route because A, Jolene would have called me lame, and B, flowers and candy cost money and I didn't have a ton of that. What I did have was a helpful mother and the knowledge that Jolene had been bugging me to make her something else ever since I brought her that piece of sweet potato pie from Thanksgiving.

I'd put the dough in the fridge to rest overnight when Jeremy—still frowning—said, "Think I should have planned something for Erica?"

I turned away so he wouldn't see me smother a laugh. "No way. Girls hate it when guys do thoughtful stuff for them."

"But we're, you know, really new. She's probably not expecting anything, right?"

I pulled out a bowl and added cream cheese, sugar, salt, and a cracked egg on top with one hand for the filling. I stared at him when I turned on the hand mixer.

"She's totally expecting something." He cupped the back of his head with both hands and tugged it down before letting his arms drop to his sides. "So I'm screwed?"

"You're not screwed. Come up with something."

"What? I can barely afford my car insurance. I can't get her anything."

That was true, and unlike me, he hadn't planned ahead. Which meant Erica was going to be SOL. Again. I groaned. "Here." I gestured for him to take over with the mixer.

"I don't have time to help you. I need to figure out what to do for Erica."

"I'm about to stick your thick head in this bowl. *This* is what you do for Erica. Mom gave me enough ingredients to make another batch in case I ruined the first one." I hadn't. "I'll help you and then you can drop it off at her house tomorrow. *After* you take me home."

Jeremy looked at the partially mixed cream cheese and sugar, not nearly as enthusiastic as he should have been, and raised an eyebrow. "Maybe I can ask Dad to lend me twenty bucks and get her a stuffed bear or something."

"Sure," I said, yanking the bowl back and attacking the contents with the mixer. "They sell those at every gas station in the country. She'll know exactly how much she means to you."

After another minute Jeremy grabbed another bowl and, after looking at the recipe I had on my phone, asked me, "What's an egg wash?"

"Hey," Jolene said when she opened the door to her apartment on Sunday afternoon. "I thought we were both going to be busy all weekend..." Her voice trailed off. "Also, why do you smell so yummy?" She leaned forward and sniffed me. "I'm having *Shaun of the Dead* thoughts right now, like I'm not 100 percent sure that I won't bite you."

I grinned and produced the still-warm-from-the-oven pastries from behind my back. "I'm a little offended that you thought I'd let Valentine's Day come and go without, you know..." I gestured with the pastry.

Jolene leaned her hip against the doorframe, a sly smile curving her lips. "Adam Moynihan, did you bake for me?" She reached for the plate, but I moved it away. Her smile, if anything, grew bigger.

"Well, now, I don't know. I spent hours over a hot stove making these for you, and—" I moved close to her, still keeping the plate out of reach "—FYI, they are so light and buttery that they literally melt in your mouth." My gaze fell to her lips when I said that, and I didn't blush even when I saw bright spots of color on her cheeks. "Maybe I should wait and see what you have for me before I hand them over."

She glanced at the pastries. "Adam. A little credit, please." Then she took the plate and left me in the hall and came back a minute later with a book in her hand.

A book by J.R.R. Tolkien with a bookmark stuck in it at slightly more than the halfway mark.

"I'm still not loving it but I'm reading it. Well, not the songs, but everything else. For you. So we can talk about it next—"

I kissed her before she could finish speaking.

TWELFTH WEEKEND

February 26–28

Jolene

I didn't wait for Adam on our next weekend. I watched from the roof as their car pulled up and he and Jeremy got out, followed by a woman I instantly knew was Adam's mom. She had his reddish-brown hair and light complexion, and there was something in the way she moved to hug each of her sons that I recognized, an innate grace and strength that I'd only ever associated with Adam before.

She held on to them way too long, and though I was too high up to see the tears on her face when she pulled back, I saw her brush them away. Adam lifted his bag and pointed to the building. He was asking her to come up with them. Jeremy added his own request, reaching for her hand and nodding his head, but she shook hers almost violently and backed up until she was pressed against the side of the car.

Adam's and Jeremy's shoulders slumped in identical movements. I expected Adam to go hug her again and apologize for asking, reassure her that it was fine if she didn't want to go up.

But he didn't. His fists clenched, and when Jeremy took a step toward our building, Adam hesitated, watching their mom before dropping his head and following his brother.

I don't know if his head fell farther when he didn't find

me waiting inside for him. I know only that, when he got upstairs, he didn't come knocking on my door or calling to me from his balcony.

I didn't know what to do with myself on Saturday. Normally, as soon as I woke up, I went over to Adam's and spent the day with him. For months that had been our routine, but I couldn't go get him that morning. And he didn't come get me. Last weekend had told me what to expect moving forward, and without Valentine's Day as an excuse for him to get away, this was how it would be. I knew I couldn't spend the whole day in my bedroom working on the film I'd made Adam for Christmas like I had the night before, and I was so focused on getting away from everything that watching that movie made me feel that I neglected to check the living room before pulling my bedroom door wide-open.

My dad wasn't there, of course not; it was Shelly.

She was dressed in a skimpy silk nightie and robe that she had to be freezing in. She walked to the coffeepot with her phone pressed to her ear, oblivious to my open door.

"—but I waited for you last night," she said, her voice equal parts hope and hurt. "You said you'd wake me up when you got home." She shivered and tugged the flimsy silk robe tighter around herself as she filled the carafe with water. "No, I know, I know, but—" She stopped talking as I imagined he cut her off. She had time to measure the coffee grounds before he let her talk again. "I thought that since it was our anniversary you might—"

I should have quietly closed my door and tiptoed back to my bed, pretend I'd never heard my dad feeding excuses to Shelly for why he apparently hadn't come home for their anniversary. It was bad enough that I'd had to watch her hunch into herself as he likely berated her for *trying to make him feel bad for doing his damn job!*

Growing up, I'd overheard him and Mom having that same fight more times than I could count.

You were the one who wanted the big house!

Because you're never here! I needed something to make me feel less alone.

Right, because I'm not just responsible for putting this ridiculous roof over your head. I'm responsible for how you feel living under it! Well then, cheers to you, Helen. I hope it finally makes you happy.

Keep your voice down or you'll wake Jolene.

That's rich. She's just another thing you said you needed until you actually got it. Buyer's remorse doesn't work so well with a kid, does it?

One or both of them would leave after that. When I was really little, there'd be another argument over who had to stay in the house with me. Mom usually lost, and I'd have to pretend to be asleep while she stood in my bedroom doorway muttering things that no kid should ever hear their mother say.

Watching Shelly, I couldn't remember if the fights between my parents had ever started as timidly as the one I saw in that kitchen. Not that Shelly and my dad were technically fighting. She wasn't raising her voice and seemed to be conceding every point to him. It was kind of pathetic, or that was what I tried to tell myself so I wouldn't feel every quiver of her chin.

Shelly's hands were shaking when she lowered her phone. She stood there, staring at the coffee maker for a long moment, before one still-shaking hand poured a cup.

"I'm sure that was fun for you," she said without turning. "Poetic justice, right? He probably missed anniversaries with your mom because he was with me, and here I am freezing in this ridiculous—" she plucked at the hem that barely covered her butt "—thing that he never even saw."

Then she laughed, and all the hairs on my arms rose. "Everyone said I was an idiot. Literally, I didn't have a single friend who told me it was okay, no matter how much I swore we were in love."

Cherry's face sprang up in my mind for the first time since my birthday, and along with it came all the fights we'd had over her being with Meneik. She and Shelly weren't the same, but their situations might have started out much more similarly than I'd ever considered. As hurt and angry as I still was, I felt hollow when I imagined a future for Cherry that even slightly resembled Shelly's present.

I shook the thought away when Shelly turned, her coffee forgotten, showing me her tearstained face. "My mother refused to meet him. Did you know that? Wouldn't let me bring him to her house. She said my father would be rolling in his grave if he could see what I'd done."

"Why don't you leave him?"

She started to smile, but it turned the other way. "I gave up everything for him. I lost my job, my family, and my friends. I destroyed your life, and even though I still think your mother is the queen bitch of the universe, I helped make her that way."

"No," I said. "You didn't." I don't know why I did it—or rather, I did, but I didn't want to think about the why. "Maybe you gave her another excuse not to hide it, but my mother has been…what she is for my entire life."

Shelly's perfect little mouth gaped at me. "Did you—you didn't—"

"You're not the reason my mother's a miserable shrew. My dad's not the reason." I thought about what Adam had said to me, and I looked down when I felt my eyes prick. "I'm not the reason either."

Somehow it all came pouring out of me, everything from those overheard fights when I was little to Mom firing Mrs. Cho because I'd made the mistake of telling her that our housekeeper loved me enough to make me a birthday cake. On and on I went, until I looked up and saw that Shelly was crying so hard that she couldn't lift her hands to cover her face.

I had to get out of the apartment after that. I dashed into

the hall, shutting the door and Shelly behind me and...then I stopped.

Normally, I'd have gone to Adam—or, more normally, I wouldn't have had to go to him, because we'd have already been together. But he was inside his apartment with his dad and brother, and I wanted that for him, I really did. They could come out at any moment, maybe on their way to breakfast, or to go play ice hockey together, or anything, and the last thing I wanted—apart from having to go back into my dad's apartment and face Shelly—was risk being outside Adam's door, like the most pathetic person who had ever lived, when they came out.

So I knocked on Guy's instead.

He opened the door mid-yawn, but it spread into a slow smile as his gaze traveled over me. "Well, if it isn't my little early bird. Where's your Adam this morning?"

"He's spending time with his dad and brother." I tugged on my braid and tried not to look at the door behind me, the one that could conceivably open at any moment. "I thought maybe we could watch a movie."

Guy leaned against his doorframe. "Sure you wouldn't rather wait out here in case he changes his mind and wants to be with you?"

I felt like squirming, and I was pretty sure he knew I felt like squirming.

"'Cause, you know, playing second fiddle to a sixteen-year-old kid—not really how I like to live my life."

"You're not," I said, tugging on my braid so hard that my scalp started to hurt. "I'm the one who told him to hang out with them."

He slowly crossed his arms. "So you could hang out with me?"

Any second, *any* second, Adam could come out. I didn't have time to let Guy amuse himself by jerking me around.

"You know what, forget it." I turned to walk away, but Guy darted out and caught my arm, and the pressure made me yelp.

"Hey, all I want is a yes or no and you can come in."

"Let go of my arm, Guy." I put enough strength into my voice that he blinked and released me. And suddenly he was all smiles.

"I was messing around, Jolene. I told you before you could always come over." He backed up and gestured for me to enter his apartment. "I'll even make you breakfast, and I don't usually do that for girls unless I also bought them dinner."

I made a face, which made Guy laugh.

"Again, I was kidding."

"Then maybe you need to watch more comedies because…" I shook my head. "Not funny."

Guy smiled and ducked his head. "I don't know if I'd call it a comedy, but I did get a screener for Wes Anderson's latest. Didn't you say you like his hyper-stylized approach to storytelling?"

I frowned, but not in the slightly offended way I had a second ago. That was exactly what I'd said about Wes Anderson. "You remembered that?"

"Sure." Guy lifted his gaze to mine. "You have great insight when it comes to films. You impressed me the first time we met, and I'm guessing you're going to keep impressing me, well, if…" He turned sideways, giving me ample room to walk past him into his apartment.

I bit the inside of my cheek.

Guy held up his hands. "Look, no pressure. I'd love to know what you think of it, but if you'd rather wait, maybe go see it in the theater with…" His eyes flicked toward Adam's door as his voice trailed off.

My throat went tight. Watching movies with Adam might not be an option anymore.

And Guy was offering me exactly what I'd asked for.

I followed him into his apartment.

Adam:

Hey.

Jolene:

Hey.

Adam:

It's so weird being here and not seeing you.

Jolene:

I've been working so I guess I didn't think about it.

Adam:

It'll be weird when you think about it. Trust me.

Jolene:

Okay.

Adam:

How's the application going so far?

Jolene:

I need to do more work on the film I made you.

Adam:

It's perfect.

Jolene:

The version I gave you was a rough cut. Trust me.

Adam:

How about the essay? Want me to look at any changes?

Jolene:

You already helped me a lot. I think I'm good with finishing it on my own.

Adam:

What about your letter? That movie critic seemed like kind of a jerk.

Jolene:

That's basically a defining trait for movie critics.

Adam:

So you'll try to talk to him?

Jolene:

I already did.

Adam:

You did? When?

Jolene:

Earlier today.

Adam:

And you asked him about writing you a letter?

Jolene:

Yeah, and he was cool about it. He needs to make sure I'm serious, so he wants to test my knowledge of cinema first. Stuff like that.

Adam:

Seriously, he's giving you homework?

Jolene:

It's not homework. He wants me to watch movies.

Adam:

Okay, but if he tries to make you watch Citizen Kane, lie and say you already saw it.

Jolene:

Citizen Kane is like the most famous movie ever made.

Adam:

It's also the dullest. I had to watch it in school once.

Jolene:

I'll watch whatever he wants. I need that letter.

Adam:

Fine, but I'm not letting you suffer through Citizen Kane alone. I'll watch it with you.

Jolene:

You're offering to watch the dullest movie ever made with me?

Adam:

So you have seen it!

Jolene:

When exactly do you plan to watch it with me?

Adam:

Maybe I can climb onto your balcony one night after my dad goes to sleep.

Jolene:

Adam. The balcony is covered in like three inches of ice. You'll die. I'll feel bad. And I'll still have to watch Citizen Kane.

Adam:

It's not three inches of ice.

Jolene:

Oh yeah? Go look.

Adam:

It's two inches tops.

Jolene:

And you can insist on that fact the whole time you are screaming and plummeting to your death.

Adam:

I'd risk it for you.

Jolene:

Duly noted, but so far he hasn't said anything about Citizen Kane.

Adam:

I think I might be able to get away for a little while tomorrow. Maybe an hour.

Jolene:

I really need to keep working on my application, but I'll let you know.

Adam:

Okay.

Jolene:

Bye.

Adam:

Bye.

Jolene

I dashed out of my apartment early on Sunday morning to avoid having to say anything to Shelly and practically ran into Adam.

"Oof," he said, his arms coming up around me to balance both of us. "You always come barreling out of your door like that?"

"I guess you wouldn't know, since you always make me come to you."

Adam dropped his arms and moved back, his neck going blotchy red.

I made a sound in the back of my throat and my stomach knotted. "I didn't mean that. I've been dealing with Shelly, and… I'm sorry, okay?"

He looked slightly mollified when I mentioned Shelly. He knew that few things could set me off like an interaction with her. But I'd still been way harsher to him than he ever deserved.

"Can we…?" I gestured at my door, making it clear that I wanted to put some distance between me and my apartment. Adam stopped when we reached his door.

I glanced between it and him and took in the suddenly sheepish way he'd shoved his hands in his pockets. "You can't hang out, can you?"

He shoved his hands deeper into his pockets.

"Five minutes again, or do we get a whole ten?" I wasn't being fair. I wasn't even being smart, because I'd nearly killed myself on our last weekend trying to convince him that I was fine spending less time together.

"I'm going to church with my dad and brother in a few minutes."

A few minutes. So not even five. "Well, that explains the necktie."

"I hate this," he said.

"Oh, I don't know." I angled my head at his chest. "I think you're pulling off the green pinstripe."

Adam didn't show a trace of annoyance at my deliberate misunderstanding. "You know what I mean."

I did know and I hated it, too. "It's okay," I said. "What can you do?"

"I'm trying to talk to my mom more, but I don't know if it's helping. She still hasn't come up to see my dad."

"I know," I said, softening my voice for the first time.

"You know?" Adam frowned before a slight smile replaced it. "You were watching for me? Why didn't you come down? You could have met her, and I wouldn't have had to wait another entire day to see you." His hands came out of his pockets and he extended the fingers of one hand to brush against the back of mine. Warmth tingled over my skin. "I wouldn't have had to wait to…" He shifted closer and the hand that brushed mine encircled it. My eyes fell to his lips at the same time his settled on mine. I rose onto my toes without thinking.

And the door opened across from us.

Guy. He had a trash bag in his hands. He saw us, his gaze sliding to where Adam held my hand, and I pulled it free.

Guy didn't say anything, just turned and headed down the stairs, but I knew with stomach-souring certainty it'd be the first thing he mentioned the next time we were alone.

The door that opened next was Adam's.

There was his dad, dressed as nicely as Adam, and Jeremy, who was in the process of fighting his own tie.

"Morning, Jolene," Adam's dad said. Jeremy was too busy fighting with his necktie to do more than glance in my direction and give me a head nod.

"Morning."

"Hey, why don't you come with us?" Adam said before his jaw flexed and he forced himself to turn to his dad like he was out of practice and the muscles in his body were resisting. "If you don't mind."

"We'd love to have you," his dad said, and I actually believed he meant it. When Adam looked back at me expectantly, it was too much. I was supposed to be giving his family the space they needed, not inserting myself into more of his life.

"Thanks, but I don't have anything to wear." I gestured at the yoga pants and oversize Chewbacca-wearing-sunglasses sweatshirt I had on.

Adam's gaze never left my face. "It doesn't matter what you wear."

And he couldn't even make it easier for me by being a jerk. "Maybe another time, okay?"

With a nod, Adam's dad held out an arm for his sons to precede him. Jeremy gave up on his tie and tucked it into his pocket before starting down the stairs.

I expected Adam to leave just as silently, but he didn't. Instead he brushed my hand again. Right in front of his dad. It made me grin as he left, though I shouldn't have let it.

And I was still grinning when Guy came back.

"Guess that went well."

I blushed as red as Adam ever did. "We were just talking."

"Sure," Guy said. "So you want to come over and just talk to me?"

The heat from thinking about Adam ran cold.

Guy laughed. "It was a joke, Jolene. Sometimes I forget how young you are."

"I didn't think it was funny."

"Right, because I need to watch more comedies." He unlocked his door and pushed it open. "I'll let you pick this time."

I perked up at that. He didn't sound like he was in a bad mood, and anything was better than going back to the apartment with Shelly. Plus, I hadn't gotten to choose a single movie that we'd watched so far, and Guy's taste ran more art house and old. He had nearly everything, and I settled on *What We Do in the Shadows*, a vampire mockumentary that might or might not have made me laugh so hard that I'd peed my pants the first time I watched it.

We were both laughing on his couch before long. Just about the time Taika Waititi was placing newspapers around his date/meal-to-be so that her blood wouldn't stain his carpet, Guy paused the movie.

"I feel like pizza. You want?"

Not glancing away from the TV, I said, "Sure, if you're buying."

"And what if I said you need to pay?"

"Then I'd say I'll have to settle for digging through your fridge instead." I started to get up but Guy tugged me back down.

"I'll cover the pizza."

I grinned. "Thanks."

And then Guy kissed me.

I pulled back immediately. "What are you doing?"

He laughed, stood up, and headed to the kitchen, where he'd left his phone. "You don't think buying the pizza's worth a kiss?" He tapped the screen. "What do you feel like? Sausage and peppers? Pesto chicken…"

Not really listening, I lifted my fingers to my lips. I looked up to find Guy's eyes on me.

"Come on, Jo. It was just a little kiss. Don't you ever kiss your friends? You looked like you were about to kiss your other neighbor earlier."

"Yeah, but he's—"

"He's what? Your boyfriend?"

"Not exactly."

"Then what's the big deal?" He slammed his phone down. "You kiss some friends but not others? Or am I wrong and we aren't friends? 'Cause you're over here a lot for someone who just wants a letter out of me. And if you're going to jump every time I sit next to you—"

"I don't—"

"—or give you a casual peck, then there's the door. I have better things to do. Maybe you should go back to your apartment and—"

"Mushrooms," I said. "Can we get mushrooms on the pizza?" My ears were ringing, and I was clutching the pillow in my lap.

Guy shook his head slightly and looked at his hands splayed on the counter.

I closed my eyes, then opened them. "And I'm sorry. You surprised me is all. You're right, it was nothing and we are friends. I do need you to write me that letter, but I also like coming over here. Please don't make me go. I don't—I have nowhere to go. Please."

We held eye contact for long seconds, then Guy picked up his phone and dialed. Still looking at me, he lifted it to his ear. I didn't start to breathe again until he said, "Yeah, for delivery. Mushrooms."

ADAM

At home on Sunday night, I was half-asleep when I heard quiet knocking on the back door in the kitchen. I rolled over in my bed to check the time. It was close to midnight. Sitting up, I listened.

I knew Mom was still up. Some nights, it was like she was keeping watch to make sure no one came in or out while she was sleeping. She'd never rest again if she knew that meant nothing bad would ever happen to her remaining sons.

From upstairs I heard her chair slide across the wooden floor in the kitchen, as though she had scooted back from the table.

I listened to her walk toward the back door and then stop before reaching it. Whoever she saw through the window didn't make her call out for Jeremy or me, but she wasn't moving either. I was out of bed in a heartbeat, hurrying down the hall, my sock-covered feet nearly slipping down the narrow, steep, twisting staircase that had been original to the house when it was built in the 1850s.

I reached the kitchen as Mom opened the door, revealing Daniel on our back porch.

Déjà vu hit me hard. There'd been so many nights growing up when I'd wake up and find Daniel in our kitchen
with Mom. Sometimes Greg would be there, too. Sometimes Daniel wouldn't even come inside. Mom always acted
like it was completely normal for him to come knocking on
our kitchen door late at night, even if he was visibly hurt.
It was like she knew that a startled or overly compassionate
response from her would send him running. I think that was
where Greg got his easy touch with animals. She'd leave the
door open and turn away, say something about how she was
getting herself a cup of tea and offer to pour him one, too.
Sometimes it would take the entire pot before he'd let her
tend whatever injury he had.

Most of the time, Daniel's injuries weren't physical though,
and talking to him, sometimes until the sun came up, was
the only comfort she could give him.

Watching Daniel, who looked so much older than he'd
been the last time he came to our back door, I knew this
visit wasn't about him seeking solace from her.

For one, Mom was the one who went still and skittish.
I'd been so happy when I ran into Daniel a few weeks ago,
even though I couldn't see him or think about him without remembering Greg—maybe because of that. But Mom
didn't want to think about Greg, or rather, she did, but on
her very controlled terms.

Daniel showing up after more than two years, forcing
those memories on her, had to be a shock. His gaze flicked
over Mom's shoulder to me, and I drew back into the shadow
of the stairway, mindful to avoid stepping on the creaky
floorboard. It felt like my being there would make things
different, maybe easier for Mom, but not in a way that might
make things better.

"Daniel?" Her back was to me, but I could imagine her

eyes cataloging his face, noticing the new scar on his eyebrow and taking in all the ways he'd changed since she saw
him last. I knew, for her, that also meant seeing the extra
years that Greg never got to have.

"Hi, Mrs. Moynihan."

Instinct snapped her into motion after that. She beckoned
him inside and put the kettle on the stove to boil, her body
seeming to tell her what to do even when her mind might
have refused.

He watched the stiff line of her shoulders and the rapid
blinking of her eyes.

"I ran into Adam in the city a few weeks ago. Did he tell
you?"

Mom's arm stilled in the process of pulling the honey bear
bottle down from the cabinet next to the fridge. "No, he
didn't mention it."

"I met a friend of his, too, a girl."

I thought I almost saw Mom smile as she turned. "Jolene."

Daniel nodded. "He seemed happy."

Mom inclined her head a little and sat down across from
him, placing two steaming mugs on the table.

"But he told me that things aren't...good."

Unflinching, Mom shook her head and stirred honey into
her mug. "No, we're okay. We're all okay. It's hard when
they go to their dad's, but we're okay."

Daniel was the one to flinch, and he did it every time she
said the word *okay*. I hadn't told him about my parents' separation, but he seemed to take that revelation in stride. He'd
liked my dad fine, but Dad moving out wouldn't necessar-
ily affect him the way it did the rest of us. I would guess it
meant something to him only because it hurt her.

"I meant to come by sooner. I must have driven by a
dozen times."

Mom focused on the swirling liquid in her mug. "I'm sure you were busy."

"I wasn't," he said, his bluntness catching her off guard so that her spoon clinked against her mug. "I thought you wouldn't want to see me."

"No." Mom squeezed her eyes shut before opening them. "That's not true."

"I didn't want you to have to see me."

She didn't react to that, as if she'd been expecting him to say something along those lines.

Daniel lowered his arms under the table. "I didn't want you to pretend to smile at me and tell me it was okay when we both know I'm the reason he's gone."

She sucked in a breath that was mostly a sob.

"Anyway, I'm leaving soon. My mom will be getting out of the hospital next month, and I've already got most of her stuff packed."

Her watery eyes focused on him. "I'm so sorry, Daniel."

"It's gonna be better, a new start...without him."

Mom reached out a hand, and her fingers lightly tapped the table, asking for his. Daniel kept his hands in his lap. "No, that's not why—" He lowered his head. "I never told you why I didn't come that night." Mom's fingers curled back, and I felt mine mirroring hers. "I never told you, because I don't have a good reason. He wasn't drinking or mad, and she wasn't scared. I just didn't want to leave her when she was happy."

Mom's shoulders shook, and Daniel's voice broke.

"That was a night I *could* have left her. I should have been here. Greg should have been in his house, and you wouldn't be sitting here now, crying. My mom, she's hurt so bad now, and I—"

Mom pushed back her chair and walked to him. At first

she just put a hand on his shoulder, and then the other came up to grip his arm. I could tell it was hard for her.

"I'm sorry," Daniel mumbled, so quietly that I had to lean forward to hear. "I'm sorry he's gone, and I'm even more sorry that you're hurting when I could have stopped it."

It looked like it killed her to fall into the chair beside him and wrap her arms around him. Her whole body was shaking.

He struggled at first, and he was big enough that he could have pushed her off if he wanted to, but he didn't. He let her hold him and press his head to her shoulder, heedless of her own tears.

"It's okay," she said. "I love you, and it's going to be okay. It's not your fault." Her gaze lifted to the ceiling. "It's going to be okay."

My fingers felt stiff when I pried them free of the banister behind me, and it wasn't until she said, "I'm going to try to be okay, too," that the tight coils of his body and mine began to loosen.

Adam:

How is it only Monday?

Jolene:

Because yesterday was Sunday?

Adam:

I was thinking maybe we could ditch school again this week. Your friend still dating that guy?

Jolene:

I honestly don't know. We're not talking.

Adam:

I know you've been trying to get through to her. That must suck.

Jolene:

I'm trying not to think about it.

Adam:

I don't suppose you have any other friends we could bribe to drive us somewhere?

Jolene:

Not really.

Adam:

I might be able to hit up one of mine. Gideon, you met him at the dance, just got his grandfather's old car. I could ask him.

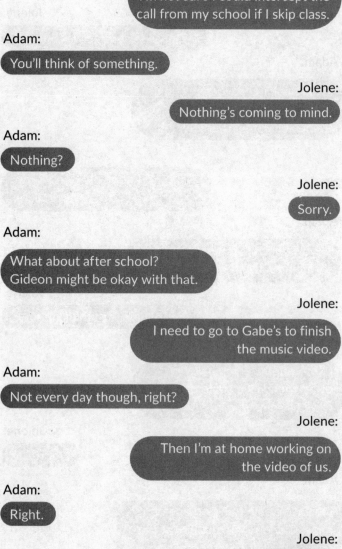

Jolene:

My mom's been home a lot so I'm not sure I could intercept the call from my school if I skip class.

Adam:

You'll think of something.

Jolene:

Nothing's coming to mind.

Adam:

Nothing?

Jolene:

Sorry.

Adam:

What about after school? Gideon might be okay with that.

Jolene:

I need to go to Gabe's to finish the music video.

Adam:

Not every day though, right?

Jolene:

Then I'm at home working on the video of us.

Adam:

Right.

Jolene:

You okay?

Adam:

I feel like something's been off between us.

Jolene:

Like...?

Adam:

You haven't made fun of me this entire conversation.

Jolene:

I'm not being mean to you so you assume something is wrong?

Adam:

Is it?

Jolene:

You're focusing on your family. I get that.

Adam:

I hate not seeing you.

Jolene:

How quickly he forgets Valentine's Day.

Adam:

Trust me, I will never forget Valentine's Day.

Jolene:

I loved that pastry thing.

Adam:

I know. I could taste it every time I kissed you that day. I loved that you're reading LOTR.

Jolene:

See? We're fine.

Adam:

It's not always gonna be like this.
I need things to get a little better
with my dad, then we'll have more
time together.

Jolene:

Before or after I leave for
my film program?

Adam:

I'm trying, okay?

Jolene:

I know. And I'm not mad.

Adam:

You can be mad.

Jolene:

That's your thing, not mine.

Adam:

Then be something. You don't
hate this?

Jolene:

It's not awesome.

Adam:

I hate not seeing you.

Jolene:

My dad's apartment is in the
same place it's always been.

Adam:

I know. I hate that, too.
You're right there and I'm not.

Jolene:

Yeah.

Adam:

I guess I'll see you in 11 days.

Jolene:

I guess so.

THIRTEENTH WEEKEND

March 12–14

ADAM

"Hey. Hey!"

It took Jeremy elbowing me to get my attention.

"Did you hear anything I said?"

I hadn't heard much of anything since leaving our house twenty minutes ago. The sun was setting and Jeremy and I were driving his car to Dad's since Mom had finally gotten hers fixed and no longer needed to drop us off.

"I said if you're already going to be this miserable with me and Dad this weekend, then take a few hours and see your girl."

"I told you I was in this. I promised." And Jolene was acting like she couldn't care less if we saw each other at all. Even her texts felt distant lately.

"'In it' doesn't mean twenty-four hours a day all weekend. Show up when we eat and don't be gone from the second you wake up to the second you go to bed. It's called balance, moron."

I didn't feel like laughing—and I'd never laughed at an insult from Jeremy before—but one corner of my mouth lifted. I was still getting used to talking with him more. Sometimes it took days before I could force myself to tell him important

things, but I still did. He'd been both pumped and pissed
when I told him about Daniel coming over and talking with
Mom. He was mad because he hadn't gotten to see Daniel,
but more than that, he saw the same potential in Mom's last
words that I had.

That afternoon when we were leaving for Dad's, she'd
even asked if we were going to go to the grief group with
him again that weekend—they had a Friday night meeting
as well as a Wednesday one—and when we nodded, she'd
looked a little wide-eyed and nervous but said we could tell
her about it if we wanted when we got home. It was a start.

It was so much of a start that I decided to take Jeremy's
advice and I gave him my bag when we reached our floor
and went straight to Jolene's door, ignoring the whipped
sound effects he made as he let himself into Dad's apartment.

I definitely caught her off guard. As she opened the door,
she was talking.

"If you can't remember something as simple as taking your
keys with you when you go to the store, then—oh. Hi. I
thought you were Shelly."

Her hair looked braided painfully tight, and she was slipping into her coat, but that first sight of me caused her whole
face to light up.

"Hey," I said, wanting to hug her, so I did. She smelled
like cigarettes, and it made me laugh. "Smoking again?"

She shrugged and moved past me into the hall. "It keeps
Shelly away, and that's easier said than done these days."

"She still opening your mail?"

Jolene shook her head. "No, she's—I don't even know.
She's trying to *talk* to me. Like, all the time."

"Talk to you how?"

"Like an actual human being. It's creeping me out."

It looked like it was more than creeping her out. She was visibly unsettled and unsure, two things she almost never was.

"Maybe she's trying to be a decent person again. I mean, you said she used to be your friend."

Jolene's spine snapped straight. "No, she *pretended* to be my friend in order to get close to my dad, so whatever she wants this time, she's not going to get it." Then she looked at me. "What are you doing here anyway?" She didn't sound mean or annoyed, just curious, and a little like she was shoring herself up for another drive-by visit.

"Things are maybe going better with my family."

"Oh?" she said, her hand reaching to grab her braid. And there was no hiding how badly she didn't want that to be true, though she tried. "Good. I mean, that's good."

We leaned against the wall between our apartments as I updated her on things with my mom. When her eyes went a little shiny, I couldn't tell if that was for me or her. I thought a little of both.

She had her braid coiled around her wrist. "That's what you've been wanting from her, isn't it? For her to try?"

"It is." It felt big, maybe bigger than I'd let on, because I didn't want to make Jolene think we might lose our weekends any sooner than we already would. Also, because my mom admitting out loud that she wanted to try was something Jolene had little hope of her own mother doing.

"Anyway, I don't have to spend the whole weekend with my dad this time. We're going to grief group tonight but not until eight. And I really miss you. Like, it's excessively pathetic how much. Ask Jeremy."

She bit back a smile. "More than five minutes of Adam time. You're going to spoil me."

I took a step toward her. "Yes, ma'am."

She laughed, and I would have kissed her except the elevator was finally being fixed and there were repair guys all over the halls and stairway. I would have taken her outside, but winter had sunk its claws into us and was still howling as it held off spring for another week. Watching each other's lips turn blue most definitely would have been a mood killer.

I also wasn't about to bring her to my apartment, where Jeremy would probably be running lines with Erica via video chat and Dad would try to make small chat.

"Do you want to maybe go to your apartment?" I asked.

"Shelly went to the grocery store, but she could be back any minute."

"Right." We'd moved closer to the stairwell, and I had to back up against the wall to let a maintenance guy past.

She chewed her lip. "I might have an idea." She didn't look thrilled by it though.

"Hey, anywhere is better than here."

"He might not be home, so don't get your hopes up."

"He?" I moved closer toward the stairs, but Jolene didn't follow.

"Yeah. You've met him, the film critic. He lives in 6-2." She pointed at the door one down and across from mine.

"Right, the homework guy." I paused, still poised to head downstairs since I still didn't understand what she was suggesting. "Do you need to pick up his recommendation letter or something?"

She was still biting her lip and staring at the door to 6-2. "He hasn't written it yet, but he's been busy."

I frowned. "So then...you want to remind him about it?"

She shook her head. "He might let us hang out, if he's home."

"How is that any better than my dad watching us from over his laptop?"

"Because he's not your dad." She half rolled her eyes in

my direction. "Or anyone's dad. And anyway, I don't see you coming up with a better idea."

I silently walked back to her. In point of fact, I did not have any better ideas, but that didn't mean I agreed we should start randomly hitting up neighbors we barely knew.

Jolene hesitated when we both stood in front of the door.

"He might not be home."

"You said that already."

"Oh, and his name is Guy."

"Okay." She must not have liked the way I said that because she looked at me and frowned. "Okay," I said again, then before she could stop me, I knocked on the door.

"What are you doing?"

"Knocking. Wasn't that the plan?"

Jolene directed her frown to the door and swallowed.

"Hey, we don't have—"

The door opened, and I didn't finish. The guy—Guy—saw Jolene first, and the way he smiled at her made me think of the stupid look on Jeremy's face the first time he saw Shelly. Or maybe I imagined it, because a second later he noticed that Jolene wasn't alone and his smile looked normal. His expression was friendly but curious when he turned back to Jolene.

"Hey," she said. "We weren't sure you'd be home."

He held his hands up as if to say we'd caught him.

"Um, you remember Adam, right?"

"Sure. Paul's kid." He nodded at me and shook my hand, all the while casting glances at Jolene, which made me cast glances at Jolene. I felt like I was missing something.

"Okay, good. I was telling Adam how we've met a few times—"

Guy raised his eyebrow at her.

"—and I remembered you said something about wanting to get to know your neighbors better, and I thought…"

I raised both my eyebrows, bouncing my gaze back and forth between the two of them. Jolene was obviously uncomfortable. She clearly didn't know this guy at all. I should have just let us spend an awkward afternoon with Dad and Jeremy. Instead, we were going to spend an awkward afternoon with this guy. A prospect he didn't look all that excited about either.

"Ah, sure," Guy said after too long a pause. "You guys want to come in?"

No, but I followed Jolene inside.

"Wow, your apartment is really cool." She looked at me with wide eyes like I needed to agree with her. It was fine, I guessed. Big TV. Massive movie collection.

"Yeah, it's cool. Hey, it's really cool that you're writing Jolene that letter for her film program application. It means a lot to her."

Jolene shot me a look like I'd said something wrong, but all Guy did was laugh.

"We need more minds like hers making movies. You guys want a Coke or something?"

We nodded, and when he stepped into the kitchen area, I tugged Jolene to my side. "What are we doing here?"

She didn't answer me.

Guy came back with our Cokes, and the sound of three cans popping open in unison broke the tension somewhat. "So are you a sophomore like Jolene?" Guy gestured to her with his can.

"Yep."

"Good times," he said. "You play any sports?"

"Baseball and some ice hockey. I used to play soccer—not like Jolene, but I'm okay."

Guy's eyes lit up, and he looked at Jolene. "I didn't know you played soccer. You probably end up with a bunch of bruises on your legs."

That was maybe the strangest response he could have made. I tried to catch Jolene's eye, but she was focused on her Coke.

"Yep. I totally bend it like Beckham." She stepped forward to a ceiling-high bookcase full of movies, and quicker than should have been possible, plucked one from the shelf. "Hey, you've got it."

"Of course." Guy looked over at me. "Keira Knightley, am I right?"

I should have smiled or nodded or something, but I didn't. The way he'd said her name was, I don't know, wrong. I didn't feel like agreeing with anything he said.

"So can we watch it?"

I raised my arm toward Jolene, as if I could get her to take her request back. I'd already been trying to chug my Coke as quickly as possible so that we could leave. How was she not picking up on how weird the vibe was? Asking if we could stick around for another couple hours... What was wrong with her?

"Be my guest."

Jolene looked past Guy to where I was mouthing the word *no* and shaking my head.

"Oh yeah, that'd be cool another time." I stepped closer to Jolene and set my empty Coke can on the coffee table. "We actually have to get going."

Jolene put the movie back slower than was strictly necessary.

"That's too bad," Guy said. "You're welcome over anytime. Adam, it was good to see you."

"Yep," I said, putting my hand on Jolene's back and steering her to the door. "Thanks for the drink."

"You, too, Jolene."

Once we were back in the hallway and the door was closed behind us, I turned to Jolene. "Promise me we will never be that bored again." Almost before I'd finished speaking, she was rounding on me.

"What was that?"

"What do you mean?"

"You were so rude." She did a rather unflattering impression of me. "'We actually have to get going.' You practically shoved me out the door."

A smile played at my lips. "Okay, first of all, is that really how I sound?"

Her answer was to push me.

"And second, *shove* is a strong word. I would say I motivated you to leave quickly."

She pushed me again.

"Hey, what do you care anyway? That guy was weird."

"He wasn't weird. You don't even know him."

"He was. Maybe you were distracted by the wall of movies and didn't notice." My smile was fading as I picked up on the fact that she wasn't feigning her irritation. "Wait, I don't know him? So he's like your best friend because you've waved at him in the lobby a few times and he's writing you a letter? Look, let's forget it. We can hang out at my apartment. I can't guarantee that Jeremy will be any better, but at least we won't have to talk to him." I turned toward my apartment, expecting Jolene to follow, but she didn't.

"Why couldn't you have been cool?" she asked, her voice strangely quiet. "We could have watched a movie. I'm telling you, you would have liked him if you gave him half a chance. Then we could have hung out sometimes, the three of us. That could have been cool."

I walked back to her, knowing I was making that face she hated, but I couldn't help it. "Yeah, 'cause I love hanging out with my dad's friends."

"He barely knows your dad."

"Who cares?" And then I fell silent, because she obviously did. I tried to smooth my face out. Maybe she was dealing with some stuff with her dad. She'd been acting off all day, more than all day.

"Okay," I said. "Yeah, maybe I could have been smoother. You caught me off guard with the whole movie thing. Don't you think two hours might have been a bit much for just meeting the guy? He's already writing you the letter. You don't need to hang out with him or anything, right?"

She was looking at me with big, shiny eyes, pleading with me, and I'd never felt denser in my life. Then she shook her head. "I just thought… Well, it doesn't matter now. I think… I think I'm going home. I'm getting a headache."

I tried and failed to convince her to come to my apartment. She wasn't mad anymore, but she kept shaking her head.

Before we went our separate ways, I caught her hand and stepped closer so I could hug her.

And then she left me.

Jolene

I stood inside my apartment, heels pressed against the back of the door, my hand wrapped around the knob behind me. I heard Shelly moving around in her and Dad's bedroom. I could tiptoe across the living room and slip into my room, and she might not think to check on me. I hadn't been lying to Adam about Shelly acting strangely since that morning I'd eavesdropped on her call with my dad and then vomited way too much personal information on her until she'd cried like she was broken. She wasn't acting broken now; she was acting determined, and avoiding each other had become a game I played by myself, one that had become so much harder since she'd started seeking me out.

There'd been more notes and texts from Dad lately, too, nearly every day, and they usually contained some bit of information from the day before, details I knew Shelly was feeding him. The one that had been waiting for me that day congratulated me on a zero-cavity dentist appointment the week before, and I didn't want to know how Shelly had found that out. The rest was always the same: *sorry...promise...excuses and lies.* I still never saw him.

Sometimes I'd spot one of his shirts or jackets lying over a chair, or an empty beer bottle on the counter that I knew belonged to him, because Shelly didn't drink. But Shelly must have cleaned before I got there. The apartment was spotless.

Ten minutes passed, twenty. I watched the hands on the clock tick past. I was sure if I went to my room and listened, I'd hear the soft murmur of Adam, Jeremy, and their dad all talking, laughing. By the sound of things, his mom's voice might be joining the mix in the not-too-distant future, only they wouldn't be at the apartment anymore. They'd be home. Together.

I squeezed my eyes shut and felt wetness on my eyelashes.

And then I was back in the hallway, wiping my eyes dry with my fingertips, not thinking about where I was going until I was knocking softly on his door.

Guy opened it after the second knock. "What happened to your friend?"

"He was the one who had to go, not me."

"You sure about that?"

I nodded. "Can I come in?" And then I added, "Please." I'd been saying that word a lot to Guy lately.

Slowly, so slowly, he moved to let me in. I jumped when the door clicked shut. "I don't think your boyfriend liked me very much."

"I told you he's not—and he didn't get to know you."

"So you think he'd like me?" Guy moved behind me, and I could feel his body heat as he stood too close. "Would he like me like you like me?"

I turned to face him and put a little distance between us. "Why wouldn't he?"

Guy answered with a flick of his eyebrows before taking a swig from his beer. It was a different brand from my dad's. Guy noticed me looking. "You want one?"

"I'm sixteen."

"I know how old you are, Jolene."

I moved farther into Guy's apartment, heading as I inevitably always did toward his movie collection. I trailed my fingers over the glossy cases. "You want to watch something?"

"Is that what you want?"

I frowned at him.

"It seems like we always do what you want." He dropped onto the couch and crossed his feet on the coffee table. Adam's empty Coke can was still on the corner.

"That's not true."

"No? So we can do what I want? Is that what you're saying?"

I felt a chill chase across my skin. My back was to him as I looked over his shelves. "You can pick the movie." He didn't answer me for the longest time, and I felt brittle and naked in front of him. He knew so much about me, my situation. And I was telling him more than I meant to every time I came back and said that same word. "Please."

He rattled off a title and I reached for it gratefully. It wasn't one I'd ever heard of, but for once I didn't care. I started the movie and settled into the far corner of the couch.

"Why are you sitting all the way over there?"

"Hmm?" I tried pretending that I was engrossed in the opening credits, but I was forced to look at him when he snatched the remote and paused the movie.

"I said, 'why are you sitting all the way over there?'"

"I like the corner."

"Really? Then why don't you put your feet up?"

"Sure." I curled my legs up sideways, but Guy grasped my ankles and pulled them across his lap.

"There, isn't that better? You can stretch out now."

"Yeah, that's better. Thanks." I reached for the remote in his hand, and he let me take it. As the movie started up again, I relaxed. It was a drama, but with one character who never failed to make me laugh in his scenes. Guy laughed at him, too, and at once it was easy between us again, just like I needed. It would have been better if Adam had been there, too, but at least I wasn't alone.

I didn't even mind when Guy started to rub my feet. I looked at him, and he didn't seem to be aware that he was doing it. I jerked when he touched a ticklish spot. He apologized, but then he did it again.

"Stop." I laughed. "I can't pay attention to the movie."

Guy held up his hands, and I turned back to the movie. The second I relaxed my guard, he grabbed my foot and started tickling me. I squealed and tried to twist away, but he yanked me down the couch as he moved his hands up to my waist, my shirt bunching up as he attacked my bare stomach. I was laughing to the point of pain by that time, but the laughter fogged my brain, clouding out the alarms that were screaming inside my head that this wasn't okay, the same ones that had been hovering around the edges of my thoughts since I entered Guy's apartment. A lot longer than that, if I was being honest with myself.

The fog started to thin when I realized that Guy had me flat on my back and he was on top of me, his weight pressing me down into the cushions. He was so much bigger than I was, so much heavier. Hot flickers of panic started to whip through me, and the laughter that he kept wringing out of me was touched with half-formed words that didn't sound like the protests I needed them to be. Suddenly he stopped tickling me. His hands were still touching me, but he wasn't laughing and he didn't want laughter from me either, if he ever had. He smashed his mouth down on mine and his tongue thrust inside. His hands were grabbing and squeezing and everywhere. I couldn't catch my breath.

If I screamed, he swallowed it.

If I kicked out, his thigh pinned my leg down.

If I bucked, he pressed me harder into the couch.

Fear froze me colder than the blizzard raging outside.

And then his hand moved to the button of my jeans. I jerked my head free and gasped the word that had been trapped inside. "Stop!" And I kicked and bucked and twisted. Nothing. He moved only because he wanted to, and this time he dragged his mouth down my neck. He licked me.

"No. Stop. Guy, I'll scream." My threat sounded pathetic in my ears. It was weak, and my throat felt raspy from laughing. I wanted to cry until I realized I already was. But the walls were thin. Guy knew that, but I repeated it out loud. Someone would hear me. I'd scream until they did.

He hurled himself to his feet.

"You're gonna scream? After you've been teasing me all this time, you're gonna act like you don't want this?" He said other things, things that battered against me as I scrambled off the couch.

"Yeah, run home, little girl. Where are you gonna go? Who's gonna care, huh?" He blocked me when I got to the door, grabbing my wrist when I reached for the handle. "You gonna tell Daddy? Tell him how you kept coming to me and begging me to let you in? How many nights, Jolene? How many?"

Too many. I remembered them all, and I felt so foolish because, even then, I'd known. I'd *known*, and I'd kept coming.

"You gonna tell your boyfriend how you kissed me? You didn't mind then, did you?" He released my hands. "No, you're not gonna tell anyone, are you? Who would you tell? Nobody cares about you, do they?" He moved aside so that I could yank open the door. "Go on. Come back when you want your letter and you're ready to grow up, Jolene."

His laughter chased me down the hall.

ADAM

*B*ees were buzzing inside my head. Or I thought they were until reality penetrated the dream I already couldn't remember. My phone was vibrating on my nightstand.

Jolene:
> Are you awake?

Adam:
> No.

Jolene:
> I'm on my balcony.

I looked toward my sliding glass door and the snow pounding angry fists against the glass. The display on my phone read 1:47 a.m.

Adam:
> You're not on your balcony.
> Frozen death is on your balcony.

She didn't text back.

I sat up, cold seeping into my skin just from looking outside. It made no sense for her to be out there. I told myself that as I flung back my blankets and, armed only with flannel pants and a T-shirt, peered through the glass. Visibility was like two inches. An entire hockey team could be out there and I wouldn't know it.

I felt each one of my teeth freeze solid when I slid the door open. "Jolene!" I called her name but the wind ripped the sound away. It didn't matter that I was still standing in my room. Snow swirled around me and licked my skin with needled tongues. Stepping out, I reached the wall and leaned over, telling myself I wouldn't see anything, not a girl shivering against the wall.

And I didn't.

Jolene wasn't shivering anymore. She was too cold.

"What are you *doing*?"

"C-can you c-come over? Or c-can I?"

"What?" I could barely hear her, but if she'd said what I thought she'd said... "No. Jolene, no. Go inside. I'll call you. Go!"

Her response was to break from her position and place her foot and hands on the railing.

"Are you trying to kill yourself?" I grabbed her shoulders and shoved her back. Instead of letting go, she gripped the railing tighter. "Jolene. *What*." I wasn't even asking her a question at that point. Either her brain had frozen with that one imperative locked in place, or something was wrong enough to make her forget that she'd nearly died the last time she climbed onto my balcony, and that hadn't been during a snowstorm. That, or she didn't care.

Both options scared the hell out of me.

"Okay, okay." I swung my leg up and hissed when my hands wrapped around the burning cold metal railing. I shifted to grip the wall, and something soft and impossibly cold pressed my hand into the brick. Jolene grabbed a fistful of my T-shirt and pulled. When I tumbled onto her balcony, I realized the soft, cold thing was her hand.

Breathing hurt, and her hand in mine was almost too frozen to hold. I pushed her toward her door, which she'd left open, so there was no warmth to welcome us when we got inside. Shoving the icy wind out when I closed the door helped, but not enough. I was still in the process of freezing. Jolene stood still as though already frozen. I ripped the thick down comforter from her bed, wrapped it around her back, and pulled her against my chest before cocooning myself in it, too.

Ice had begun forming on the exposed hairs on my arms, and as I looked at Jolene, that ice seemed to stab deep inside me. Her eyelashes had frosted over and glistening tracks of frozen tears trailed down her cheeks.

We both started to melt as we sank to the floor in front of her bed. My teeth were chattering; her lips were gray. I didn't know what I was saying to her as I started rubbing warmth back into her hands, her arms, her back. She said nothing as I coaxed circulation back into her limbs. I didn't stop until her teeth were chattering, the sound a sharp clicking that was so fast that it almost sounded like my phone vibrating.

"Are you going to tell me why you were freezing to death outside?"

We were sitting shoulder to shoulder, so she didn't have to move much to let her head drop to my shoulder. "No."

Glancing at her face, I saw that the color was returning to her lips, but she didn't feel all the way thawed out. Little shivering tremors still racked her body, so I wrapped my arm around her waist, sharing my body heat. I forced my tongue to the roof of my mouth so that I wouldn't say something rash in response to her one-word answer. With gut-twisting panic, I thought back to the look on her face when she'd grabbed the balcony railing. She'd have done it. She'd been that desperate. I hadn't been that afraid since the night we'd gotten the call about the accident that killed my brother. So I didn't say anything else. I added another arm, and I held her.

I wanted to make her tell me, to shake her and scream at her and hold her all at once. I wanted her to hold me. I still felt threads of terror stitching through me until I could almost see them under my skin. I'd already known I loved her. But I didn't know until that moment when she'd started to climb to me that I'd die for her.

"Just so you know," I said, hearing the way my voice shook, "you're my favorite person. In every way, you are my favorite."

After a minute, I leaned forward to flip open the laptop that she'd left on the floor. I turned on the first movie I found, then settled back into the comforter with her as the opening credits of *Napoleon Dynamite* started to play. Her frozen tears had melted away, but new ones fell silently as we watched the movie.

Jolene

I woke up on the floor. With a person for a pillow.

We'd sort of folded into each other. Adam's head was resting on the crook of his arm, which was draped over my hip; mine was cushioned on his thigh. The comforter that he had wrapped us in was constricted tightly around my arms and pinned under Adam's weight. When I tried to extract myself, I had to tug hard, which succeeded in freeing my arms but also waking him.

Adam shifted so that I could untangle the rest of myself and sit up. He blinked several times and arched his back, then righted himself, too. Weak sunlight spilled into my room through the glass doors. It lit a path that stretched toward us but didn't quite reach. There was no real warmth from the early-morning sun.

"You stayed all night." My voice cracked when I spoke. Not because I was struggling to control my emotions—I felt more numb than anything—but because I'd abused it the night before with laughter that had turned into something else. "Did you mean to?"

"I wasn't going to leave, so yeah, I meant to."

I'd let so much cold into my room the night before that the air still felt chilly once we were no longer pressed together. I shivered. "You're going to get in trouble." I didn't want Adam to pay for helping me, but even had I been thinking clearly the night before, I still would have gone to him. I'd needed him more than I'd worried about what his dad would do later.

Adam leaned away, not from me but toward my laptop to wake up the screen and check the time. It was still early. Maybe early enough for him to sneak back home—through the front door this time. If he left right then, if he was quiet... but he didn't get up.

"Is it too late?" I asked.

Adam shook his head. "Probably not."

"Then you should go." But I didn't push him or in any way urge him to move, apart from my words.

We were back in the same position we'd started in the night before. Sitting on the floor against the foot of my bed, shoulder to shoulder, except we weren't touching. It had been so easy to lean on him in the dark, but I couldn't shift even an inch to my left that morning.

"Doesn't matter anyway." When I looked at him, Adam plucked at the side of his pants. "I didn't think to grab my keys."

When he moved, I was able to see him in a way I hadn't during the night. Adam was wearing a short-sleeve T-shirt and the same red plaid pajama pants he'd worn on his birthday. And he was barefoot. He'd gone out into a blizzard for me with nothing but thin cotton covering him. He'd crawled across an ice-covered wall to reach me. Because I'd needed him. Because I was stupid, so stupid. I hunched into myself as my stomach clenched.

"Hey, hey. It's all right." Adam's hand slid over to grasp mine, to thread our fingers together. "I'm not complaining."

The thing that broke me, that thawed my numbness, was that he meant it. He'd gladly get in trouble for me, and we both knew he was going to get in some trouble. He wasn't agitated or mad or anything like that. He was completely relaxed, holding my hand like he didn't have a care in the world beyond being there with me.

"What you said last night, about me being your favorite person, did you mean it?"

"You know I did." The answer came so easily to him. He didn't even think about it. He wasn't trying to comfort me, keep me from freaking out and running into a blizzard again. He didn't have to say it again, but he did. I closed my eyes, because he was so bright.

"Sometimes I just think about you and I feel better. I don't even have to see you or touch you—" Adam squeezed my hand "—and I feel warm. How do you do that?"

"I'm the physical embodiment of Prozac."

Adam didn't laugh.

"You're better than I am." I forced myself to look at him, letting him look at me. "Your mom, your dad, Jeremy, even Erica knows that. Everyone who knows you loves you. They want you around. They fight over you—*you*, not what you represent, but you. I never knew Greg, but I know he loved you, too. Because how could he not? How could anyone not?" I pulled my hand free and immediately missed his warmth. I wasn't to anyone what he was to everyone. The breath I took then was painful, hollow, empty, and cold.

I suddenly realized I could still taste Guy in my mouth. I scrambled out of the comforter, tripped, and ran into the bathroom. I brushed my teeth until my gums bled. And then I brushed them again. Adam was there, watching me.

"I just need a minute," I told him. And he didn't push me. He closed the door behind him and said without words that he'd be waiting outside.

I cleaned myself up. Washed my face, brushed my teeth a third time, and combed my hair. I thought about rebraiding it, but then I thought about Adam and the urge left me.

Adam was sitting on my bed with his legs crossed. It was the exact position I'd been in that first night that he'd decided to be my friend, to keep me instead of throwing me away. He'd become my favorite person that night, and he did all over again as I stared at him.

"Bit of a role reversal." I climbed onto the bed and sat facing him, so that we were knee to knee. "You're sneaking into my room now."

Adam looked into my eyes. "You needed me. I came." And then, even though it was awkward—and I could tell he realized it was awkward about halfway through—Adam leaned forward, across his bent knees and mine, and he hugged me. We both had to stretch forward to reach, but we did. I needed to be held and to know that, even though it wasn't fair, I was his favorite person.

I wasn't anyone's favorite, but I was Adam's, and that was everything.

I should have tried harder to make him leave, to urge him to go, and at least try to get home before his dad realized he was gone. But when I moved to climb off the bed, Adam tugged me back.

And I went.

ADAM

I'd never lain on a bed with a girl before. I kept eyeing the closed door like her dad would kick it down any second and beat the ever-living hell out of me. That was what he should do. He should be worrying about his daughter, be aware that she had a guy in her bedroom. He should know me and, to a degree, terrify me. That was what dads were supposed to do to guys who were interested in their daughters.

But Jolene's dad didn't know I existed. He barely knew *she* existed. He didn't care that she'd been crying, or that something had hurt her. I swore in that moment, with Jolene lying next to me and her long, loose hair tickling the back of my hand, that I would kick in his teeth if I ever met him. "You should come home with me later. My dad will be mad enough to yell at both of us. If you're really lucky, he'll ground you, too—maybe even confiscate your phone."

Jolene laughed a little, and the moment made her hair slip forward over her shoulders. She was so beautiful my breath caught.

Then the smiles faded. The reality wasn't as funny. If—

when—I got grounded, we both knew I wouldn't be the only one punished.

"How long do you think?"

I rolled onto my back. "The last time I sneaked out all night to see a girl, I had a full beard by the time they let me out, so…"

Jolene pushed up on her elbow. "There isn't a single part of that sentence I believe."

"Her name was Stephanie and it was so worth it."

That got me a laugh.

"Maybe you can convince your dad you sneaked out early this morning?"

"That might work." I'd have to persuade Jeremy to back me up, but things had been okay between us lately so that wasn't as ludicrous as it would have been even a month ago. Lying next to her in that moment though, I didn't care how much trouble I got in.

"And what about me?" Jolene asked. "Am I worth it?"

I started to say yes. To say something ridiculous, like being with her would be worth never seeing the sun again, so she'd keep laughing. But I didn't. Jolene wasn't the type to fish for compliments. She was more the type to pay them to herself. At first, I'd thought she was sort of conceited, but as I'd gotten to know her, I'd realized the opposite was true. She made them a joke. But they weren't. She was beautiful and funny and all these other good things that I tried to tell her, that she needed to hear. But I didn't say anything. Instead I lifted my head, fit my hand under her jaw, and kissed her.

I felt her breath suck in as my lips touched hers, actually felt some of the air in my lungs slip into hers. The sensation made me jump a little, but I didn't pull away. And the thing that made me fight not to smile against her mouth was that she didn't pull away either.

Kissing Jolene again was so much more than I thought it would be—and I'd thought about it a lot. It sent my blood racing and my heart pounding. I shifted closer and let another demanding instinct urge me to kiss her deeper.

But that time she did pull away.

"Sorry," I said before she could pull back even an inch. "I didn't mean—"

But she didn't let me finish. She ducked her head into my shoulder and wrapped her arms around my waist. I didn't need instinct to hold her, too. I settled back and she followed. I could feel my pulse and imagined she could, too.

Jolene breathed deeply, then she lifted her face to look at me. "You're my favorite person, too." She gazed at me until I thought she was going to cry.

"I feel like I did something wrong."

"You didn't," she said, and I didn't like the way she emphasized the word *you.* "I—"

A heavy pounding knock sounded on the front door and without thinking I tightened my arms around Jolene. Then it sounded again. The third pounding cut off midway and I heard a sound that sent a chill of dread down my spine.

"I'm sorry it's so early but I need to talk to Jolene. We can't find Adam."

"I think she's still sleeping, but we can wake her if we have to."

I tried to move when I heard Dad and Shelly's footsteps cross the room, I swear I tried, but Jolene and I were wrapped together and there was a blanket twisted around both our legs. She moved one way and I went the other and I ended up half on top of her when the door opened.

Jolene

Adam's dad didn't drag him off my bed and out of the room. No, it was much worse than that. He stood there silently watching as Adam climbed off me.

I'd only glimpsed Adam's dad's face when the door opened, and his expression was one of desperation and fear. I immediately thought of Greg, and whether it had been a minute or ten since Adam's dad discovered he wasn't in his bed, I knew for a man who had already lost one son, it had been an eternity.

It was almost comical how his features shifted. There was that one bright burst of relief when he'd had to catch his weight on the doorframe, but it had been followed so quickly by cold, hard disappointment that laughter was the furthest thing from my mind.

Adam tried to explain that it wasn't what it looked like *while he was climbing off me.*

Yeah, that went over well. His dad didn't say a word.

Shelly, for once in her life, was speechless, too.

Adam shot me a glance before leaving. He was smart

enough not to say anything to me. His dad was clearly beyond words at that point, otherwise I'd have tried to say
something myself.

When they left, I told Shelly the truth.

"I don't care if you believe me or not. Nothing happened.
He came over last night and we fell asleep watching a movie."

"I believe you," she said. "You're stupid and he's going to
get in a lot of trouble because of it, but I believe you."

My shoulders sagged. She was right. I didn't want to think
about that, so I deflected. "Think my dad'll be that mad?"

Shelly hesitated. "I should probably tell him."

I stared at her as I scooted off the bed. "That was a rhetorical question, Shelly. We both know he doesn't care."

"He does." She took a hesitant step into my room. "He
should. I've been talking to him about being more involved,
and he's going to try, Jolene. He's just so busy."

That was such a load, and we both knew it. "Do you
know how many days it's been since I've seen him? Actually *seen* him, beyond the rare glimpse in the morning on
his way out the door?"

Shelly lowered her gaze and plucked the exact number
from my mind. "One hundred and ninety-four."

I gaped at her. Nobody knew that but me. Dad might,
I supposed, but something told me he was "too busy" to
count. I hadn't even told Adam. But Shelly knew, which
meant she'd been keeping track, and I couldn't for the life
of me fathom why.

"Why do you know that?" I moved toward her.

She caught her hands up in front of her, wringing them.
"I didn't know it was going to be like this. I thought—"

"What? You thought what?"

"Can we stop?" she asked. "Can we stop being enemies?
I never wanted that."

"You just wanted a married man and you used me to get him. So no," I said, reaching for my doorknob and forcing my eyes to remain bone-dry when hers flooded. "We don't stop. How could you think for a single moment that I could possibly stop?"

I shut the door in her face and after looking around the empty room where minutes before Adam had been holding me, I opened the door to my balcony and let the bracing wind lash at me until my cheeks felt numb. And then I forced that feeling to spread to the rest of me.

Shelly left shortly after that. I didn't know or care where. Adam's dad had been yelling at him earlier, but they must have migrated to the other bedroom, because it'd been a while since I'd heard anything. I paced my room and chewed my nails till they bled. He'd find some way to let me know what happened, wouldn't he? Once he calmed down and let Adam explain, his dad wouldn't keep us apart forever, right? I tried to reason with myself but it didn't help.

The thing that finally drove me from my room was another fist pounding on the front door.

I honestly hoped it was Adam's dad. I was ready to tell him everything if it meant I could still see Adam.

But it wasn't.

Jeremy craned his neck to peer past me into my apartment. "Is Shelly home?"

I had barely uttered the word *no* when Jeremy pushed past me. "What happened with your dad?"

Jeremy crossed his arms and looked me over. "Well, you don't *look* stupid…"

I pushed the front door shut and gritted my teeth. "I know Adam's in trouble. What I don't know is how much."

"Yeah, but you can guess, can't you?" When my only response was a glare, Jeremy went on, "He's grounded until the end of time, but that was a given. No phone, no internet, no life. Thanks to you, my little brother is going to be a shut-in until he graduates."

I dropped into the dining chair next to me, my indignation forgotten. I looked to my future weekends at Dad's, and I saw myself running out the clock in my room, watching movie after movie with nothing to focus on except the number of fingernails that I hadn't chewed to the quick. Mom's wouldn't be any better now that Mrs. Cho was gone. I'd have school but soccer was over and Cherry and I weren't talking, and I had all the footage I needed for Venomous Squid so I wouldn't see Gabe or the guys as much. There'd be no more texting with Adam. No more Adam, period. It was like having the wind knocked out of me. "He can't."

"Uh, yeah, he can. Do you even care what you put my dad through last night? I mean, do you?" He broke off with a note of disgust that made me flinch. "Adam and our dad were starting to make progress and in one stupid night, you destroyed all that. You deserve this. Adam, too. But our dad didn't."

My heart took the hit from his words and pain lanced through me. "I'm sorry," I said. "Please don't be mad at Adam about this. Something happened last night and I didn't know who else to go to. You have to tell your dad it wasn't Adam's fault."

Jeremy sighed. "Yeah, it was. Unless you physically prevented him from going home last night, it was his fault. Whatever excuse you try to come up with makes Adam look cowardly as well as stupid. Trust me, stupid is plenty." Then he walked back to the door and opened it. "You don't have anyone to blame but yourselves."

Tears spilled over onto my cheeks. *No*, I thought. *That*

can't happen. I can't lose him and ruin everything he wants. I was already on my feet, striding toward the door as if Jeremy had opened it for me.

"What do you think you're doing? I told you he's grounded. He can't see you."

"I need to talk to your dad."

"Yeah, that's a bad idea." Jeremy stretched his arm across the door, barring me when I stepped forward.

When I didn't relent, he sighed again and dropped his arm. "I'm also supposed to tell you that Adam's waiting for you on the balcony."

I didn't stop to yell at Jeremy for withholding that crucial bit of information. It was just another thing that didn't matter. Instead I shoved him into the hall and slammed the door before running to the balcony.

"Adam?" I couldn't lean far enough out to fully see into his balcony, but I heard him perfectly.

"I'm here."

I let all the air out of my lungs, the still-freezing temperature turning it into fogged clouds. "Your brother just told me."

"I figured he would be less than forthcoming. I had my doubts about him telling you at all."

"He's pretty mad."

"He'll get over it." Adam's hand crossed over the railing in front of me, and I covered it with my own.

"I'm sorry."

"I'm not."

"You don't even know what you got in trouble for," I said.

"It was for you. That's all I need to know."

My heart swelled, then shriveled in the space of a single heartbeat. I lifted my hand free and clutched my elbows tight to my chest. "I did something stupid last night."

"I was there," Adam said. "I have the frostbite to prove it."

"No." I shook my head. He was trying to help me, even then. I owed him more than the teasing excuse he was trying to give me. "I did something before that."

He already knew that, or he at least knew something.

"I went somewhere I shouldn't have, and something happened." I gagged on the memory of Guy's hands on me, his mouth… My stomach twisted and would have emptied itself if there'd been anything in it. "I'm not this girl. I'm not this stupid. I don't know why I kept going back. It was so stupid, because I *knew*. I kept lying to myself because I—I don't know." I went on like that, my words becoming vaguer and harsher as I spoke. "And I'm sorry I texted you like I did. I couldn't think of anyone else."

Adam was silent for a long time. A really long time. Too long. "Are you hurt?" he asked at last.

"No." My voice was so quiet that wouldn't have carried to him if he was even an inch farther away.

"Are you safe?"

I told him I was.

And then Adam said something that made me flinch. "Jolene, where did you go?"

I didn't answer, because we both knew my options had been limited. It had been late; there had been a blizzard. And he was smart. He figured it out between one heartbeat and the next.

"What did he do?"

I didn't even try to lie.

ADAM

When I got back inside my bedroom, I felt frozen solid. My legs didn't move right and my chest ached. Even after the warmth from the heater soaked into my bones, I still felt that way.

Dad was on the phone with Mom. He must have been pacing outside my door because I could hear him perfectly.

"Yes, all night, I saw them myself… I agree… Sarah, I've already talked to him, but he isn't saying much… Yes… He's in his room… Nothing, he says, but would he tell me? Not yet, but I will. I've never actually seen her father, but I'll get in touch with him somehow…"

I almost laughed. Jolene's dad wasn't going to care, assuming my dad could find him. Jolene hadn't even seen him in months. Fire suddenly raced through my muscles and my hands formed into fists.

"Now's good. Jeremy's here… We can meet somewhere if you'd rather I not come to the house… Okay. I'll be there in thirty minutes." A fist knocked on my door. "Adam?"

I opened it.

"I'm going to the house to talk with your mom. I don't

know when I'll be back, but you're not allowed to leave this apartment, do you understand me?"

"Yes, sir."

He gave me a nod, then he walked over to where Jeremy was dozing on the couch and relayed the same info. He left Jeremy with my phone and reminded him that I wasn't to use it. If Jeremy opened his eyes, I didn't see it, but he did take the phone.

Then Dad was gone.

I think I waited a full minute before moving toward Jeremy, but my blood was still pounding in my ears and it was possible my sense of time was off.

"Hey." I kicked at the lump that was my sleeping brother.

"What!" Jeremy rolled over to glare at me.

"I need my phone."

Jeremy tucked it under his pillow and started to lie down again. "Yeah, well, good luck with that."

"I'm not messing around. Give it to me or I'll take it from you."

One eye opened. Then the other. Jeremy sat up, pulling my phone out and holding it in his lap. "Maybe you aren't getting it, but you seriously screwed up more than your life last night." He shoved me back a step without standing. "You're always talking about what Greg would do when calling out me or Dad. What do you think he'd say to you right now, huh?" He shook his head and glanced down at my phone, swiping the screen to unlock it. "Forget it. I'm sick of you always acting like everyone else is the problem. Grow up, Adam. And here." He tapped the phone a couple times and tossed it onto the coffee table. "Here's your stupid voice mail from your equally stupid girlfri—"

"Adam, Adam, Adam." Greg's half-teasing voice started playing and Jeremy and I both froze. "Why do you even have a phone? So, listen, I'm bringing another dog home and I haven't found a home for Baloo, so obviously Mom and Dad can't know."

Jeremy's gaze lifted to mine, his mouth opened like he wanted to ask a question but didn't want to risk talking over our brother's voice.

"I need you to move Baloo to the other cage in the barn, the one with the blue dog bed. But watch his leg, because he'll bite you if you pull his stitches. Maybe get Jeremy to help—"

Jeremy's face twitched and he sat forward, his hand drifting toward but not touching the phone when Greg said his name.

Caught between the memory like I always was and the sight of Jeremy hearing Greg's voice, I didn't move as the rest of the message played. I didn't even stop him when he replayed it.

"How do you have this?" he asked when it ended the second time, but what he really meant was *how do you have this but you've never played it for me?*

I took a slow step toward him, intending to pick up the phone and reassure myself that the voice mail was still safe and saved, but the second I moved, Jeremy looked up. His eyes were flooded, and he simultaneously looked like I'd given him the greatest gift of his life and tried to keep it from him all at once.

My stomach twisted. It wasn't like I'd set out to keep it from him. After Greg died and I realized it was the last message he'd ever send me, I'd listened to it over and over again until it became a ritual. Whenever I thought about Jeremy and how he might want to hear it, I'd tell myself that he probably had a saved voice mail of his own.

But watching Jeremy replay Greg's message for the third time, I saw instantly how wrong I'd been.

I sat down next to my brother, seeing the way his eyes swam as he got to hear our brother again. "Jer, I'm sorry."

Jeremy nodded, not taking his eyes from the phone. The

air I drew into my lungs turned thick and heavy, as though it fought every breath I took, not wanting to be inside me anymore than I did. And I didn't know how to make it better.

"I should have played it for you from the start."

He sniffed, then rubbed his eyes with the back of his arm, and nodded again. Or he started to nod but the gesture morphed into something more ambiguous. "We were better with him, the three of us, you know?"

I sucked my lips in, nodding when the pressure built behind my eyes and the words wouldn't come.

"He knew what to say to you." Jeremy turned to me, his eyes still wet. He slapped his palm with the back of the other hand to punctuate his next words. "Like, every time, he knew what to say to you. That's not me. I don't know how to talk to you. If it'd been me instead of him gone—" He choked on his own words and forced his eyes wide as he glanced away. "This wouldn't have happened." He made a gesture that encompassed not just Dad's apartment and the fact that our family was living apart, but also me and him and the way our relationship had frayed over the past couple years. "He'd never have let it get like this, and I tried, but I'm not him. I don't know how to be him with Mom or Dad. Or you." He shook his head. "You think I don't get that, that you're the only one who's smart enough to see how much better he was at everything, but I know."

It was so wrong that I wanted to laugh, and the sound that came out of me was much harsher, more broken than a laugh. "And you think I know what to say to you? To any of you?" Jeremy wasn't the only one who came up short. And it wasn't that I thought I was so much smarter than him by realizing how far short we fell compared to Greg, it was that I hoped he didn't feel it, too.

Because it felt like this gut-twisting emptiness. The grief was bad enough, but knowing that Greg had left behind a role that Jeremy and I were expected to fill for each other—one we couldn't possibly take on—was sometimes worse in a way.

"I'll never be as good as he was. I push, and I push, and even when I'm telling myself to stop—" I stabbed my fingers into my sternum "—I push harder. I make you mad, because I don't know how to do anything else." I sucked in as much of the thick air as I could, feeling my chest rise and hurt. Because everything hurt. All the time. "How did he do it, huh?" The words came out as a whisper, soft yet guttural. "Tell me, 'cause I can't figure it out any more than you can."

I was so close to losing that last bit of hold I had over myself. My eyes were welling up, and I knew the second I blinked, they'd spill over. And I still couldn't breathe right. The air wouldn't come, and then it'd come too fast, too much. "It's not just you. I'm not him either."

Jeremy considered me for a moment, staring hard, seeing everything, so much more than I'd ever given him credit for. Then he snorted. "I'm the older brother—the oldest brother now. I'm supposed to keep you in line and have your back. I'm supposed to be the one you can come talk to when stuff gets messed up."

"And I'm supposed to talk *you* down, have *your* back. I'm supposed to be someone you can talk to, too."

"Yeah." Jeremy scoffed and he pulled off the near laugh far better than I had. "Except you're an arrogant little punk most of the time."

A sound came out of me, more a surprised exhale than anything, but the sound that followed on its heels lifted my mouth on one side. I glanced sideways at him. "And you're a short-tempered idiot."

He laughed. So did I. True laughter. Some of the tightness loosened in my chest.

"I'm sorry," I said. "I'm not ever gonna be him, but I'll try to be better than I've been."

"Yeah?" He lifted an eyebrow. "'Cause you sucked a lot this past year."

I made sure Jeremy saw me rotate my jaw in annoyance and he cracked a smile.

"I guess I have to. You've been a little better here lately. I don't want you to think I don't see that, but that crap last night?" He shook his head. "Greg would have torn you a new one, too."

Remembering why last night had happened, my jaw stayed tight. "No, Greg would have gone with me to kick someone's ass."

Jeremy frowned. "Who, Dad?"

"You think I'd have risked ruining everything good that's happening with all of us to start something with Dad? That Jolene would let me if I tried?"

His frown started to smooth and then drew sharply back together as he turned his head to the wall that divided our apartment from Jolene's. "She said something happened..." His face was perfectly smooth, almost scarily so, when he turned back to me. "To her? Somebody... Do you know?"

My hands clenched into fists. "Yeah, I know."

He nodded. In less than a heartbeat, he was on his feet, cracking his neck from side to side. "Well, all right."

My gaze followed him up. "What, just like that? You're not gonna ask...?"

He extended a hand to me. "Do I need to?"

The last bit of pressure in my chest left as I realized he didn't. I needed him to have my back and he had it, no questions asked. Because he was my brother. Not the one I lost, the one he could never replace for me any more than I could for him, but the one I still had. He didn't need to be Greg. *I* didn't need to be Greg. It only took us two years to understand that sometimes, more than sometimes, it was that simple.

I drew in a deep breath and took my brother's hand.

He only raised an eyebrow at me when I walked out into the hall and stopped in front of Guy's apartment.

"You sure?"

"Yes."

My one-word answer was good enough for Jeremy. Together we pounded the door until it opened.

Guy's look of confusion lifted when he passed over Jeremy and saw me. Something of my intent must have been clear on my face, because Guy held both his palms up toward us.

"Oh, hey, Adam, right? Listen, I don't know what Jolene told you, but she's a little messed up and—"

I cut him off with my fist. I didn't have the mass that my brother did, but Guy hadn't been expecting me to deck him, and he staggered back. I didn't advance, but Jeremy did. He landed a solid gut punch and Guy went down to one knee. I didn't hesitate before kicking him in the nuts so hard that Guy nearly threw up.

I'd thought we'd beat him to a pulp, but now that I was standing over him while he whimpered on the floor, the urge left. Instead I went down next to him and lowered my voice so that my brother wouldn't hear. "Stay away from Jolene. Don't *ever* touch another girl, you sick piece of rat filth. And you need to find another place to live." I stood up and walked to his massive shelf of movies. As soon as Jeremy saw what I intended to do, he went to the other side. Together, we knocked it onto the floor with a crash.

Guy was still gasping and trying to catch his breath when we left.

"You good?" Jeremy asked in the hallway.

"Yeah," I said. "And thanks."

Jeremy glanced back at Guy's apartment. "You sure we hit him hard enough?"

I shook out my hand, trying to bring the feeling back. "I don't think hard enough exists."

FOURTEENTH WEEKEND

March 26–28

Jolene

Adam was wearing a sleeping bag the next time I saw him, like, literally wearing it. Winter had finally started to admit defeat, but it was still more than cold outside.

"That's a good look," I told him as we stood on our respective balconies. It had been the longest two weeks I could ever remember.

"How are you?" he asked.

I wished he hadn't. I didn't want to talk about it and had been racked with regret ever since I told him. Knowing that Adam knew made everything with Guy feel more real.

"I'm fine. Do you have any idea how boring these last two weeks have been?"

"I missed you, too," Adam said. Sometimes Adam's bald statements made me uncomfortable. I could never come right out and tell him I missed him like that.

"Are you still persona non grata with your family?"

"Ah, no, not exactly. Jeremy and I are actually good. Better than we've been since my parents split. I think he may have said something to my dad, too, because he and my mom decided I'm only going to be grounded for the month. Next time I'm here, we won't have to freeze to death to talk."

"Really? Your brother went to bat for you?"

"And he said I can get a onetime use of his phone, so if something important comes up, we can talk. He'll text you from his phone so you have the number."

"It's disgusting how much people like you. When I last saw Jeremy, he was practically making the sign of the cross at me. How do you do it, and can you teach me?" I had to lean farther out to catch Adam's smile. His expression shifted into something else, like when you see the sunrise.

"Something else happened, or is happening. My mom came to support group with us. Twice. She and my dad are talking about meeting with someone together, too. I'm really proud of her. She's not, you know, instantly better or anything, and she hasn't talked at any of the meetings yet, but she was better than me the first time I went. She sat in a chair and everything. I mean, that's good, right?"

My stomach sank and I had to look down so he wouldn't see my face crumble. "Yeah."

"And my dad's been coming to dinner nearly every night. I don't know if they're specifically working toward reconciling, or if they're just trying to see how they feel around each other again. But today, when my mom watched Jeremy and me drive away, it was the first time she didn't cry. This is what I wanted from her, from both of them—to try." He shrugged and looked at me.

I tried to return his smile but it wobbled.

"That isn't what I wanted us to talk about. Or not the only thing."

Warning lights started flashing in my head and I let Adam see a chill shake through my body. "I didn't think to wear my sleeping bag. I'm going to have to head in and thaw out. Plus you have family dinner soon, so, later?"

Adam was clearly reluctant to let me go, but I couldn't

say another word. I kept my smile on till I slid the door and curtain closed behind me, then I let myself sink to the floor.

Whole-body sobs shook me. They were so loud that they echoed around my room. And they fed each subsequent sob, growing louder and almost violent until I forced my hands to my mouth. I tried to muffle the sound, stem the tears and gasps for air, but I couldn't.

How horrible was I that my stomach sank when Adam told me about his parents? I should have been happy for him, for them, especially his mom. If there was a chance his family could be put back together, I should be happy.

But I wasn't.

The moment he'd said the word *reconciling*, daggers had seemed to pierce my chest, sliding deep and cutting bone. I'd never have that. Adam's broken family was more than mine had ever been whole. They were mending. Soon his dad would move back home, and I'd be more alone than before Adam came. The thought was so unbearable that I gagged on it.

I heard nothing but the audible sound of my own misery. Not the door opening nor the soft footsteps drawing near. When a hand settled on my shoulder, I didn't look up before curling into the offered arm and burying my face into a shoulder.

Her soft lilac perfume penetrated my senses before my eyes or ears recognized Shelly. Even when I realized who was crouched down and stroking my hair, I couldn't let go. I was too wretched to reject comfort of any kind when I was so seldom offered it.

A thought punctured my misery. Shelly was starved almost as much as I was. She had no family, no steady job, nothing but Dad and the scraps of affection he gave her.

Slowly, agonizingly slowly, my sobs ebbed. Weariness

began to replace despair. Little things began to register, like the jade pendant of Shelly's necklace digging into my cheek, the uncomfortable angle of my leg folded beneath me, the muscles in my hands, still clenched in her shirt, beginning to cramp. Other random things. Any one by itself might not have been enough, but the culmination made me pull back and reveal the damage my tears had done. The wet fabric and smeared black mascara, I'd expected; the tears streaming down Shelly's face, I hadn't.

"Why are you crying?"

Her hand lifted to her cheek, like she needed to test the truth of my words. When her fingers came away wet, she pushed to her feet and hurried into my bathroom. I saw her lean over the sink and splash water on her face, then dry it with a hand towel. When she returned and held out the towel, I took it.

"I'd thought we'd be friends eventually," she said. "I really did."

I gave her a look that she had no trouble interpreting.

"I know. I didn't see back then. I didn't want to."

The towel was damp from where she'd dried her face, and the coolness felt good against my flushed skin. When I had a firm hold on my emotions, I half extended the towel toward her. "I'm sorry I ruined your shirt. I'll pay for a new one."

Her brows drew together and she shook her head slightly. "Jo, I—I don't care about a stupid shirt. I care about—" She bit the word off, knowing she'd kill the momentary cease-fire that hung tenuously between us. "Are you okay?"

I starred at her with my swollen red eyes. "No, Shelly. I'm not okay. I haven't been okay for a long time, but that's not your problem, is it?"

She looked down at floor. "I'm not a bad person," she whispered. "I'm really not. I never set out to hurt anyone."

Like me. Like my mother.

I couldn't yell at her the way I normally did, not when her shoulder was wet from my tears. But I couldn't console her either, not when she'd played a role in all our lives ending up this way. "I loved you, and you used me to get to my dad." My voice cracked but I kept going. "You committed adultery with him, helped him lie to my mom, and now you play warden with me twice a month so he can continue to screw her over, whether she deserves it or not. You say you didn't want to hurt anyone, but you did. You still are."

"I know," she said so softly I barely heard it. "Would you believe me if I said I was sorry?"

I wanted it to be that easy, but all the pieces of me were broken inside and a word wouldn't put them back together. "Sorry doesn't change anything."

"I'm sorry, Jolene." And then she started to tear up again. "Is he worth it, really?"

It took her close to a minute, but she reined it in. "No, he's not. I lost everything I ever cared about because of him, people and time that I'll never get back." She looked down at the towel she still held, the one that was smeared with my mascara as well as hers. "Why were you crying?"

"No." My bluntness made her flinch. "I can't do that with you. You're not going to braid my hair while I tell you that Adam's dad is probably going to move back home soon, or that I lost my friendship with Cherry, or that the Roman Polanski wannabe across the hall isn't going to write me the letter I need to get into the film program. It's never going to be the way it was. So stop trying. Please."

As always, Shelly was spot-on with the takeaway. "Who's Roman Polanski?"

I slowly closed my eyes and then shot them open again when Guy's face filled my mind. My stomach launched itself into my throat. "He's a director who likes teenage girls. Just forget it." I started to push to my feet, but Shelly caught my hand.

"You mean Guy, don't you?"

I stilled, and my eyes started to sting, more than sting. "Please, just leave me alone."

Her gaze flicked back and forth between mine and my eyes filled up faster. "Jo. If something happened, I need you to tell me so I can help you. Hate me again in an hour if you need to but right now…"

The suddenly soft tone of her voice sent a tear rolling down my face. The second it did, I decided to remember—just for a little while—that Shelly used to be my friend.

IN BETWEEN

Jolene:

Can I talk to Adam?

Jeremy:

Hold on.

Jeremy:

It's Adam.

Jolene:

Was it you?

Jeremy:

Was what me?

Jolene:

Shelly told me somebody beat up Guy. Was it you?

Jeremy:

Yes. I was going to tell you.

Jeremy:

I wasn't thinking. I should have waited and talked to you. It was right after you told me. I didn't think.

Jeremy:

But he's moving. You won't have to see him in the hall.

Jeremy:

Say something.

Jeremy:

Are you mad at me?

Jeremy:

Jolene?

Jeremy:

I couldn't stand that he hurt you.
I wanted to hurt him. And I
needed him to know that you
weren't alone. You're not.

Jeremy:

I looked up some stuff online
and there's info about how to
report people.

Jolene:

I don't want to talk about it.

Jeremy:

He shouldn't get away with
what he did to you.

Jolene:

All he did was kiss me.

Jeremy:

He did something you didn't
want. That's assault.

Jeremy:

On top of that you're a minor.

Jeremy:

You wouldn't have to do it alone.
I'm here. I'm always going to be
here. We can talk to my parents or
Mrs. Cho or whoever you want.

Jolene:

Stop. First Shelly, and now you?

Jeremy:

You told Shelly?

Jolene:

I didn't plan on it but yes. She wants me to report him.

Jeremy:

I can't believe I'm saying this but I agree with Shelly.

Jolene:

I just want to forget about it.

Jeremy:

Okay. But I'm here if you change your mind. Bizarrely it sounds like Shelly is, too.

Jolene:

I don't know right now.

Jeremy:

Okay.

Jolene:

And you need to delete these texts from Jeremy's phone.

Jeremy:

I will.

Jeremy:

I just want you to know I'm here.

Jeremy:

I'll do anything for you.

Jolene:

I know.

Jolene:

Thanks.

Jolene

I set my phone down, then curled my legs up, and rested my cheek on my knee. For once, I was glad that my bedroom at my mom's felt like it belonged to someone else. As my gaze traveled around the room, there were few memories associated with the soulless space. Apart from Mrs. Cho coming in to clean, I was the only one who spent time there. I'd never wanted to have friends over, not even Cherry.

At the thought of her, I lowered one leg, then the other, and after a moment's hesitation, I walked over to open my closet. Smashed in the corner of a shelf was the holographic gift bag I'd thrown up there over two months ago.

I gnawed on my lip and plucked it down. Crumpled white tissue paper floated to the floor as I revealed a hinged box at the bottom that was no bigger than my palm.

It creaked slightly when I opened it and inside was a necklace with a tiny film camera charm on the end. I lifted the charm in my fingers as a tear slid down my cheek.

Gabe and Cherry's mom opened the door when I knocked twenty minutes later. "Hi, sweetie. We haven't seen enough of you lately." She reached for my hand and gave it a squeeze as I mumbled a vague excuse about homework. "You just missed Gabe. You want to text him and see if he can swing back for you? He and Grady and Dexter were going to grab something to eat."

I shook my head. "Can you just give this to him for me?" I held out a flash drive. "It's the finished music video for Venomous Squid."

She smiled wide. "You're such a good friend for helping them with this. Gabe says you're a genius."

I gave her a tight-lipped smile in return and my fingers trailed up to clutch the charm resting against my chest. "I was also hoping you might let me see Cherry. I know she's grounded but—"

Their mom frowned and cut me off. "Cherry's not grounded anymore. She didn't tell you?"

The charm dug into my palm as I clutched it tighter. "We haven't been talking, so…"

The frown smoothed and her eyes softened. "She's in her room." She backed up to open the door wider for me. "Go on."

Upstairs, my footsteps halted a few feet from Cherry's open door. I'd almost turned around and left when her mom told me Cherry was no longer grounded. That meant she could have tried to call me or at least text me to say she was sorry. But she hadn't. Which meant maybe she wasn't. My foot inched back from her door. Maybe all these weeks she'd been avoiding me as much as I'd been avoiding her.

But then I thought about Shelly and what I'd agreed to do the next day and realized that I'd never get through it if I backed away from this situation now.

Cherry's eyes widened when she saw me. She clicked the TV off and swung her legs off the bed.

"Hey," I said. "Your mom let me up."

She nodded. "Gabe's not here."

"I know. I came by to see you. I mean, I did drop off the music video, too, but—"

"You finished it?"

I nodded. "A while ago. I just—"

"—didn't want to come over." I saw her swallow and her hands made fists in the comforter on either side of her. "Jo, I—"

"Wait, okay?" I took a step into her room, still clutching my necklace. There weren't enough deep breaths in the world for what I had to say but I took one anyway. And when it wasn't enough I took another. I was mad at her. More than mad, I was broken by her. But standing in her room with its hand-me-down furniture and the collection of stuffed animals nearly crowding her off the bed some of that fell away, not all, but a lot.

I took a few more steps and then lowered myself to sit on the opposite corner of the bed from her so I could pluck up a flamingo—her favorite animal—that I'd given her for her last birthday. I'd sewn a soccer ball to its hand and used markers to recreate our school's mascot on its belly. It turned out awful, and I'd wanted to chuck it but Cherry had insisted it take a place of honor on her bed.

And it was still there.

My heart ached as I looked at the flamingo, and it ached more when I glanced at Cherry.

"I know you're not grounded anymore. You could've tried to talk to me."

Her head slumped further.

"I don't get it. I thought eventually you'd come over and we'd fight it out and be okay again. But you didn't." My voice broke. "And I know you don't want me to talk about Meneik—*I* don't want to talk about Meneik, but I'm going to because I don't care if you hate me for it. I don't like him. I don't like the way he treats you or the way he forces you to act to keep him happy. Whether you want me in your life or not, and whether I'm mad at you or not, I care about you.

I don't want you to look back in five years and regret your life." My heart lodged itself in my throat when I remembered Shelly telling me that she'd lost everything because of my dad. "I've seen that, and I don't want that for you."

Cherry glanced down at her knees, her shoulders hunching as though she was bracing herself. "Are you done?"

"No." I tossed the flamingo down. "I'm not done. Cherry, I—I've been going through some stuff." My throat closed off so my words came out choked. "I could've used a friend to tell me the truth when I was lying to myself." I thought about all the warning signs with Guy and how maybe if I'd told someone, they'd have helped me see him for what he was long before that final night in his apartment. "Because it turns out it's a lot easier to point out somebody else's mistakes than recognize your own." My eyes were threatening to start swimming, so I bounced my gaze all over her room, her closet, her window, her dresser.

And I stopped.

Standing, I walked to the dresser and stared at the mirror hanging above it, the one that had been so crammed with photos, concert tickets, and notes she and Gabe always left for each other. I'd been in her room enough times to have them memorized, but even if I hadn't, I'd have noticed the glaring gaps.

All the photos of Meneik were gone. Whenever they'd broken up before, she'd never get around to taking them down before they were on again.

I spun to face her and didn't need to ask the question when the answer had been staring me in the face.

"Turns out I didn't need you to see Meneik," Cherry said, her voice less flat and more empty. "Do you know what he said when I showed up at his door?"

My stomach turned over.

"It was my fault for getting grounded, that if I really loved him, I'd have figured out a way to be with him sooner, even if that meant leaving my family. And I don't know if it was all the time I'd spent away from him or thinking about the horrible things I'd said to you and everyone else—things he was yelling at me—" I heard her voice thicken. "But I finally realized that you were right, all of you."

I pressed my lips together to steady them. "It's over?"

She nodded. "And I'm sorry. I didn't mean what I said. It was awful and heartless." When she lifted her head, her eyes were swimming. "And it wasn't true."

My chest felt too tight as I stared at her. I didn't need an apology. I'd repeated that to myself the whole way over, but I know that part of my heart would have broken if she'd let me leave without saying those words and meaning them.

"After Meneik, I told myself I waited too long, that it was too late to say sorry and—" She broke off when she saw my necklace and then her face crumbled and we were both moving toward each other, meeting in a hug that felt like we'd never gone a single day fighting.

"Never," I told her.

"I missed you."

"Me, too."

"Promise you'll always tell me when I'm messing up?"

"If you'll tell me."

She nodded. "But you saw through Meneik from the start. You'd have never let some guy manipulate you like I did." She felt me stiffen and drew back. "What?" she said, taking in the way my face had gone slack.

I sucked as much air into my lungs as I could, hoping to make the next part easier. I even tried to smile but it broke before my lips could lift.

Shelly let the two officers into Dad's apartment and, after introducing everyone, she sat next to me on the couch and didn't move for the next two hours while they questioned me.

If I hadn't had my hands clenched tightly in my lap, I think she'd have tried to hold one as I relived not only the last time I was in Guy's apartment, but every interaction we'd had since the first time we met.

To her credit, Shelly never once reacted. She didn't gasp or sigh or so much as twitch while I spoke, my voice growing softer as the unbelievable stupidity of my actions hit me all over again.

The officers were kind, too. They never acted like they thought I was lying or embellishing. They wrote down my answers, asked questions that didn't feel nearly as invasive as I'd been expecting, and they were straightforward with me about what was going to happen when I asked.

Guy would be interviewed next, but I already knew that his version of the events was going to contradict everything I said. And it turned out Guy was very clever. All his insistence on keeping our "friendship" secret meant there were no witnesses who'd ever seen us together. There were also no phone records, no inappropriate texts or voice mails. His kissing and groping hadn't left physical marks on me, and I'd waited weeks before reporting him. There was nothing to prove my story over his.

"Okay, so what if he denies everything?" Shelly asked, scooting forward so that she was barely sitting on the edge of the couch as her gaze darted back and forth between the two officers. "You can arrest him based on what Jolene told you, right? I mean, right?"

"Unless he admits to kissing or touching Jolene, I'm sorry, no," said one of the officers, a young blonde woman with striking blue eyes. She turned to me. "You're the first person to make allegations against him, so unless he says something happened or we find a witnesses or evidence—"

"It's my word against his," I said, feeling hollow and small.

"Jolene, I believe you're telling the truth, and whatever else happens, there is now an official record documenting your story. That report is going to follow him for the rest of his life."

She told me I was brave and important and that because I'd come forward, any other girl who reported him would have my story to stand alongside hers.

I nodded, feeling more numb than anything as they left and Shelly shut the door behind them. She stayed there, leaned her back against the door until I realized what she was doing and my face went hot.

"Right," I said, pushing to my feet and grabbing my bag. "It's not my dad's weekend and you probably have stuff you need to do."

Shelly bit her lip. "I want to tell you I'm proud of you, but I'm betting I'm the last person you want to hear that from." She took a step toward me. "I also want to tell you that it's wrong that your dad wasn't here."

I couldn't keep my eyes from glancing at the kitchen counter and the note Dad had left me.

Can't make it today. I'll make it up to you next time.
Knock 'em dead, champ.

I wasn't sure if he was confusing the events of the day with a soccer game or he really meant he'd try to make it to my next sexual assault police interview. Honestly, neither one changed how I felt about him.

Shelly had read the note over my shoulder, and for a second I'd thought she might throw up.

But then the cops had shown up, and we'd had to forget about the note. I'd try at least. There was an ugly, dark part of my brain that had it memorized though.

"And while I'm sure I know the answer, I'm going to offer anyway." Shelly sucked in a deep breath and held it before saying, "I'll go with you if you want to tell your mom. Her lawyers are going to be notified, but if you want to tell her yourself..."

Mom's lawyers were going to be out for blood and they were finally going to have cause given that this had all happened on "Dad's watch." I didn't want to think about that so I let myself imagine Shelly's offer, what that meeting might look like, and the injuries and indignities that my mom would inflict on her if she came with me. For some reason, it wasn't as fun to think about as it used to be.

"She'd probably try to run you over with her car," I said.

Shelly didn't react. "I know."

"And you're still offering?"

"Yes."

Something stung the back of my eyes hearing that. "I think I'll let the lawyers do the honors."

Shelly started to take another step toward me, and I could tell that if I let her take that one, she'd take another, and another, and she wouldn't stop until she was right in front of me. And then she'd push me into a choice I could never make. It was one thing to let her hug me when I was breaking apart and crying on the floor, but when I was standing and feeling...not brave, exactly, but not weak anymore either. It would be something very different.

"Shelly, don't." She halted mid-step. "Please don't."

Her teeth dug into her lower lip before she nodded. "I know."

She did know; we both did. Whatever she did for me now couldn't undo what she'd done. Dance dresses and holding me while I cried and letting her shoulder press into mine while I relived one of the worst things that had ever happened to me, those were good things. But we were tainted by a past and present that I couldn't forget. At least, not while I was still living it every other weekend. Not while she silently read my dad's notes and reported to his lawyers.

I couldn't.

"Can I...?" She pointed past me to her bedroom. "I need to show you something, and I promise that will be it, okay?"

She barely waited for my wary nod before crossing the room. I heard the closet opening, and a moment later she was back and holding a bag that was nearly as big as she was.

A packed bag.

I frowned.

"I'm leaving." Shelly grunted under the weight of the bag and I felt the reverberation in the floor when she dropped it. "I don't want to live like this anymore. I don't want to be this person, not for myself and not for you either."

I kept frowning, but only because I was afraid of the expression my face would make if I stopped. "When?" I glanced at the bag.

"I bought the bag the day after you told me about Guy. I've been packing slowly ever since so your dad won't notice."

My heart started beating faster when I processed what she was saying. "Why didn't you leave then?"

"Because of today," she said in the softest voice. "I wasn't going to leave you to go through this alone. I know you think you're tough and you don't need anyone, but I think that's because you've never really had anyone. And you should, Jo. You deserve to have so many people. People better than me."

The stinging behind my eyes intensified, and my frown began to tremble. I don't know if I would have been able to stop her if she'd tried to hug me then, but she didn't. Instead, she reached into her pocket and pulled out a folded piece of paper.

"I already know how this is going to go, which is why I'm sending an email to your dad's lawyers the second I walk out this door. I can't do much, but unless they want me going to your mom's lawyers first thing in the morning, they'll do what I want."

I stiffened when she came toward me, but she stopped an arm's length away and offered me the folded piece of paper.

"That's Mrs. Cho's new number. It took me a while to track her down since her old number was from a phone that your mom was paying for, but there's only so many Korean churches in this city, and when I told my mom I was leaving your dad, she helped me look."

I took the paper with a shaky hand, and Shelly drew back, shoving both hands into her back pockets.

"Anyway, she hasn't found a new job yet, and once I'm gone, your dad is going to need somebody to be here with you. I know it's not perfect, but…"

I opened the paper and saw Mrs. Cho's number. And Shelly's beneath it.

Shelly hurried to add, "My number's only so you can call me if the lawyers try to get out of the rest. I don't think they will, but they are lawyers, so… Oh, and I just called Mrs. Cho and she's on her way over, so you won't have to be alone or go back to your mom's right away unless you want to. She's really excited to see you again."

The words and numbers started to blur the longer I looked at them.

"So, um, yeah. I guess that's it. I don't entirely know if that bag is going to fit through the door, but thank God the elevator is fixed, right?" She tried to laugh, but it was forced.

Still staring at the paper, I sensed Shelly moving, groaning as she picked up her heavy bag and shuffled toward the door with it. I heard the hinge squeak as she opened the door, and the sound of fabric scratching as she forced the bag into the hall.

"I hope good things for you, Jolene. Better things than you can possibly imagine."

And then, softly, the door closed behind her.

I caught her as the elevator doors were opening. She turned, and I saw that the tears streaming down her face matched my own.

"I was supposed to get to hate you forever."

One side of her mouth lifted. "You still can."

I shook my head. And I hugged her.

FIFTEENTH WEEKEND

April 9–11

ADAM

I was heading down the hall toward Jolene's apartment with dragging feet when my phone buzzed.

Jolene:
Hey.

Adam:
Hi. I'm knocking at your door.

Jolene:
Good luck with that.

Adam:
Are you gonna let me in? I need to talk to you about something.

Jolene:
I'm not there.

Adam:
Where are you?

Jolene:
Behind you.

I turned, and saw her coming up the stairs, her hair half pulled back and half loose. I moved quicker than she did and we met in the middle of the hall. I knew I held her too tight, but she didn't complain.

"It's okay," she said after I released her from a hug. "I already heard your dad is moving home."

I expected my gut to bungee more than it did, probably because I'd expected the news to hurt her as much as it had both hurt and thrilled me. My dad moving home was great, but losing my weekends with Jolene... But *she* didn't look devastated.

"I would have called you but—"

"You only just got your phone back."

"Yeah."

"That's awesome, Adam." She hugged me again, and it felt like there wasn't a single part of her that didn't mean it. "I'm happy for you."

"Really?" I said. "Because I'm happy for my family, but I hate that this...is ending."

She looked away, then grimaced when she noticed that we were standing in front of Guy's apartment. She moved us until we were in front of mine.

I couldn't help it. I glanced back at Guy's door. I knew he was gone, but still. "Did you tell your parents?"

"Everybody knows and everyone is blaming everyone else." Jolene tugged the sleeve of my shirt so that I'd follow her down to sit on the ground.

"That can't have been a fun conversation."

Jolene shrugged. "I wouldn't know. I let the lawyers do the honors with my parents." She sighed before speaking again. "I, um, ended up reporting him to the police. Shelly was with me when a couple officers interviewed me, and she... wasn't horrible about it." She hunched her shoulders ever so slightly. "The officers talked to me again after interviewing Guy, and he denied everything. He said he barely knew me and that after I tried to come on to him he kept his distance so as not to encourage me."

"That son of a—" I wasn't aware that I'd started to push to my feet until Jolene stopped me with a hand on my forearm.

"Adam." She said my name softly and it helped to slow the rage-induced adrenaline coursing through my body. "He's gone, remember?"

"He belongs in a cell," I gritted out, lowering back to the ground.

"Yeah, well, he has a squeaky-clean record, and there's no proof—"

"There's you!" I said, feeling my face burn for very different reasons than it usually did around her.

Jolene's face went hard. "Honestly, I'm just glad he's gone. Actually, no. I'm glad he's gone *and* I'm glad that his record won't be so squeaky-clean if anyone else ever reports him." She slid her hand off her lap to brush against mine. "According to Shelly, his face was bruised enough that maybe no one will ever have to."

I looked down, watching her fingers reach for mine, and forced mine to unclench. My knuckles had been bruised for a few days after hitting Guy, but the skin was fine now. "I didn't hit him hard enough."

She laced her fingers through mine and I could feel her gaze on me. Then she leaned forward and pressed her lips to my cheek. The soft, sweet touch dimmed the fury still shouting at me to find Guy and make him hurt. Her fingers were so small compared to mine, she was so small and he'd— shame, slick and heavy, kept my head from lifting to see hers.

"I'm sorry that I wasn't there, that I didn't understand

when you brought us to his apartment. I would never have left you."

"I know," she said, laying her head on my shoulder. "And it's not your fault."

"It's not yours," I said, jerking up to find her face, the need to make sure she knew that superseding everything else.

Her nod was stiff and she didn't say the words, but I had to hope that someday soon she'd be able to. Slowly, a smile lifted her mouth.

"Does it make me a bad person that I'm glad you hit him?"

"No, and I did more than hit him. I kicked him in the nuts so hard he nearly puked."

Jolene's smile stretched wider. "Did you really?"

"Yeah. Jeremy hit him, too."

"Jeremy was with you? He hates me."

"He doesn't hate you. In fact, he wanted me to give you this." I shifted so I could reach into my back pocket and hand a ticket to her. "It's for the play. Opening night is next week."

Jolene took it and raised an eyebrow. "The play your ex-girlfriend Erica is also in?"

"Trust me, she is completely over all that. Last night at dinner, she and Jeremy were—"

"She's eating dinner at your house now?"

"Just a few times so far, but we've talked and we're good. She'll tell you the same thing if you come to the play. Will you?"

Jolene looked at the ticket without saying anything.

"I know it's not the same as a whole weekend, but you could come for dinner and go to the play with my family."

She bit her lip.

"Or, you don't have to come to dinner if you don't want. My mom will be crushed but she'll understand."

Jolene's eyes were a little shiny. "What about you, will you be crushed?"

"Completely." That made her laugh, though I wasn't remotely kidding.

"I'm glad Jeremy went with you," she said, referring to Guy. "It has to be a big-time brother bonding moment to beat up a sexual predator together, huh?"

She meant the comment lightly, but she wasn't wrong. Things with Jeremy and me had changed that day for the better. I could actually see a future where we were friends as well as brothers. With an odd but not unpleasant ache in my heart, I knew Greg would have been happy to see our relationship shifting. "Yeah, I think so." I glanced over at her. "I guess things are pretty different for you now, too?"

"You could say that."

"But things are better with Shelly, right?"

"Actually, Shelly's gone. I don't think she even left my dad a note." There was a touch of bitterness in her voice when she said that last word, but it was gone the next second, replaced by something that sounded almost sad but couldn't have been, because she was talking about Shelly. "Anyway, she's gone and, just like she predicted, my parents' lawyers went for each other's jugulars."

"Who won?"

Jolene was gazing down the hall toward her dad's apartment and frowning. "I guess I did." She shook her head. "Or at least, neither of my parents did. My mom's lawyers initially tried to go after my dad for negligence, but then his lawyers got Tom to divulge a bunch of stuff about my mom, and it ended in a stalemate. It would have all come down to Shelly, except when she left my dad, she promised not to help my mom, as long as he agreed to do three things for me."

I mirrored Jolene's earlier frown.

"Yeah, that was me for a straight week," Jolene said, noting my expression. "I hated her for so long, you know? I don't know how I'm supposed to feel about her now, since she helped me when she could have so easily helped only herself. I'm still working through it." Then she sighed and smiled at me. "Well, aren't you going to ask me?"

My brain was tripping over that turn of events, but something about the way Jolene's eyes were boring into me kicked the right question to my lips. "What did you ask for?"

"Just so you know, Shelly didn't get me a blank check. I had to keep my requests within reason. The first thing was so much easier than it could have been, because Shelly's mom found her for me before she left—"

"Who?"

Jolene grinned wide. "Someone has to stay with me at my dad's, and since even he doesn't rebound that quickly, I got him to hire Mrs. Cho. *And* he can't fire her, no matter how many future girlfriends parade through the place."

Then my smile came, easy and as full as hers. I caught her up in a hug that nearly tugged her into my lap.

Jolene made a fake grunting noise. "I think you're almost happier than Mrs. Cho was."

"Good," I said, still not letting go. "She should be happy to get you back. She was, wasn't she?"

"Yeah, she was. I guess you were right about my mom lying." Jolene squeezed me tighter, strong enough that I almost didn't have to fake a grunt. Then she released me suddenly and leaned back, cool as ever, a smile playing at her lips.

"Ready to hear about wish number two?"

"I'm still really happy about wish number one."

Her smile grew. "It's the money and the time away for the film program."

"Jo—" My own smile started to spread but then dimmed. "What about the letter?"

Her smile slipped, but not all the way. "Venomous Squid wrote me one. It's not the most cohesive recommendation letter since they traded off between paragraphs, but they talked about the music videos I made for them and basically credited all of their success to my artistic brilliance. Like, that's an actual line from the letter."

I grinned. "I still don't love their music, but I'm totally buying their first album."

"It was actually Cherry's idea. We had a chance to talk when I dropped off the music video last week. It started off a little rough and we're not 100 percent back to how things were but I'm starting to think we might get there." Jolene drew her knees up and hugged them. "She broke it off with Meneik. She and Gabe have been talking a lot since my birthday. And her mom. And her dad. And her grandmother. And they got through to her."

"And you," I said, bumping her shoulder.

"And me," she agreed. "I told her, not everything, not yet anyway, but she immediately thought of having the band write me a totally unconventional letter. It'll have to be enough. It *will* be enough. And if it's not, then I'll find another film program, and another after that if I have to. I'm not giving up. Maybe I won't win an Oscar by the time I'm twenty-five, but I'm going to make movies."

"I know," I said without missing a beat.

"You really believe that, don't you?" She inhaled and exhaled, her smile returning in full force. "Are you ready to hear about wish number three? I got my Lexus back! Not the exact same one, obviously, but…" She dangled her keys up high in front of us. "And my mom can't make him take this one back. My dad had to up her alimony to ensure that, but I don't care. Anyway, if I'm going to have to drive half an hour to see you all the time, we can split the gas."

"Fifteen minutes," I said, finally throwing her off balance for once. I shifted to pull my wallet out and I held my brand-spanking-new driver's license out to her.

"You got it!"

"Your complete shock is doing wonders for my self-esteem."

Jolene pulled her own license out and had me mirror the way she was holding hers under her chin. Then she laid her head on my shoulder and mine dropped against hers as she lifted her camera out in front of us. "Okay, this is better." I slid an arm around the small of her back and breathed in the subtle honeysuckle scent of her hair.

"Say 'bikes are for chumps!'"

The camera flashed but even after she lowered it, she kept her head on my shoulder.

"We don't have to send pics to my mom anymore."

"Maybe they can just be for us now."

I'd been so afraid of seeing her today, having to look at her when I told her I wasn't coming back. I didn't know if she'd try to brush me off or if she'd let me glimpse any of the pain I was expecting to inflict on her. I didn't think I'd get to hold her while she absently traced the edges of my license and teased me about how I probably now had my picture framed at the DMV for bestest test taker ever.

I never thought I'd be laughing or that my heart would feel so full.

When she finally lifted her head, she loosely linked her arms around my neck, and there was a hint of pink flushing her cheeks. "I would have driven half an hour."

"And I would have biked five."

Jolene smiled at me, and the gap in her teeth did all kinds

of wild stuff to my heart. I didn't mean to stare at her lips, but after not seeing her for two weeks, I couldn't seem to help it.

"You really want to kiss me, don't you?"

Heat danced up my neck, and I was glad that she saw it, because she smiled wider.

"Yeah. Constantly. Always."

She stiffened slightly and pulled back until she was sitting on her heels. When she reached for her hair in that nervous way of hers, I covered her wrists with my hands before she could start braiding it.

"Hey. Where'd you go?"

She lowered her hands to her lap and squinted hard at me. "You can't just say you'll always want me. I mean, it's gonna be different, you know that, right? We've been fine seeing each other a couple weekends a month—okay, we've been more than fine," she allowed when I started to say the exact same thing. "But now you want me to meet your mom, and what happens when you realize that you only like me in small doses and—"

I kissed her. I mean I *seriously* kissed her. My hands went to her jaw and sealed her mouth with mine. I didn't have to worry if it was the right move, because her hand came up to curl around my wrist, holding on to me. My pulse exploded and my heart raced. We were both gasping when we broke apart.

"That's not an answer either," she said in an unsteady voice that had me fighting the urge to kiss her again. But she needed words from me more.

"Yeah, it is." I brought her palm to my chest so that she could feel my heart beating, fast and strong, for her. "All that stuff I told you about our futures... I want the video chats when we're at college. I want the holidays where we fly out to meet each other, even if it's only for a couple hours before we have to fly back. I want the summers together doing I-don't-even-care-what." When she tried to lower her head, I bent mine to hold her gaze. "I want to be there for your first movie, and you need to be there for me to talk me down when I want to chuck my first book. And later when it's published to middling reviews."

She laughed a little at that.

"And I know you're gonna break my heart at some point. I might even break yours." I pressed her hand more firmly against my chest. "But it's yours to break and mend and hopefully not break again, because, like you've said many times, I have fragile boy emotions." My fingers slid up to her chin and urged her to look at me. My pulse kicked impossibly higher when I drank in the features I knew better than my own at that point. "I want all of *you*. Prickly, funny, sarcastic, brilliant, and sometimes a little mean you. And I'm not gonna make a joke here even though I can feel you squirming. There's nothing funny about the way you make me feel. I love you, Jolene. I love you like a movie with the perfect lighting and the sweeping camera, the kind where the music swells and—Jo...?" My voice trailed off and my heart came to a slamming halt because she was shaking her head and tears suddenly spilled silently down her face.

"No," she said. "Not like that." She gazed at me, her eyes flicking fast back and forth between mine. "All my life I've wanted to change things, to make them perfect and safe and unreal, because my reality was a mess. But I've never done that with you. I've never needed to. I *want* this still somewhat dark hallway with the laugh track from somebody's TV drifting through the walls. I *want* the thin carpet and the weird smell from whoever burned microwave popcorn earlier. And I don't care about camera angles so long as I get to see any part of you." Her fingers dug into my shirt before inching up to brush my jaw. "Adam, I never needed a movie with you, because when you love someone—and I can say it now a million times if you want—it's already perfect."

I tasted her tears when she brought her trembling lips to mine, sweeter than any apple pie, and then felt the whoosh of air when my arms locked tight around her ribs. My heart thundered, and I didn't care about the blood that was no doubt rushing to my face.

And she was laughing against my mouth, kissing me, then pulling back long enough to meet my gaze before kissing me again.

I brushed her cheek dry with my thumb when she finally pulled away, and I couldn't help grinning at her like an idiot.

She smiled and dropped her forehead against mine. "You gonna make that face every time we kiss?"

"Oh, this isn't for the kiss. I think I just proved who'll be crying at the airport when we both leave for college."

Jolene's whole body shook when she laughed. "My money's still on you, but I guess we'll see."

That was the last time I kissed Jolene in the Oak Village apartment building. But I did kiss her at her new apartment after watching the first of many movies with the famous Mrs. Cho, and at my house the next week when she helped me with the dishes after dinner with my whole family. And at Jeremy's awful play, where she and Erica were not only civil to each other but actually made plans for all of us to go on a double date. And at Venomous Squid's show the next month. And a million times after that.

If I'm lucky, I'll be kissing Jolene for the rest of my life.

Jolene would say "I guess we'll see."

I'm saying I feel lucky.

Jolene's Essay

My name is Jolene Timber, and I'm a filmmaker.

I'm not an aspiring filmmaker. I am one now, presently, currently. I was a filmmaker long before I picked up a camera.

When I was little and my parents were fighting, I'd change the story in my head. When I watched my mom yelling at my dad for the cliché lipstick marks she'd found on his collar while he poured himself a drink and told her she knew where the door was, I'd rewrite the story, reframe the shot, even rescore the music I could hear in my head. Sometimes it wasn't lipstick that she found on his collar; sometimes it was blood, and before she could ask him about it, a gunshot would shatter the window behind her and I'd slow the frame rate down to catch her hair blowing as the bullet whizzed past, and then I'd rush it back to normal speed as my dad tackled her before a second shot fired. They'd both be breathless, staring at each other from the ground as an incongruously happy song played in the background, something from a kids' show on the TV that I'd left on. He'd spin and pull a gun from his jacket, taking out the assassin that had been sent to kill our whole family, while my mother ran to shield my body with her own.

Maybe it's not the most original idea, but I think I was around eight when I mentally shot that film. I've developed some since then, as you'll see in my included short films. My point is that I've been making films since I first understood that, if I didn't like a story, I could change it. I could make my father the hero instead of the cheater, my mother the protector instead of the woman who saw me watching from the top of the stairs and baited him until he blamed me for his many affairs. I could cut the scenes I didn't like and reshoot the ones I did. I could light them, edit them, control them until they were exactly what I wanted them to be. And when I discovered that I could do that for an audience and not just to escape a reality that I wanted to deny, that was when I began making the films that I'd only ever imagined before.

I thought they would all reflect the lifelong need that I've felt to escape, that the stories and feelings I wanted to create would be antidotes to my own life, but that's not how I feel anymore, and those aren't the only films I want to make.

I'd be lying if I said I've fully abandoned retelling my own stories. As long as I live with either of my parents, it's what I have to do. Maybe even after that. I don't know. I do know that I want more. I deserve more.

I want to tell love stories that maybe end as broken and as messy as they started. And ones that end happy and hopeful, as the girl realizes that happily-ever-after isn't just a silver screen fantasy. And I want to adapt books—one in particular, but I have to wait for him to write it first.

Whether you accept me into your program or not—and you should—I have to make movies, so I will. Other people have to eat and breathe, but I have to make movies. I have to tell stories, because I can't live any other way.

My name is Jolene Timber, and I'm a filmmaker.

★ ★ ★ ★ ★

AUTHOR NOTE

Jolene's story, though fictional, is true for too many people. On average, there are 321,500 victims (age twelve or older) of rape and sexual assault each year in the United States. Or to put it another way, every ninety-eight seconds, another person experiences sexual assault. The term *sexual assault* refers to sexual contact or behavior that occurs without the explicit consent of the victim. Out of every one thousand sexual assaults, 310 are reported to the police, and of those cases, 93 percent of juvenile victims knew the perpetrator.

If you need help or need to talk to someone, RAINN (Rape, Abuse & Incest National Network), the nation's largest anti-sexual-violence organization, operates the National Sexual Assault Hotline, which offers free, confidential help and information 24/7 by phone (800-656-HOPE) and online (rainn.org and rainn.org/es).

ACKNOWLEDGMENTS

People often ask me where the ideas for my books come from and my answer is always different: a single scene that popped into my head of a girl sitting on her roof at night talking to the older boy next door (*If I Fix You*), or an article about a DNA test that accidentally revealed an unknown sibling (*The First to Know*), or a simple prompt to write a summer love story that, to me, needed to involve a girl falling for the brother of *her* brother's murder victim (*Even If I Fall*).

Every Other Weekend was inspired by an old episode of *The Wonder Years* where Kevin falls for a girl he meets on vacation and then has to leave her behind when he comes home. I started wondering about what it might have been like if they'd continued to see each other regularly, but briefly, and forged a relationship that was separate from their "real" lives back home. Adam and Jolene's story evolved radically from that inspiration—they always do—and there are so many people who helped me along the way.

My agent, Kim Lionetti. Thank you for your unwavering faith in me and for your willingness to let me run with this story in particular.

My editor, Natashya Wilson. I think this has been our most challenging book to date because it's essentially two books, Adam's story and Jolene's story, combined into one. I love how fiercely you loved Jolene from the start and how you completely fell for Adam, but more than that, I love how hard you pushed me to make this book do them justice.

Thank you to the phenomenally hardworking team at Inkyard Press and HarperCollins, including Gigi Lau for art direction and Marissa Korda for the spectacular cover art and design (the pigeons are EVERYTHING!), Justine Sha, Brittany Mitchell, Stephanie Choo, Chris Wolfgang, Ingrid Dolan, Shara Alexander, Linette Kim, Bess Braswell, Andrea Pappenheimer, Heather Foy, and the entire Harper Children's sales team.

To my longtime critique partners, Sarah Guillory and Kate Goodwin, and to my Pitch Wars mentee turned critique partner, Rebecca Rode. Sarah and Kate, you guys have read this book in so many different forms and you told me which parts were crap even as you cheered me on to fix them. Best. CPs. Ever. And, Rebecca, I can't wait to start inflicting, I mean sharing, future first drafts with you.

To my sister Mary Groen, who has asked me weekly for the past six years when this book was going to be ready because it was her favorite. The answer is now, today. Because of you.

To my sister Rachel and my brother Sam. Thanks for giving me so many good sibling stories to draw from.

To my parents, Gary and Suzanne Johnson. It is the greatest privilege of my life to make you proud.

To my family, Jill, Ross, Ken, Rick and Jeri, the Depew family, and my honorary brother Nate. I love you all so much.

To all my nieces and nephews, Grady (thanks for giving me the best band name ever), Rory, Sadie, Gideon, Ainsley, Ivy, Dexter, and Os. I have finally written all of you into one of my books! You're now contractually obligated to say I'm your favorite aunt for eternity.

Thank you to my longtime friend and police officer, Laura Cervantes, for all of your help with certain aspects of this story. Any mistakes are my own.

To everyone who asked for more Daniel, thanks for letting me step back into his life a little. If you haven't already and you want to read more about him, his story continues in *If I Fix You*.

I thank God for all the people who've read my books and told their friends about them, posted reviews, shared on social media, or written me letters. I wouldn't be able to do this amazing job without you. Thank you.